ᵀʰᵉ *Fourth Generation*

Bob Bancks

Paradise
Creek
Books

Paradise Creek Books
Seattle, Washington
Elgin, Iowa
www.ParadiseCreekBooks.com

Paradise Creek Books

Seattle, Washington

Elgin, Iowa

www.ParadiseCreekBooks.com

Printed in the United States of America

First Publication: December 2012

ISBN # 978-0-9836652-8-1

The Fourth Generation

Bob Bancks

Preface

Emil Paul Maas came to the United States in 1910, when he was eighteen. After working for a large landowner for two years, he started farming a small acreage in Muscatine County, Iowa. At a little Methodist stone church, he met Williamena (Minnie) Mae Thoene [Tay-nie]. They married and had four children: Bess, Thelma, Leona, and George.

George was born in 1926 and was the heir apparent to head the second generation of the Maas Farm family. At seventeen, he joined the Army to fight in World War II. While George was overseas, his father died in late 1943.

Minnie and the three girls continued farming until George returned and fell in love with his high school sweetheart, Madeline (Madge) Linn Wilkerson. He and Madge had two children, Sue and Paul. Paul would head the third generation on the farm—and foster the fourth generation for the Maas family of farmers.

This is their story.

Chapter One
The Beginning

The three Maas children were all grown up and no longer thought of in the community as just the children of Sara and Paul. They were now young adults, looking to find their place in the world.

Ed had chosen to continue running the farm. He had met his wife, Carol, one summer while detasseling seed corn. They lived just up the road at the old Becker place.

Tim was about to finish his degree in Agronomy and was excited about moving away. Jenny was just starting Iowa State.

The Maas children, like many farm children, had few playmates from outside the farm. They worked and played with each other as they grew up together. That closeness forged a strong bond among all the family members. Sara made sure family values and togetherness were top of the list of things she hoped to teach her children. God had blessed her and Paul with three wonderful children, and she had worked hard to help them grow to be responsible adults.

It was hot in Ames and carrying all the clothes and furniture Jenny thought she would need in her room in Oak Hall was tiring for Sara and Paul, but Mom could tell Jenny was excited. It was her first year at Iowa State.

Tim would be finishing up his degree this year, so it was all old hat to him. He even had his own apartment. He lived with a bunch of guys south of campus. All he had to bring was some clothes and his laptop. By four o'clock, everything was in the room and Sara and Paul took their two college students to dinner.

Afterward, there were tearful goodbyes, Sara and Paul began the long drive home. On the way, Paul did most of the talking, receiving only short answers from Sara. They stopped at the rest stop on I-80, where Paul bought a soft drink from a vending machine. As they hit the road again, he looked over and saw Sara sound asleep.

The next morning at breakfast Paul told her, "Ed and I are going to a seed corn field day in Washington. You're welcome to ride along if you'd like."

"No, I've got some sewing to do, and Jenny's room needs a thorough cleaning," Sara replied.

At 7:30, Ed picked up his Dad and they headed for the field day. Sara decided to sit on the porch swing for a while, letting the cool morning breeze blow across her face before she began sewing. Down the road, she saw the top of the school bus. It didn't slow as it passed the Maas driveway. For many years, it had stopped to pick up one or all three of the Maas children.

Sara remembered putting Ed on the bus for the first time. She was holding Jenny in her arms and Tim was by her side as her eldest son climbed into the big yellow bus. Next it was Tim, and finally, it was Jenny's turn.

As the children got older, Sara would just sit or stand on the porch and wave as they boarded the bus, but today was different. There would be no Maas children riding the bus. There was no more exciting news to hear when they got home. It would be quiet.

She thought she had prepared herself for the inevitable, but had she? She had raised three farm children. There were cuts and scratches, bumps and bruises. There were times of joy to celebrate and times of sadness to endure. She had healed broken spirits and broken hearts.

Now she had to let them go.

They were young adults, entering a world of promise. She could advise, but not make their decisions anymore. She sat on the swing for a long time, tears running down her cheeks. She reached into her pocket and brought out an old crumpled tissue to blow her nose, wishing time could be stopped, but she knew it wasn't possible.

When she finally went back inside, she put off cleaning Jenny's room. At 3:30, she returned to the porch swing so she could watch the bus go by again—and again it didn't even slow down. A cloud of dust billowed up from behind as it roared down the road.

Paul found her still sitting on the swing when he returned.

"How was your day, hon?" he asked.

"Oh, fine," was her answer, but he knew she wasn't telling the truth.

He sat beside her and put his arm around her shoulders. "It was tough today, wasn't it?"

"Yes," she said softly. "I just can't believe everyone is gone. I hope I raised them right."

"You did just fine, honey, just fine. I'm proud of you and our kids. God has really blessed us. Now why don't we go to supper at the Elms tonight and talk about it. I never should have gone today. You go in and put on some makeup and a clean blouse, OK?"

Sara smiled at her husband and said, "Okay, Big Boy, Let's start a new chapter in our lives."

When they returned that night, they changed into their pajamas and sat in the den, waiting for the evening news. Paul and Sara were all alone in the big farmhouse for the first time. In the silence of the quiet house, Sara wondered aloud, "When does a parent begin to have influence? I hope I began to touch them from the very beginning."

"And you'll continue to touch them as long as they live," Paul assured his wife as she dabbed at her eyes with a handkerchief.

"Remember when I was pregnant with Ed?" Sara reminisced. "I didn't even know what labor pains were. If it hadn't been for your mom, I would have had him in the kitchen."

"Do I!" Paul said with a smile. "I thought we'd never make it to Muscatine in time. Tim came even faster, and I thought you were going to have Jen in the car! Those were fun times. We've raised three wonderful kids. Sure, we had some trying times, but I wouldn't have changed a thing. Now we're going to have a good life, just the two of us, for a long time. Hon, I loved you when I met you, and I love you even more now. I can't fathom being without you. We can live our lives together and take care of all the grandkids."

Chapter Two
Rusty and the Boys

The next morning, after Paul had gone out to do chores, Sara sat in the kitchen, drinking her second cup of coffee. As she sat, her mind drifted back to a time when Eddie was still in grade school—and to the day Rusty came to live with them.

Rusty arrived one damp May afternoon just as Eddie was getting home from school. The dog simply met him when he got off the bus and wandered up the lane with him, as if it was the most natural thing in the world.

When Eddie went into the house, Rusty just laid down on the porch by the back door. Sara didn't even know Rusty was there until she opened the door and almost stepped on the poor scraggly dog.

"Shoo! Get out of here!" Sara scolded, but Rusty merely stood, moved about ten feet away, then turned and looked at Sara with the saddest face she'd ever seen.

"Where did you come from?" Sara asked, her voice softening.

She figured Rusty was what farmers call a *walk-on*. People who had pets they couldn't keep sometimes dumped them off in the country to let them fend for themselves. Generally, the dogs or cats found their way to someone's door or barn.

Sara was just about to go back into the house and get the broom when Eddie bounded out the door and cried, "Can we keep him, Mom, please? He followed me home when I got off the bus, and we haven't had a dog since Susie died. I'll take care of him, Mom. Really, I will."

Soon little Tim was also at the door. He squatted down and Rusty immediately walked toward him. As Sara watched the scene unfold, she had to admit Rusty was sort of cute—or would be, once they got him cleaned up. He had some golden lab in him, along with who knew how many other breeds. The fur on his shoulders and ears had a tinge of red, and he was definitely friendly enough.

As Sara bent down to pet Rusty, she said, "I bet you're hungry.

Let's see if we can find some old dog food for you."

As the boys stayed behind on the porch, Sara went to the basement and scrounged around for some food and a couple old pans. Just as she was setting down pans of food and water, Grandpa George arrived.

"Where did that thing come from?" he grumbled. "Are you planning to keep him?"

"I don't know," Sara replied tentatively. "We'll see what Paul says when he comes in."

It wasn't long before Paul arrived, and as soon as they saw their father, both boys started running in his direction, asking if they could keep the dog.

Paul smiled at his sons' enthusiasm and said, "Well, I don't know. First let's have a look at him." Paul took one look at the skinny mutt and said, "You know, he looks rusty to me with all that red hair on his shoulders."

"That's what we'll call him, Dad!" Eddie said happily. "Can we keep Rusty, please?"

Paul smiled again. "Why not? All farms need a good dog, but you boys will have to feed him and brush him and give him a bath now and then."

"We will, we promise!" Eddie agreed.

Rusty had found a new home and he proved to be a worthy addition to the farm. He barked whenever a car or truck came up the driveway. When the cattle got out and were about to make a break for the road, it was Rusty who barked and growled and prevented their escape. He followed Paul out to the pasture and learned to ride in the go-getter. Best of all, he was a constant companion for the boys.

Later that summer, on a warm humid morning when the corn was tall, Sara was out in the garden, before the children would be waking up. Rusty had followed her and was sitting close while Sara dead-headed the coneflowers and zinnias. All of a sudden, Rusty's ears perked up. Then he ran to the closed garden gate and began barking.

"What do you hear, Rusty?" Sara said. "I don't hear anything."

Undaunted, Rusty kept up his clamor until Sara finally opened the gate for him. He tore out of the garden and raced toward the barn, where he stopped at the gate to the silo shed and began to bark again. Sara followed Rusty and as she drew nearer, she could hear the silage unloader churning. Then she heard Paul calling her name. She threw open the gate and ran around the bunk to the unloader, where she found Paul caught between the silo and the feeder belt. One leg was bare and the other was at an odd angle against the gear reduction box, his jeans wrapped tightly in the gears.

"Quick! Turn off the feeder belt!" Paul shouted. "Then turn off the unloader!"

Sara hurried to the control box and quickly pulled the disconnect, bringing the entire operation to a halt. She returned to Paul and began scooping the silage away from his body.

"Cut my pants off so I can get my leg down," Paul said, obviously in pain.

Luckily, Sara still had her flower pruners in her pocket and began to cut the twisted fabric of Paul's jeans until his leg finally dropped free.

As Paul let out a huge sigh of relief, Sara asked, "What happened, hon?"

"I stepped over the conveyor, like I've done hundreds of times before, but I slipped on the wet silage and fell forward. I caught myself, but my pant leg got caught in the gears and the thing started to grind my pants right off me. I've heard of guys getting caught like this, so I unbuckled my belt and unbuttoned my jeans so the machine would take them off. As my pants wound around the gears, I started to take off my shoes, and I got one off, but wasn't fast enough with the other one. The conveyor pulled my leg up and wound it tighter and tighter, and I couldn't get a hold of anything to shut off the machine. How'd you hear me above the noise?"

"I didn't," Sara said, shaking her head. "It was Rusty. He wouldn't stop barking, and as soon as I let him out, he headed for the silo shed, so I followed him. It was only after I came around the corner of the barn that I heard you calling. You sit on this bushel basket and I'll get the go-getter and give you a ride back to the house. I don't think you can walk across the gravel without shoes."

Sara hurried to the shop, got the go-getter, and then helped Paul into the back. When Rusty jumped in beside him, Paul put his arms around the dog and said, "Thanks, buddy. You're a good dog."

Once they reached the back door and were about to start up the three steps to the kitchen, Paul said, "Do you suppose I could take a shower? I've got silage all over me and it itches. I probably smell, too. I think I can make it downstairs."

"Okay, but I'm going down in front of you so you won't fall."

Paul hopped down the stairs on one leg and limped to a chair. Sara turned on the shower and adjusted the water temperature. When she turned back to Paul, he already had taken off his t-shirt. She helped him remove one sock and cut off the other with her garden shears. Then she helped him strip off his underwear and get into the shower. Paul braced himself against the wall as best he could, intense pain shooting through his leg.

As Sara washed his back and legs, he turned toward her to have her bathe his front, then grabbed her shoulders. Sara saw that his eyes were rolling back in his head. He was passing out. She grabbed him, doing her best to prevent him from falling, and sat him down in the corner of the shower. With one arm she reached up and turned off the water. With the other, she tried to cradle his head to prevent it from hitting the tile floor.

Then she remembered, when someone fainted, it was important to get their head below their heart. She literally dragged Paul out of the shower, put his good leg up on a chair, and knelt above him, looking down and saying, "Paul, honey, are you alright?"

It took a few moments, but Paul finally opened his eyes, looked up as Sara, and said softly, "What happened?"

"You passed out in the shower. You scared me! I never had anyone pass out on me before," Sara said, fighting back her tears.

Paul looked up at his wife, then down at his body and said, "Looks like I forgot to get dressed."

"Well, sort of," Sara said with a smile. "Let me dry you off and see if I can find you some shorts in the laundry basket. Then I need to get myself out of these wet things."

She dried Paul off and helped him into his shorts. Then she removed her t-shirt and jeans and dried herself off with a towel.

"Do you think you can make it upstairs?" she asked.

"Yes, if I take it slow."

She helped Paul to his feet and they slowly started toward the steps. Leaning heavily on the railing, Paul managed to hop up the stairs and into the den, where Sara got him settled with his injured leg up on pillows.

"I'm going upstairs to put on some dry clothes," Sara said after she was sure Paul was comfortable.

"You don't have to put on clothes for me," Paul said with a smile. "I like you undressed. In fact, you can take them all off if you want."

She smiled and said sarcastically, "Don't you ever stop thinking about sex? It's a good thing we got you fixed or we'd have a dozen kids by now."

They both laughed for the first time since the accident. They were a perfect match and liked to kid each other. Sara went upstairs, and when she returned with a t-shirt and khaki shorts for Paul, she said, "Try to put these on. I'm calling your folks to see if they can finish chores and watch the kids. I think we'd better take you to the emergency room."

Madge and George came right over, took one look at Paul's leg, and agreed he should go to the hospital. George helped Paul into the car and Sara drove to Muscatine, where x-rays showed no bones had been broken.

Paul's twisted pant leg had crushed many capillaries in his leg and it would take some time to heal. Dr. Barnes gave him a choice of being admitted to the hospital or going home to lay flat on his back with his leg elevated above his heart. Paul chose to go home, and he promised to behave himself and follow the doctor's orders.

When they got back to the farm, George told them he was going to need help removing the jeans from the gearbox. They were wound so tightly he would have to loosen the gears from the shaft to clear them. Sara told him she'd be right out after she changed her clothes.

For several days Paul was confined to the sofa, getting up only to go to the bathroom, and even then Sara had to help him. He had to wear a tight surgical hose for several days and his leg turned many colors of black, blue, and angry purple. The children were also very helpful, running errands, getting him drinks of water, and gathering the mail every day. In a week, Dr. Barnes told Paul he could start putting weight on his leg, and from that day on, he began to recover, though it was slow going.

Meanwhile, Rusty was the hero of the farm. One day, Sara found the boys sitting on the front steps with Rusty between them. Eddie had his arm around Rusty's neck and Tim was resting his head on Rusty's back. It was a perfect picture of contentment. This brought tears to Sara's eyes, knowing Rusty had showed up on the farm at just the right time.

In late August, the corn was very tall. Sara was rocking Jenny to sleep while Eddie played with his toy tractors in the sandbox outside. She could also hear Tim in the front yard throwing a ball for Rusty to fetch. As Jenny drifted off, Sara closed her eyes for a few moments, and when she awoke, it seemed very quiet outside.

She put the sleeping Jenny on her bed and looked outside. She could see Eddie, still playing in the sandbox; however, she didn't see Tim or Rusty. She went out to the front porch and looked around the yard. There was no sign of Tim. The children weren't supposed to go out of the yard, but the big gate on the west side was slightly ajar.

As she stood on the porch wondering, she saw Rusty come running out of the cornfield. She smiled, thinking that Tim had probably gone into the cornfield to fetch Rusty's ball, which had accidently gone over the fence.

She called out, "Tim, where are you?"

Rusty looked at her for a moment, then turned and darted back into the cornfield, followed by Sara. She called again, but there was no answer. She could hear Rusty running ahead, but this time she didn't follow him. Tim knew his way around a cornfield and he'd eventually come out. She turned and walked back to the house, where she found Jenny awake.

When Eddie came in for a snack, he asked, "Where's Tim, Mom?"

"I think he's in the cornfield and I'm starting to get a little worried," Sara replied.

"Don't worry, Mom," Eddie said. "Tim can find his way out."

An hour went by, but Tim hadn't returned. It was four o'clock and the temperature was in the nineties. When Paul came in for a break, Sara told him about Tim. Paul quickly ran out into the field, calling Tim's name. When he stopped and listened, all he could hear was the rustle of the corn leaves.

After a few moments, Rusty came running up to him. Paul looked down at the dog and said, "Where's Tim, Rusty? Take me to him."

Rusty looked up, turned and ran back in the direction from which he'd come. Paul tried to follow, but he soon lost track of Rusty. He glanced at his watch. It was getting late, so Paul returned to the house and decided to call 911.

After he had explained the problem to the dispatcher, she said, "I'll call the fire department and we'll have them out there as soon as possible."

Joe Hansen, the fire chief, owned the hardware and lumber store in town. When he heard it was a lost child situation, he had one of his employees, who was also a fireman, gather all the plastic pipe he could find and load it into the store van.

Then he told Sue, the store's clerk and accountant, "Go into the back room and get all the flashlights and batteries you can find. Then call John's Grocery and have them bring all the bottles of water they have to the Paul Maas farm."

He called the football coach, who was still at school, and asked, "How many boys are still at practice? Can they come and help? We'll need all the help we can get. Little Tim Maas is lost in a cornfield and we've got to find him before dark."

After he got off the phone, Coach Brus hollered at his team, "How many of you guys can help search for a little boy who's lost in a cornfield?"

All the young men raised their hands, and within a few minutes, dozens of vehicles, loaded with players, cheerleaders, girlfriends, and anyone else who wanted to help, were on their way to the Maas farm. When they arrived, Joe was barking orders over a bullhorn from his perch in the loader bucket of Paul's tractor, which Paul had raised so Joe could be seen by everyone. There were nearly sixty volunteers in the yard, waiting for instructions.

"Everyone grab a flashlight and put new batteries in them," Joe said. "If you haven't got your own flashlight, take a new one. Next, everyone line up down the lane. Every third person grab a plastic pipe and hold it up like a flagpole. Starting at the far end of the field, go into the field until you get off the end rows. Starting with the fourth row, count every four rows. That will be your row. Don't get off your row, and be sure to look on both sides of your row! It's getting dark, so Tim will probably be scared and crouched close to the ground. Those people with the pipes, hold them up high so I can see where you are. Nobody start down their row until I say so, understand? If you find Tim, raise your pipe high and holler."

When everyone was ready, Joe said, "Okay, everyone go into the field. I'll tell you when to start walking."

When the group was in place, Joe gave the order to begin the search and the volunteers started down the long rows, their pipes held high. Joe watched intently from his perch, calling out for some volunteers to slow down and for others to walk more quickly. Twenty minutes went by, then thirty, then forty-five. Sara and Madge stayed in the yard with Jenny and Ed, praying for good news. Finally, after darkness had completely set in, there was a shout from the field.

"I found him!"

About three hundred yards into the field, a pipe began to wave frantically as cheers erupted among the volunteers. In the midst of the noise, Rusty could be heard barking loudly from somewhere in the field.

Within minutes, Jake Smith, a linebacker who worked part-time on the Maas farm, emerged from the field, carrying little Tim in his strong arms. Rusty was at his side, now carrying the tennis ball they'd been playing with.

"The dog was right by his side when I found him," said Jake. "He even growled when I tried to pick Tim up. I tell you, Rusty is some kind of dog."

One by one, the volunteers emerged from the cornfield, and as they did, they were handed a bottle of water. Jake walked up the lane with Tim and handed him to Sara.

Tim looked up at the tears in his mother's eyes and said, "What ya crying for, Mom? I was alright. Rusty was with me all the time."

"Yes, I know. He's a special dog," Sara said, hugging her little boy tightly.

Paul let Joe down from bucket and thanked him for his help.

"Happy to be at your service. It's nice to have these things come out alright—and you should thank those football players, too. They sure made the job a lot easier," Joe replied.

Paul nodded, then added, "I will, but I wish I could pay you or maybe the department something in return."

"Paul, you support us by your taxes," said Joe, "but we do need a little extra every once in a while. Right now we're trying to buy an oxygen tank re-filler. We could use a little help with that."

"How about a thousand dollars?" Paul said happily.

"That would be great!" Joe replied. "Thank you very much."

"But what about all those flashlights?" Paul asked.

"Heck, those will actually make me money," Joe said. "Everyone in town will want to buy the flashlight they used in the search. I'll have more customers than I can handle."

"Well, how about you give everyone a flashlight and I'll pay for them," Paul volunteered.

"Say, that's even a better deal," Joe agreed. "Thanks a lot, Paul."

Joe put the bullhorn to his mouth and announced, "You can all keep the flashlights, compliments of the Maas'."

It took about an hour for the crowd to leave. Since Rusty had been a hero again, Sara cooked an extra hamburger that night—and gave it to him.

As she tucked Tim into bed that night, Sara asked, "Why did you go into the cornfield? You know you're not supposed to leave the yard."

Tim looked at her, sighed, then replied, "Me and Rusty were playing fetch, and when I threw the ball as hard as I could, it didn't go straight. It went into the cornfield. At first, I let Rusty out to go find it; but when he came back without the ball, I went out to help him look for it. I found the ball, but pretty soon I was lost. I'm sorry, Mommy."

"I know you were trying to help Rusty, and we knew Rusty knew where you were, but we couldn't follow him fast enough," Sara said with a smile. "He's a good dog. Now you go to sleep. It's all over now."

The next morning, as he did every morning, Rusty was waiting for Paul when he came out of the house to do chores. Rusty especially loved checking the cattle, but he made sure he was always outside the fence as he barked at the steers. Whenever Paul went to the pasture, Rusty rode in the seat of the pickup or the go-getter.

Rusty was always with the children when they were outside. He followed them to the school bus stop each morning and waited until the bus disappeared over the hill before he returned to the house. At three-thirty in the afternoon, he waited for the bus to return. Even if it was raining or snowing, Rusty was always there.

Whenever someone pulled into the driveway, Rusty let Sara know with a friendly bark. Only once did he growl at a stranger. Sara was getting ready for a dentist's appointment and was upstairs getting ready when she heard Rusty growl. She looked out the window and saw an old pickup parked in the driveway. She watched as a man got out, walked over to the shop, and came out with an armload of tools. As he went back into the building for another load, Sara quickly called 911.

When the dispatcher answered, Sara told her a man was stealing tools out of their shop.

"Don't leave the house, Sara!" the dispatcher said firmly. "I'll have someone out there right away—and lock your doors!"

Sara ran downstairs and locked the back door. Then she called Paul on the CB radio, but he didn't answer. She went back upstairs to watch the thief and was horrified when she saw him walking toward the house. He was about to open the yard gate when Rusty rushed toward him.

Cursing, the man tried to brush by Rusty, but the dog stood his ground. The man walked back to his truck and returned with a large wrench. Sara knew what the man was planning to do, so she quickly went to the closet and grabbed Paul's shotgun. She didn't know how to use it, but she was not going to let that man hurt Rusty.

She found a box of shells on the top shelf and jammed one into the chamber, then opened the window and shouted, "Hey! Stop right where you are or I'll shoot!"

The man looked up, saw the gun, then began backing up. "Now look, lady. I'm not going to do anything. I'll just leave, okay?"

"No! I saw the tools you stole, so you just stay right where you are!" Sara shouted, aiming the shotgun at the man.

When the intruder suddenly turned and started running toward his truck, Sara pulled the trigger. Gravel flew up to the right of the frightened man, who froze, turned around, and put his hands in the air as Sara reloaded the shotgun.

Pointing the shotgun again, Sara shouted, "Don't move a muscle. Next time I won't miss!"

The man stood with his hands up high, as Rusty continued to growl. In just a few moments, two squad cars came roaring up the lane. Two deputies jumped out and grabbed the thief.

Sara, seeing the deputies had everything under control, went downstairs and walked out of the house, still holding the shotgun in her hands. The deputies smiled at the sight of mild-mannered Sara holding a weapon. Her hair was a mess, she was wearing some old jeans she'd put on in a hurry, and her blouse wasn't buttoned straight.

One of the deputies said, "Nice job, Sara. We've been trying to catch this guy for some time. He usually just steals stuff out of shops and garages; but if he thinks no one's home, he cleans out the farmhouse, too. How did you know he was here?'

"Rusty started to growl, and he never growls," Sara replied. "I heard him growling, so I looked out and saw this guy from the upstairs window. I didn't grab the gun until he threatened Rusty. That's where I drew the line. Rusty protects us, so I had to protect Rusty."

Just as the deputies were getting ready to leave, Paul pulled up the lane. He jumped out of the truck and said, "What's going on here?"

"Oh, nothing, Paul," one of the deputies responded. "Your wife and your dog just captured a thief we've been trying to catch for a long time. He's lucky she didn't fill his hind end with buckshot."

Paul looked at Sara and asked, "Are you alright?"

"I'm fine, just a little shaken," Sara said, reaching down to scratch Rusty behind the ears. "It would have been much worse if it wasn't for Rusty. Looks like he's a hero again."

Everyone laughed, except the guy in the backseat of the squad car.

The deputies said they'd send someone to pick up the thief's truck, then drove away. As they disappeared down the driveway, Sara turned and kissed Paul. Then she bent down and kissed Rusty on the top of his head.

"You're a mess," Paul said, noticing her disheveled condition. "What were you doing when this guy showed up?"

"Oh, my gosh!" Sara said. "I forgot I was to be at the dentist by now. I'd better call them right away, though they'll never believe my excuse."

"Maybe you should give me the shotgun now," Paul said with a smile. "I don't want you to shoot yourself."

"Hey, the kids won't be home for another hour yet. It's too late to go to the dentist. How about coming up and helping me change out of these rags? I could stand a little calming down, if you know what I mean," Sara said with a wink as she started to unbutton her blouse.

Paul smiled and replied, "You know, I'm sort of nervous myself."

As they walked hand-in-hand into the house, they heard the phone ring. It was a reporter from the *Muscatine Journal*. She'd heard about the incident and wanted details. Sara talked to the reporter for twenty minutes, and by the time she hung up, Paul was already back outside.

The headline on front page of the *Journal* read: "Farm Wife Nabs Tool Thief" Sara had become a celebrity. There was even a photo of Sara—and Rusty.

Chapter Three
Three Bikes Have We

Farm children have some disadvantages because they don't have neighborhood friends next door at their beckon call to play with. They do, however, have plenty of space, since their playground is the whole farm. There are creeks, woods, ponds, haymows, and pastures.

The Maas children played together, even though there was an age difference. The bond formed between brothers and sister was strong. When they were very young, they were supposed to stay in the yard, but being children, that rule wasn't always obeyed.

Paul was always doing things on the spur of the moment. One day he was in charge of the children while Sara attended a church meeting. They made a parts run to the John Deere dealer during the time when the John Deere company first decided to start selling bicycles. At the store, the children oohed and aahed over the bright green bikes. By the time they left to head toward Grandma Madge's, there were three shiny new bikes in the back of the pickup.

Grandma Madge lived on a quiet street in Wilton, so learning to ride there would be safer and on a hard surface road. Paul started each child out by hanging on to the back fender or the seat.

As he got each of them going, he shouted, "Keep pedaling, keep pedaling!"

When the child was traveling faster than he could run, Dad let go, but he kept shouting, "Keep pedaling!"

Soon all three children were riding with ease. They all wore new helmets in case they fell. After having cake and ice cream at Grandma's, they returned home to show Mom what they had learned.

Although she was impressed, she warned, "Be careful on the gravel. It can throw you."

Eddie was the first to start down the lane, calling over his shoulder, "I'll get the mail!"

"You don't have to. I already got it!" Sara shouted back, but just as she said it, Eddie hit a chuckhole in the gravel lane.

His bike made a ninety-degree turn and headed for the fence. A second later, Eddie, bike, and a fence post met. Eddie slammed his shoulder into the post, but jumped up quickly and examined his new bike. It had survived the crash with only the mirror knocked out of place. To his joy, there were no scratches.

He stood and waved to his mom to show that he was okay; however, as he waved, he felt a sharp pain in his shoulder. He slowly walked back to the house, pushing his bike. Mom could see that he was in a lot of pain by the way he was wincing.

"Are you alright?" she asked.

"I think I hurt my shoulder," Eddie replied.

Sara removed his shirt and found several scratches on his upper back. Every time he moved his arm, the pain shot through his shoulder.

"Let's go inside and put an ice pack on your shoulder," she told her son. Then she turned to the other children and said, "You two be careful or you'll end up the same way."

By late in the afternoon, Eddie's pain hadn't subsided.

"I think we'd better go to the emergency room and have your shoulder checked out," Sara said. "I'll have Tim go out to the barn and tell your dad where we're going."

Sara and Eddie got into the car and headed for the ER in Muscatine. When they arrived, they discovered it must have been a bad day for children. The emergency room was full. It took an hour before the doctor could finally see them. He took an x-ray, which showed Eddie had broken his collarbone. There weren't a lot of options for fixing a broken collarbone except immobilizing the arm and shoulder with a sling.

"Eddie's young," the doctor said. "He'll heal quickly. In a couple of weeks, he'll be as good as new, but he'll have to stop riding his bike for a while."

This was just one of many mishaps happening to the Maas crew.

Aside from getting lost in the cornfield, Tim seldom got into trouble. Eddie seemed to be the leader, Tim was the brain, and Jenny was a tomboy in the purest sense. Having two older brothers and a lot of freedom on the farm helped. She was afraid of nothing. Once she grabbed on to an electric fence. She was definitely shocked by that touch—but it was all part of the learning process. Her daring got her in trouble many times.

Chapter Four
Snakes Alive

Early one morning in June, Sara and Jenny were picking strawberries. After about fifteen minutes, Jenny lost interest. Sara knew it was going to happen and never scolded or chided her children. She just figured that even if she only got a little help, it was better than none at all.

Jenny left the garden and went to play at the back of the garage. Sara thought she'd be safe, so she went back to picking the red fruit.

The next words she heard were, "Mom, will this snake hurt me?"

Sara looked up to see the head of a bull snake about eight inches in front of her face. As she screamed and fell back, her hand hit the side of the berry basket, sending strawberries flying every direction.

As she sat on the ground, trying not to show fear, Sara asked, "Jenny, where did you get that thing?"

"It's not a thing, Mom. It's a snake."

"And a darned big one, too. Why don't you just let him go out by the cornfield?" Sara suggested.

"No, Mom. I want to keep him as a pet."

"No, Jenny, you can't do that. You can keep him until your dad and your brothers come home, but then you've got to let him go. Wild animals, including snakes, should be left in the wild. That's God's plan."

Secretly, Sara added, "and let God be responsible for his animals," but she didn't say it out loud. Instead, she said, "I'll tell you what. Let's put your snake in a bucket. When Dad comes home, you and he can let it loose on the sand dune. How's that?"

Jenny sighed and said sadly, "But, Mom, I already have a name for him—Sneaky, like in a song I heard at school." Then she sighed again and added, "I do suppose he should go free, though."

"That's my girl. You stay here. I'll go find a big bucket with a lid."

Sara hurried to the garage and found a bucket with a snap-on lid which looked clean inside. Jenny was still holding the snake when she got back. The snake had relaxed a bit and was curled around Jenny's arm. It had to be at least three feet long.

As Jenny carefully unwound Sneaky and dropped him into the bucket, she asked, "Won't he die in there? He has to have air."

"You're right," Sara conceded. "Let's go over to the shop and fix that."

They carried the bucket to the shop, where Sara found an electric drill and put several holes in the lid. This seemed to satisfy Jenny.

"Now, you set the snake in the shade by the backdoor, and come back out to the garden and help me finish," Sara instructed her daughter. "We also have to pick up the berries I spilled."

They were just finishing their picking , as Paul and the boys pulled up the drive.

Jenny immediately ran toward them, hollering, "Daddy, Daddy! I've got a snake in a bucket. Want to see? I named it Sneaky. It's big and brown. Mom says we should take it to the dune and let it go."

Paul looked at his wife and smiled. He could tell she wanted no part of the reptile.

"Okay, Punkin, I'll have a look," he said, looking down at Jenny. "Do you know what kind of snake it is?'

"Mom says it's a bull snake."

"Well, bull snakes are good snakes. They eat mice and voles and other small animals. We shouldn't kill it, but it's a wild thing that belongs outside. I think the dune would be the perfect place for him. Let's take a look."

Tim, and Eddie crowded around the bucket as Dad slowly opened the lid. The snake was coiled around the side of the pail. He made a jump at the edge, but it was slick and tall, so he fell back.

"Eddie, you run and get a tape measure from the shop," Paul said. "Let's see just how long this critter is."

As Eddie ran toward the shop, Paul went into the house and put on some leather gloves. When Eddie returned, Paul grabbed the snake's head and pulled it out of the bucket. The snake whipped around trying to free itself, but Paul grabbed its tail and stretched it out. Eddie handed one end of the tape to Tim and they measured the snake—three feet ten and a half inches.

"That's a mighty big snake for a little girl. How'd you ever catch it?" Paul asked.

"It was sleeping in a little hole by the garage. I just grabbed its head and caught him," Jenny replied. Then she added with a laugh, "I really scared Mom when I showed it to her."

Paul looked over at Sara and smiled, but it was obvious she wanted that snake out of the yard and far, far away.

"I'll tell you what," said Paul. "Why don't all of us go out to the dune and release it—and Jenny, you can have the honor of letting it out of the bucket."

"I think I'll stay here at the house," Sara said firmly. "I've got a lot of berries to clean."

So Paul and the kids scrunched into the go-getter with the bucket in the back and headed for the dune. Paul carried the bucket to the top of the dune, tipped the container over, and Jenny slowly opened the top. At first the snake didn't move. It seemed comfortable in the bucket. Then Tim picked up the bottom of the pail and the snake slid forward and fell out. It lay still in the grass for a few seconds, then slithered into the underbrush.

"'Bye, Sneaky Snake," said Jenny softly. "Be careful, and eat a lot of mice."

As they rode back to the house, Paul told Jenny that maybe she should just leave the next snake she found alone and not scare her mother. A smiling Jenny agreed.

It wasn't the only time Jenny got involved with a snake. One day during recess at school, she and her friends were in a circle, giggling and talking little girl talk, when Bobby Kissel, the meanest boy in third grade, snuck up behind one of the girls and dangled a snake into her face. It wasn't a big snake, but it was enough to scare all the girls—except Jenny. When Bobby pushed the snake toward Jenny, she grabbed his hand and pushed it right back into his face. As she pinned Bobby against the fence, Bobby screamed and let go of the snake. Jenny grabbed it and was just about to put it down Bobby's shirt when Mrs. Olsen arrived on the scene to see what all the commotion was about.

"Jenny Maas! Don't you dare put that snake down Bobby's shirt!" shouted Mrs. Olsen. "You let that snake go over by the edge of the schoolyard right now—then go inside. Both you and Bobby are headed for Mr. Moore's office."

Jenny dutifully carried the critter to the edge of the yard and let him go. When she returned, Mrs. Olsen already had Bobby by the arm and was leading him back into the building. They all met in the principal's office.

Mr. Moore looked at Bobby first and asked, "What is this all about, Mr. Kissel?"

"Jenny was going to put a snake down my shirt," Bobby said, trying to look as innocent as possible.

"Is this true, Miss Maas?" asked the principal, turning his attention to Jenny.

"Yes, Mr. Moore, but Bobby was pestering us with the snake before I got it. I just grabbed it from him."

"Was there anyone else there to witness this event?" asked the principal.

"Yes, there was Susie Smith, Gloria Hennessy, Sandy Jones, Lucy Cole, and me," replied Jenny.

"Mrs. Olsen, could you bring in the others?"

A few minutes later, Mrs. Olsen returned with the other girls. Mr. Moore listened to their stories, knowing Bobby had a reputation for getting into trouble and Jenny was a fine student. It appeared Jenny had been trying to teach Bobby a much-needed lesson, but he couldn't let the deed go unpunished.

He sat back in his chair and thought for a moment, then said, "Okay, here's the deal. Bobby, because you started this fracas, you'll stay indoors in the detention room for one week, understood? Miss Maas, since you were trying to protect your friends, your punishment will be less. You can't just go around stuffing snakes down people's shirts; therefore, you'll spend one week in the science room with Mr. Howe during your free period to help him clean cages and care for all the animals he has in the room."

Bobby looked glum at the verdict, but Jenny's eyes twinkled as she said, "Yes, Mr. Moore. I can do that."

Jenny was overjoyed. It wasn't going to feel like punishment. After all, Jenny loved the science room. In fact, science was her favorite class. Taking care of animals and plants was right up her alley.

Mr. Moore had one more request. "I want both of you to say you're sorry and that you won't do it again. Jenny, you start."

"I'm sorry, Bobby. I won't bother you again."

Mr. Moore turned his attention to Bobby. "Now, Bobby, you tell

Jenny and the rest of the girls you're sorry and you won't do it again."

Bobby agreed and apologized.

The ironic thing was the next year Bobby Kissel and Jenny became good friends. Bobby's dad raised rabbits, and when Jenny decided to raise rabbits for a 4-H project, she and Bobby showed against each other and with each other. Several times Jenny even rode to shows with the Kissels.

Chapter Five
Ants in the Pants

Summers could sometimes be boring—unless Jenny was around. One early June afternoon, she asked Sara if she and Tim could go to the pasture. Eddie was at church camp for three days and there seemed to be nothing to do.

"I don't want you two going down there by yourselves," Sara replied. "I'm not doing much, so let's all get in the go-getter and I'll read while you guys play. We'll go down by the sand bar. The creek might be a little chilly yet, so all you can do is wade."

After packing some cookies and drinks, they headed for the pasture, where Sara found a warm spot in the sun to read. She curled up in her lawn chair while Jenny and Tim waded in the creek. They made bark boats and floated them in the fast-moving water. In the more shallow part of the stream, they piled rocks to make a small waterfall. Soon the creek became boring, so they moved up on the bank. Sara had been watching them, but she was growing drowsy, so she shut her eyes, just for a bit. Meanwhile, the adventurers roamed farther and farther away from her chair.

Eventually, they came upon a large ant mound. As Jenny took a stick and started to poke at the mound, Tim said warily, "I don't think you should do that."

"Oh, ants won't hurt you," Jenny scoffed, poking a little deeper.

The ants flew into a frenzy. Tim and Jenny soon had ants climbing all over their bare feet and legs. Moments later, the ants were inside their pant legs—and beginning to bite.

"Ow! Mom!" the children screamed as they began to jump up and down, which only made the ants madder and made them bite even more.

Sara came running and quickly pulled the children about twenty feet away from the ant mound as they continued to scream in pain. Sara unsnapped their pants and stripped them off. With the waist bands gone, the ants began to crawl under their shirts, as well, so Sara pulled them off and desperately began to brush the ants off. Then she picked up the kids, one under each arm, and ran toward the creek. She threw them into the water and began washing the angry ants from their bodies.

A few minutes later it was all over; but now she had two wet, cold children and was wet to the knees herself. She hauled them out of the water and led them over to her chair, scolding, "You stand right there in the sun while I get your clothes."

Sara returned to the ant mound and picked up the children's clothes, shaking them furiously as she walked back toward her chair. She turned the clothes inside out to make sure there were no more ants, then looked at her shivering children and said, "Okay, take off your underwear because they're soaked. You can wear your pants and shirts home without underwear."

Tim and Jenny looked at each other. They'd seen each other naked before, but that was in the house—and when they were much younger. Now they were six and eight.

"Come on, come on!" Sara ordered. "We haven't got all day. You'll feel warmer in dry clothes."

When they still hesitated, Sara grabbed Jenny, ripped down her underpants, and threw them on the chair. She had trouble getting Jenny's outer pants turned right side out, so she grabbed Tim and stripped off his underwear, as well. There they stood in the pasture, in full sunlight, bare as baby birds, while their mother straightened out their clothes. Jenny giggled as she looked at Tim. Then he smiled and started to laugh.

"What are you two giggling about?' Sara asked.

"I don't know," Jenny replied. "It's just kind of funny standing out here with nothing on—but I'm still cold."

"Well, run over to the old willow and back while I straighten out your clothes," said Sara. "That'll warm you up."

"But, Mom, we're naked!" Tim complained.

"Listen, God knows you're naked, I know you're naked, and Jenny knows you're naked, but guess what? None of us care. Now git!" barked Sara.

"Come on, Tim, I'll race you," Jenny challenged as she took off running, followed by Tim.

Jenny reached the willow first and waited for her brother. When he touched the tree, she raced back to her mother, her long pigtails bouncing on her bare back. As Sara caught Jenny in her arms and helped her put her top back on, she noticed a number of ant bites on Jenny's legs. When Tim arrived, she examined his legs also.

"When we get back to the house, we'll put some calamine lotion on those bites," Sara said. "Hurry and get your jeans on."

"That was fun!" Jenny exclaimed. "I like running around with nothing on. Can me and Tim do it again?"

"Maybe," Sara replied, "but this was sort of an unusual circumstance. Let's hope you don't go poking in any more ant mounds."

"Will you do it with us next time, Mom?"

"Oh, no!" Sara said, shaking her head. "Young brothers and sisters can run around with nothing on, but not with anybody else—and certainly not with their parents. Someday you'll understand."

They climbed into the go-getter and went back to the house, where Sara hustled them into the upstairs shower. She showered Jenny first because she had the most bites. While Tim showered, Sara dabbed calamine lotion on Jenny's bites. Then she did the same with Tim.

While the lotion dried, Sara gave Jenny her summer nightgown to wear. It wouldn't rub the bites as much as pajamas. For Tim, she found one of Paul's t-shirts, which covered him all the way to his knees. Tim and Jenny played Monopoly until suppertime. At the table, Jenny claimed the bites itched when she sat, and she asked if she could eat standing up, Sara said yes.

Before bedtime, Jenny was still itching, so Sara dabbed some more calamine lotion on her daughter and gave her some antihistamine, which also made Jenny sleepy. Sara finally carried her daughter upstairs and rocked her to sleep in the old rocking chair.

As Sara later told Paul about what had happened in the pasture and how the children had enjoyed running bare in the grass, she was smiling.

"The only thing wrong was, you wished you could have joined them, right?" Paul teased.

With a wink, Sara said, "You got it."

Chapter Six
The Fence

The pasture is the largest playground a kid can imagine. After all, how many town kids have a 200-acre backyard with a creek and a pond? If you could avoid the cows and their leftovers, you could imagine anything. On the east side of the pasture was a small grove of trees with many exposed roots. It was a great place for playing cowboys and bad guys. The middle had two large hills which were perfect for sledding. The kids could slide down one and part way up the other, then return. The north hill generally had the best sledding because the sun didn't melt the snow and it stayed frozen all winter.

One December afternoon, the three Maas kids were sledding in the pasture. It was a Saturday and Mom was in town shopping, so Eddie was in charge. Instead of going back to the buildings through the pasture lane, they decided to take a shortcut and head across the harvested bean field. They were talking and singing as they crossed—until they came to the final fence.

The fence was 32" woven wire topped by three strands of four-point barbed wire. If one person held the two bottom wires apart, the others could crawl through the gap. This was easier than climbing over the fence at the post.

Eddie held the wires first for Jenny to go through, then Tim. But as Tim held the wire for Eddie, he lost his grip just as his brother was swinging his leg over the barbed wire. The wire sprung back, catching Eddie's pant leg, causing him to fall with his leg sticking straight up. Jenny and Tim tried to free the pant leg, trying not to tear Eddie's jeans, but to no avail. Next they tried to lift Eddie in order to take the pressure off the fabric, and that didn't work either.

"Jenny, you go see if Mom is home," Eddie ordered.

Jenny took off running as Tim and Eddie returned to struggle with the pant leg.

Then Eddie got an idea. "Tim, untie my boots and take them off."

"Why?"

"You'll see."

As Tim untied his brother's boots, Eddie unbuckled his flannel-lined jeans. Tim slipped off the boot from his brother's foot and Eddie's leg slid out. Then he pulled the other leg out. In a few seconds, Eddie was sitting in the snow—in his underwear and stocking feet. He and Tim quickly started working on the pant leg, but Tim couldn't help laughing at Ed.

"Hurry up! I'm freezing," Ed growled.

He was just putting his boots back on when Jenny arrived.

"Mom's not home," she reported. Then, noticing Eddie was free, she asked, "Say, how'd you get loose?"

"It's a long story, Jenny," Eddie replied. "A really long, cold story."

Chapter Seven
Cow Tank

When anyone needed help, it was always Ed they called on. He helped Jenny with her homework and her 4-H projects. Since he was the oldest, he was also the designated babysitter.

When Ed was old enough to drive, he became the chauffer. He drove Jenny and Tim to music lessons, choir practice, dance lessons, and early bird classes at school. Even when Jenny grew up, it was Ed who helped her when she needed it. When Jenny's car needed repair, it was Ed she called. If the lawnmower didn't start, she called Ed.

On the other hand, Tim was Jenny's confidential advisor. If there were issues she thought her mother couldn't handle, Jenny talked to Tim. If Sara wasn't around and Jenny needed the back of her dress buttoned, she'd ask Tim for help. He'd even tell her if what she was wearing was inappropriate, since he didn't want his sister showing too much cleavage or too much leg.

One warm day in late March, Sara was in Muscatine helping Grandma Emma while Paul was with Grandpa George at a seed corn meeting. Ed and Tim were working with their 4-H calves in the barn. Jenny, a month away from turning eleven, was outside, at the edge of the lot. It was her daring personality that caused her to try walking the fence rail.

The rail was a two-inch by four-inch piece of wood nailed on top of the posts of a wooden fence which stretched from the main cattle yard gate to the barn, about two hundred feet. Grandpa George called it his *talking fence*. It was one he leaned on as he and the neighbors talked cattle. If you were a kid, you could sit on the four-inch surface and watch the men work the cattle.

The rail was an easy walk, except over the concrete water tank in the middle. One half was in the cattle lot and the other half was outside. The reason it was built this way was because before tractors and diesel-powered engines, horses did the heavy work around the farm—and they needed water. Instead of opening the gate to the cow yard and making the horses drink with the cows, they were allowed to drink on the outside of the lot, in the portion of the water tank outside the fence.

That part of the tank hadn't been used in years, so Paul and Grandpa George covered it with a wooden lid. This not only kept the water warmer and free of trash. It also kept people (and especially children) from falling in. The fence spanned the tank, but the stretch was further than normal. The wooden cover had become weakened by years of disuse and the constant moisture underneath.

As Jenny approached the center of the span, the board snapped and she fell onto the rotted lid covering the tank. She bounced once, then the lid disintegrated and she plunged into the cold water, catching her leg on one of the lid's now exposed nails. She went under the water and came up quickly. Fortunately, the water wasn't very deep, maybe two feet at most, but she couldn't free her pant leg from the nail. She tried to pull herself up, but the rotten, slick lumber wouldn't allow her to get a grip with her wet fingers.

She screamed, "Ed! Tim! Help!"

Ed and Tim quickly came running out of the barn.

"Where are you?" Ed called.

"Over here in the water tank!" she answered. "I'm stuck!"

The boys rushed to the tank and found Jenny struggling to keep her head above water. Ed reached in and grabbed the hood on her coat. He tried to pick her up, but the weight of her water-soaked clothes and her pinched leg prevented him. Tim tried to pull the rotted boards away, but they stubbornly stayed put.

"Run over to the shop and get a hammer and wrecking bar," Ed told Tim.

When Tim returned, he attacked the boards while Ed kept Jenny's head above water. They finally made the opening big enough to lift Jenny; however, her leg was still pinched. Tim got out his pocket knife and began to cut Jenny's jeans. As he ripped the denim away, he saw she had a big gash on her thigh.

"We've got to get her out of here—now!" Tim shouted.

Ed continued to struggle, but there wasn't room enough for him to get under Jenny's shoulders, so he stepped into the tank, followed by Tim. Together they lifted the remaining piece of the lid and secured it with a broken 2x4. Struggling in the cold water, they carefully hoisted their sister out and laid her on the ground. Tim knelt by her cut leg, grabbed his handkerchief, and placed it on the wound, which was bleeding heavily. Ed also offered his hankie. Jenny was cold and her leg was throbbing, but she didn't cry. She just moaned.

"We have to get her to the house and out of these wet clothes," Tim said. "Let's make a basket with our arms and she can sit in it until we get to the back door."

They formed a seat with their arms and carried Jenny to the house as quickly as they could. Although the policy was all dirty people undressed in the basement, it was an emergency. They'd clean up everything later. They laid Jenny on the kitchen floor and Ed pulled off her boots and socks. Then he removed her coat and gloves.

The next items were her inner clothes, but he just couldn't do it. Instead, he told Tim, "I'll call Mom while you take off her jeans and top and underwear. I'll get her robe and some bandages for her leg."

"Okay, but bring me some warm water so I can clean the cut," Tim replied. Then he added, "Hey, wait a minute! Look at the mess on the floor. We're tracking mud all over. Mom will be mad."

In their hurry to take care of their sister, they had forgotten to take off their shoes, caps, coats, and sweatshirts. They quickly took off their shoes and socks, then their wet jeans. When they went back to the task at hand, they continued to run around in their flannel shirts and underwear. Tim helped Jenny to a sitting position and pulled off her soaked t-shirt.

"I'm going to have to take off your undershirt, too," he told her, "and your jeans."

"That's okay," Jenny said, shivering from the cold. "I've got to get out of these wet things, but be careful of my leg. It really hurts. Is it a bad gash? I can't see it very well."

Tim lifted her undershirt off, and carefully undid the snap and zipper of her jeans. He put his arm around her waist to raise her up and slid the jeans down her legs. Slowly, he inched the fabric over the deep cut, being careful not touch the makeshift bandage. He refrained from removing her underpants. He figured they would dry quickly. When Ed returned, he brought Jenny's sweats and let Tim help her into her top.

"I called Grandma Emma. Grandpa said she and Mom won't be back until four. Do you want me to call Grandma Madge? How's Jenny's leg? I brought some bandages from the medicine cabinet. I'll get a pan of warm water so you can wash her leg. How are you feeling Jen?" Ed rattled on, obviously flustered.

Tim gave his older brother a disgusted look and said, "Why don't you get some dry duds on and start picking up this mess? Go upstairs and change. I'll take care of Jenny."

Ed quickly disappeared to find some dry clothes as Tim turned his attention back to his little sister. He helped her lay on her side while he washed the wound. She only whimpered a couple times—until he poured some hydrogen peroxide on the cut. Then she really let out a scream!

He pushed the skin together and placed a piece of gauze over the opening. Then he wrapped tape completely around her thigh to hold her wound together. When he had finished, he had her sit up so he could help her put on her sweat pants.

As he helped her stand up, Tim asked, "Do you think, you can make it to the den?"

"Yes," she replied, smiling weakly.

He put his arm around Jenny's waist and helped her into the den and onto the sofa, where he covered her with a blanket and tucked it around her. Jenny smiled at her older brother and began to giggle.

"What's so funny?" Tim asked.

"You are," she said. "Just look at you. All you have on is a flannel shirt and shorts, and your shorts are wetter than mine. Aren't you cold? Go get some dry clothes on. I'll be alright. Tell Ed I'm decent now, so he can make me some hot chocolate. I never thought he was so shy."

After Tim had dashed upstairs, Ed came back down. He felt much better now Jenny was dressed.

"What happened, Ed?" Jenny teased. "Couldn't you stand to see me naked?"

"I guess not," Ed confessed, and quickly changed the subject. "Mom will be home soon. I'd better get the kitchen cleaned up before she gets here—and I think the calves are still tied out. I'll wait until Mom gets home before I tend to them."

"Go out and finish your chores," Jenny said. "Tim can take care of me."

With that, Ed turned and left the den.

When Tim returned, he asked, "How you doing, sis?"

"I'm fine, but I wish Mom was here," Jenny replied. "My leg

hurts really bad."

Tim picked her up and sat on the couch, holding her in his arms as she put her head on his shoulder and sobbed. Tim stroked her hair gently until her crying stopped.

Then she looked up at him and said, "Tim, guess what?"

"What?" Tim asked.

"I have to go to the bathroom. Can you help me?"

Tim rolled his eyes, but dutifully helped her to the downstairs bath.

"I can't sit down with my bad leg," Jenny whined.

"Okay, I'll get a couple of books to put under your foot. They will lift your leg so it won't touch the edge of the seat," Tim said, " but I'm not going stay and watch you pee. You call me when you're finished."

"Alright, but can you help me pull my underpants down?"

As Tim slowly inched Jenny's underwear over the cut, she cried, "Ow! That hurts!"

"I'm sorry," Tim said, "but it's the best I can do."

"Take it easy, but hurry up!" Jenny demanded. "I really have to go!"

"I've got an idea. Just give me a second," Tim said.

He hurried to the sewing room and got a pair of Sara's scissors. Then he went back to the bathroom and cut the elastic on the side of Jenny's bandaged leg. Her underpants slid off easily and he helped her sit down before leaving the room.

In a few minutes, Tim heard Jenny call, "I'm done! You can come in now."

Tim entered, only to find Jenny still on the stool. He looked at his sister and said, "I thought you said you were done."

"I am."

"But you're still on the pot."

"I can't get off. You've got to help me."

Tim helped her up. They decided to ditch the underpants. Tim told her she'd just have to go without—at least until their mother came home. He pulled up Jenny's sweats and helped her back to the den, hoping Sara would be home soon. He'd seen enough of his sister that day.

Ed was carrying an armload of wet clothes down to the laundry room when Sara burst through the door. She looked at Ed and the wet clothes, then at the dirty kitchen floor as she asked, "Is everyone alright? Grandpa said Jenny was hurt and had cut her leg."

"We're pretty good now," Ed replied. "Jenny fell into the water tank and cut her leg when she fell through the lid. We got her out and brought her to the house, and Tim did a real good job of taking care of her. Maybe you should check out her cut. She may need stitches. She's in the den. I'll put these clothes in the laundry room and then go out and put the calves away. Tell Tim he doesn't have to help. I'll do it."

Sara hurried to the den and found Jenny sitting on the sofa with her leg propped up on a pillow.

"Hi, Mom!" Jenny said cheerfully. "You ought to see my leg. It really hurts bad."

Jenny tried to stand, but her leg hurt too badly, so Tim helped her to her feet.

"She's got a real bad cut on her thigh," Tim said. "I think she should see Dr. Barnes. I'll show you."

"I'll take a look," Sara replied. "You can leave, Tim."

Jenny shook her head and said, "He can stay, Mom. There's nothing he hasn't seen in the last twenty minutes."

Even so, Tim left as Sara slid Jenny's sweatpants down. She looked at the bandage and couldn't believe the skill and maturity Tim had shown. However, as she lifted the bandage, she gasped. The cut was about three inches long and was quite deep.

"Jenny, how did you do this? You'll definitely need stitches," Sara said firmly. "I'll call Dr. Barnes' office to see if we can get you in. I've got to hand it to your brother, though. He did a good job. Where was Ed when all this happened?"

"Oh, he was there, Mom. He got me out of the tank after I fell and carried me in, but when it came to getting me out of my wet clothes, he just couldn't take it," Jenny said with a giggle. "I guess he'd never seen a naked woman before. It didn't seem to bother Tim, though."

"I can see that," Sara said. "He definitely took good care of you. I'll go call the doctor."

Sara made an appointment and told Tim what to fix for supper in case they were late getting back. He said he'd clean the floor and start some laundry before he started his chores.

"Don't worry about your chores," Sara said. "Your big brother said he'd do them for you tonight."

It was late by the time Jenny and Mom returned. All three men were waiting to hear the latest news. Jenny proudly announced she had gotten twelve stitches in her leg.

"Tell them the rest of the story, Jen," Sara said with a smile.

"Well, I can't show you my bandage because we left in such a hurry I forgot to put on any underpants," Jenny explained, "but I'll go up and get some right away."

Everyone laughed as Jenny turned and started up the stairs, aided by Sara.

At the supper table, Jenny explained she had been walking the fence when the board broke, sending her into the water tank. She thanked her brothers for saving her and she especially thanked Tim for taking care of her once they got inside the house.

Her final comment was, "How many brothers would carry their wet little sister into the house, take all her clothes off, cut off her underwear, and dress her cuts, thinking it was their duty—without being embarrassed? Oh, and by the way, Dr. Barnes said you did a great job, Tim. She said you ought to become a doctor—and, Ed, you kept me from drowning while Tim ripped the boards off. I love you both."

When the story had been told, Paul said, "I think we've all been lucky today because Jenny didn't drown and her injuries weren't serious. I'm so glad you boys fished her out and took care of her. God was watching over all three of you today, and you should thank Him tonight in your prayers. I know I will. Tomorrow we'll make the tank lid stronger and tighter so no one has to go through this again—but, Jen, you'd better be more careful next time."

Although the stitches came out after a couple of weeks, Jen would always have a scar—which she proudly claimed was a battle scar from being a farm kid.

Chapter Eight
(Dirty Work

Farm children are sometimes called upon to do unusual tasks, especially when it comes to fixing machinery. Grain combines are the biggest culprits. They tend to have nooks and crannies, and when a bearing burns out or a belt breaks, replacement may be difficult. This was the case of replacing the bearings and hangers for the grain sieves and chaffers in the back of the Maas combine. The space was small, but Paul finally managed to take out the broken part. Then he hurried to the machinery dealer.

The parts man said, "I haven't got the part in stock. I've never heard of that particular piece breaking. We can have it here tomorrow, or you can go to another dealer. Let me see who might have one. You should probably replace both sides while you're at it. Ah, here we go! There are two bearings and hangers in Tipton. Do you want me to call and have them save both for you?"

"Tell them I'll be there in thirty minutes," Paul replied.

As he headed for Tipton, Paul called home and talked to George. "Flatten down the sieve, put an old carpet over it, and get Ed. He's small enough to crawl in there and put in those carriage bolts. I have to go to Tipton for the parts. I should be home in an hour."

When he returned, Ed and George were waiting. Dad showed Ed where to push the bolts through. Then he'd have to hold the bolts in the holes until they could tighten them on the outside. After Ed had squirmed inside, George handed him a trouble light. He could see the drift pins Paul had slipped into the openings. Ed shoved in the first bolt and held it tight—one down, five to go. They switched sides and started again, and in just a few minutes, the rig was repaired. Grandpa grabbed Ed's legs and gently pulled him out of the bowels of the combine. Then Paul started the machine and it ran perfectly.

Paul hollered from the cab, "Thanks, son. We couldn't have done it without you."

Ed smiled and waved. He was itchy and dusty, but he had helped his dad.

When he arrived at the back door, Sara wouldn't let him in the house. "Take those filthy clothes off in the garage and put them in a bucket. Then head downstairs for a shower," she scolded.

She made Ed strip down to his underwear and socks, then gathered his outerwear and threw them in the washer by themselves. Ed showered and felt better now that the dust was gone.

Tim wasn't so fortunate during his escapade with a fertilizer applicator. Paul had decided to try a total liquid fertilizer program for the corn that spring. He rented a machine from a fertilizer company and applied a mixture of nitrogen called urea and super phosphate plus nitrogen mix called DAP. It was a great fertilizer, but difficult to work with. It was sticky and tended to settle out. After a few passes in the field, the applicator's pump stopped working properly.

The space was tight and Tim was elected to crawl under the machine and turn off the valves. He scooted under easily. George turned on the pump, not realizing, Tim had turned the wrong valve. The hose broke and sprayed Tim with gooey caustic fertilizer. It didn't take long for Tim to escape, but he was covered from the chest down. Standing in a pool of fertilizer, he didn't know what to do, but George hustled him to the back door and called Sara.

She took one look and gasped, "Take off as much as you can outside and meet me in the upstairs bathroom. I'll check my health book to see what we have to do."

George helped Tim out of his outer clothes and Tim headed up stairs in just his t-shirt and undershorts. Sara already had the shower running when he arrived.

"The book says to wash good and make sure we get all the fertilizer off. You don't mind me helping, do you?" Sara asked.

"I guess not," Tim replied, although he was a little embarrassed.

"Good. You do your front and I'll wash your backside. Hurry, before the fertilizer soaks into your skin."

Tim wasn't too sure about removing his shorts, but after all, she was his mom. While washing Tim's backside, Sara noticed some redness already appearing in his tender areas. She helped him dry off and went for some aloe gel.

When she returned, she said, "The book says to give you some

Tylenol to ease the pain. I don't think you should wear any underwear for now. We want to get as much air to the burn as possible."

"It's starting to burn already, especially between my legs," Tim whined.

"Rub some ointment on, hon," said Sara.

Turning slightly red-faced, Tim said, "Maybe you should do it, Mom."

"Okay, if you don't mind."

Sara gently applied the gel. At supper that night, Tim could barely sit down. Sara gave him another Tylenol and helped him to bed.

Tim slept well until about 1:00, then called, "Mom, could you come in here, please?"

Moms are always alert to the cries of their young, so Sara was up in a jiffy. When she walked into Tim's room, he said, "Mom, I'm burning up. My balls are on fire. I can't sleep."

"Let me take a look," Sara said, pulling his pajama bottoms down.

Tim's genitals were fiery red and had small blisters. Sara hurried to the bathroom and wet a washrag with cool water.

Awakened by the commotion, Paul asked, "What's up?"

"It's Tim," Sara replied. "Maybe you should take a look."

Paul followed Sara to Tim's room, where he found his son in serious pain.

"I read somewhere that if you dissolve aspirin in warm water and apply it to a burn, it can take the fire out," said Paul. "Let's give it a try."

Thankfully, the aspirin solution did help. They gave Tim another Tylenol and Sara put a towel under his hips and laid a cool towel over his lower body. That also helped, and Tim finally drifted off to sleep— when morning came, the burn was no better.

"We need to go to see Dr. Barnes," Sara announced.

When they were ushered into an examination room, Dr. Barnes' nurse, Cassie, handed Sara a gown, looked at Tim and said, "Okay, take everything off."

At times Cassie seemed to be a little gruff, and this was one of those times. Mom helped Tim undress and into the gown, but Tim was a little embarrassed because it was meant for a smaller child and barely covered him. He pulled it down as far as he could.

When Dr. Barnes sailed in, her white coat flying, she looked at

Tim and teased, "I hear you took a bath in some fertilizer and now you can't sit down. Let's see if we can put that fire out. Lay back on the table and we'll see what's going on."

She lifted the gown, then shook her head and said, "Oh, my goodness! You do have a problem, but it's not serious. Let me get some gel and we'll get you fixed up."

Dr. Barnes hurried out of the room and returned in a few minutes. She put on a pair of latex gloves, applied the gel, and told Sara, "I'll write a prescription for this gel and also for some pain medicine. If this doesn't go away in a couple of days, call me."

Turning her attention to Tim, she said, "You should be feeling much better by tomorrow. The burns are bad, but they'll heal fast. In the meantime, stay away from fertilizer and don't wear any underwear for the next couple days. Take a shower twice a day and apply the cream until all the redness is gone, okay?"

"Yes, ma'am," Tim said with a smile, knowing he'd be glad to get rid of the burning feeling.

When he got home, Sara fixed up a pair of his Dad's boxer shorts for him to wear around the house. Jenny teased him about having "chicken legs" because the boxers looked so huge around his skinny legs. Tim stayed close to the house for several days until the burning finally stopped.

All the Maas children had their own "helping fix something" episodes. Many were non-eventful, like driving cattle. When the stock cows were moved from pasture to pasture, instead of tormenting both the cows and the farmers, they were driven from place to place. The go-getter was a big help and one of the neighbors had horses, so they could keep strays to a minimum.

The children were stationed at various gate holes and driveways along the way, and most of the time all they had to do was stand in the middle of the opening and wave their arms to keep the herd moving.

Whenever cattle or hogs escaped, it was all hands on deck. Everyone pitched in, waving and hollering, holding gates open, or keeping the remaining animals wherever they were supposed to be. Every event was different.

Once as the family was involved in a cattle drive, a cow nicknamed Old Blue got separated from her calf, and somehow the calf got behind Ed. Old Blue saw her calf and was determined to be reunited.

Ed waved and screamed, and he even hit the cow with a club he was carrying, but it didn't deter the thousand-pound mother in the slightest. Old Blue wasn't interested in attacking Ed. She was only concerned about her calf. She lowered her head, bellowed, and charged.

Ed jumped to the side, but was not quick enough. Old Blue caught him with the stub horn on the side of her head and then with her huge shoulder. Ed was fortunate not to be trampled by the thundering hooves or the outcome would have been much worse.

As it was, he managed to scream, "Help!" before he was flung against the barn and knocked unconscious.

Paul came running to Ed's aid, shouting, "Sara, come quick! Old Blue just trampled Ed. He's between the barn and the tight board fence." Then he knelt down and said, "Lay still, son. Let me check you over before you try to move."

Paul felt Ed's legs and arms, which seemed to be alright. When Sara arrived, she sat down and laid her son's head in her lap.

When Ed started to come around, he looked up at his mother and said, "My chest. It hurts terrible."

Sara lifted Ed's shirt and saw a big mark on his side where Old Blue's horn had scraped his ribcage. "I think we should call an ambulance," she said, looking over at Paul. "If we try to move him, we might cause more internal damage."

Paul nodded and headed for the shop phone, saying, "You stay here with Ed till the ambulance arrives. The rest of us will finish rounding up the cows."

For her part, Old Blue, satisfied by being back with her calf, was calmly guided back into the herd. Most of the cows had already returned to the lot when the episode began, so after Old Blue and her calf strolled into the lot, it was just a matter of closing the gate.

The town fire engine and ambulance soon arrived with sirens roaring and lights flashing. The EMTs carefully slid Ed onto a back board and onto a gurney. It didn't take long to get him into the back of the ambulance.

"Do you want to ride with us, Mrs. Maas?" one of the EMTs asked.

"Sure," she answered, "but let me get my purse. It's in the house. I won't be long."

Sara rushed into the house, forgetting she was wearing her dirty work shoes. She made big mud tracks across the kitchen floor. She muttered something about being forgetful and having to mop the floor when she returned. She kicked them off and slipped on some tennis shoes.

Back to the ambulance in less than three minutes, she said, "Okay, let's go."

"Man, you're quick!" exclaimed an EMT.

"I'm a farmwife. It goes with the territory," Sara said with a smile.

"I'll meet you in town in a few minutes," Paul told Sara as the ambulance doors closed.

At the hospital, Ed was rushed to the ER, where a nurse, with Sara's help, stripped him to his undershorts. Because of damage to his ribs, they cut off his t-shirt. Ed was frightened, not knowing what they were going to do to him. Dr. Sue Smith examined him, poking and pushing before deciding to order an MRI to check for internal injuries.

The x-ray technician was calm and helpful. He let Sara stay in the room with Ed and explained all about the MRI chamber. The scans showed five broken or cracked ribs, a bruised spleen, and some slight kidney damage. Because of his age, none of Ed's injuries were life-threatening. He'd be sore for several days, but he would heal completely.

Dr. Smith taped Ed's ribcage and gave Ed some pain medicine. Ed stayed in the hospital overnight. When asked about it later, Ed said he'd never forget the sight of Old Blue, her eyes red with rage, coming at him.

Jenny may have been the only Maas girl and she wasn't exempt from helping hold wrenches. One day Paul decided to replace the bottom boot on a feed ingredient bin. The bin had a steep taper and small opening at the bottom. The trick was to have all the round-headed bolts inside the bin so the feed wouldn't hang up on the sides.

When they built the bin, the bolts were easily fastened because the top of the bin rings had yet to be installed. However, replacing bolts on the assembled bin presented the problem because of the small opening at the bottom and the steep sides inside.

Paul figured Jenny, with her slim nine-year-old body, could get into the bin and push the bolts through. She was also light enough not to distort the sides. Getting her out of the bin was the challenge. Once the boot had been bolted on, there was no escape through the bottom. The only way out was through the top.

Paul devised a plan in which he would lower a rope with a loop in the end from the top. Jenny would then put her foot in the loop and grab onto the rope so they could pull her out the top. Before she entered, Paul tied knots in the back of the dust mask to make it fit Jenny's small face. Then she crawled into the opening, her pockets full of bolts. Paul and Ed were on the outside with drift pins to line up the holes.

As Jenny shoved the bolts through, she would hold them tight against the metal until either Dad or Ed had a nut tightened on the bolt. When one of the holes didn't line up, Ed gave the drift pin a good whack with his hammer. Inside the bin, the sound was deafening and dust from the walls floated down.

"Stop that, Ed!" Jenny hollered, "You're knocking down all the dust and making my ears ring."

"Sorry, but I need to get the holes lined up somehow," Ed said.

It was hot inside the bin. Her sweaty hair was plastered against her face. Jenny moved her feet inside the bin, trying to brace them against the sides. Her movement caused a small piece of feed to fall. It broke into many dusty, mildew-laden pieces, causing her to cough and spit. The moldy feed was sour-tasting, even through her mask.

"How many bolts left?" Jenny called out.

"Four. Then we'll get you out," Paul replied.

By that point, dust and mold had infiltrated Jenny's t-shirt and covered her legs—and it itched. She wished she had worn long pants instead of shorts. She finally shoved the last bolt in and held it tight.

"All done!" she heard her dad call from outside bin. "We'll get you out in a jiff!"

When Paul climbed to the top of the bin and looked down, all he could see was the top of Jenny's head. It was white from dust and mold. He lowered the rope and told her to grab hold while he pulled her up. Just a few seconds later, Jenny emerged through the opening.

Paul lifted his daughter out by her armpits and set her on the top of the bin. To Jenny, the smell of fresh air was wonderful as she sat trying to catch her breath. As she looked at herself, she could see she was white all over.

"Well, I guess I get a trip to the garage," Jenny said playfully. "Mom won't let me in the house looking like this."

"You're right there, Punkin," Paul agreed. "I'll get Mom to help you."

Ed laughed when he saw his sister. "You're as white as a ghost and you smell like sour wet corn," he teased.

Jenny turned up her nose and said, "Well, you couldn't have done it without me."

She stomped off toward the garage, where she was met by her mother, who said, "Okay, off with those clothes—and I mean everything. I'll go get you a towel."

Jenny happily stripped off her clothes. She had heard her brothers talk about standing in the garage with nothing on, and now she was going to get to do it—but she hadn't realized how cold she was going to be without clothes. Someone had forgotten to shut the overhead door and a cold breeze was blowing in.

As she stood shivering, Jenny thought, "Mom sure is slow. I think I'll run into the house this way. No one will see me. It is just a little ways."

As she opened the side door and stepped out, the sunshine felt warm, so she stood for a few seconds before taking off. It was about thirty feet to the back door. She took off running, and she had almost made it to the house when Ed stepped out of the shop and saw his "streaking" little sister. He let out a long wolf whistle just as Jenny made it to the door. She turned toward him, waved, and stuck out her tongue, making him laugh. His kid sister would do anything and nothing seemed to embarrass her.

When Jenny walked into the house, Sara was on the telephone. She gave her mom a dirty look as she ran past, heading upstairs to take a shower. Sara laughed as her naked daughter hurried by. She was all white except for her feet and where her underpants had been, and her face looked like a raccoon, only in reverse coloring.

Jenny was almost finished with her shower when Sara walked into the bathroom. "Your hair is still gray from the dust," said Sara. "You'll have to wash it again. I'll help this time."

"Who was so important on the phone that you couldn't come out and get me?" Jenny whined. "I was freezing to death out there, so I had to run in here with nothing on—and Ed saw me. Now he's gonna kid me all week. Thanks a lot."

"It was Grandma Madge. Your great-aunt Thelma is sick and she needs some help cleaning her house. I volunteered you to help her tomorrow."

"You volunteered me?" Jenny said in surprise. "I thought I had a day off. What'll I have to do?"

"You just have to dust and run the sweeper," Sara replied, "and don't worry, I'll be going with you. Afterward, I thought we might go to Northpark Mall. Maybe we can look at some new school clothes."

"Ooh, now that sounds better!" Jenny said, her tone brightening. "I need some new shoes."

Sara dumped a big glob of shampoo onto Jenny's head and began to scrub vigorously. As she rinsed her daughter's hair, she said, "I think we got it. You're all squeaky clean. Now dry off and get dressed. I don't think you'll need to wrap up in a towel. It sounds like you've shown enough of yourself today anyway—and I'll tell Ed not to pick on you too much."

"It's a good thing we live way back from the road or I couldn't go streaking," Jenny said with a smile.

When Paul came in for supper, he told Jenny how proud he was of her. "The job would have taken a lot longer if you hadn't helped."

Jenny beamed with pride. She had proved, a little girl could be a big help around the farm.

Ed chimed in, "The next time you go streaking, little sister, warn me. I'll run and get Tim. He'll wanna watch, too."

"That'll be enough, Ed," warned Sara. "I was on the phone and Jenny was getting cold out there. She had no choice but to run in here naked."

"But she sure was cute in her birthday suit, Mom."

"Well, next time you can just close your eyes, 'cause I'm just going to walk and not run," Jenny said firmly. "You won't bother me a bit."

Everyone chuckled as the smug young girl's face turned bright red. Maybe she had been embarrassed, after all.

Chapter Nine
The Bean Buggy

The summer brought many different jobs. One of the most dreaded was bean walking. Until Roundup resistant soybeans were developed in 1996, weeds in the bean fields had to be hand-pulled or sprayed with chemicals individually.

Some farmers developed small tractor-like machines with seats on rails. Each person riding on a seat controlled an herbicide nozzle, and whenever a weed appeared in their row, they gave it a squirt. The weed would then die within a week.

The Maas farm had a machine which held five people—four riders and a driver. They called it their bean buggy. The driver was usually Grandpa George or Paul. The riders were the Maas children and friends who wanted to earn a few bucks. Jenny always had friends available. Occasionally, Sara would take a turn driving, especially when the riders were all girls. There were few jobs for teenyboppers at that time, and girls were eager to make a little money.

The days were long and hot, but like detasseling corn, there was only a small window of time to do the job. Grandpa George would get his helpers situated on their seats and check each nozzle to make sure it was working. He always carried plenty of water, and every hour the crew took a break.

When the boys rode, they soon had their shirts off, and the girls envied them. They wanted to work on their all-important tans, too. One day, Jenny and her girl pals were the only ones available to ride the bean buggy. Jenny got on her seat and immediately took off her blouse. She was wearing her bathing suit top underneath. After her experiment, the rest of the riders began wearing bathing suit tops when they rode the bean buggy. They also tried wearing just their bathing suits, but the seats were too sticky when they wore bikini bottoms.

Poor Grandpa George often tired of putting up with the giggly young women, so he dreamed up an excuse to do something else. Sara was then drafted to drive the bean buggy.

The final bean field was across the creek and very isolated. Paul had driven the bean buggy down to that field late the previous evening. The girls arrived and Sara loaded them into the pickup to haul them to the field.

The day started out cloudy. Everyone was wearing shorts and tank tops and not swimsuits. Sara phoned home and told Paul to fix his own lunch, since she and the girls wouldn't be coming in for lunch.

When she hopped up onto the driver's seat of the bean buggy, it was wet with dew. She swore softly, then realized she'd dry quickly once the sun came out. The girls took notice and wiped their seats before sitting down.

Next came the check of the pump and nozzles—and the pump wouldn't start. Sara got off the bean buggy, wiggled some wires, and checked the pump battery. Nothing! She started the tractor motor. It coughed and sputtered, but finally caught with a loud backfire from the exhaust, causing the girls to jump. The auxiliary battery stared to smoke. Things were not going well.

Sara called Paul and reported, "The pump won't go and the battery is throwing off sparks. I've tried everything I know. You'll have to come down and fix it."

"I'll be down in a jiffy," Paul replied. "Check to see if the main switch to the pump is turned off."

Paul arrived and found the pump had been left on. That was why the auxiliary battery was dead. He rewired the pump to run off the tractor battery, then checked everything out, and it all worked. The girls hopped into their seats as Sara climbed into hers. Paul watched for a bit to make sure the machine was working correctly before he headed back toward the farmstead.

Sara had packed a lunch for everyone. They had wanted to be done early, but now they were running late. The sun came out in late morning and the wind died down, making it very hot in the creek bottom. Heat waves spiraled up from the beans rows.

At noon, Sara stopped the buggy under a black cherry tree. Both she and her riders were sweltering. She looked at the young women, who were in varying stages of puberty. Jenny and Cindy were as straight as bean poles, with just small buds on their chests. On a day like that, they didn't bother wearing bras. On the other hand, Lydia and Nancy were developing nice figures.

All the girls were wearing baseball caps and sunglasses. Sara was the only one wearing jeans and a sleeveless blouse. The girls were wearing shorts, which was fine because Sara always made everyone wash their legs before they went home in case they had accidentally sprayed any of the chemicals on their legs.

The crew drank from the water container on the back of the buggy. Each had her own cup. The water was warm and stale, but wet. Their hair stuck to the sides of their faces. Sara found an old towel and wiped her forehead as they ate their lunch and swatted flies.

"Girls," she finally announced, "we have only three rounds left, and it's really hot out here. You girls are better prepared for this heat than I am. You're wearing shorts and cool tops, but I'm not. If you don't mind, I'm taking off my bra. I know you think bras are cool at your age, but wait until you get old, like me. I'll tell you, they were invented by the devil himself, just to torture women. I used to go braless a lot when I would drive tractor in this field by myself. There are no men for miles. You can do whatever you like."

Sara unbuttoned her blouse, took it off, unhooked her bra, and hung it behind the seat like a flag. Then she slipped her blouse back on, minus the bra. She didn't even button it. She just tied the ends together to make a halter. She sighed in relief as the cool breeze caressed her chest. She thought about taking off her jeans, but decided maybe it would be going a bit too far, so she just rolled up her pant legs.

"Okay," she said, "let's get back on the rig and finish this field."

"Mom's just having a hot flash," Jenny teased. "Older women do things like that when they're going through the change of life."

"I heard that, young lady!" Sara shot back. "You just wait until you're my age. Then it won't be so funny."

They finally finished the field at three o'clock. Their blouses and t-shirts were soaked with sweat. Even the backs of their shorts were wet from sitting on the hot seats and their legs were almost black from a combination of dust and sweat. All of them were glad to see the old pickup.

Jenny asked, "Mom, can we go swimming in the pond after we're done?"

"Sure, why not? We can get all this dust washed off."

"But we didn't bring our swimsuits. Mrs. Maas. What will we

do?" one of the girls whined.

Without hesitation, Sara replied, "Who needs swimsuits? This is an all-girl crew. I see no need for swimsuits, do you, Jenny?"

Jenny said, "No, ma'am. We can swim in our skin."

With that, they headed for the end of the field and piled into the truck. Sara put in a call to Paul, saying, "We're done here. You can come get the buggy, but give us about an hour. The girls and I are going for a dip in the pond. No men allowed."

When Sara parked the truck at the pond gate, the girls ran toward the picnic area and the beach. Jenny had her top off before she even reached the picnic table. She continued to strip off her clothes as she ran, since she'd done this before with her mother. Sara was the last one to make it to the picnic table, where Cindy and Nancy were peeling out of their sweaty clothes. Lydia was the only one reluctant to disrobe. She was standing alone when Sara reached the picnic table.

"Don't you want to go swimming, Lydia?" Sara asked.

"Well, I think I do, Mrs. Maas, but I don't look like the other girls. They're all skinny and white, but I'm brown and fat—and I have breasts."

Sara looked at Lydia and smiled. "Lydia, you have a beautiful body," she said softly. You have lovely brown skin and dark hair, and beautiful brown eyes. God made you a wonderful person. Don't ever be ashamed of what He has given you. If you don't want to go skinny-dipping, I'll sit here with you."

It wasn't long until the other three noticed Sara and Lydia were sitting out.

"Aren't you two coming in?" Nancy called from the pond.

"Lydia isn't quite ready for this, so I'm going to sit here with her," Sara replied.

For a few moments, the three girls in the water talked quietly among themselves. Then they emerged from the water and approached Lydia.

"If you're not coming in, then we're coming out," Nancy said when they reached the picnic table. We're a crew, and we all do things together or we don't do them at all. Lydie, we won't laugh at you—I promise."

Then, with a mischievous smile, Nancy said, "Here, we'll help you!"

The other two girls lunged forward and helped Nancy pull Lydia's top over her head. Then they attacked her shorts and Lydia was soon in just her undies.

"Well, we're half way there!" Cindy said, laughing happily.

She turned Lydia around and unhooked her bra, and with three naked girlfriends around her, Lydia quickly lost her self-consciousness. Jenny took her hand and together they ran back toward the pond, where they were soon splashing and swimming amid sounds of happy laughter.

After a few minutes, Lydia looked back at Sara and called, "Aren't you coming in, Mrs. Maas?"

"Only if you want me to."

"Come on in! The water's fine!" Lydia said with a broad smile.

It didn't take any more coaxing. Sara joined the girls and swam over to the dock. Then she dove off the dock and swam back across. The girls were having a wonderful time skinny-dipping—something they'd never done before.

They played in the water for a half hour, then Sara suggested they dry off on the beach. They air dried as the sun began to set and put their clothes on. They climbed into the truck for the ride back to the house.

It was a day they would talk about for weeks to come.

Chapter Ten
Wild Ride

In late August the third cutting of hay was ready. Paul had mowed the lush green alfalfa, thinking it would be ready to bale in a couple of days, but cloudy weather slowed the drying process. Most of the cutting was to be baled into small square bales, to be used mainly for the cows when they were calving and for starting out feeder calves.

When it came time for the actual baling, the usual crew of teenage boys Paul counted on was busy with football practice and not available. Grandpa George was at the state fair. School had just started. Ed and Tim had to be picked up at school to save them the long ride home. Therefore, they could help bale. In the alfalfa field there would be three hundred bales, at most. It was a bit hilly, but Paul thought he and the boys could bale themselves if they took it slow.

Ed was thirteen at the time and had proven he could drive around the yard. Paul and Tim would load while Sara and Jenny pulled the loads home. Instead of putting the cab tractor on the baler, Paul hitched up the older 3020 John Deere. It would be Ed's tractor to drive. He was accustomed to the older tractor. Sara and Jenny would have the cab tractor.

The second windrow of the field was the first to be baled, and Sara drove first. She showed Ed how to stay close to the windrow without touching. It was best if the pickup tines on the baler were always to the outside of the row, because the hay would feed into the machine more smoothly.

She let Ed drive the last hundred yards or so and everything was going fine. There was a steep slope at one end of the field, but it didn't present a problem since they were always going uphill while baling. Everything was wrapped up and racked. The women had pulled the next to the last load to the buildings. Ed was down to the last windrow, but it had to be baled in the reverse direction. The outside row was too close to the edge of the hay field for the tractor and baler, so Ed would have to go down the steep slope.

The bale rack was about three-quarter full as Ed started down the slope. The hard dry ground was poor for traction and the 3020's tires were old and worn. Ed hadn't gone fifty feet when the trouble started. The weight of the baler and load of bales began to push the tractor down the slope—and Ed made an inexperienced driver's mistake. He disengaged the clutch, allowing the tractor to free wheel. He stood on the brakes and looked back at his dad in panic.

"Let the clutch back out!" Paul hollered.

When Ed did as his dad suggested, the tires tried to grip the hard surface. As they did, the rig slowed down with a jerk, sending the bales on the rack surging forward. Paul quickly shoved Tim off the rack and onto the ground. Then he jumped off and ran downhill as fast as he could.

The baler jackknifed around the rear wheel of the 3020 as the hayrack, minus a number of bales, shoved against the tail end of the baler. The bale chute caught under the rack and twisted until the support chains snapped. Just as the baler slid around the rear tire, the power shaft snapped and started to flop around dangerously.

Paul wanted to climb aboard the sliding tractor, but the rotating power shaft prevented him from jumping on from behind.

"Turn off the PTO!" Paul shouted.

"I'm trying!" Ed shouted back.

The rig finally reached the bottom of the hill, where Ed shoved in the clutch while Paul jumped aboard, flipped off the PTO and rammed the shifter into park.

Amid a cloud of dust, a badly shaken Ed looked at his dad and started to cry.

"I'm sorry, Dad," Ed whined.

"Don't worry, son. Nobody's hurt, and we can fix machinery easier than bodies. Now let's see if we can straighten out this mess. You sit on the fender while I drive ahead."

As Paul inched the 3020 forward, the baler trailed off to one side and the hayrack bounced up over the bale chute. Then he got off the tractor to survey the damage.

Seeing Tim limping toward them, Paul said, "Did you get hurt when I shoved you off the rack?"

"A little, but it's just my leg," Tim replied. "I think I landed on it wrong."

"Sorry, son, but I had to get you out of the way. I didn't know if Ed was going to be able to get this rig slowed down before he drove into the ditch."

"I know, Dad," Tim said. "I'll be alright."

Ed climbed down from the tractor and walked behind his dad, surveying the damage. The PTO shaft was broken, the baler tongue was bent into a U-shape, the bale chute was crumpled like a tin can, and the wagon tongue was twisted into an S-curve. The bales still on the rack were scattered everywhere, and there were bales lying all along the path of the mishap.

Just then, Sara and Jenny appeared at the crest of the hill. At first, they sat still, until Paul motioned for them to come down the hill.

Sara got out of the 4440 and asked anxiously, "Is everyone alright?"

"Everyone's fine, but I'm afraid the baler and rack are gonna need some attention," Paul replied. "Ed lost control going downhill, but it wasn't his fault. We had too much weight behind such a small tractor going downhill and things started to slide. Pull your empty rack next to this one. We'll transfer the bales and pick up the ones that aren't broken off the ground."

Mom looked at Ed, who was still shaking.

She went over and gave him a big hug. "It's alright, honey," she said. "Accidents happen. I'll bet you'll never forget this as long as you live. There will probably be other times, but every time you bale this piece of ground, you'll remember your wild ride down the hill."

That was enough baling for one day. In fact, Paul decided not to unload the hay. It could wait until Saturday afternoon. They would have to borrow the neighbor's baler to finish up. Even Paul had been a little shaken up by the incident. He drove the wounded machine to the shop and parked it. It would take several days and a couple of trips to the welder's shop to get the baler back to its original condition.

Paul learned to use a bigger, heavier tractor on the baler from that day on and maybe a more experienced driver.

Chapter Eleven
Calves and Rabbits

Jenny turned ten in April, which meant she wasn't eligible to show animals until the next season. In October when the calves were weaned, she and Grandpa George picked a calf from the herd. He wasn't all-black like the other Angus calves. He had a tinge of white on the tips of the hair around his shoulders, which gave him a grayish look. Because of his coloring, Jenny named him Smokey.

She diligently fed and cared for her calf, and with the help of Grandpa George and her brothers, she broke him to lead. Smokey was a great project and Jenny loved him.

When fair time came, Smokey, along with Ed and Tim's steers, was loaded onto a trailer for the ride to West Liberty. They tied the steers in the 4-H section of the barn with other club members.

The second day was weigh-in day. All animals had been weighed during Christmas break and tagged. Smokey tipped the scales at 1,120 pounds. He had gained just over two pounds a day. He didn't win the rate of gain contest, but he placed in the top ten. Jenny wasn't sure how good Smokey would show, but Grandpa George was. He was very happy and even bragged a bit.

Day three was a rest day and a day to wash the steers. Washing steers was always a boy-watching day for girls. The boys would shed their shirts as they worked with their animals. In the heat of the day, their muscles would ripple while girls stood around, talking and giggling.

If you were a girl like Jenny, you would take the far wash rack or wait until the big shots were done. Jenny was lucky. She had two older brothers looking out for her. By afternoon, she would find out which class and at what time she was to show.

Friday was show day, so everyone was up early. Power combs and blowers were used to primp the steers so they would look their best in the show ring. Jenny and Smokey were scheduled for the seventh class at about 10:30. Ed was showing in the same class. Tim had one steer showing earlier and one later.

Animals moved in and out of the barn to the show ring. The call came for the seventh class. Grandpa George helped Jenny lead her steer to the show ring, where Smokey preformed perfectly. He followed the other animals around the ring as the judge eyed every steer closely. The judge motioned for the animals to line up side-by-side so he could view them from the rear.

Finally, after an agonizing pause, he chose the first four, and Jenny found herself standing in fifth place. She held Smokey's head as high as she could, keeping her eyes on the judge while glancing over at Grandpa George from time to time. She coiled the lead strap in her small hand, the loop on the end sliding down her arm.

Perhaps a bee stung Smokey at that moment or maybe a horse fly bit him, but he suddenly jumped into the air and bolted forward, dragging Jenny along behind. She tried to jerk on the strap to stop him, but her body was just too small. He tore off around the edge of the ring with Jenny's hand caught in the strap. She was pinched between the 1,100-pound steer and the guard rail.

Smokey had dragged her about twenty feet before she finally freed herself and fell to the ground. One of the ring helpers dashed toward the runaway steer. Ed quickly handed his lead strap to the young man next to him and chased after Smokey. He finally caught him by the flailing strap and dug his heels in just as the ring helper also grabbed hold of the strap and helped pull Smokey to a stop.

Smokey had forgotten why he was running by this time and had calmed down. Tim and Paul came running from the area where they had been waiting for the next class to be announced. Tim raced to help Ed with Smokey while Paul's eyes searched the ring for Jenny.

By now the judge and another ring helper were at her side and Sara was trying to pick her way down to the ring. Jenny was on the ground, not quite sure what to do. She was stunned and hurt.

"Don't move, miss," the judge said quietly. "Just lay still. Your mom will be here soon."

As Jenny looked up at the judge, her pain was starting to come. "My wrist!" she said, "It hurts terrible—and my side."

A moment later, Paul was at her side. As he knelt next to his daughter, the judge said, "I think we'd better call an ambulance. The steer really squashed her against the fence."

Jenny's new white-and-green t-shirt was streaked with dirt and her face was plastered with sawdust from the ring. Her hand was at an awkward angle. Sara climbed over the fence and raced to her daughter's side.

She brushed the hair away from Jenny's face and the sawdust from her cheeks. Sara whispered, "You're going to be alright, baby. The ambulance will be here shortly."

The judge made an announcement over the loudspeaker. "Will all exhibitors line your animals up along the opposite side of the ring? We want to give the EMTs plenty of room."

An ambulance had just arrived for exhibition at the Red Cross tent, so the EMTs were in the ring in a matter of minutes, rolling a gurney across the ring. One of the EMTs checked Jenny's vital signs. He motioned for Paul and a couple of other men to slide their hands under Jenny's body.

"On the count of three, I want everyone to lift her up and shift her to the back board. Then we'll lift her onto the gurney," the EMT ordered. "Ready? One, two, three, up and over. Fine! Thank you, gentlemen. We'll handle it from here."

The EMT then looked at Sara and asked, "Are you her mother?"

"Yes," Sara answered.

"Would you like to ride with us to Iowa City?"

"Most definitely! Let me get my purse."

By this time Grandma Madge had made it to the edge of the ring. She handed Sara her purse and Sara followed the EMTs to the ambulance.

As she climbed into the ambulance, Paul called to her, "Call as soon as you find out anything!"

It was a fast, noisy ride of about twenty minutes to the hospital, where the staff wheeled Jenny into the ER. Sara filled out the admission forms and hurried back to the ER. A nurse had already helped Jenny into a hospital gown and was washing the dirt off her face while assuring Jenny that her mom would be there soon.

The doctor who examined Jenny thought she might have a broken wrist and some damaged ribs. He ordered x-rays. In less than an hour, the results showed no broken ribs, but she did have a broken right wrist, which would require a cast. Her injuries could all be taken care of in the ER and then she'd be released.

Back at the fairgrounds, the show went on. The judge and the show committee decided Tim could continue to show Smokey in the class. Everyone in the ring was jittery, so the judge quickly placed the steers, finally moving Tim and Smokey into fourth place.

In his analysis of the class, the judge said, "This was a difficult class to place. There was no true top or bottom. Every animal had its pluses and minuses. The top four are like peas in a pod. It was unfortunate the young lady's steer bolted. I've seen it happen at other shows. There seems to be no reason for an animal to bolt like that, but it happens. We have to remember they're just animals and we don't know what goes through their minds. My hope is the young lady will be alright and she continues to show. I think we should give her and her family a hand for the way they handled the situation."

As the crowd applauded, Paul and Grandpa George waved to acknowledge their well wishes.

After lunch, Sara called Paul with the news. He was glad it wasn't as bad as it could have been. Jenny wouldn't have to stay in the hospital. He could pick Sara and Jenny up as soon as the show was over.

Tim and Ed were both showing in the intermediate showmanship class, and the competition was intense. Ed had just missed first place the year before and he was determined to do better.

While the class was being judged, Paul circled around to the judge's table and whispered to the announcer, "My daughter is alright. A few bruises and a broken wrist."

The announcer replied, "Why don't you tell everyone after this class?"

A few minutes later, the judge took the microphone and said, "Today we have a group of young people who have shown me they've devoted a lot of time and effort toward taking care of and showing their animals. Some of you need to pay more attention to the judge and the ringers, but others have done well. This has been a long day for everyone.

"Today one young man was far and away the most attentive and showed his animal to the best of its ability. That young man gave up his calf to catch a runaway steer earlier. He has shown poise and maturity. He's number thirty-six. I believe his name is Ed Maas. Congratulations, Ed. The runner-up in this class is another tall, slim young man—number thirty-seven. I didn't catch your name, but you did a good job today. To the rest of the class, everyone showed well. It was a very good class of young exhibitors."

The judge handed the microphone back to the announcer, who called out the names of the winners. "First place in the intermediate class was Ed Maas. Runner-up was Tim Maas. We hope to see both of you back here next year in the senior class. Now, Paul Maas, the father of the little girl who was injured, would like to say a few words."

Paul took the microphone and said, "Ladies and gentlemen, I've received a call from my wife at the hospital. My daughter, Jenny, is alright. She has a few bruises and a broken wrist, but she'll be released as soon as I get to Iowa City. I want to thank everyone who helped get her steer calmed down and for your concern. Thank you."

Before Paul left the ring, the judge walked over to him and said, "You're raising a great group of kids, Paul. I had no clue both of those young men in the ring were your sons. Congratulations."

It wasn't long before Jenny was back to being a tomboy again. The next year, she picked out two calves for her project. At weigh-in time over Christmas break, they loaded up the calves and headed for the scales at the local sale barn.

As Jenny was leading her calves to the scale, one of them bolted and ran ahead. This time Jenny let go of the leash and someone up front corralled the animal. The second calf decided to try the same stunt, jumping into the air and landing on Jenny's foot. She screamed in pain while Paul and Grandpa George raced to her rescue. They helped weigh her calves and reload them into the livestock trailer.

All the way home, Jenny complained about her foot. As soon as they were home, Paul told her to go into the house and have mom look at it. He and her brothers would put the calves away.

As Sara examined Jenny's foot, she could see the calf had come down on her instep. It looked like it called for another trip to the ER, so Sara quickly changed her clothes and the two of them hurried out the door.

As they got into the car, Sara called to Paul, "I'm taking Jenny to the hospital. Her foot might be broken."

Dad waved from the barn door as they drove away.

After x-rays showed no broken bones, the doctor wrapped Jenny's foot and told her to stay off it for the next three days. On the way home, Jenny was very quiet.

"A penny for your thoughts," said Sara.

"Well, I was just thinking," Jenny replied hesitantly. "Do you think Dad and Grandpa would feel bad if I didn't show calves next year? I've had some pretty bad experiences lately and Andrea Howe asked me if I'd consider raising rabbits as a project."

"Rabbits?" Sara exclaimed, looking at her daughter. "What do you know about rabbits?"

"Nothing," Jenny said, "but I could learn. Andrea's dad raises them for a lab in Iowa City, and I'm sure he'd help."

"Rabbits," Sara said again. "Well, I never." Then she thought for a moment before adding, "But you know what? I didn't have a clue about chickens at one time, either, and I raised them alright. If that's what you'd like to try, I say go for it. Your dad and grandpa might be a little disappointed, but I think they'll understand."

In April, Jenny went to Andrea's and picked out some white Satin rabbits. Mr. Howe helped her get the necessary cages, feeders, waters, and feed. Paul let her use a corner of the old dairy barn. They hung the cages from the ceiling.

She'd only had them home for a week when Mr. Howe asked if Jenny wanted to go to the annual Easter rabbit show at a mall in Galesburg, Illinois.

"I guess so," replied Jenny. "I'll ask my mom, but I'm sure it'll be alright. I've never been to a rabbit show before. What do I have to bring?"

Mr. Howe said, "I'll loan you some carrying cages. I'm sure you'll enjoy it."

Saturday, Jenny and Sara loaded Jenny's two rabbits into the back of Mr. Howe's van. When they arrived in Galesburg, they saw many breeds of rabbits. Before the show ended, a rabbit showman named Al Iverson approached Jenny.

"Would you be interested in having some colored rabbits?" Al asked.

As Jenny eyes lit up, Sara asked, "How much will it cost?"

"Nothing," Al replied. "I'm trying to develop a strain of Satins called coppers, and I'd like to see if I can make them breed true. Right now I have black, gray, and blue, along with my coppers and reds. I'd like to give the blacks, grays, and blue to some new breeders. I've already given some away, but I still have some left. Stan Howe told me you might be interested."

After calling home to get Paul's okay, Jenny and Sara brought home eight Satin rabbits—two blacks, four grays, and their original two whites. Before they left the mall, Mr. Iverson gave them a quick lesson in genetics. Black crossed with a white equaled a gray. Gray crossed with a white equaled a blue. Gray crossed with a blue might get white, black, super blue, or gray.

Jenny also learned she could house does together, but not bucks, so more cages and pens were built. The next week Jenny started her 4-H project in earnest. Within thirty-one days, she was having little bunnies. Mr. Howe and Andrea came over and helped set up a breeding and weaning schedule.

Soon Jenny was overrun with rabbits, so she put up a notice at the local feed store, saying, "Live or dressed rabbits. Will deliver. Jenny Maas. 563-744-8930."

Within a few days, she had orders to fill. Tim helped butcher the rabbits, and at first it was difficult to kill her fuzzy little friends, but she knew she had to do it. She quickly acquired a number of customers. She didn't get rich, but it helped with the feed bills.

Besides selling rabbits for meat, she also had to choose the right ones to show. Mr. Iverson held a clinic at his rabbit barn for 4-H members and demonstrated how to pick out and show a good rabbit. Jenny soon won blue ribbons at several shows.

At a show in Cedar Rapids, she chose to take a black Satin buck, which won its first class. Between the first class and the championship round, a fellow rabbit breeder approached Jenny and asked if he could examine her buck.

Jenny pulled the bunny out of its cage. The man felt it and brushed its fur. He asked, "Would you be willing to sell this buck?"

Jenny looked at him and asked, "You really want to buy one of my rabbits?"

"I sure do, young lady," the man replied. "This is a very good rabbit and I need some new blood lines for my group. I'm willing to give you sixty dollars for him."

"Sixty dollars!" Jenny blurted out.

"If you're willing, I'll even let you keep him until the show is over," the man said with a smile. "How's that?"

Jenny glanced at her mother, and said, "It's a deal. Sixty dollars, and I get to show him today."

The man shook Jenny's hand and said, "Deal! I'll be around after the show."

In the championship round, the buck won the grand champion ribbon. Now Jenny wasn't so sure she wanted to sell her prize rabbit, but a deal was a deal. She had shook hands with the buyer, just like she'd seen her dad and Grandpa George do many times with cattle buyers.

The man came up to her and introduced himself. "I'm John Ruckstack. I breed rabbits for Blue Bonnet Feeds. I assure you your rabbit will be a great addition to our hutch." Smiling, he handed Jenny three twenties and a five-dollar bill. "The extra five is for being such a good businesswoman."

As they were packing up to go home, Mr. Iverson said, "I heard you sold your black buck to John Ruckstack."

"Yes, did we do wrong?" Sara asked.

"Heavens, no," Mr. Iverson said. "He's the most knowledgeable rabbit man in the United States. You should be honored to have your rabbit become part of his breeding group. Congratulations. You should have no problem selling rabbits in the future. That was quite an endorsement from an expert."

Jenny beamed all the way home. Her rabbits were going to be as good as the boys' calves—and they wouldn't break any of her bones, although she did receive several scratches from the rabbits' sharp toenails.

Jenny's rabbit project lasted four years, until Jenny became an eighth grader. She was so busy with school activities it became obvious that her mom was caring for the rabbits and not Jenny. Sara didn't complain, but before winter arrived that year, Jenny decided it was time to move on. She loved her rabbits, but simply didn't have time for them. She decided to sell them. With her winning reputation, she had no problem finding buyers. Instead of selling her equipment, she gave each buyer some of it.

The next year would begin another chapter in Jenny's 4-H book.

Chapter Twelve
Thin Ice

In early December, it snowed four inches—just enough for good sledding. The pond wasn't frozen before the snow arrived, but two days after the snow, it was cold and the pond was covered with a smooth glassy surface.

Saturday afternoon, Ed, Tim, and Jenny headed for the pasture to try sledding on the hillsides. Rusty tagged along. The slope behind the pond looked most promising. It was a short, steep slope. The ground under the snow was frozen, so their sled runners didn't cut into the soil. They sledded for an hour then it was time to go back to the house.

Instead of going around the pond, they cut across the north end. To get to the picnic table and the road home, they had to go around a finger of water. Rusty took the short cut and started across the new ice. He slipped a bit, but was soon happily trotting on the ice. Jenny decided to join him and make her trip shorter.

"You'd better not go out on the ice yet, Jenny," Ed warned. "Dad hasn't tested it yet."

"It's supporting Rusty," Jenny countered. "Look how smooth it is, and it's only a few feet across. I'll make it, and then I'll wait for you scaredy-cats on the other side."

With that, Jenny stepped onto the slick surface. Rusty came running over toward her, but he couldn't stop and slid into her legs, knocking her down. When she fell, the ice cracked. Jenny panicked and struggled to get to her feet.

"Lay flat on the ice, Jen!" Ed shouted. "Spread yourself out! I'll get a stick for you to grab on to and I'll pull you in."

Ed found a long willow branch and laid it on the ice. Then he reached out as far as he dared, but Rusty thought it was something to fetch and rushed to grab the tip.

"No, Rusty! Let it be!" Tim shouted.

The weight of the dog and Jenny proved to be too much for the thin ice. It cracked menacingly, and a moment later, the piece on which Jenny was lying shattered, sending Jenny into the icy water.

As their sister disappeared under the water, both boys screamed. When she surfaced and began to splash around, Rusty jumped in to save her. She grabbed on to his fur, but she was too heavy and they both went under.

"Ed! Tim! Help me!" Jenny cried when she surfaced again.

Ed plunged onto the ice, which broke instantly, but he was undeterred. He waded out to Jenny, breaking the ice as he went. Luckily, the bottom of the pond was only five feet deep at this point, so he could keep his head above water. As Jenny struggled to hold on to a piece of ice, Ed reached out, took her hand, and began pulling her toward the shore.

When they drew near, Tim held out the willow branch for Ed to grab. As Tim pulled with all his might, he was pulled into the water, too, but only up to his knees. Ed now was holding Jenny by the hood of her parka, and she was floating behind him. Seconds later, everyone was safe on shore, but Ed and Jenny were soaked to the skin.

"Tim, you run home and have Dad come get us in the go-getter," Ed ordered. "We'll start walking, but it's gonna be slow. Why don't you take off your boots? You can run faster without them, and they're full of water anyway."

Tim kicked off his boots and headed for the house at a dead run. He found his dad in the shop.

"Dad! Jenny fell in the pond, and Ed and I got her out, but they're both soaked. Ed sent me to get you and the go-getter," Tim gasped, out of breath from his long run.

Paul shut down the welder and hopped onto the go-getter, saying, "Tim, you push the door opener, then go and get Mom. Have her meet me at the pasture gate with the pickup. The ride home on the go-getter might be too cold for Ed and Jenny. Hurry! Also tell Mom to put the truck in four-wheel drive."

As Paul fired up the go-getter and roared out of the shop, Tim pushed the down button on the shop door and sprinted toward the house, shouting for his mom as he ran.

Sara met him at the backdoor. "What's the matter? Is someone hurt?"

"Jenny fell through the ice," Tim said, speaking so fast it was hard to understand. "Ed got her out, but they're both wet and cold. Dad went to get them on the go-getter. He wants you to meet him at the pasture gate in the pickup. He also said to put it into four-wheel drive. Hurry!"

Sara grabbed a hooded sweatshirt and ran to the pickup.

As Tim jumped into the passenger seat, he said, "I'll ride home with Dad. I only got my feet wet."

Paul found Ed and Jenny halfway up the long hill to the gate, where they'd had to stop due to the cold. Jenny was crying as her dad lifted her into the seat next to him and buckled her in. Ed climbed into the dump box in the back. Then Paul spun the go-getter around and roared back toward the house.

Sara and Tim were waiting at the gate. She unbuckled Jenny and carried her to the truck while Paul helped Ed walk around to the other side of the cab and get in.

As Sara fired up the truck, Jenny blurted out, "Where's Rusty? He went through the ice with me and held me up until Ed got to me. You've got to get him."

"Don't worry, Punkin," said Sara. "Tim and Dad will go back and get him, but right now we have to get you two warmed up."

As the pickup sped toward the house, Paul and Tim headed back toward the pond to see if they could find Rusty. When they got there, Rusty was still lying in the shallow water at the edge of the pond. He was so exhausted he was unable to pull himself out completely. Paul jumped out of the go-getter and waded into the water to retrieve the dog.

Laying Rusty in the back of the go-getter, Paul told his son, "We'll come back tomorrow for the sleds. We've got to get you and Rusty back to the house."

Once in the house, Sara quickly ushered Ed and Jen downstairs, saying, "Let's get you two out of these wet things."

She sat Jenny down on a chair and pulled off her water-filled boots, then her shoes and socks. Jenny tried to unzip her coat, but her fingers were too numb, so Sara stood her up and stripped off her coat and sweatshirt.

Then she looked at Ed and said, "Come on, Ed. Get those wet things off."

"I can't, Mom," Ed said, shaking his head. "My fingers are so cold, they won't work."

"Sit down here on the chair. I'll help you. Jenny, you take off your top and jeans."

Sara pulled off Ed's wet boots and helped him remove his jacket and sweatshirt. As she started to unbutton his flannel shirt, he said, "I think I can get my shirt, Mom. You help Jenny."

Sara nodded, then turned toward Jenny and quickly had her daughter down to her underwear. When she turned to look at Ed, she saw he was having trouble with his jeans. She undid the button and helped him slide the jeans down.

As Ed stepped out of the jeans, Sara said, "Okay, so far, so good. Now, off with the underwear. I'll get some old towels for you to wrap yourself in. You can take a hot shower upstairs."

Sara was a little upset at Ed's hesitation, but she was also thankful that her children were only cold and not frost-bitten. She hurried to the laundry cupboard and rummaged through the towel supply, expecting to find two naked kids when she returned. Instead, they were just as she had left them.

Sara exploded, "This is no time to be modest! You got yourselves into this predicament, not me—now strip!"

The tone of their mother's voice told Ed and Jenny she meant business, so they slowly removed their wet underwear, obviously embarrassed. Moving quickly, Sara wrapped Jenny first and then Ed. Jenny was so cold, she had to be carried up the stairs. Ed painfully followed, his legs feeling like stumps.

Once they were in the upstairs bathroom, Sara turned on the shower and tested the water. "Now, I want both of you to get into the shower and warm up while I go find some dry clothes."

"Both of us?" Ed exclaimed in surprise.

"Yes, both of you—unless you want to sit around and freeze to death," Sara said firmly. "Come on, Ed. She's just your sister. You'll get used to it in a minute or two."

Jenny was almost giggling. It didn't bother her in the least to take a shower with her brother.

She ducked into the shower stall, then called, "Come on, Ed. It feels good. Don't worry, I'll close my eyes, and I won't tell anyone."

Ed had no choice but to follow his sister, and the warm water did feel good on his cold body. Maybe his mom was right. It wasn't that bad to be showering with his little sister. After all, she was family, and he really was glad that she was alright.

They stood together under the shower and let it warm their cold bodies until Sara brought some dry clothes into the bathroom and announced, "I hear your dad and Tim outside. I'm going down and see if they found Rusty. When you're warm enough, get out and put these clothes on. Then go to the den. I'll fix you some hot chocolate. Okay?"

"Okay, Mom," they both replied.

Sara hurried down to the kitchen, where Paul and Tim were just coming through the back door. Paul was carrying Rusty, who hung limply in his arms. They went downstairs to the laundry room. Paul laid Rusty on some of the towels Sara had found for Ed and Jenny. Then he hung a heat lamp over the listless dog. Rusty's breathing was very shallow. They'd have to wait to see if he would recover. Only time would tell.

Looking at Paul and Tim, she could tell that they were nearly as wet as the other two. Paul was soaked to the waist and Tim was wet from holding Rusty in his lap on the way back to the house.

"My land," Sara said, "I'll be washing clothes till midnight tonight. Take everything off and meet me upstairs. I've got Ed and Jenny in the shower now, but I'll get them out so you can get in. Can you get your clothes off by yourselves or do I need to help?"

They indicated they could handle the chore themselves.

Ed and Jenny still weren't out of the shower when Sara returned. She reached in and turned off the water, saying, "Alright, you two, out! Your dad and brother need to warm up now."

Ed and Jenny were heading to the den when they met their dad and Tim coming upstairs, wrapped in towels the same way they had been. It didn't take Paul and Tim as long to warm up, and soon they were all in the den for a welcome cup of hot chocolate.

The days are short in December, so Paul soon had to go back outside to do chores. Before he left, he scolded Jenny for disobeying his rules. She also lost her computer privileges for a week, except for schoolwork.

When Paul had gone outside, Sara and the kids all went down to the laundry room to check on Rusty. He was still lying motionless, almost deathlike.

Jenny bent down and whispered, "Rusty, are you alright?"

Rusty opened one eye and slowly wagged his tail. This brought smiles to everyone's faces, but they all knew Rusty would be spending the rest of the night right where he was.

The Maas children were growing up. Soon all of them would be in high school and their shared escapades would be fewer, but never forgotten. Episodes such as these would bond the three siblings forever.

Chapter Thirteen
Sweet Corn Cousins

It was sweet corn time and the cousins were visiting. Ed, Missy, and Robin would be together again. Everyone showed up the night before. Tom and Kristy stayed with Tom's folks, Sue and Jeff stayed in Wilton with Paul's folks, and all the cousins slept at the farm. Aunt Sara would be serving her special chocolate pancakes for breakfast.

Early Saturday morning, the adults and Sue's boys were out to pick sweet corn. Everyone wore long-sleeve shirts to avoid getting cut by the corn leaves. George drove the tractor and hayrack while the pickers tossed ears onto the rack. Soon the rack was full and the group headed back to the house.

Back at the house, the younger children were finally waking up. Everyone knew they'd have to help shuck the huge pile of sweet corn on the rack. Even four-year-old Josh tried to help.

As soon as several ears were husked, the girls had the task of brushing and picking off the corn silk. On occasion, there were comments like "Gross" and "Ugh." Meaning someone had found an earworm or some corn smut. The pile of clean ears went into a square laundry basket and was hauled to the basement for processing.

About 10:30, the corn husking was finished and the children were released from their duties. Tim's friend, Pete Petersen, called to ask if Tim could go with him to a ballgame in Davenport. It was Kid's Day at John O'Donnell Stadium and he had an extra ticket. When Tim asked his mom, she said it was okay as long as he was back by 6:00. Pete told Tim they would pick him up at eleven. Tim hurried upstairs to change and Sara gave him some money for food at the ballgame.

Missy, Robin, and Eddie were also set free. The first place they headed for was the haymow to see a new litter of kittens. They played with the fuzzy animals for awhile. Missy spotted a pile of loose straw in the corner. She jumped into it, and soon they were all seeing who could jump from the highest bale.

Eddie pulled the hay carrier down the track and swung out on the rope hanging from it before dropping down into the hay pile. The girls discovered they could hang on to the rope better if they were barefoot. They did flips and flops into the pile, time after time. The only problem was the straw was dusty and itchy—and the haymow was getting quite warm.

When the trio arrived back in the basement where the corn was being processed, Sara saw them first and rolled her eyes. Seeing their dirty faces, she asked, "Where have you kids been?"

"Up in the haymow and we're itchy now," Eddie replied.

Aunt Sue smiled and said, "I'll take care of them, Sara. You keep everything going here." She stood and told the kids, "Okay, you three. Into the laundry room and strip your clothes off. You're going to have to take a shower, and I'll wash those dirty, itchy clothes. "

Missy looked at Robin, Robin looked at Eddie, then they all looked at Aunt Sue as she said, "Hurry up! Let's get those clothes off!"

Once in the laundry room, Aunt Sue stripped off Missy's shorts, then she glared at the other two, so they began to reluctantly pull off their shorts, too.

In the other room, Sara, Kristy, and Madge were cleaning up after the sweet corn processing. They could hear the conversation in the laundry room.

Kristy whispered to Sara, "I wonder how far Sue's going to take this undressing?"

"I don't know, but this could be interesting," Sara whispered back. "You don't care if she goes all the way, do you?"

"I guess not, but Robin has never seen a naked little boy. At least, I don't think she has."

In the laundry room, Missy whined, "But, Mom, he's—"

"Hush!" Sue interrupted, pulling Missy's shirt over her head. "Just get those clothes off."

Eddie and Robin had taken off their shorts and were standing in their underpants and t-shirts. Missy was naked except for her underpants and was trying to cover her chest with her arms as Sue reached into the shower and turned on the water.

When she turned around and saw that Eddie and Robin hadn't moved, she demanded, "Come on, you two, let's get moving."

Eddie removed his shirt and looked at Missy. He shrugged his shoulders as if to say, "I'm just doing what your mother says."

Robin took off her top. Now they were all wearing nothing but their underwear. Certainly Aunt Sue wasn't going to make them get completely naked. Knowing her mother meant business, Missy turned away from Eddie, put her fingers in the waistband of her underpants, and started pushing down. How humiliating!

All of a sudden, Sue hollered, "Sara! Come quick! I've got to show you something."

As Sara and Kristy rushed into the room, they saw the almost naked trio standing there. Sue exclaimed, "Sara, there's a boy in this room. Is he yours? I didn't know you had a boy. I know he's a boy, because he has Scooby Doo underwear on. He can't take a shower with the girls."

Sara looked at Eddie and smiled. She could tell he was very much relieved to see her. "Oh," she said, trying not to laugh, "Yup, he's mine alright. I'll get him right out of here. Come on, Eddie. You can sit out in the other room while the girls shower. Then you can take yours."-

Aunt Sue had pulled a fast one on the kids, and all three grownups knew it. Sara grabbed an old shirt and led Eddie out of the room.

As he was sitting on a chair outside the shower room, Eddie asked his mom, "Didn't Aunt Sue know I was a boy?"

Sara laughed, then said, "She was just playing a joke on you three, Eddie. She has three boys of her own. I'm pretty sure she knows the difference by now."

In the other room, Eddie could hear Missy and Robin talking and giggling.

"Did you see his cute underpants?" Missy asked.

"Yeah, and I didn't know boys wore such cute underwear," Robin replied, then added, "I'm glad we didn't have to go all the way. You really had me worried, Aunt Sue."

"I had you worried, huh? Well, I hope it stays that way," Sue replied, "but I must admit all of you followed orders and didn't question me. Robin, have you ever seen a naked boy? Missy has, because she has brothers. "

"No, ma'am," Robin answered.

"Well, someday you will. Mark my word, you will," Sue said with a smile.

When the girls had finished their shower, Sue wrapped big towels around them. Then she said, "Kristy, will you take the girls upstairs and find them some clean clothes? I'll stay down here and help Sara clean up. All right, Eddie, you're next. I'll get the water ready."

Eddie looked at his mother and she mouthed the words, "Go ahead. I'll be right in."

As Eddie walked in, Aunt Sue looked at him and said, "That was a close one, wasn't it? I mean, having to almost shower with girls."

"Yes, Aunt Sue."

"I put a towel on the chair for when you get out. I'll see you in a few minutes."

Eddie quickly undressed and ducked into the shower. The big wooden door on the shower was too tall for him to see over, so if someone entered he could hear them but not see them. He finished quickly and opened the door—and was happy to see his mom standing there and not Aunt Sue. Sara wrapped a towel around his waist twice and sent him up to his room. He crept up the stairs, hoping the girls wouldn't see him; however, he met Missy at the top of the stairs.

"I think you have cute underwear, Eddie," she teased. "Want to show them to me again? I won't tell."

"Never!" he replied as he ran to his bedroom and slammed the door, determined to find underwear that didn't have Scooby Doo on them.

At lunch, the three eight-year-olds ate at a card table set for them. When they got into a heated discussion, Sara walked over and asked, "What seems to be the problem, kids?"

"Well, Eddie claims he's a cousin to both Robin and me, but Robin and me aren't cousins. If not, what are we?" asked Missy, wrinkling her nose.

"Well, Eddie's right. Aunt Kristy is my brother's wife and Aunt Sue is his dad's sister, but they're not aunts or uncles to either of you. That makes you two just really good friends."

"So what do I call Robin and my parents if they're not relatives?" Missy asked.

"I guess you should call them Mrs. and Mr. McWilliams or Mr. and Mrs. Taft."

Robin said, "But Missy and me are more than just friends. Can't we be something else?"

Sara thought a moment, then said, "How about sweet corn cousins, since you're always here at sweet corn time."

"That's a good name!" Missy agreed. "Sweet corn cousins. I think we should make a pact."

Missy was always into pacts. Every time a decision was made, she had to make a pact.

When Sara returned to the adult table, Sue asked, "What's going on over there?"

Smiling, Sara answered, "Oh, they're just trying to figure who they are. You know we're sort of an unusual group. I mean, you and Kristy are my sisters-in-law, but you're just friends, and that's confusing to eight-year-olds."

"I suppose it is," Kristy agreed. "We get along so well we don't realize we're not related completely."

Sue said, "Do you remember the year we were all pregnant at sweet corn time? I was due in two weeks, Kristy in a month, and Sara, you were six months along. I could barely waddle and my feet were so swollen."

Kristy laughed and added, "Yeah, and remember when you sat in the old lawn chair and it broke? There you were, lying on your back with your feet in the air. Your maternity top was flopped up over your head, exposing your big belly. Both Paul and Jeff had to help you to your feet."

"Oh, my, do I!" Sue said, joining in the laughter. "They had to roll me over on my side because they couldn't pull me straight up. I finally got up on my hands and knees. I bet I looked like an old sow about to farrow. I was laughing so hard. I almost wet my pants. Jeff had to hurry me to the downstairs bathroom before I embarrassed myself even more."

Laughing, Sara added, "Boy, those were the days."

Lunch was a variety of casseroles because there hadn't been time for any of them to cook in the morning. After lunch, the women retired to the front porch and the men found some lawn chairs and sat in the shade of the oak trees in the front yard. Little Josh needed a nap while Wendy played dolls with Jenny, but the sweet corn cousins were bored.

"Can we go to the creek, Aunt Sara?" Missy asked.

"It's all right with me if it's alright with your mothers," Sara replied.

Sue told the girls not to get wet or muddy, since they'd already gone through one set of clothes. The girls promised. Sara gave them a small thermos of water and some cups. She put it all in a bucket, along with an alarm clock.

"When the clock goes off, come right home, okay?" Sara warned. "We're having a wiener roast and homemade ice cream for supper, so don't be late."

The kids agreed and headed for the pasture. The creek wasn't as much fun as they'd hoped. The water was low and the cows had messed up some of the best wading spots. They floated some hickory shells, but the deer flies and gnats were bad and the air in the creek bottom was hot and sticky.

"Let's go up to the pond," suggested Missy.

"We can't go swimming. My mom isn't here," Eddie reminded her.

"Her rule is that you can't go swimming alone," Missy countered, "but there are three of us and we won't go in the deep water. We'll just wade. Come on, it'll be cooler up there."

"Okay, I guess it'll be alright," Eddie said reluctantly.

When they reached the beach by the pond, Robin said, "Now remember, Missy, we're not supposed to get wet or dirty."

"I know, and we won't," Missy replied.

The water was cool and fresh. A cool breeze blew across the pond as they waded out as far as they dared. Then Missy instigated her plan, saying, "You know, if we took our clothes off, we wouldn't get them wet or dirty."

"What? You're kidding, aren't you?" Robin asked.

"Heck , no!" Missy said. "Look, we saw each other in our underpants this morning, so why not go the rest of the way?"

"But you're girls and I'm not!" Eddie said in surprise.

"Well, la de da," Missy said sarcastically. "When did you figure that out? We know you wear Scooby Doo underwear, too. Have you got Scooby Doo underwear on now?"

"No, but I'm not gonna show you!"

"Come on, scaredy cat," Missy teased. "Who's going to see you? Just me and Robin. We'll take ours off, won't we, Robin?"

"Um, I don't know," Robin said hesitantly. "Maybe we shouldn't."

"Well, I'm not afraid," Missy challenged. "You already saw me in my underpants, and I almost had them off."

Missy took off her shorts and top and then, standing in just her underpants, she said. "Come on, you two. At least take off your shorts. We're cousins, and we have a pact. Remember?"

Eddie and Robin looked at each other and started to remove their shorts. When they hesitated again, Missy grabbed Robin's top and pulled it over her head, saying, "See? There's nothing to it. Now you, Eddie. I won't tease you anymore. I promise."

The girls danced around the beach in their underpants for a few moments, then approached Eddie. Missy grabbed him and Robin pulled his shirt off—but they weren't finished.

Missy, who was the biggest of the three, grabbed Eddie in a bear hug and said, "Take off his underpants, Robin, I'll hold him."

Eddie struggled, but to no avail as Robin stripped off his underwear. When Missy let him go, he tried to cover himself. The girls were between him and the water, but he made a dash between them and splashed out into the pond until he was waist deep as both girls laughed. Then he turned around and began to cry.

"You said you wouldn't tease me. How come you get to see me butt-naked and I don't get to see you?"

Robin said, "I'm sorry, Eddie. You're right, it isn't fair."

She slipped off her underpants and splashed into the pond, leaving Missy alone on the beach, but Missy wasn't about to be outdone.

"I'll show you I'm not afraid for you to see me naked," she announced.

She picked up the other two kids' underwear, ran over to the picnic table, and laid them on top. Then she stripped off her own and ran toward the water trying to do a cartwheel along the way. She almost made it, but she fell sideways into the sand and mud. Then she got up laughing and finished her run into the water.

They splashed and pushed each other around, no longer caring they were bare. Their slick bodies sparkled in the sunlight. They swam until they were tired, then started ashore.

At the edge of the water, Missy stopped and grabbed the other two and said, "We have to make a pact. We can never tell any of our mothers about going skinny-dipping. Let's all hold hands and make a vow."

They put their arms around each other's shoulders and made a solemn pledge to be, as Missy said, "Cousins to the end of time." Then they walked back to the table, their arms linked together, with Eddie in the middle. While acting silly and trying to make scissor steps, Robin tripped over Eddie's feet and they all fell into a pile. They lay laughing for a few minutes.

"I guess we'll have to go back into the water and clean off," Robin finally said.

"Right!" said Missy, standing and racing back toward the water.

After rinsing off, they walked back to the picnic table and sat on the benches to dry. Their conversation ranged from old teachers to what their moms would do if they found out what they'd done. When they were dry, they started to get dressed.

"How much time's left on the clock?" asked Missy.

"About twenty minutes," Eddie replied.

"Good. We don't want to go back too soon. Robin and I have to dry our hair."

Missy laid on the top of the table and Robin on the seat, their hair hanging over the edges. As Missy studied the sky and trees, she saw a paper wasp nest hanging on a limb in a box elder tree.

"What's that, Eddie?" she asked, pointing to the nest.

"That's a wasp nest. My friend, Ben, has one hanging inside his garage, but it's not active. His dad knocked it out of a tree in the winter."

"Do you suppose this one's active?"

"I don't know, but I'm not going to find out. Wasps sting, you know."

"I don't see any wasps around it now. Let's try to knock it down."

"I don't think that's a good idea, Missy."

Missy didn't heed Eddie's warning. She got up, found a long stick, and approached the nest while Robin and Eddie stayed behind and watched. She gave the nest a good whack. It didn't fall, but it swung violently. Within seconds, wasps began pouring out of the opening in the bottom.

Missy turned to run, but she wasn't fast enough. Several wasps landed on her back and shoulders and began to sting her.

Eddie shouted, "Quick! Jump in the pond! Robin, you, too!"

As they splashed into the pond, Eddie said, "Dive under the

water! They can't sting us under there."

They submerged and held their breath as long as possible. When they came up for air, they looked around and saw wasps continuing to circle overhead, so they submerged again. Then they came up again, the wasps had finally given up.

"Now what do we do?" asked Robin. "We're soaked, and we don't have time to dry out."

Eddie said, "You girls walk along the shore while I get your shoes and the thermos."

The girls slowly crept away from the pond while Eddie got their shoes, but he couldn't retrieve the thermos. It still had wasps swarming around. By the time Eddie joined them, Missy was crying in pain from the stings she had received.

"Rub mud on them," said Eddie. "That's what the Indians used to do."

Robin helped Missy get her top off while Eddie went back to the pond for some mud. They packed the mud on her back, and it did seem to help.

"Robin, you and Missy stay here," Eddie said. "I'll run and get Mom. She can come and get you in the go-getter."

"Okay, but hurry," Missy whined.

As Eddie approached the yard, Sara asked, "What happened to you? Where are the girls? How did you get so wet?"

"Missy tried to knock down a wasp nest and it was full of wasps, so she got stung bad. She and Robin are waiting for you to come and get them in the go-getter."

"Oh, my gosh!" Sara gasped. "Sue! Missy's hurt. Eddie says she got stung by wasps."

Sue came running and joined Sara in the go-getter. They found the girls sitting alongside the road. Missy was still topless and her back was covered with mud.

"How come you've got your top off?" Sue asked.

"Eddie said the Indians put mud on stings, so he put some mud on my back."

Sue picked up her muddy daughter and held her in the seat while Robin climbed into the back. In the meantime, Eddie told Aunt Kristy about the situation. When they returned, Kristy met Sara, Sue, and the girls at the kitchen door.

"You and Sue take care of the girls. I'll take Eddie back and get the thermos and other things," Sara told Kristy. "See if Madge has a remedy for stings. We'll be back soon."

Eddie rode back to the pond with his mom, and they were happy to see the wasps had finally forgotten their adversaries and returned to their nest. Sara retrieved the thermos and clock. She looked around the beach area and saw footprints leading in and out of the water. She said nothing about it.

In the basement back at the house, Missy and Robin were hearing how disgusted their moms were because they were going to need a second shower in one day. They were also out of clothes. The girls would have to wear pajamas until their clothes were washed and dried.

Missy was the biggest mess, since Eddie had smeared mud all over her shoulders and back. Both girls' hair was full of sand. Kristy got the shower started, then helped her daughter finish undressing. She noticed mud on Robin's upper legs and underpants. She knew the trio had been forced to jump into the water to avoid the wasps, but how had the mud gotten so far up on Robin's leg, and why was there so much sand in her hair?

"Robin," Kristy asked, "How come you have mud up here on your fanny?"

Robin didn't reply. She just ducked her head and remained silent.

Sue asked, "Missy, your undies are full of sand. How did this happen?"

Now both girls were hanging their heads.

"Robin, answer me!" Kristy ordered sharply.

Robin looked at her mom, her lower lip beginning to quiver, and said, "Missy made us swear never to tell."

Sue turned to her daughter and demanded, "Okay, Missy, out with it. What did you girls do?"

Missy whined, "We didn't do anything bad, Mom."

Sue paused a moment, then said, "I know what you did. You went skinny-dipping—and with Eddie, didn't you? Wait until I tell your Aunt Sara. I'm right, aren't I?"

As both girls nodded, Sue looked at Kristy, who just rolled her eyes and smiled. Sue took Kristy's smile to mean she was alright with the skinny-dipping.

After a long pause, Sue finally said, "Well, girls, did you have fun?"

Both girls looked up at Sue in surprise. Were they really off the hook?

Sue then added, "I wonder what your Aunt Sara will say about this. You and Eddie, swimming naked together. Well, it's too late now. Get in the shower, then head upstairs. Missy, you stop in the kitchen and let Grandma Madge treat your bites."

The girls were in their pajamas when Eddie and Sara returned. When Kristy broke the news, Sara looked at Eddie, who quickly looked down at the floor.

Instead of scolding him, Sara asked, "Well, Eddie, was playing naked with your girl cousins worth it? I don't think it's bad at your age, but I wouldn't recommend it eight years from now—or at least, don't tell me if you do it then."

Eddie looked up at his mom and sighed deeply, knowing he wasn't going to get into trouble.

"Now go downstairs and clean up," Sara said. "We'll have supper when the men get home."

Eddie hurried downstairs and into the laundry room. He tore off his shirt and shorts and took off his underwear as he started the shower. Then, out of the restroom came Aunt Sue—and he found himself standing naked in front of her.

As he froze, Sue just smile and said, "Well, we meet again, Eddie, and this time without your Scooby Do underwear. I guess I was right. You *are* a boy. Now go take your shower while I put your clothes in the washer with the girls'. I'll see ya later."

Eddie could hear Aunt Sue chuckling as she went upstairs. When he finished his shower, he wrapped a towel around himself and headed upstairs. It had been quite a day for him and his girl cousins.

Later that evening, after wieners and ice cream, the mothers and Madge sat around the picnic table. Sue broke the silence, saying, "Kristy, do you approve of our little skinny-dippers?"

"I don't want to say I approve, but at this age it's a good experience," Kristy said. "They're starting sex education in school, and kids are curious. I'm glad they satisfied that curiosity with someone they know and trust. Robin's probably far ahead of her older sister. The funny thing is, I'm sure, after the first few moments, they forgot all about being a boy or a girl. Still, I think the next time I let Robin go to the creek with

Eddie and Missy, I'll have her wear her swimsuit."

Madge laughed and added, "From my experience, that doesn't always guarantee they'll keep it on, especially when they get older. Isn't that right, Sara? "

Sara's face turned bright red as she replied, "Yes, Madge, but that was a long time ago."

Sue asked in surprise, "You and Paul went skinny-dipping? Good! I never told Mom, but Jeff and I did it several times before we were married. It was almost as much fun as sex."

All four women laughed until tears rolled down their cheeks.

* * *

The families met one more time over Labor Day. This time it was in Pella, and the sweet corn cousins spent their time riding their bikes around town. On Sunday, everyone made the short trip to Adventureland in Altoona, where the kids rode nearly every ride.

It would be next summer before they would be together again, and then Tim would tag along. When sweet corn time came, the sweet corn cousins helped, but things had changed. Missy and Robin were becoming young women. They were still bent on having fun, but the creek and pond now seemed immature. They still went to the pasture, but it was only to get away from the adults. They hiked all over the hills and ended up at the pond picnic table, where they sat, talked, and laughed for hours.

Only once did the subject of swimming come up. There would be no skinny-dipping, although the thought crossed their minds a time or two. Missy suggested they swim in their underwear, but Robin, whose body was a bit more developed than Missy's, nixed the idea. She claimed she'd have to go get her suit before going swimming. The sweet corn cousins had grown up, and previous summers were just something they could laugh about.

Chapter Fourteen
Snowy Christmas

The Maas family went to Waterloo for Thanksgiving. Christmas would be celebrated on the farm. It was an every-other-year event. This year Christmas fell on Friday, which meant a longer time to be together. On Christmas Eve, they attended Sara's home church's evening service with her parents. John and Emma planned to stay overnight at the farm, so they could watch the children open their gifts in the morning.

Sara was up early on Christmas morning, fixing rolls and an egg casserole for breakfast. Paul found his wife in her pajamas and robe when he came into the kitchen.

He gave her a peck on the back of her neck and said, "Merry Christmas, honey. Everything smells good. I'll do chores as fast as I can."

He spun her around, opened her robe, and hugged her tightly. He liked to feel her body close to his. He kissed her passionately and slipped his hand under her pajama top.

"Not now, Big Boy," she said with a playful smile. "You've got chores to do and I've got to fix breakfast. Besides, your parents will be here any moment. Now get going!"

Sara was right. Paul hadn't been gone more than five minutes when George and Madge pulled in the driveway. Paul helped bring their gifts and food in from the car. The ground was white with snow.

"Why don't you put your car in the shed, Dad?" said Paul. "They say we're going to get another four inches of snow before evening. I put John's car in the shop. I'll go open the door."

By the time Madge had set her food down, Emma walked into the kitchen, ready to help. Madge poured her a cup of coffee and sat down with Emma as Sara continued getting breakfast prepared.

"Do you think I should put the prime rib in?" Sara asked.

They always had prime rib on Christmas Day. It was a Maas family tradition. Madge got up from the table and helped Sara carry the meat to the oven. It would take at least five hours to cook.

John came into the kitchen, and George came through the back door after parking the car. The four grandparents sat and drank coffee while waiting for Paul to finish chores. It was quiet at the moment, but they all knew the children would be up shortly and bedlam would erupt.

"I'm the only one not dressed," Sara said. "I'd better get upstairs and see if the kids are awake."

As she reached the top of the stairs, she found the children just waking up.

"Do we have to get dressed?" Jenny asked.

"No, your PJs will be fine," Sara replied. "You can dress later. I'll be down as soon as I get dressed."

It was seven before Paul came in from chores. By that time, the kids had all their presents piled up and were busy shaking and feeling them. Grandpa John kidded them by imagining all sorts of ridiculous gifts which might be inside the packages.

When they were given the okay to begin, it didn't take long for the wrapping paper to disappear and the boxes opened. Jenny was just getting into her Barbie doll phase, Tim liked games which made him think, and both boys were into farm toys. The Ertl Company made a lot of money from the Maas family, and the boys especially liked the toys with green and yellow paint.

In the midst of the commotion, the phone rang. It was Sue, saying they were just leaving Waterloo and would be there in about three hours. She told Sara it was just starting to snow in Waterloo and hoped they wouldn't have to drive in snow all the way.

When Sara hung up, she turned on the TV. The weatherman said snow was forecast all day. The main band of snow was expected to go south of Iowa, through southern Illinois, but if it moved on a more northerly track, it would catch eastern Iowa. There was the possibility of twelve to fourteen inches.

Sue, Jeff, and family arrived at about noon because of the slick roads. They unloaded the car in about four inches of new snow as it floated down in big flakes.

"We brought our toboggan, just in case we get enough snow," one of nephews said excitedly. Paul and Seth untied the toboggan and carried it in the garage.

Everyone went inside. It was 1:00 before the Christmas feast was ready. Paul gave the blessing, thanking God for the many blessings He had bestowed on everyone present. He thanked God for sending Jesus. Sharing of food was a way of celebrating His birthday.

When he had finished, everyone said, "Amen!"

George carved the prime rib into nice thick slices. It was roasted to perfection. Emma brought her famous orange and pineapple Jell-O salad. Madge had made her banana cream pie and Aunt Sue's specialty was Great-Grandma Minnie's escalloped oysters. Not everyone liked this particular dish, but George and Paul loved it. Tim tried it, because he'd try anything once.

Everyone ate until they were stuffed. The men tried to retire to the den; however, Seth and Noah had received a new TV game called Donkey Kong. The boys were dominating the den. The girls headed upstairs to Jenny's room. The men had to settle for the living room, which meant the ladies would sit around the kitchen table.

Outside, the snow continued to fall and the wind was picking up. Paul came into the kitchen and turned on the little TV on the counter to check the weather. They learned there was ten inches of snow on the ground and another five or six expected.

"Maybe I should go over and check on the calves at Becker's," he told Sara. "I'll get someone to go with me. I bet Seth would like to ride on my new toy. I'll ask him."

Paul walked into the den and said, "Hey, Seth, would you like to ride over to Becker's with me?"

Seth looked up and replied, "No, thanks, Uncle Paul. I think I'll stay here."

"Okay, Noah, how about you?" Paul asked. "I've got a new snowmobile in the shed. We can ride over on it."

"I didn't know you had a snowmobile, Uncle Paul!" Noah said excitedly. "I'd love to go."

"Okay, get your snow pants on," said Paul. "I've got a helmet for you."

Seth gave his uncle a dirty look. He knew he'd just had a trick played on him.

"You and your dad can ride when we get back," Paul said with a smile. "Tim and Ed will have a lot of time to ride later on."

Paul and Noah suited up and headed to the shed where the snowmobile was housed. It was a shiny new Polaris. Noah hopped on behind his uncle and hung on as Paul gunned the engine and began speeding down the lane. It was about a mile and a half to Becker's.

As they approached, they saw the house was dark. Mrs. Becker probably wasn't home, but just to make sure, Paul called her daughter in Muscatine.

"Hello, Cindy. This is Paul Maas. I'm at your mom's and the house is dark. I hope she's at your house and not in trouble here."

"Yes, Paul, she's here," Cindy replied. "She'll be staying overnight. I'll bring her home in the morning. Thanks for thinking about her."

"Before you come back, call me," Paul said. "I'll plow the lane, but with all this snow, it may take a while."

"Okay, I'll do that," said Cindy. "Merry Christmas to your family."

"Same to you and your mom. I'll talk to you in the morning. Goodbye."

Noah and Paul checked the calves and gave them a little extra feed. Noah was delighted when his uncle let him drive home. As they pulled up the lane, the snow was beginning to drift it shut. In some places it was already three to four feet deep.

When they got to the house, Paul asked Jeff, "Want to take it for a ride?"

"Sure," Jeff said happily. "Come on, Seth. Let's go."

Jeff and Seth put on the helmets and were soon speeding off into the twilight, headed for the big bean field. After watching them leave, Paul went to the barn to check the cows. The snow continued to fall as he worked, and Paul listened for the rig, but the wind drowned out any engine noise.

Thirty minutes later, Paul had finished his chores, but the pair hadn't returned. It was getting dark. Paul went into the shop and plugged in the tractor with the snow blower. He knew Jeff had his cell phone if they got into trouble, so Paul wasn't worried yet.

He went to the house, stood by the kitchen window, and waited for ten minutes. He was about to head out on the go-getter when he saw headlights coming around the barn. The wayward pair put the rig in the shed and came inside.

"Where have you guys been?" asked Paul, "Did you get lost?"

"No," Jeff answered simply, but Seth let the cat out of the bag.

"Yes, we did, Uncle Paul. Dad just doesn't want to admit it."

Paul chuckled as he asked, "What happened?"

"Well," Jeff said with a sheepish grin, "We went to the end of the field and started back. Then I decided to do some circles, and I guess I got disoriented. It was so dark out there and the snow was blowing. I took off for the end of the field, following the rows, and soon I was at the fence. Instead of turning right, I went left. Then, before we knew it we were at the far end of the field. To get back, we slowed down and followed the fence back. We could barely see ten feet in front of us. It took a little longer than I planned."

Seth said, "I think Dad was a little worried when we almost hit the far fence."

"Well, the storm is getting worse and nobody's going anywhere tonight," Jeff conceded.

There was more than enough leftover food for supper. After the dishes were finished, Sue gathered everyone around the dining room table for a game of UNO. Sometimes the game got a little nasty, but it was all in fun.

Everyone stopped to listen when the evening news came on. There were weather problems throughout the Midwest. Interstate 80 was closed west of Walcott and travel wasn't recommended east of the Quad Cities. The snow had ended, but the wind would be gusting to forty miles an hour.

The wind was howling around the house and banging at the windows and doors, as if it was trying to get into the house to get warm. It was time to find places for everyone to sleep. The adults confiscated the upstairs while kids were everywhere downstairs. Because of Donkey Kong, the boys headed for the den. Little Josh decided to bunk with Missy and Jenny in the living room.

It was 11:00 when Sue slid the door open to the den and stood in her borrowed robe and slippers, her hands on her hips, ordering, "Alright, you guys. Turn off the TV."

She went into kitchen for a drink, but when she came back, the TV was still on. She marched through the den, turned off the TV, and grabbed the controls.

"Now go to sleep!" she growled as she took the game controller with her.

The boys snickered, knowing Aunt Sue had forgotten the TV

remote. They could still watch the late movie, which they did.

The next morning dawned cold, but calm. The drifted snow had been sculptured into white crystal waves, eight to ten feet deep in some places. After a hardy breakfast, it was all hands on deck. Everyone except the grandmas headed outside to help shovel.

Paul and George manned the tractor and skid loader, and by noon the lane was clear; however, the county road was still blocked. It would take a while before it would be cleared.

This time Seth rode with Paul to the Becker place on the snowmobile. When they returned, Paul had Sara call Cindy to tell her to keep her mother a couple more days.

By nightfall, the county had cleared the road, creating snowdrifts higher than a car. The grandparents headed home to check on their homes and get a good night's sleep, but Jeff and Sue decided to take another day off so they could enjoy the snow.

What a Christmas it had been!

Chapter Fifteen
Family Camping

Farmers, believe it or not, have a difficult time taking vacations. Because they're self-employed and responsible for their own operations, there never seems to be enough time to get all the jobs completed. Every time they think they're caught up, something else needs to be done.

Most farmers will fit into one of two categories: those who are workaholics and never take a day off and those who realize the job will be there tomorrow. Paul was in the latter group, and annual vacations were always a part of his plans.

In the early years of their marriage, Sara and Paul stayed close to home on their vacations, partly because it was difficult to travel with babies. However, when Jenny turned three, they ventured to the Black Hills of South Dakota. Finding motel rooms and eating out all the time caused both sleeping and eating problems. A lot of money was wasted on food the kids wouldn't eat. McDonald's and other fast food venues were the norm.

After dealing with upset stomachs and noisy rooms, Sara and Paul decided to try camping the next year. First, it was with tents and cook stoves, which involved a lot of work for Sara. One week they camped at Backbone State Park near Strawberry Point, Iowa. Since they were their own bosses, they went midweek in August. The van was loaded with a big tent, a cook stove, a cooler, and lots of clothes.

The park had a nice sandy beach and plenty of hiking trails. They selected a site not far from the shower house and restrooms. By the time everything was set up, Sara and Paul were soaked with perspiration. Sara brought out sandwiches and drinks from home. Afterward, Ed, Tim, and Jenny spread a blanket out on the grass and fell asleep.

Paul woke everyone at 2:00 and said, "Let's go swimming. The beach is open until five."

The boys ducked into the tent and put on their swim trunks while Sara and Jenny changed in the van. The beach was on the other side of the park and easily reached by car.

The day was beautiful and the water was warm. The sky was

blue, punctuated by a few fluffy white clouds. The family stayed on the beach until it closed, then drove back to the campground, where Sara dug out clean clothes and everyone went to the main building to take showers.

Paul built a campfire and helped Sara fire up the camp stove. For supper, they had wieners and baked beans. As the fire died, Sara brought out marshmallows and Hershey bars for s'mores. They were messy, but delicious.

Just as they were getting ready to put the kids to bed, they heard thunder. The camping area was amid shade trees, preventing a clear view of the sky. Paul helped put away the cooking utensils and Sara hung the swim suits on a line to dry. They could see flashes of lightning overhead. Paul and Sara had just crawled into their dual sleeping bag and fallen asleep when they were awakened by an announcement from a loudspeaker on a ranger's truck.

"There's a severe storm heading our way," the ranger said. "It should be here in about thirty minutes, with high winds, hail, and heavy rain. We suggest all campers gather at the shower house."

The message was repeated several times as the ranger slowly drove through the park. Paul and Sara quickly pulled on some shorts and jeans and woke the kids. The family loaded into the van to go to the shower house.

At the shelter house, they found a motley-looking group of tired campers. Everyone was in their pajamas or robes, the women weren't wearing makeup, and the men were unshaven.

Although the storm was dangerous, it was also exciting. Amid flashes of lightning, they could see the trees outside beginning to strain against the rising wind. They also began to see entire tents flying by the window, rolling along the ground like gigantic tumbleweeds. The wind was soon joined by torrential rain. The roads soon were flooded and as huge streams of water poured off the shower house roof, water started to make its way into the building, and soon many people found themselves standing in water.

Then, as quickly as it had come, the storm was over. The torrent turned into light rain, then to gentle drizzle, and finally to a fine mist. Finally, at about 1:00 in the morning, the ranger announced an all-clear.

The family climbed back into their van and headed back toward their campsite, having to carefully drive around several downed branches along the way. When they arrived, they all let out a collective sigh of relief. Their tent was still there and all in one piece—but it was now sitting in a large puddle of water. As Sara entered the tent, she shook her head. All the bedding was soaked.

"Well, kids," Paul announced, "looks like we'll be sleeping in the van tonight. Jenny, you take the backseat. You boys will be on the floor and Mom and I will tilt the front seats back."

Sara suggested, " We should get the sleeping bags out of the tent and lay them over the top of the van."

Paul agreed, and as the kids settled into their sleeping positions, Paul and Sara removed the wet bedding from the tent and put it on top of the van. It was past 2:00 when they finally joined the kids and settled in for the night.

The kids slept fine, but it was a long night for the adults. When the new day dawned clear and bright, Paul surveyed the campsite as the kids continued to sleep, and asked Sara, "Do you think we can dry this stuff out?"

"No!" Sara answered quickly. "We might get it dry, but it'll smell. I say we go home and try this again some other time."

Paul nodded. "Sounds like a plan. Let's pack up. We can eat breakfast somewhere on the way home."

"I'm not going inside to eat," Sara countered. "I don't even have a bra to wear."

"Well, you look fine to me," Paul said with a smile.

"Yeah, but I'm still not going into a restaurant, Big Boy," Sara said. "I'll wake the kids and we'll get out of here."

They stopped at Hardy's in Manchester and ordered breakfast at the drive-thru. Sara wouldn't have to go inside. Once they got home, Sara spent the entire day washing and drying bedding and clothes while Paul and the boys unfolded the tent and washed it with the power washer. This would be their last tent camping experience. The next day the whole family began visiting recreational trailer dealers to find a pop-up camper. It would still feel like a tent adventure, but they'd all be off the ground.

The pop-up trailer they bought lasted for several trips, including Mackinac Island, Cape Hatteras, and Pike's Peak. Their most enjoyable camping was at the Iowa State Fair. It was very crowded there; however, since a high percentage of the fairgoers were farmers, there was little danger of losing a child. Everyone looks out for each other's children. Ed and Tim soon made friends from a camper three units down the row and Jenny found a girlfriend next door.

The shuttle wagons carrying visitors to and from the fairground were always full, but there always seemed to be room for one more. Paul spent quite a bit of time in the cattle barns while Sara and the kids toured the rest of the fair. They spent a long time in the Children's Forest and at the petting zoo. Over the next six years, a trip to the state fair became an annual affair for the Maas family.

It was the trip to Yellowstone which prompted another change in the family's camping style. The trip went fine and Yellowstone and the Grand Tetons were fabulous. Paul even made arrangements with a dude ranch for horseback rides through the forest.

On the way home, they stopped at Thermopolis, Wyoming, where they spent a day at a water park and soaked in the hot springs. They had been away for eight days, so it was time to start for home. In Cheyenne, they stopped at a campground on a hill overlooking the city and surrounding mountains.

While they were eating supper, they could see storm clouds beginning to build and clouds of dust rolling before the wind in the valley below. When the storm finally hit, there was no rain, but lots of wind, which rocked the camper violently. They watched tents fly by and wondered if their pop-up would be next. No warnings were issued, but they wondered if they should go to the camp's shelter house.

Paul had an idea. He parked the van on the windward side, thus breaking the wind. The pop-up still rocked, although it was less. Everyone endured the long night, but no one slept very soundly. Jenny was especially scared and crawled under the covers beside her mother.

After breakfast the next morning, they headed for Iowa. Unfortunately, they caught up with the cold front near North Platte. On the Nebraska prairie, thunderstorms can become quite violent. They kept driving, and by 10:00 they were in Omaha with the storm still on their heels.

It was 1:00 in the morning when they passed through Des Moines. The kids were asleep in back as Paul filled the gas tank at a twenty-four-hour station. He drove the last leg of the trip home with everyone else asleep. He smiled as he listened to the rhythmic breathing of his family.

Sara awoke just as he was pulling off the highway and onto the gravel road for home. It was 3:00 in the morning when they finally pulled up to the house. The family crawled out of the van, grabbed their pillows, and went inside to fall into their own beds.

In September, Sara put in her request for a solid-sided trailer, which would mean not only a new trailer, but also a new van big enough to pull it. She convinced Paul the old van was due for retirement. After some shopping, they pulled home a twenty-five-foot camper which would become their home away from home for the next several vacations. Wind and rain no longer were a problem and the women of the family had their own bathroom and shower.

Their next vacations included Walt Disney World, the Smokey Mountains, Washington DC, Gulf Shores, Alabama, Mesa Verde National Park, and several other national parks. The length of the trips varied from seven to fourteen days.

The severe drought of 1988 caused the Maas family to curtail spending in 1989 until the crop was harvested, meaning their only vacation would be four days at the state fair. Paul decided to compensate for the loss of vacation by parking the camper at the farm pond, jokingly renaming the site "Little South Dakota."

He started by filling the water tank used for supplying the sprayer and pulling it to the grove by the pond. Next he rigged up a shower by hanging a garden hose in a tree and attaching a shower head to the end. He hooked a battery-powered pump to move the water through the hose. The heat of the sun would warm the water. He placed a wooden pallet on the ground to stand on while taking a shower.

Paul was proud of his shower, but when Sara saw it she suggested the addition of a curtain. Since there was no way to attach a curtain, Paul brought three sheets of particle board of varying heights to place around the shower. The front piece was five feet tall, but the side pieces were shorter, only covering the person taking a shower from the waist up. This meant if Sara or Jenny was taking a shower there was to be no peeking.

Blocks were placed under one set of wheels to level the camper. A generator would power the lights, TV, and air conditioning if needed. Late at night, Paul turned the generator off to save fuel and to lessen the noise. For restroom needs, Paul brought an old outhouse he had found behind a shed at the Becker place. He set it up behind some honeysuckle bushes.

Placement of the outhouse was crucial because the door was gone. This meant everyone had to warn the rest of the family when they were going to use the outhouse. After a few mishaps, Sara found an old rug to hang over the door.

They had picnics and swam, followed by cool showers, because the water in the tank never warmed. They sat around the campfire and roasted marshmallows. All in all, it was a beautiful campsite, with shade trees, a small sandy beach, and a three-acre pond. It also provided a quick and easy getaway for the family.

One day, Paul and the boys were at a 4-H field day to learn more about grooming and showing calves. By three in the afternoon, Sara had finished her chores and asked Jenny, "Would you like to go to the camper early? You can play in the water while I read."

Jenny happily agreed. All her friends were busy, so an afternoon with her mom would be nice. They jumped into the go-getter and headed for the pond, where Jenny ran into the camper to put on her swimsuit. A few minutes later, she returned with a long face.

"What's the matter?" Sara asked.

"My swimming suit must be back at the house," Jenny replied. "I don't see it in here."

"You know what?" Sara said. "I took everyone's suits back to the house last time to wash them. I must have missed yours when I picked them up for the return trip. Tell you what, honey. There's no one around. Why don't you go swimming in your underwear? "

Jenny loved the idea. She liked doing daring things. She stripped off her top and shorts and headed for the water while Sara unfolded a lawn chair and sat in the sun to read. She also took off her blouse and rolled up her shorts to get more sun.

"Mom, can I go skinny-dipping?" Jenny called from the edge of the pond.

"Sure, why not?"

Jenny scurried to shore and took off her underpants, then dashed back into the cool water. When Sara grew tired of reading, she spread a towel on the sand, lay down on her stomach, and unhooked her bra. The sun was hot, so she eventually wiggled out of her shorts and fell asleep.

Seeing her mom was sleeping, Jenny crept up to her with a small pail of water and began to pour the contents onto her back. As Sara jerked up, Jenny giggled.

Giving her daughter a dirty look, Sara said, "I'll get you for that! You just wait."

Jenny ran toward the water with Mom in hot pursuit. At the water's edge, Sara paused, watched her naked daughter splashing happily for a second. She slipped off her own undies and flipped them into the chair before joining Jenny in the water.

"If you can go skinny-dipping, so can I," said Sara as she reached out, picked Jenny up, and threw her into deeper water. They splashed and swam for about hour, then Sara went back to shore to check her watch.

"We'd better quit," Sara announced. "Dad and the boys will be home soon and we don't want them to catch us out here skinny-dipping."

Sara turned on the water pump so Jenny could shower, and Jenny gasped as the cool water hit her back. When Jenny finished, Sara handed her a towel. She was about to step into the enclosure herself, when her CB radio blared. It was Paul, saying he and the boys would be home in about an hour. They were going to Happy Joe's with the Petersens for pizza and would bring home the leftovers.

Sara smiled. This meant supper would be late, but it also meant she wouldn't have to cook.

"Jenny, that was Dad," Sara told her daughter. "They're going to be late. Put your towel on the beach, and as soon as I finish my shower, I'll join you. We'll sunbathe naked, since no one will be home for a while."

Jenny was elated. It was something else she'd never done before and she was happy to join her mom. They basked in the warm sunshine until they heard the pickup coming. They both hurried into the camper to get dressed.

The guys arrived with a small Canadian bacon pizza. It was still warm and no one had touched it. Evidently, they had felt guilty about going to Happy Joe's without them. The boys were hot and sticky and had animal hair all over their jeans and t-shirts.

'How'd you eat with all that hair on you?" Sara asked. "Paul, how could you go into a restaurant with the boys looking like that?"

Paul gave her a sheepish grin and said nothing. He knew she was right.

"You boys take your shoes, socks, jeans and t-shirts off by the water tank and throw them in the back of go-getter," Sara ordered. "Then jump in the pond in your underwear so you can get the filthy hair off of you."

As the boys happily threw their clothes in the go-getter and headed for the water, Sara looked at Paul and said, "And what about you, Big Boy? You don't look much better than they do."

"But I just watched and held the ropes," Paul protested.

"Well, you don't smell very good," Sara said firmly.

Paul smiled, then stripped down to his shorts and headed for the pond. As he walked by the lawn chair, he paused, then bent over and picked up Sara's underwear and bra.

Holding them up for her to see, he said, "Well, well. How do you suppose these got here?" Smiling mischievously, he added, "You don't suppose a pair of ladies were skinny-dipping here today, do you?"

Sara smiled back and said defiantly, "Yes, we did and we had fun, too."

As Paul and the boys splashed in the pond, Jenny and Sara ate their pizza. One by one, the men left the pond to take their showers. Sara purposely set their towels on the tires of the water wagon so they'd have to walk a few feet with nothing on to retrieve them. She always liked to tease.

As evening rolled around, both Jenny and Sara changed into their pajamas. Sara preferred button tops. She claimed pullovers were too confining.

As the sun began to set, Paul started the generator to run the lights and air conditioning. The boys were tired from their long day and went inside to go to bed. Sara, Paul, and Jenny stayed outside to watch the embers of the campfire die. Jenny fell asleep in her mother's arms and Paul carried her inside.

Because he was awakened by his Dad putting Jenny to bed, Ed peered out the window. He could see his parents sitting close together, talking. Seeing their obvious affection for each other, he thought, "When I get married, I want to be like Mom and Dad."

As he watched, his dad did a silly dance in front of his mom, then pulled her to her feet and began to dance with her. They danced slowly around the fire. He kissed her tenderly. Against the backdrop of the glowing embers, he saw his dad slip his mom's top from her shoulders with her back to the camper. They kissed again, then slipped off into the darkness. A few moments later, he heard them laughing and splashing in the pond.

Next thing Ed knew, it was morning and Mom and Dad were in their bed at the opposite end of the trailer. He decided not to ask about the previous night. After all, it was their love affair and not his. His time would come one day—and he could only hope he'd someday know the same kind of love his parents had always shared.

Chapter Sixteen
Relationships

Like many young people, the Maas children attended a number of youth camps. Ed, being the oldest, started in the fifth grade at a primitive camp in Wyoming, Iowa. The campers cooked, ate, and slept in the woods for five days. They even had to dig their own latrine. Not being able to use a bathroom with a stool was quite an adventure, especially for some of the town girls.

In the middle of the week, they were deluged with four inches of rain. On the last night, because the bedding still wasn't dry, the counselors decided to sound the retreat and allow everyone to sleep on cots in the mess hall. Even so, everyone had a blast!

Tim attended his first camp as a gangly five-foot-ten, twelve-year-old. His body would never seem to do what he wanted, but his claim to fame was music. He had a nice tenor voice and the chorus director at West Junior High claimed he had perfect pitch.

Noah's Ark was the theme of the camp. On the first day, the campers were divided into groups, and each group adopted the name of an animal. Within each group, males and females were paired together, like in the biblical story, doing most tasks and playing most games together. The counselors, Tanya and Mitch, helped the shy campers pair up.

Mitch looked at Tim and said, "You're a giraffe because you're tall and have a long neck."

The girls giggled at the comment as the counselors turned their gaze toward them.

"Who wants to be a girl giraffe?" Mitch asked.

There was an awkward pause during which no one replied. Then, from the back of the group, a voice said, "I will."

It turned out to be a perfect fit. The girl who spoke was a tall blonde with her long hair pulled back. She wore glasses and was as straight as a bean pole.

"What's your name, Miss Giraffe?" Mitch asked.

"Angela Vander Ploog," the girl said. "I'm from Oskaloosa."

"Well, Angela from Oskaloosa, meet your partner," Mitch announced. Then he turned to Tim and said, "By the way, what is your name? I forgot to ask."

"Tim Maas, from Muscatine."

Tim and Angela shook hands and stepped aside while everyone else was paired off.

Tanya then explained what the campers would be doing. If a team game was being played, all the animals in a specific group were on that team—such as mammals, reptiles, and birds. When jobs like washing dishes or cleaning the bathrooms were scheduled, the pairs would work together. The only time the pairs wouldn't be together was when they went to bed or to the bathroom. Again there were giggles as the format was explained.

"Now for the next ten minutes, I want you sit with your partner and ask questions like: Where do you live? Do you have siblings? How big is your school? And, of course, do you love Jesus?"

Tim sat on a bench with his long legs stretched out in front of him. Angela sat across from him.

"Do you play basketball?" was Angela's first question.

"Yeah, but I like music better," Tim replied. "My brother plays sports, but I could do without them."

"Do you play an instrument?" Angela continued.

"I try to play the harmonica, but I like singing best."

"Oh."

There was an uncomfortable silence, then Angela volunteered, "I like to sing, too. I also play the guitar and piano, and if you don't mind, could you call me Angie? Everybody does."

"OK," said Tim. "Do you have any brother or sisters?"

"Three brothers, all older, and one little sister."

"How about you?" Angie asked. "Do you have any other family besides your brother?"

"Mom, Dad, and my sister, Jenny."

Angie nodded, then asked, "Oh, and I'm supposed to ask if you love Jesus."

"Yeah, I suppose so."

The conversation continued with short questions and answers

until Mitch called time. Some campers found they hadn't been paired well and were allowed to switch partners.

After the evening meal, the mammals were on cleanup duty. Tim and Angie wiped the tables and set the chairs straight. They had short devotions in each group, and everyone went out to the campfire vespers. Mitch and Tanya soon took note of the musicians in the group. The next morning, they asked for volunteers to form a singing group. Angie immediately volunteered.

Then Mitch asked the campers, "All right, everyone. When we sang last night, you heard who could carry a tune, so if they're not already up here, who do you think should?"

"Tim can sing," said Angie.

Tim smiled as he shyly walked up front. Others were also suggested, and the final group included eight campers.

"Okay," Mitch said, "you're the chosen few. You won't have to do KP for three days. Instead, you'll be practicing some songs to teach the others. Tanya will lead you. Come up with a name for the group and we'll be expecting to hear from you shortly. The rest of us are going to the south end of the camp to pick up trash and mark trails."

There were groans and moans, but the non-singers dutifully followed Mitch down the trail. The singers stayed behind. Tanya sang the melody and asked them to follow. In a short time, they were singing the tune. The second time through, Angie sang harmony in her alto voice and Tim added a tenor. With Tim and Angie leading the way, the others joined in; and by the time the others returned, the group had decided to call themselves Noah's Pooper Scoopers.

Most of the games and work events were team-oriented, so the pairings were only used for the three-legged race, the wheelbarrow race, and tag team races in the pool. Camp ended sooner than the campers would have liked, but soon it was time to say goodbye. Tim, being a gentleman, helped Angie carry her bedding and dirty clothes to her parents' car. When she introduced Tim to her folks, Tim shook their hands, then turned to go to his own parents' van.

He had just turn the corner of Angie's car when she caught up with him and said, "Tim, I have something for you."

Tim turned around and asked, "Really? What is it?"

"This," Angie said, giving him a peck on the cheek. "I hope to see you again."

Tim could feel his face getting warm. He'd never been kissed by anyone other than his mom or sister. Angie smiled as his face turned red.

Though Tim never expected to see Angie again, he returned to the camp the next summer, but Angie wasn't there. His last year of junior high, he decided to attend a basketball camp with Ed; however, in April, Mrs. Henry, the school's youth advisor, offered Tim the possibility to attend a Christian music camp at Luther College in Decorah. She thought with his tenor voice and music composition ability he might be interested. It would be a ten-day camp. He was unsure until his music teacher, Miss Leach, called his mom and told her of the great opportunity.

Sara quickly made the decision. Tim would be going. She told Tim, "Basketball's great, but music will last you forever."

The camp went from June 23rd to July 3rd. It would be over just in time to help with detasseling. Sara and Jenny drove Tim to Decorah and got him checked in. He was assigned a roommate in one of the dorm rooms, a boy named Peter Vandewalle, from Oskaloosa.

When Tim met Peter, he asked, "Do you happen to know Angie Vander Ploog?"

"I sure do," Peter replied. "She and I came to this camp together. She's really musical."

Tim could barely believe his ears. Angie was there! At the first evening meal, Dr. Anderson, head of the vocal department outlined the camp's goals. It wouldn't be just for fun. Even though there would time for mixing and recreation in the evenings, everyone would be expected to be at all rehearsals and individual lessons.

While Dr. Anderson spoke, Tim scanned the crowd for Angie, but he didn't see her. An hour after the opening ceremonies, there was a mixer dance, and a girl asked Tim to dance. Midway through the song, he heard a familiar voice behind him.

"May I cut in?"

It was Angie. She had gotten rid of her glasses and her hair was long, golden, and straight. She was also the tallest girl there.

As they danced, Angie asked, "How have you been? Looks like you've grown a bit."

"Looks like you have, too," Tim said with a smile.

He couldn't take his eyes off her. He thought she was beautiful as they swayed to the music.

"Are you here for vocals?" she asked.

"Yeah, and for composition."

"I'm here for vocals and piano. Maybe I'll be able to play something you write."

"Maybe."

The week was very busy with little down time. When there was time for relaxing, it was shortened by homework. Tim and Angie saw little of each other until two days before the end of camp. He showed Angie his latest piece of music, and she played it on the piano.

"The melody's wonderful. May I work on it by myself?" she asked, and Tim agreed.

Finally came the time to show the parents what the campers had accomplished. Each division had its own concert. The orchestra went first, then the mass chorus, and finally the band. After a short intermission, individuals were given a chance to perform their works.

Tim had worked hard on a composition he called "The Girl with the Golden Hair." He'd only had time to write just the melody before he gave it to Angie. She had then added chords and trills. When it came time for Angie to play, the piano flowed beneath her expert touch.

When she finished, there was dead silence for a second or two, then the audience's applause began to increase until there were cheers and whistles and everyone rose to their feet.

Angie stood and acknowledged the applause, then motioned for a microphone.

In a shaky, nervous voice, she said, "Ladies and gentlemen, thank you for your generous applause. I would like you to meet the composer of this piece. He's a dear friend of mine. Tim Maas, would you please come up and take a bow for this fabulous piece of music?"

Tim had found a seat in the rear of the auditorium, but he stood and slowly walked down the aisle to the stage as the applause erupted again. Angie held out her hand and led him to center stage, where they both bowed to the audience. When Angie looked over at Tim, her face was beaming. She hugged him and gave him another peck on the cheek.

"Thank you for your music, Tim. I hope we meet again," she whispered.

It was a great finish to a wonderful camp. Sara, Paul, and Jenny were proud of their son and brother. Angie brought her parents over to meet Tim's parents. They exchanged pleasantries. Tim and Angie promised each other they'd stay in touch. They did for a while, but distance and going to different schools made it difficult. High school activities soon replaced their letters and e-mails.

Angie and Tim met again briefly at All-State Chorus festival and at some music contests. When they graduated, Tim went to Iowa State. Angie e-mailed to let him know she'd received a scholarship to Luther. She wished him well—and Tim did the same.

Chapter Seventeen
Teenagers and Romance

When Ed started high school at Muscatine, Maas family life changed dramatically. Football practice started in early August, which meant family vacation time became a thing of the past—maybe a few days at the state fair, but that was all.

Ed's freshman year was the beginning of his athletic career. He made the football, basketball, and baseball teams, but of the three, basketball seemed to offer his best shot at playing full-time.

Ed turned sixteen in November of his sophomore year. Coach Miller, the basketball coach, pulled some strings to enable Ed to take driver education classes during the fall semester, which helped with transportation in mid-January. Ed stood 6'4" on his sixteenth birthday. He was also developing a beard.

He had an excellent shot from behind the three-point line and Coach Miller had plans for his prodigy. He knew Ed's younger brother would be joining the team the next year. Tim was already 6'4" and wasn't done growing yet. The coach was confident the Maas brothers would one day become a force to reckon with.

Before Ed got his driver's license, he had to wait for his neighbor, Ben Scott, to give him a ride home. He did homework in the coach's office while waiting, and it was during that time he met Coach Miller's daughter, Renee.

Renee wasn't a star athlete—she left her athletic talents to her four sisters. In fact, Renee didn't like sports at all. She chose dramatics and stage crew as her extracurricular activities.

Her father was disappointed, but he accepted her choice, telling anyone who asked, "Not everyone can be an athlete, and there's no sense trying to make one out of someone who doesn't have the heart for it."

Renee was the exact opposite of Ed in temperament. She was bubbly and loquacious, and she helped bring Ed out of his shell. When they were studying together, she would kid him about not having a girlfriend when every girl in school wanted to date him.

In late February, there was a school dance in which the girls paid for the dance, dinner, and flowers. Renee asked Ed to be her date for the dance, and he accepted.

When Ed got home, he announced, "I've got a date for the Sadie Hawkins dance."

"Who is she?" asked Sara.

"Renee Miller, the coach's daughter," Ed said happily, then added, "but, Mom, I don't know how to dance. What am I going to do?"

"Well, I'd have a difficult time teaching you the dances young folks do now," replied Sara, "but maybe Jenny can help."

"But Jenny's just a teenybopper, Mom. She only dances with other girls."

"Okay," Sara conceded. "Would you be embarrassed if I called your Aunt Sue and asked if Missy could teach you? She's your age. We could drive up and see them next weekend and you two could go to her room or down to the basement and practice. We moms would butt out until you're finished. What do you say?"

"Sounds like a plan, Mom. I'll try it."

They arrived at Aunt Sue's just before lunch. Missy was her usual bubbly self and happy for a chance to teach her cousin how to dance. She and Ed went downstairs to the family room, where Missy started the lesson with a slow dance.

"Take you left hand and hold it like this," she instructed, "and put your right hand on my waist, right here."

As the music played, Missy tried to get Ed to flow with the rhythm, but he was stiff and obviously uncomfortable. Before deciding he was hopeless, Missy had an idea.

"Ed," she said, "do you remember the time Robin, you, and me went skinny-dipping?"

"Do I! I'll never forget it."

"Okay, good," said Missy. "Remember how we were all a little nervous at first, then forgot about being girls or boys and just had fun."

"You don't want me to get naked again, do you?" Ed teased.

"No, silly," Missy said with a smile. "I'm just saying you have to let go of your inhibitions and just dance as if no one's looking. Dance as if you're just playing in the water and not caring about anything else.

Just loosen up."

"Okay, I'll try."

Missy started the song again and Ed immediately began to flow more smoothly with the rhythm of the music.

"Now, my dear cousin," Missy said with a mischievous smile, "this is what Renee might do during your second dance."

Missy put her arms around Ed's neck and moved in close. He could feel the curves of her body against his as she swayed slowly, rubbing against him. She made moon eyes at him and laid her head on his shoulder. Missy took his free hand and placed it on her lower back. She continued to guide his hand until it was just below her waist. Then she patted his fingers.

When the record stopped, she stepped back and said, "I think you'll do just fine, Cousin Ed. Just go no lower than the flat part of a woman's backside. Man, I wish you were my boyfriend and not my cousin. We could have a good old time."

Ed easily caught on to the rock and roll dances. He didn't have to touch the girl at all, except maybe her hand occasionally. Missy called her mom and Aunt Sara down to show them Ed's progress, although they avoided the close slow dance. It might have been a bit too much. When they were done, both mothers applauded.

On the night of the dance, Ed picked up Renee. They met their friends at the dance. Missy had taught Ed well and he wowed Renee and her friends. He danced with many girls during the evening, as well, but he saved the last dance for Renee. Just as Missy had predicted, she wrapped her arms around his neck and moved in close. He put both arms around her waist as she laid her head on his chest, since she wasn't tall enough to reach his shoulder. As they swayed together, Ed remembered Missy's instruction and put his hand on the flat part of Renee's back, just below her waist.

Renee almost purred with approval. "Where did you learn to dance like this?"

"It just comes natural for me," he lied while silently thanking Missy.

The dance was over at 11:00, but instead of going out with the gang, Ed told Renee he had to be home before midnight—Coach Miller's orders.

Renee chuckled, "My dad sure has you guys' number. He was

always after my sisters, too. Still, you should follow his orders. I know I have to."

Ed drove Renee home and walked her to the door, where he said, "I had a really good time tonight. Thanks for inviting me. Maybe we could go to a movie next week. We don't have a Saturday game."

"I'd be delighted," Renee said, smiling sweetly. "You're the nicest guy I've ever met."

"It's a date then. See ya at school Monday."

Ed then turned and walked away, leaving Renee standing dumbfounded on the porch. Ed was the first boy she'd ever dated who hadn't expected a goodnight kiss. Her sisters had told her about such men, but she never thought they were telling her the truth.

Ed and Renee dated the rest of the school year. They attended dances, school plays and movies. Ed always walked her to her door, said goodbye, and left. Even when Renee invited him in, he sat on the sofa and watched a ballgame with her dad. Sometimes Renee urged her dad to leave so she could sit close to Ed, but Ed never took advantage of their alone time.

During summer break, Renee had a job at a Wisconsin resort owned by her uncle. On the night before she was to leave, she and Ed double dated with Ben and Sally. Ed was the driver. Ed didn't really like Ben because he was always foul-mouthed and belittled women, but he could tolerate him on a double date.

They decided to go to the Quad Cities to a huge theater complex. After the movie, they went to eat at a restaurant called Casper's. It was noisy and full of video games and other games of skill. At 11:00, just before they left, Ed called home and woke his parents up.

"We're just leaving Davenport," he told his sleepy mom, "so I'll be a little late."

"Okay," Sara replied, stifling a yawn. "I left the porch light on. Drive careful."

The long ride home was quiet. Ben and Sally were in the backseat, and Ed and Renee could hear rustling and giggling. When they let Ben and Sally off at Sally's house, Sally's top was all askew. Ed told Ben he'd pick him up on his way home, then they headed toward Renee's home on Iowa Avenue.

When Ed walked Renee to the door, she invited him in, but he declined, saying, "I've got to get going. I have to get Ben home before the midnight curfew. The cops will be out."

"Oh, you've got a little time," Renee said, pulling him into the house. Then she grabbed him by both arms and looked him directly in the eyes. "Ed Maas, we've been dating for five months, and I've been waiting patiently for you to kiss me. Now, come here."

She pulled his head down and planted a big kiss on his lips. Ed had never been kissed on the mouth by anyone—on the cheek maybe, but not on the mouth. Immediately, he took a cue from the movies and kissed her again. He liked the way she pressed her body against his.

After another long kiss and embrace, he again said he had to go. He hurried to his car and drove over to Sally's to pick up Ben, where he found Ben and Sally making out on the porch.

"Come on, Ben, break it up! It's time to go," he thought, but Ben dallied until the porch light finally came on. Apparently Sally's parents had also been waiting up. It was past midnight.

Ed drove Ben straight to his house and then turned onto Houser Street. He wanted to get out of town as fast as possible, without speeding. He turned onto Mulberry Avenue. As he passed the nursing home, he saw a car in the driveway, but he kept on driving. He was almost safe.

All of a sudden, he saw red lights flashing in his rearview mirror. He quickly checked his speedometer. He hadn't been speeding. He pulled over and waited as a policeman approached the van.

"Are you alone?' he asked.

"Yes, sir."

"Do you know you're passed curfew?"

"Yes, sir."

"Where are going now?"

"Home, sir."

"How far is that, young man?"

"About ten miles, sir."

The policeman looked at Ed's driver's license and asked, "Are you related to George Maas?"

"Yes, sir, he's my grandfather."

"Well, I don't want to be ticketing George Maas's grandson," the officer said with a smile, "so I'll let you off with a warning this time— but you'd better be getting home."

"Yes, sir, thank you, sir."

"And say hi to your grandfather for me. Tell him Officer Warren thinks he's one of the best supervisors around."

The officer went back to his car and turned off his lights. He motioned for Ed to go ahead. Ed pulled out slowly, crossed the bypass, and hurried home, knowing his grandpa had saved his neck that night!

Renee left the next day, but Ed had his 4-H and FFA projects to work on, so he'd be busy. In July, he and Tim contracted several acres of seed corn to detassel, and August brought the fairs. The next time Ed saw Renee was after football practice one afternoon. Coach Miller was also Muscatine High's athletic director and was at many of the practices.

As Ed and Renee began dating again, kissing and petting became part of the ritual at the end of almost every date.

Between her junior and senior year, Renee was again scheduled to work in Wisconsin for the summer, but she provided an interesting exit. On Memorial Day weekend, Ed went to Renee's for the day. She and her little sister, Susie, were home alone. Their parents had gone to visit their grandparents.

After the three of them had eaten lunch, Susie was invited to go swimming with a friend and her family, leaving Renee and Ed alone. They watched some TV, but after awhile, Ed suggested going out to the farm.

"Sure," Renee agreed, "but I'll have to change. I can't go out there in this miniskirt and flip-flops. I should put on a different top, too." Then she smiled coyly and added, "Why don't you help me pick out what to wear?"

"Really?" Ed said in surprise.

"Yeah. I want to see what you like. Come on," Renee said, taking his hand and leading him to her bedroom.

Renee pointed to her bed and said, "Sit there while I pick out some duds." She went to her closet and tossed a top, some blue jeans, and a pair tennis shoes onto the bed. "Will those be alright?"

"I think they'll be fine," Ed replied.

Renee stepped behind a changing screen. The only part of her body Ed could see was her head. Renee pulled her top over her head and threw it on the floor in front of Ed. Then she threw her miniskirt out.

Looking over the top of the screen, Renee said, "Shoot! I left my clothes on the bed. Could you bring them over here?"

Ed nodded, picked up her clothes, and walked over to the

changing screen. As he handed the clothes over the screen, he couldn't help but get a good view of Renee in her underwear.

Smiling broadly, Renee said, "There's a penalty for peeking, you know."

"What's that?" Ed asked.

"You have to take off your shirt so I can get a thrill, too."

As Ed took off his t-shirt, Renee said, "That's better."

Ed turned, walked back to the bed, sat down, and waited.

A moment later, Renee said innocently, "Ed, honey, close your eyes. I have to get a different bra. Don't you peek while I go to my dresser! I don't want you to see me in my bikini underwear."

Ed dutifully closed his eyes, but Renee gently took hold of his hand as she walked past and placed it on her hip. Ed couldn't help but open one eye, and what he saw was Renee standing topless directly in front of him. The surprise of seeing her topless caused him to open both eyes, and Renee pulled him to his feet and pressed her body against his chest, pretending to be embarrassed.

Then her tone changed as she said, "Ed, honey, kiss me! Hold me tight!"

As Ed bent down and kissed her, she guided his hands to her waist. She pushed his hands onto her hips and tried to work his fingers inside her panties, but he resisted. She put her forehead on his chest, looked down, and undid Ed's shorts.

"No, not now, Renee," Ed said. "Not yet!"

Renee continued her seduction, pushing down his shorts and sending them to the floor, leaving Ed in just his boxers.

He stepped back, shaking his head and saying, "No!"

Renee was getting irritated. She had never expected resistance. After all, her sisters had told her, "Get them in their shorts and they'll do anything you want, especially if you're almost naked yourself. Boys like naked girls."

Renee's sisters knew what they were talking about. They had all gotten pregnant before they married.

Renee pushed Ed down onto her bed, and before he could react, she was on top of him.

"Don't move," she ordered.

Ed was amazed by what was happening as he lay on his back looking up at her half-naked body. The only time he'd ever seen a naked woman was in a friend's *Playboy* magazine, although he had seen Jenny a couple of times as she dashed from the bathroom to her room, but she was his sister, and that was different.

Renee slid her bikini panties down her legs and struck a sexy pose by putting her hands under her breasts and lifting them.

"You like?" she asked.

Before Ed could answer, she was on top of him again, attacking his undershorts.

"Oh, no you don't, Renee," Ed said. "I'm not going to do this. I don't know exactly what you have in mind, but I can guess. You're going to have to find someone else. Now put your clothes on. I'm leaving. Maybe we should cool it for a while—or at least you should. I'm not going to be a willing man like your sisters' boyfriends or lovers."

Ed rolled off the bed, grabbed his clothes, and headed for the door as Renee watched. She made no attempt to get dressed. She jumped up and beat him to the door.

As she slammed it shut, she shouted, "Oh, no! You're not going anywhere. I want to see you naked. You saw me and liked it. Now it's my turn. "

Ed looked at her, but said nothing as he began to get dressed. He put his hands under her arms and lifted her off the floor. He momentarily held her at arm's length as he looked at her body, then tossed her onto her bed.

"You should take better care of such a lovely body, Renee. Be careful who you get naked in front of," Ed said. "The next guy might take you up on your offer. I'm sorry, but I don't want this kind of relationship. Goodbye."

He turned and walked out the door. As he got into his car, he looked up at Renee's bedroom window and saw her standing naked with the curtains open. He just rolled his eyes and shook his head.

"How could I have been so dumb?" he asked himself.

It would be different without Renee, but he'd have to get used to it. When he pulled out into the street in front of Renee's house, he floored his old Dodge and the tires squealed a little. Maybe the Dodge wanted to get away, too.

Chapter Eighteen
Carol

Ed soon forgot Renee. One day, Pioneer Seed Corn Company called, needing some roguers—people to rid their seed fields of undesirable corn plants by hand-hoeing. They asked Ed to be a crew boss. His crew consisted of twins Jason and Jake, and Nora, Sue, Cindy, and Barb from Muscatine. They were joined by Maria and Carol from Wilton. Maria was a dark-haired, brown-eyed Hispanic girl, and Carol was a tall brunette with hazel eyes.

Roguing was difficult physical work. They walked for miles through fields, looking for out-of-place plants, which they hoed out. If there were several plants together, Ed would help.

On the fourth day, the weather was forecast as being good until late afternoon, but by 2:00 the clouds began to build. There were four crews working in the field, which meant there were thirty-six people out in the open. Rain wouldn't stop their work, but thunderstorms would, since it was dangerous to be in an open field when lightning was present.

Louie, the bus driver, was on the radio, and when he received news of the impending danger, he honked the horn. Ed looked up at the sky and saw the storm approaching.

"Everybody head for the bus! Forget the corn! We'll come back tomorrow!" Ed shouted.

The crew started trotting toward the bus. Soon it began to rain. Ed's crew was the last to reach the bus. Everyone got soaked, since the rain was coming down in buckets. Louie started to pull out of the field, but the ground was wet and the tires started to spin.

Ed hollered, "Everyone out to push!"

Grumbling, the riders got out and began to push the bus. They were already wet, so a little more rain didn't bother them. As soon as Louie got the bus on the gravel road, everyone climbed back aboard. Now they were not only wet and cold, but also muddy.

After everyone was safe in the crew shed, Louie shook his head when he saw the floor of his bus covered with mud.

"Louie, I'll wash out the bus," Ed said with a smile.

Louie thanked Ed and happily took him up on his offer, since he hated power washing. Ed pulled the bus around behind the crew shed and hooked up the washer as crew members inside the shed phoned for rides back home.

Ed was almost finished when Don, the rouging supervisor, stuck his head inside the bus and said, "Hey, Ed, can you take one of your crew members home? Her ride won't be here for at least two hours and she's really cold. She lives in Wilton."

"Sure," Ed replied. "I'll be done in a minute. Tell her to meet me at the door."

Ed pulled his old Dodge in front of the crew shed and Carol appeared at the door. Her arms pulled tightly across her chest. She was shivering, as she got into the vehicle. Ed reached into the backseat and grabbed an old flannel shirt.

"Here, put this on," he said. "It will warm you up."

"Thank you," Carol said as she wrapped the shirt around her shoulders.

"Your name's Carol, right?"

"Right."

"Where's your friend, Maria?"

"Her mother's ill, so she couldn't come today. My mom's playing cards and she wouldn't want to leave early. It would cramp her style," Carol said with a touch of sarcasm.

"Where do you live in Wilton?"

"Just three blocks west of the high school."

As Ed pulled up in front of Carol's house, she began to remove the flannel shirt.

"That's okay," Ed said. "Keep it until tomorrow. Why don't I pick you up in the morning?"

"Okay, what time?"

"About 6:15. I have to check in before the crew to find out which field we're going to."

Ed picked Carol up every morning for the next week, and by Friday night he had learned much about her. She was an only child, her dad sold insurance, and her mom was a socialite.

Saturday was a short day, and when Ed dropped Carol off, he

asked, "Would you want to go to a movie tonight?"

"Okay, where are we going?"

"The cinema in Davenport. There should be something worth seeing there. I'll pick you up at seven."

When Ed arrived that night, Carol appeared at the door in a light blue dress and flats. Her hair was tied in a pony tail. She looked like something from a 1960s movie.

In the car, Ed said, "You sure look nice. I've only seen you in your work clothes."

They went to a movie, then for a snack at the Steak 'n Shake. When Ed walked Carol to the door, she stood on her tiptoes and gave him a peck on the cheek.

"I had a great time, Ed. Thank you," she said with a smile.

Ed nodded and said, "Me, too. I'll see you on Monday. We'll start detasseling in the first fields."

Ed and Carol dated the rest of the summer and saw each other only on weekends during the school year. Carol did invite Ed to a couple of dances at Wilton High and Ed took her to some events in Muscatine, such as the school play. Both of them felt out of place at the other's school. It was like being the new kid on the block. Everyone pointed at them and talked behind their backs. They waited until Carol had graduated before their dating became serious.

***

During his last year of football, Ed drove Byron Hougham home every night after practice. Byron had gotten too many speeding tickets and had lost his license. Byron's dad was an attorney in Muscatine and had gotten Byron out of trouble several times, but even he couldn't get Byron's license back.

Practice one Thursday ended early. Coach Harper wanted everyone to get plenty of rest before the long trip to Clinton the next day. Ed and his friend Kent waited for Byron in the parking lot. Byron appeared late as usual, with Brett Pointer, the quarterback. Brett's dad was an attorney in the same firm as Byron's dad.

Byron called to Ed as he got into Brett's Camaro, "Brett's going to take me home. We're going to cruise a bit. See you tomorrow."

Ed looked at Kent and shook his head. They both had chores and homework to do.

The next morning, Ed was summoned to the principal's office.

When he entered, he saw Kent sitting in a chair outside the office.

"What's going on?" Ed asked softly.

"I'm not sure, but Brett and Byron are in the principal's office now with Coach Harper."

A few minutes later, the coach summoned Kent and Ed to his office, where he asked, "Did you know where Brett and Byron were going after practice?"

"No, they just told us they were going cruising. Why?" Ed replied.

Coach Harper sighed and said, "Good, because after practice I passed by Louie's Bar on the way home and saw Brett's car in the parking lot. I was curious, so I went in, and I found Brett, Byron, and Brett's older brother, Mike, sitting in a booth, drinking beer and smoking. They gave me all kinds of excuses, but I kicked both of them off the team on the spot. I just wanted you to verify you two didn't know anything about it. There are rules, and every player must abide by them—no exceptions. I know I'll have some upset dads calling me, but I can't help it. Sam Fennelly will be our quarterback for the rest of the year. You can go back to your classes now. I'll make the announcement before we leave for Clinton."

The Muskies stumbled through the game that night, and they lost by a touchdown.

On Monday in Chemistry class, Byron brushed by Ed and growled, "I'll get you for this someday, Maas. Just you wait and see."

Ed looked up at Byron, shrugged his shoulders, and said, "I had nothing to do with it."

Despite a disappointing season for the team, Ed made first team all-conference as a defensive back.

During the football season, he saw Renee several times. Their conversations were cordial, but cool. After the first basketball practice, Renee was in the coach's office, as usual. She asked her dad to have Ed come to the office. The other players, except Tim, made cat calls and whoops. Tim had heard about the last encounter with Renee and felt sorry for his brother.

As Ed started toward the office, Tim told him, "I'll wait in the car for you. Stick to your guns, Big Bro."

When Ed entered the office, Renee was sitting at the coach's desk. He looked at her and said, "Hello, Renee. Your dad said you wanted to see me."

"Yes, Ed. I just wanted to tell you despite our difficulty last May, I still think you're a great guy. In fact, I think you're super. I met a guy at my uncle's resort last summer and we hit it off right away—but he was aggressive. One night he and I went to a dance and stopped at his place on the way home. It was a bad decision! I was barely inside the house when he started to maul me. He was up under my skirt, and even when I told him to slow down, he kept undressing me. It didn't take long before I was undressed in his bedroom.

"For some silly reason, I thought of you and what you said to me about taking care of my body. Your refusal last May made me realize I was wrong. The sex thing should be left for special people and not every Tom, Dick, or Harry who comes down the road."

"When the guy went into the bathroom, I grabbed my clothes and ran. I was glad we were in the country, because I had nothing on when I left the house. I ran naked until I saw some car lights coming down the road. I dashed behind a bush and got dressed. Thank goodness the guy never came after me, but it was a long walk back to the resort."

"I just wanted you to know your firmness changed my life. I started to attend a different church—one with a great youth group—and I found a really nice boy there. Because of you, I've decided to save myself for my future husband and not end up like my sisters."

"I love you, Ed, but not like the love I first tried to share with you. I love you for being who you are and for being honest with me. I'll always be your friend, if you don't mind. The girl who catches you will be very lucky. I just wanted to thank you for saving me!"

When she had finished, Renee stood, walked over to Ed, and gave him a kiss on the cheek. Then she said, "You can go now. I hope you'll only remember me as your first girlfriend and not for what happened on our last date."

Ed smiled and said, "Those were kind words, Renee. I'm glad you found someone, and I promise I'll never forget you—and yes, we can be friends."

Then he turned and left the office.

Basketball started in early November, but Tim missed two games because of All-State Chorus. The first game in December was also the first conference game.

The combination of the Maas brothers and Jeff Petersen, the

best guard in the league, made the Muskies hard to beat. The only team in the conference to challenge them was the North Scott Lancers. They had a high school all-American on their team who received a number of scholarship offers from major universities.

When Muscatine played in Eldridge, home of North Scott High School, they were beaten handily. At home, the game went into overtime, but North Scott won again—by two points. The winning shot was by their star, Kevin Stab. North Scott went undefeated the rest of the season.

The two teams met again on a neutral floor in Davenport for the sub-state finals, in front of a standing-room-only crowd. There's an old adage in sports: everyone has a best game sometime in their career. This night, both Maas brothers had theirs.

Ed was deadly from three-point land and Tim blocked more shots than he'd ever done—including a number of Kevin Stub's. Stab eventually became frustrated and lunged at Tim like a bull; however, Tim stood his ground and Stab was charged with an offensive foul. He picked up another offensive foul later. He became so aggravated he kicked Tim while he was still lying on the floor, which added a technical foul. During the last minute of the third quarter, he protested a block by Tim and was ejected from the game. After that, Muscatine took over the game and won handily, earning a trip to the state tournament in Des Moines! Muskie fans talked about the game for weeks afterward.

Although Muscatine didn't win the state title, they won the consolation game and received the third place trophy. It was a good year for Ed, Tim, and the Muskies. The Maas brothers were both honored with all-state recognition.

* * *

During Easter break, Kent invited him to a picnic at Wild Cat Den State Park, sponsored by the Parent's Athletic Club.

When he arrived, he discovered Byron Hougham was also there. Bryon's mom was on the committee, so he had been invited. The PAC cleaned up the tables and headed home before all the students were back from walking the park's trails.

As Ed started for his car, he heard Byron shout, "Hey, Maas, Can I get a ride home?"

Though Ed hesitated, he eventually said, "I guess so, but I'm going right home."

Byron hopped in and they headed for Muscatine on the New Era blacktop. Just outside of town, Byron pulled out a cigarette.

"Hey, I don't like people smoking in my car, Byron," Ed said firmly. "Put it out."

Byron just smiled and took another drag. When the smoke reached Ed's nose, he realized it wasn't a cigarette—it was pot. Byron smoking marijuana in Ed's car! Ed didn't want to force Byron out of the car in the middle of nowhere, so he waited until he reached the intersection of 38 and 61.

He pulled into a parking lot just beyond the crossroads.

He turned to Byron and shouted, "Alright! Get out. You're walking the rest of the way."

When Byron refused, Ed shut off the engine, got out, and stormed to the other side of the car. He yanked open the door, grabbed Byron's arm, and jerked him out. Just as Byron was falling to the ground, a squad car pulled up. Although Ed didn't see him do it, Byron tossed his stash into the backseat.

"You fellas having a problem here?" the officer asked.

"Not really," answered Ed.

The officer poked his head through an open window of the Dodge and said, "I smell pot. You guys weren't having a little party, were you? I think I'd better search your car."

Both boys stood silently while the officer looked, and quickly found the marijuana in the backseat. Picking it up and showing it to the boys, he asked, "Who belongs to this?"

"It's not mine," Ed replied, "Its' Byron's. That's why I was throwing him out my car. I was giving him a ride home and he lit up a joint. I don't do that kind of stuff. "

"Now, officer, you're not going to believe this guy, are you?" Byron said in an innocent tone. "You just found the pot in the backseat of his car."

"Well, let's go downtown and see if we can straighten this out," the officer said.

At the police station, both boys were allowed to call their parents. Byron's dad arrived first and began to negotiate with the police.

When Paul arrived, Byron's dad told him, "Don't worry, Mr. Maas. I'll get the boys off on a lesser charge and we'll all be on our way."

"We'll discuss this later," Paul said dismissively. "First I want to talk with my son."

Paul found Ed sitting alone on a bench looking glum. He sat next to his son and said, "I want to hear your side of the story, Ed. Then we'll decide what to do."

Ed explained the situation exactly as it had happened, finishing with, "Dad, I don't do drugs. You know that! Byron's lying! He's been out to get me since last October, and now he's got his chance. He thinks I told the coach where he was the night he got kicked off the team."

"I believe you, son," said Paul. "Now we've got to figure out some way of solving this."

As Paul returned to the main room, Mr. Hougham approached him again, saying, "If the boys plead guilty, I can get them off with just community service. I know the judge."

"Mr. Hougham, my son is innocent, so I think we'll just wait a bit before we make any snap judgments," Paul replied.

Mr. Hougham sputtered a reply which included several four-letter words. The sergeant entered the room and asked Mr. Hougham to return to the interrogation room. He also spoke softly to the officer at the desk. When he was gone, Paul asked to use a phone to call his lawyer.

"I don't think the call will be necessary, Mr. Mass," the desk sergeant said. "We found a pouch of cocaine in young Mr. Hougham's jacket. When we showed it to him, he confessed the whole thing. Ed won't be charged with anything. Officer Henley is getting your son right now.

"We've been trying to catch Mr. Hougham's son for quite a while, and during his confession, with his dad standing beside him, he gave us the names of dealers in the area. I know we won't stop the drug war, but maybe we'll slow it down a bit. It seems Byron Hougham and Brett Pointer are the main suppliers for the high school. Your son is a good kid. It's too bad he got caught up in this."

Ed and Paul then signed out and retrieved Ed's car from the pound.

When Ed reported for baseball practice on Monday, the school was alive with rumors. Ed had to explain the whole episode to Coach Willys. After practice, the coach told the whole team what had happened. Ed wouldn't be kicked off the team, and over time, the arrest would become a distant memory.

Chapter Nineteen
Tim and Kate

Tim could do both chorus and basketball as a freshman, but during his sophomore year, he had to make some choices. He was a candidate for show choir and Mrs. Potts wanted his tenor voice, but he also would be a starter on the sophomore basketball team. He solved the dilemma by giving up show choir and settling for the a cappella choir, which didn't conflict with basketball practice.

Coach Miller and Mrs. Leach were pleased and Tim was satisfied. Tim grew considerably during his freshman year. Sara wondered if it was due to the steroids he'd had to take to rid his lungs of mucous, but regardless of the reason, he had sprouted up seven inches by his sophomore year, reaching 6'9" by October.

In early January, Coach Miller moved Tim up to the varsity, meaning Ed and Tim would be on the same team. With Tim patrolling under the basket and Ed's outside shooting, the Muskies had the potential to be a good team, but they were young and more experience teams handled them easily. The Muskie season was over early.

Singing with the choir in the spring musical, Tim met a girl with dark red hair, a sweet smile, and a face full of freckles. Her name was Kathleen Reilly. She had lived in Muscatine for three months and her dad, who was actually her stepfather, worked for Stanley Engineering.

Kathleen's step father met her mom, a widow with two children, Kathleen and her younger brother, Ian, while working on a project in South Africa. They got married and he brought them all back to Muscatine when the project was finished.

Kathleen was an alto and sat next to the tenors. She was tall herself and liked to kid Tim about his height. In return, he kidded her about her South African accent. When scenes required couples, Tim asked Kate if she'd be his partner. She agreed.

It wasn't an immediate romance. Kate worked as a checkout

in the local Hy-Vee store. It seemed whenever Tim had time to see her she was working and whenever she had time he was either practicing basketball or tied up at home with chores.

By that time, Ed and Tim shared a car, but Ed usually had first dibs on it. If a date was important enough, Tim could drive the family van or the good pickup. He usually chose the pickup, partly because Kate liked to ride in a pickup.

Kate and Tim became good friends, but it was more of a brother-sister relationship than a romantic one. A few times during summer, Tim brought Kate out to the farm. On one occasion, she had both Saturday and Sunday off, so Tim her invited her to stay overnight.

"Where would I sleep?" she asked.

"In my sister's room. She has twin beds. Ed's girlfriends bunk with her all the time," Tim replied.

Kate ended up staying Saturday night, and on Sunday after early church, Tim took her to the pond for a picnic. Kate borrowed one of Jenny's bathing suits. She wasn't a great swimmer herself, but she admired Tim's strong swimming skills. He had achieved lifeguard status, although he never worked as one.

In October of Tim's junior year, a quartet featuring Tim and Kate tried out for All-State Chorus. They were the only quartet chosen from Muscatine. The concert was held at Hilton Coliseum on the Iowa State campus during Thanksgiving break. Both sets of parents rode to Ames together to hear the performance. The long ride provided the opportunity for them to become acquainted.

Tim's junior year was his best year of basketball. Muscatine went to state that year. After basketball, Tim excelled in the a cappella choir and Kate had a small role in the school musical. Tim and Kate became inseparable.

During summer break, Kate and her mom planned to return to South Africa to see their family members. It would be August before she would return. After she left, Tim moped around the farm until Sara finally got after him.

"Criminy sakes, Tim," she scolded. "She'll only be gone for eight weeks."

It was to be a tragic summer on the farm. In June, Grandpa George suffocated in the grain bin, and both Tim and Ed had to help their dad more than ever since Paul had always relied on George whenever he needed help around the farm. Ed quit baseball to help out, but baseball had never been his best sport anyway.

In July, Grandpa John died of a heart attack. Grandma Em found him lying in the yard. Having two grandpas die in one summer meant Christmas would never be the same again.

* * *

When fall arrived, Ed left for Iowa State, leaving an empty place at the family dinner table. Tim and Kate both made All-State Chorus again this year. Kate even had a solo spot in one number. Basketball was okay this year; however, with the departure of the best point guard in the conference, Jeremy Cousins, and brother Ed, wins were hard to come by.

Kate and Tim had big parts in the spring musical—a variety show. The show choir, the a cappella choir, and some small ensembles from the band performed.

Tim and Kate sang several duets, but their show-stopper was their rendition of "Side by Side." They started from opposite sides of the stage and met in the middle. Their performance and actions led the audience to believe the couple was truly in love—and they weren't far from wrong. At the end of the song, they received a standing ovation.

During senior week, Kate won a scholarship to Cornell College in Mt. Vernon, Iowa. Tim planned to attend Iowa State. On Wednesday after graduation rehearsal, there was the Senior Picnic, which everyone had to attend. It would be the last event the entire class would attend beside graduation. Many of the attendees decided to go to the sand pits south of town after the picnic. The pits were a popular teenage hangout in the summer.

Tim and Kate jumped into his pickup so they could go home and get their swim gear. They stopped at Kate's first, then drove out to the farm for Tim's trunks. Kate followed him into the kitchen.

"I'll round up some pop and snacks while you go up and get your swimming trunks," Kate said.

When Tim returned, dressed for swimming, he yawned and said, "Gee, I'm tired. I hope I can stay awake this afternoon. "

Kate looked at him in surprise and asked, "Are you going to the pits in those?"

"I couldn't find my regular swimming trunks and Mom hasn't gotten the summer shorts out yet," Tim confided. "These were all I could find. It won't hurt if I get them wet. "

"But they look like they're two sizes too small," Kate said with a smile. "Aren't you afraid they'll shrink when they get wet and you won't be able walk, let alone squeeze something? How about going to the farm pond instead? We can lay on the beach by the picnic table and you could take a nap."

Tim looked happy with her suggestion, but he asked, "Are you sure you don't want to go back to town? I really do have a backache and the back of my neck hurts. I think I need a couple aspirin."

"I'd rather spend the afternoon alone with you than with a bunch of silly seniors," Kate replied with a smile.

"Great!" said Tim. "Let's go. I'll grab the old comforter so we can lay on the sand."

When they arrived at the pond, Tim carried the blanket to the beach and spread it out. Kate followed with the picnic supplies and her beach bag. Tim took off his shirt and then laid face down on the blanket. Kate removed her beach jacket, revealing a two-piece bathing suit. The top was revealing, but the bottoms were little boy pants.

"You'd better put some suntan lotion on," Kate suggested. "I'll do your back."

"I'll do you first," Tim said.

"You can do my back, but I'll do my legs," Kate said. "Then you're going to let Dr. Kate give you a massage."

Kate turned her back toward Tim, then reached around and unhooked her top. She held it in place with one hand while pulling her hair aside with the other. Tim lathered his hands with lotion and started on her shoulders, slipping her shoulder straps down her arms. When he was done, he took two fingers and lightly ran them up her back from her waist to her neck.

It sent chills up her spine and Kate said, "Don't do that. You give me geese pimples."

"You mean goose bumps, don't you?" Tim asked, "And what's this maroon patch on your waist?"

"A birthmark," she replied. "That's why I don't wear bikini bottoms. People ask too many questions. Hook my top back up and I'll show it to you."

After Tim had re-hooked her top, Kate leaned over on one hip and pulled her pants down over the other hip. The birthmark looked like a reddish blue question mark.

"Sort of hideous, isn't it?" she said, sitting up. "These boy pants cover it fairly well. Now it's your turn. I'll do your back first. Lay on your stomach."

"You're sure bossy," Tim teased.

"Well, as tired as you are, I need to be," she countered with a smile. "Now, Mr. Tim, step into Dr. Kate's office and show me where it hurts."

Tim pointed to his neck and his lower back. "I think I overdid when Dad had me help load the bean drill. He thinks because I'm six-nine I can throw bags of beans higher. I think I twisted my back."

"I'm going to give you my resume first. My mum is a masseuse. That's how she met Dad. He hurt his back playing tennis at a club and she treated him. He liked it so much he asked if he could make an appointment. She told him she couldn't do it at the club, but she could at her private parlor in our home. He started to come to our house regularly for treatments, and soon they began dating. I used to help Mum when she treated women by fetching towels and oil. I even gave Mum massages sometimes, so you see, I know what I'm doing."

"Okay, it sounds great to me," Tim conceded.

"Now, relax and trust me—and do what I ask, okay?"

"Yes, ma'am."

"The first thing for you to do is take off those tight shorts."

"But I'm wearing briefs, not boxers."

"All the better. Less fabric to work around. I promise I won't peek. Here's a small towel. Lie face down on it and I'll tell you everything I'm doing or going to do. Relax and let my hands smooth out those sore muscles."

She started with his shoulders and explained each move as she worked her way down his long back. After a few minutes, she asked, "Tim, are you still with me?"

"Yes, but barely. It feels so good. You're wonderful."

"I'm going to slide your shorts down a bit so I can work your lower back, okay?"

"Sure, you can do anything you want. I'm so relaxed, I'll probably fall asleep."

"I may slip your shorts off. You trust me, don't you?"

"Yeah, but I won't need to turn over, will I?"

"No."

Kate lowered his shorts about two inches. She stopped just above the cleavage of his buttocks. Slowly, she worked the shorts lower until she finally put her hands under his hips, and she slipped his shorts off. She slid his shorts down his legs and then covered his hips with his t-shirt.

Next she rolled him over on his back, making sure he was always covered, although she did take a quick peek—a masseuse's privilege. Then she lifted his head, put it in her lap, and massaged his temples and face. As Tim opened one eye, all he could see was auburn hair and a swim suit top almost touching his face. He closed his eyes again and soon started to snore.

Kate placed a small pillow under his head and covered his eyes with a cloth. She put her lips close to his ear and whispered, "Tim, do you mind if I sunbathe like I used to in South Africa?"

He mumbled, "I don't care, just let me get some sleep."

"Okay, I just wanted your approval."

Tim didn't realize in South Africa, Kate had sunbathed nude. She removed her suit, lay down on the blanket, and fell asleep beside Tim. After about an hour, a fly started to bother Tim. He swatted at it, but missed. When he put his hand on Kate's hip, he felt nothing but skin. He moved his fingers to her waist. Nothing.

Slowly, he turned his head, opened one eye, and couldn't believe what he was seeing. He opened both eyes and saw Kate was stretched out with her arms above her head. The mounds of her breasts showed beneath her arm pits. He didn't know what to do.

He touched her waist and whispered, "Kate, wake up."

Kate stirred and asked sleepily, "What is it?"

"You don't have any clothes on," he stammered.

"My, how clever you are!" she said with a smile. "I asked if I could sunbathe like I used to in South Africa, and you said it was okay, so here I am." Looking into Tim's eyes, Kate rolled over and asked, "Haven't you seen a girl in the nude before?"

Tim was still in shock, but he managed to say, "Your breasts are covered with freckles, too."

Kate laughed and said, "Well, maybe you should take a look at yourself. I don't believe you're fully dressed either."

Tim looked down and for the first time noticed he was as naked as Kate. The t-shirt had slipped off. Self-consciously, he tried to cover himself with his hand for a moment, then his embarrassment seemed to disappear. After all, if Kate wasn't embarrassed, why should he be?

They both sat up and Kate put her arms around her legs as they talked about the next year a bit. She said, "I'm hot. Let's go for a swim."

She took hold of his hand and led him to the water. They walked in waist deep and Kate pulled Tim to her, pressed her body against his, and kissed him passionately.

"I love you, Tim Maas," she cooed.

Tim smiled. It was a wonderful moment.

"Let's swim a little," she suggested.

They swam for a while, then walked back toward the beach. As Kate walked ahead of him, Tim was mesmerized by her beauty. His eyes followed her every step as she walked to the picnic table, retrieved her beach bag, and motioned him to the blanket.

They knelt facing each other. Kate laid her hand on his shoulder and pulled him closer. Tim stroked her reddish hair, then smoothed her hair down the back of her neck. His hands soon found themselves on her freckled shoulders. Next he moved down her side and under her breast. He felt under the curve of her breast and eventually touched her nipple. Neither of them spoke.

Kate leaned forward, took Tim's hand, and studied it. She played with the few hairs on his chest and toyed with his bellybutton. As Tim lay down on the blanket, Kate moved on top and kissed him again. As she rose up on her arms, her freckled breasts hung down.

She moved forward and lowered one breast right above Tim's lips. He kissed it, then put his hand on her back and pulled her closer, swirling his tongue around the nipple. A few moments later, Kate moved him to her other side and he sucked the other nipple as she closed her eyes and sighed.

She smiled as she straddled his waist and reached inside her beach bag, asking. "Do you know what this is? It's a condom."

"I don't think we should, Kate," Tim said hesitantly.

"I think we should," she countered. "The time is right, and we must savor this moment! I'm on the pill, so it will be all right."

"Have you ever done it before?" Tim asked.

"No, but I've watched my mum's videos," Kate said with a smile. "You're my first."

Kate opened the package and soon the condom was in place and they were making sweet love in the warm sunshine, enjoying each other's bodies. When it was over, they lay next to each other, basking in the glow of the moment.

"That was heavenly," Kate said. "It seals our love for each other. I could never love another man."

They agreed such lovemaking should be reserved for special occasions. They dressed and returned to the house. It had been the best day of their young lives.

The next Monday, Tim started to work for a seed corn company and Kate worked all day at Hy-Vee. It rained on Thursday, so Tim got off work early. He called Kate at the store and she told him she'd be off at 8:00. She agreed to meet him and Kent at the Cheri Top drive-in at 8:30.

The Cheri Top was a favorite teen hangout on the edge of town, not far from the sand pits. Kate and Cissy, Kent's friend, showed up a little late, but Tim didn't mind. Instead of staying in their cars, they sat at a table in front of the restaurant. Along with several other teenagers, they laughed and talked as they drank their Cokes.

At 9:30, Kate announce, "Time for me to go home. I've got an early shift tomorrow. Let's go, Cissy."

"Yeah, I'd better get home, too," Tim said.

They headed to their cars, where Kate gave Tim a goodnight kiss. Kate and Cissy started to drive away, with Tim and Kent beside them as they approached the highway. Tim playfully gunned the motor of the pickup and waved as Kate started to pull out, blowing him a farewell kiss.

Just as Kate pulled the car onto the highway, a black four-wheel drive pickup came roaring out of the darkness. It smashed in the driver's side door of Kate's car, sending the car spinning backward, where it collided with Tim's pickup. The air was filled with the sound of grinding metal and breaking glass. Without stopping to survey the damage, the driver of the other vehicle slammed his truck into reverse and roared backward—until he rammed a pole. Trying to get away he slammed his truck into forward gear, sending the truck careening into a water-filled ditch on the other side of the road.

The other teenagers, who had seen the accident, came running to help. They pulled Kent out of Tim's pickup. He was scratched and bruised, but Tim's leg was wedged under the steering wheel and couldn't be freed. Everyone decided to wait for help, since the manager of the Cheri Top had called 911.

Tim looked over at Kate's mangled car, unable to move. He could see Cissy, her face covered with blood and her arm sticking out of the window at a grotesque angle.

He could also see Kate, her head in Cissy's lap, her beautiful red hair drenched in blood. Both girls were pale, silent, and unmoving.

"Kate!" Tim screamed, but there was no answer.

The EMTs arrived and while several of them worked to free Tim's leg, others were busy with Kate and Cissy. Tim moaned again when he saw an EMT shake his head and cover Kate with a white sheet.

Cissy was alive, but just barely as the EMTs gently pulled her from the wreckage and rolled her toward an ambulance. From the second ambulance, Tim saw the driver of the black pickup appear at the edge of the highway, so drunk he could hardly stand. There didn't seem to be a scratch on him, even though he had just killed one person and injured three others.

At home, Sara and Paul were sitting in front of the TV, watching the Cubs get shellacked again. Jenny was upstairs on her computer. During the seventh inning stretch, a reporter broke in.

"There has been a bad accident in Muscatine involving several teenagers. It occurred at the Cheri Top drive-in. We're sending a camera crew there now, and we'll have full details on the 10:00 news."

Sara and Paul looked at each other. "Wasn't Tim at the Cheri Top tonight?" asked Sara.

"Yeah," said Paul. "I wonder if he saw anything."

Just then, the phone rang. Paul answered, "Hello? Maas Residence."

"Paul Maas?"

"Yes."

"Mr. Mass, this Sergeant Joe Hanly of the Muscatine Police Department. I'm calling to tell you your son, Tim, has been in an automobile accident. He's been taken to Muscatine Memorial Hospital. Could you please go to the hospital as soon as possible? Because your son's a minor, they'll need parental consent before any treatment can be administered."

"Alright," Paul said excitedly. "Do you know the extent of his injuries?"

"No, I only know he's in stable condition and his injuries are not life-threatening."

"Thank you, officer. We'll be there as soon as possible."

"When you arrive, check with the officer on duty. He'll need some identification."

As he hung up, Paul turned to Sara and said, "That was the police. Tim's been an accident and they want us to go to the hospital as soon as possible."

Paul and Sara hurried upstairs to change, since they'd been ready for bed.

When Jenny heard the commotion, she called, "What's going on?"

"Tim's been in a accident. We're going to the hospital," Sara replied.

"May I go?" she asked, "I don't want to be left home alone."

"Well, I guess so, but hurry and get dressed," said Sara. "I'll leave a note for Ed."

Within minutes they were speeding toward Muscatine. The reception room was crowded with teenagers, parents, and reporters. They found Kent's parents already there.

Paul checked in and an officer led them down the hall to the ER. On the way, they passed a small room where they saw the Reillys sitting. Sara waved at Melinda Reilly as she hurried past, and though she didn't know why, she could tell by Melinda's eyes that she'd been crying.

There was no time to stop. In the ER, the desk nurse informed them Tim was in bed four. When they drew back the curtain, they saw Tim lying motionless, his face cut and bruised. His left arm and left leg were restrained by temporary braces.

When he saw them, Tim said weakly, "Hi, Mom. Hi, Dad."

Sara quickly moved to the head of the bed so she could hear him better. She touched his head lightly and caressed his hair as Paul and Jenny looked on in shock and horror. A nurse came into the room with papers to sign. The doctor wanted to take x-rays and maybe do a CAT scan.

After Tim had been wheeled to the x-ray department, the Maases sat in the hallway to wait. As they waited, Jill Paustian, Kent's mom, walked up and sat down beside Sara.

"How's Tim?" Jill asked.

"We don't know yet," Sara replied sullenly. "They're taking x-rays now." Then she looked at Jill and said, "Was Kent hurt, too?"

"No, Kent was lucky," Jill replied. "He only got cuts and bruises. No broken bones. We think he'll be released yet tonight."

"Do you know what happened?" Sara asked.

"Not all of it," Jill said, "but I know there's some bad news." As Sara listened in silence, Jill said slowly, "Kent's friend, Cissy, is in surgery right now. She has head injuries and several broken bones. She was riding in Kate Reilly's car when a truck hit them."

"What about Kate? Is she alright?" Sara asked anxiously.

Jill sighed, unsure what to say. "Sara," she said hesitantly, "I hate to be the one to tell you, but Kate was killed." As Sara recoiled in horror, Jill continued, "A truck hit the driver's side of Kate's car and crushed her. She died instantly."

"No!" Sara shrieked as Paul put his arm around her. "It can't be true! Does Tim know?"

"I think so," said Jill. "Tim was still in his pickup when they checked on Kate, and Kent knows."

"Oh, my god!" Sara sobbed. "The other driver—how is he?"

"Not a scratch. He was drunk and driving without his headlights on. Kent said Kate never saw him coming. The guy was so drunk that he tried to get away, but he ended up in the ditch across the road. The cops arrested him as he was staggering back."

As Sara sobbed on Paul's shoulder, another woman walked up to them. Jill recognized her as Cissy's mother, Shelia Holmes. She introduced Shelia to Sara and Paul, and when Jill asked Shelia about Cissy, she broke down. Sara had Jenny stand up so Shelia could have her chair.

After she'd composed herself somewhat, Shelia said, "Cissy's in surgery now. She has a broken wrist and several broken ribs—but she also suffered a severe trauma to her head and her brain is starting to swell. The doctors are cutting open part of her skull to relieve the pressure. They're going to keep her in a coma until the swelling goes down. Hopefully, she won't suffer any brain damage, but we won't know for days."

Sara looked at Shelia and said softly, "I'm so sorry."

Shelia dabbed at her eyes with a handkerchief and said, "You just never know. One day your child is vibrant and beautiful and the next you have to pray she'll live. Cissy and Kate were such good friends. She'll be devastated when she finds out Kate was killed."

"I know," said Sara, "and we don't know if Tim knows yet, either. We should all pray for Kate's folks. This is all so unbelievable."

The group lapsed into silence for a long moment, until the ER doctor emerged from the x-ray room. "Mr. and Mrs. Mass, Tim has a broken left shoulder and collar bone, a broken forearm, and several cracked bones in his left wrist. He also has a dislocated kneecap and a broken ankle. The CAT scan showed no internal injuries. I feel he should stay here overnight, and tomorrow we'll set the breaks and put them in a cast. You're welcome to stay with him tonight if you'd like."

After they had wheeled Tim back into his curtained room, the Maas' decided Sara would stay with Tim while Paul and Jenny went back home. They'd return in the morning with Ed.

Tim listened in silence as they worked out their plan of action, then looked up and asked his mother, "Kate was killed in the accident, wasn't she?"

Sara shook her head helplessly and said, "Yes, she was, son. I'm so sorry."

A tear rolled down Tim's cheek as he said, "I knew it. She never had a chance. I saw them cover her with a sheet while I was trapped in the truck." He broke down and managed to say through his sobs, "Why, Mom? I loved her. I really did."

"Tim, honey," Sara said, stroking her son's hair, "we never know why these things happen. Sometimes I wonder if God even knows. I know He cares, but why He tests us this way is a mystery."

After Paul and Jenny left, Sara sat by Tim's bedside, talking to him gently, even though he was sleeping due to the pain medicine. The curtained parted and as Sara looked up, she saw it was Melinda Reilly. Sara sprang from her chair, crossed the little room, and hugged Melinda.

Melinda sobbed, "Oh, Sara, Kate had her whole life ahead of her, and she was so fond of Tim. How could this happen? What am I going to do now?"

"I can't answer that," Sara said, her own tears flowing. "No one can. Is there anything I can do to help?"

"No," Melinda said softly. Then she looked down at Tim and asked, "Does he know?"

"He knows," Sara replied, "and he wanted me to tell you how much he loved Kate."

"I know this is an odd time to tell you this, but we're going to delay Kate's funeral until Tim can come," said Melinda. "It won't be until next week anyway. I'll call you with our plans. I have to go now, Sara. Pray for me. I'll need all the help I can get."

They hugged again, then Melinda turned and left. Tim had a restless, pain-filled night and was almost comatose by morning. The surgeons set his broken bones and put a cast on his left arm from his shoulder to his wrist. His leg was in a cast from mid-thigh to his ankle. All they could do for his ribs was to wrap them in gauze. His left eye was black and swollen.

When Jenny, Paul, and Ed entered Tim's room in the morning, Jenny didn't know whether to laugh or cry. Her brother was a mess.

Putting on a brave face, Jenny said, "I want to be the first to sign all your casts. First I want to sign at the top of your leg cast."

She lifted the sheet carefully, pretending she was going to lift it completely, but she stopped just short of embarrassing her brother. She also tickled his toes.

Knowing Jenny was trying to cheer him up, Tim smiled and said, "Please don't tickle me. My ribs hurt when I laugh."

Tim was finally released on Saturday, but the hospital had to order special crutches to accommodate his height. At home, he could make the upstairs with help, which meant he could sleep in his own bed. Paul and Ed had to take turns helping Tim to the bathroom.

On Sunday night, Melinda Reilly called to check on Tim, and as luck would have it, Tim took the call. His voice cracked as he said he would make it to Kate's funeral on Tuesday, even if he had to be loaded into the back of a pickup. He and Melinda talked for awhile, then she asked to speak to his mom.

After Tim handed Sara the phone, Melinda said, "Sara, Doug and I would like your family to sit with us at Kate's funeral. We'd also like you to come before the service. We think Tim will probably want to say his goodbyes in private."

"Thank you, Melinda," Sara said softly. "We'll do whatever you'd like us to do—and thank you for thinking of Tim."

The Maases attended the visitation at the Methodist church without Tim. Many young people attended. They didn't get home until

10:00 that night.

The next morning, the funeral was scheduled for 10:00, but Tim was up and getting ready at seven. He could shave himself, but dressing was more difficult. Sara had split a leg on a pair of khakis and the sleeve on one of his shirts.

"Mom," he called from his room, "could you come up and help me?"

As Sara entered Tim's room, she found him standing on one leg trying to pull his shorts up over his cast. In spite of herself, Sara had to laugh.

"The last time I saw you in a predicament like this, you were covered with fertilizer," she said as she stepped forward to lend a hand.

The Maases arrived at the church at nine and Ed helped Tim up the steps of the entrance. Kate's brother, Ian, met them at the door and gave Tim a hug. Then Tim slowly made his way down the aisle, where Melinda and Doug met him in front of Kate's casket.

Luckily, Kate's face hadn't been damaged in the accident, but she had a big bandage around her neck to hide a gash to her throat. She was wearing a high-collared dress—a blue one which Tim had always liked. Her auburn hair lay perfectly on each side of her face.

Tim stood looking at Kate in silence for several minutes. She would be with him no more. How he wished he could hold her just once more. He remembered her throwing him a kiss just before the pickup slammed into her car.

Tears rolling down his face, he edged closer, and with his right hand, he reached into the casket and placed a ring in Kate's folded hands. It was the promise ring he had planned to give her on their next date.

He bent his head down and whispered, "Goodbye, my love. I'll never forget you."

He kissed her cheek and slowly backed away. He took a seat in the front pew with the others.

The church was full by ten. Pastor Henry tried to make sense of the tragic event by reminding the mourners they had to trust God and accept His will.

As he concluded his talk, the pastor looked directly at Tim and said, "We must move on. Kate wouldn't want us to mourn for her for very long. She knew Jesus and she trusted in Him. She'd want you to do the same. She loved life, and especially you. God bless you, Tim. We all pray you heal, both physically and mentally. I know this is difficult for a young man to understand, but you will someday." Then he looked up at the gathering and added, "Someday we all will."

They buried Kate in Greenwood Cemetery, and Tim laid the last flower on her casket.

A week later, Sheila Holmes called the Maas residence and asked to speak to Tim. When he took the phone, she asked, "Could you come and visit Cissy? She's out of her coma and the doctors say she's out of danger, but it'll take a long time for her to recover completely."

"Sure, Mrs. Holmes, I'd love to see her," Tim said. "Would tomorrow be okay?"

* * *

Tim walked into Cissy's room about 2:00 the next afternoon with Ed's help.

"I'll wait for you out here," Ed said, turning to leave.

Cissy's head was wrapped in gauze and there were several tubes in her arms. Her right arm was in a cast and there was a cast from her ankle to her thigh on the right side.

Seeing the cast on Tim's left leg, Cissy smiled and said, "Looks like we'd make a good pair in a three-legged race."

Tim smiled as he approached the bed. Cissy reached out, took hold of his good hand, and pulled him close, saying softly, "We'll get through this together, Tim. Kate was my best friend, and she talked about you all the time and the things the two of you were going to do together."

Cissy paused for a moment, then added, "She even told me about the last time she was at your farm."

"She did?" Tim said in surprise. "What did she say?"

"Oh nothing," Cissy said coyly. "She just said she gave you a massage and fell asleep while sunbathing nude. Then you guys went skinny-dipping. That's all. Is there more?"

"No," Tim said, breathing a silent sigh of relief. "That was pretty much it."

They talked for about thirty minutes. Cissy asked, "Are you still going to Iowa State this fall? I guess I'm going to spend a year at Muscatine Community because of all the therapy I'm going to have to go through. Kent says he'll stay here, too."

"That's good," Tim said with a smile. "I'm glad. As for me, I should be fairly well healed by fall and Ed will be there in case I have problems."

With that, Tim struggled to his feet and said, "Well, I guess I'll get going. Let's keep in touch, okay? I hope your hand heals so you can play the piano again."

"Thanks," said Cissy with a smile, "and remember what I told you. We'll get through this together."

Chapter Twenty
Jenny's Summer

When Jenny turned fifteen, she was almost six feet tall and weighed barely 110 pounds. She was too old to want to stay at home and work with her mom, but not old enough to drive to a job in town. One morning, just after summer vacation started, a neighbor pulled into the farmyard in an old station wagon. He slowly approached the back door, looking around nervously before he knocked. Sara answered the door and recognized the man immediately. It was Bob Beamer from down the road.

"Hi, Bob," she said. "Come on in and have a seat."

After Bob sat at the kitchen table, Sara brought him a cup of coffee and asked, "Now, what can I do for you?"

Bob looked uncomfortable as he began, "It's my wife, Anna. She's very sick and I need some help." Trying not to break down, he continued, "As you know, we have five children, all under the age of twelve. Anna had some trouble having the last one—Jeremy, who's now a little over two years old. There's something wrong with her female organs. I don't know what. The doctor told us to wait and let time do the healing, but it never happened. Last week she hemorrhaged badly. She's very weak because she has lost a lot of blood. We're going up to the Mayo Clinic in three days. I can send Jeremy to her sister's, but the other four want to stay home and help me. We sell produce at the farmers' market in Muscatine, Davenport, and Iowa City. To tell you the truth, I need them more than they know."

As Sara nodded her understanding, Bob went on. "Here's the thing, Sara. I was wondering if maybe Jenny might be available to help at our house until Anna recovers. It might take all summer and I'd pay her well for her work. She'd have to cook meals and wash clothes, bathe the kids, put them to bed, and care for them. There are also some ladies from our church who'd come from time to time to help, but she'd be pretty much in charge whenever I'm not there."

Bob paused, then looked at Sara and asked, "What do you think?"

Sara looked at Bob and said softly, "I think we should ask Jenny. I could help, too, if she ran into any problems. Jenny's up in her bedroom." Sara went to the bottom of the stairs and called, "Jenny, could you come down here for a minute, please?"

When Jenny walked into the kitchen, Sara said, "You know Bob Beamer, right?" As Jenny nodded, Sara added, "Bob, go ahead and make your proposal. Then we'll let Jenny decide what she wants to do."

Bob again outlined the situation, though he added he and his wife believed in limiting the children's television time because of the violence and lack of modesty on the screen. In fact, there would be no TV at all during the summer. He also asked Jenny to leave her cell phone at home, followed by a request to refrain from wearing shorts, since their church frowned on women wearing clothes they considered immodest.

Finally, he ended by saying, "You'd have every weekend off and we'd pay you $400 a week for as long as you're needed."

Jenny listened attentively. When Bob was through, Sara looked at Jenny and said, "It's a tall order for a young woman, but if you want to take it on, it's okay by me."

Looking at Bob, Jenny said, "I think I could take care of the four older children, Mr. Beamer, but I'm a little concerned about of taking care of a toddler."

"Well, my wife's sister has volunteered to take Jeremy until Anna's feeling better, so you'd only be watching the four of them. The girls will be able to help, too. Miriam already does the laundry. We don't have a microwave—Anna didn't want one of those things—but we have everything else you'd need. Anna could help, too, when she feels up to it."

Smiling, Jenny said, "Okay, I'll give it a try, Mr. Beamer. Where would I sleep?"

"In the girls' room with Miriam and Hannah. The boys sleep across the hall in their room, and Nathaniel sleeps in the back room."

"Who's Nathaniel?" asked Jenny.

"Sorry, I forgot to mention him. He's my nephew. He'll be there all summer to help with the garden and chores. He's seventeen. I hope this doesn't change your decision."

Sara said, "I have no problem with it. Jen has two older brothers and she handles them with ease. How about you? Jen."

"It's fine with me."

"Could you come over tomorrow and meet the family?" Bob asked. "Sara, you come along, too. Thank you both. The Lord has just lifted a great burden from me. "

"Okay, see you tomorrow about eight," said Jenny.

With the agreement reached, Mr. Beamer left. Then Jenny turned toward her mother and said excitedly, "A job for the whole summer— and at $400 a week! I'll be rich."

"I think you can do it, hon," said Sara, "but it's going to give you a workout."

The next day Sara and Jenny drove to the Beamer farm about three miles up the road. It was well maintained. The house was old, but had been remodeled several times. The lawn was spacious and led down to a small pond surrounded by trees. The pond wouldn't lend itself to swimming because of its size. Between a pair of oak trees, suspended from an iron beam, was a large porch swing. It would be nice to sit by the pond on warm summer afternoons.

Because of their faith, the Beamers generally kept to themselves. They believed in dressing modestly, and the women of their faith always wore dresses or skirts and blouses. They never wore jewelry or makeup. Their hair was neatly piled atop their heads and the men had short haircuts and were always neatly shaven. Their children attended public school until eighth grade, then the children were given an option to go further or to stay home and help. They were not against higher education—they just believe it wasn't always necessary.

When Sara and Jenny pulled up to the house, the two older girls came out, followed by the boys, Sam and Noah. "Come on in and meet our mother," said Miriam. "She isn't feeling well and can't come out."

They found Mrs. Beamer sitting on a sofa in a little room off the kitchen.

"Good morning, Mrs. Beamer," Jenny said politely. "How are you feeling?"

"A little better, now that you're here." Anna replied.

Sara stepped forward and took Anna's hand. "Hello, Anna. I want you to know if there's anything Jen can't handle, I'll be just down the road, so don't worry."

Anna told Jenny, "Miriam can show you around. I'm so weak I can hardly move." Then she turned to Sara and said, "Sara, do you have time to sit and talk for awhile?"

Miriam led Jenny around the house and was especially proud of the girl's room and the bed where Jenny would sleep. It was right below a window. She also showed her the kitchen, bathroom, and even the basement. As Sara and Jenny left about an hour later, Jenny told Anna she'd be back the next morning at ten.

When they got back home, Jenny immediately began to pack blue jeans and t-shirts, as well as a few blouses she thought would be appropriate. She decided one pair of tennis shoes would be enough. By 3:00 that afternoon, she was packed and ready. She was so excited about the next day she had a difficult time sleeping that night.

The next morning she said goodbye to everyone as if she was leaving on a major trip.

"You're only going down the road, Jen," teased Tim.

When Jenny arrived at the Beamer farm, Miriam helped her put her clothes in a dresser. Then Jenny went downstairs in her newest jeans and top to start her job. Mrs. Beamer coached from a chair as Jenny and the girls fixed lunch.

It was at lunch when Jenny first met Nate Yoder. He was a tall, muscular young man with dark hair and deep brown eyes. He smiled as he was introduced to Jenny and she smiled back. When Jenny was placing the food on the table, Nate's hand brushed her leg.

"Was that intentional or just an accident?" she wondered, but she dismissed it as an accident.

There was the usual small talk at the table. Mr. Beamer seemed pleased Jenny had fit in so quickly. He told her various ladies from the church would stop in every other day to help with the cooking while he and Anna were at the Mayo Clinic.

At 6:00 the next morning, Bob and Anna left for Rochester. Jenny roused Miriam and they started breakfast. Nate had risen earlier and was already milking the cows.

When Nate came in at about 7:00 to eat, Jenny was standing by the stove frying eggs. He passed close to her and as he walked by, his hand touched her hip.

She looked at him and thought, "What's he doing?"

Later in the morning, Mrs. Beatty arrived with her two girls. She was a jovial woman who claimed she'd never seen such a tall girl who was also as pretty as Jenny.

As promised, women from the church came by every other day to help. First came, Rachel, then Ruth, then Sara, then Bernice, and finally, Beulah. Jenny felt odd wearing jeans and t-shirts around them. One day, she asked Beulah if she would make her some skirts and dresses—and especially a nightgown. It would make her feel more like one of the family.

"I feel funny in my pajamas with legs," Jenny explained. "I can pay you later."

"Sure, honey," Beulah said a broad smile. "I'd be glad to, and don't worry about the money. I like to sew. I'll use soft fabric for the nightie. In the summer, we wear gowns which come to the knee. Let's go into the other room and take some measurements. I'll have to adjust my patterns for such a tall young woman."

The next week, Beulah presented Jenny with four skirts, five blouses, two dresses, and the softest nightgown she had ever felt. They all fit perfectly.

"Do you want any underwear?" Beulah asked. "Most of us wear a camisole under our clothes instead of bras. We think they give you more freedom."

Jenny thought for a moment and responded, "Okay, I'll try one."

"Then let's go into the sewing room again for more measurements. You'll have to remove your top and bra for a good fit."

"Okay," Jenny said, knowing she was soon going to be even more like one of the church women.

Two days later, Beulah brought four pretty camisoles, each with lace around the top, and told Jenny, "You'll need to try one of them on to see if it fits."

Jenny went upstairs and put on the new undergarment. Then she hurried downstairs to show Beulah. Beulah pinned the garment here and there to make it fit better. She was almost done when Nate came through the door.

As Jenny tried to cover herself, Beulah bellowed, "Get out of here, Nate Yoder! You're not supposed to be in here right now."

However, Nate stood where he was, looking at Jenny—until Beulah grabbed a broom and started chasing him, shouting, "You get out of here or I'll call Bob!"

Covering his head for protection, Nate scampered out the door, laughing all the way.

"That Nate!" Beulah warned. "He's going to get into trouble some time. He was sent here by his dad to get him away from a girl next door. You be careful around him, you hear?"

"I've got two big brothers. I think I'll be alright," Jenny assured her.

* * *

The summer eventually settled into a routine: up at 5:30, fixing breakfast for Bob and Nate, waking the girls at 7:00, starting laundry and cleaning, rousing the boys at 7:30, feeding the kids and herself, then working in the garden if there was time.

In the third week of June, Anna finally came home from Mayo. She'd had several surgical procedures, so she needed rest and couldn't lift anything, but just having her around was a relief for Jenny. Anna and Bob still made weekly trips to Muscatine to their family physician.

In a few more weeks, little Jeremy would return, and Anna was eager to have her little boy home. Anna told Jenny several times a day how much she appreciated her help and how much the girls loved her.

The routine became a little more hectic when the fruits and vegetables began needing more attention. Bob sold produce at three farmers' markets: Iowa City on Wednesdays and Muscatine and Davenport on Saturdays. On Saturdays he left Nate and part of the produce in Muscatine, then he went on to Davenport with the rest. It required harvesting late at night and early in the morning to make sure the produce was fresh.

On the last Saturday in June, the demand for labor was critical, and since Jenny was a farm girl, she understood about harvesting pressure. At 4:30 that morning, Anna woke Jenny and Miriam. They stumbled out of bed, dressed, and headed for the garden in their bare feet. It had rained overnight and the ground was muddy, but it would be easier to wash feet than shoes.

Nate and Bob loaded the van while Miriam and Jenny finished picking green beans at the end of a field. They were just about finished when lightning began to flash to the west. Jenny told Miriam to head for the packing shed with their first two baskets. She'd finish the row and come as quickly as she could. She didn't realize the storm was closer than she thought.

First came the wind, then a few big drops, followed by a torrential downpour. Bob came running in a raincoat. He grabbed the baskets and told Jenny to head for the shed. By the time Jenny reached the building she was soaked and her dress clung to her like a wet paper towel.

"We still have to load these into the van," Bob told Nate and Jenny. "I sent Miriam to the house because Jeremy was crying."

"Well, I'm soaked already, so I'll help," Jenny shouted over the sound of the pounding rain.

Now Jenny was the only one without a raincoat, but she didn't care. She wouldn't have to go to the market. After everything was loaded, Nate decided he wanted to change shirts, so he dashed to the back porch and removed his shirt. Jenny was right behind him. As Nate disappeared inside, Jenny stayed on the porch. She wanted to wait until her clothes dripped a little before she went back into the house.

A few moments later, Nate returned and saw Jenny was shivering. To her shock, he began to unbutton her dress, saying, "We've got to get you out of these wet clothes."

"Leave me alone!" Jenny shouted, slapping at his hand, but Nate immediately went back to unbuttoning her dress.

"Nate Yoder, you stay away from me—now!" she screamed.

This time he backed off, raising his hands as if she had a gun. Then he snarled, "My, my! Aren't we testy today? I was only trying to help."

Jenny glared at him as she began to rebutton her top. "All you want is to see me in my underwear—now get out of here!"

From the van, Bob called, "Come on, Nate, we have to get going."

Nate smiled as he turned to go, sending a shudder through her body. She stood and watched as the van disappeared down the road, then turned and walked into the house.

Anna was waiting for her in the kitchen. "Did he hurt you, Jenny?" she asked.

"No."

"Did he touch you?"

"Yes, he tried to unbutton my dress," Jenny said, trying to hold back her tears.

As Jenny started toward her room to get some dry clothes, Anna caught her arm and pulled her back. "Nate's been known to do things like that. I'll have Bob talk to him when they get home. I'd give you a hug, but you're too wet. Why don't you take off your dress down here? You can run upstairs in your underwear before the boys get up. Then we'll talk some more."

"Okay."

Jenny slipped out of her dress and laid it over the back of a chair. Anna touched her shoulder gently and said, "Okay, now I'll give you a hug. Jenny, please don't leave us. I need you."

As Jenny dashed from the kitchen, she nearly ran into Miriam, who was holding Jeremy in her arms. Miriam asked in surprise, "What happened to your dress?"

"It's a long story, Miriam," Jenny said softly, since it looked like Jeremy was almost asleep. "I'll tell you all about it later. Right now I have to get upstairs before the boys wake up."

Jenny changed clothes and returned to the kitchen to help fix breakfast, then went to wake the others. The rain was subsiding and the sky was clearing in the west.

The morning was filled with the usual chores. When Sam came back from the hen house, he was all muddy. He said he'd fallen in the slippery mud of the chicken yard, but Anna suspected he had probably been checking the depth of the water in the dusting holes created by the hens. She made him strip off his filthy pants before he could come into the kitchen. The girls made fun of him as he dashed through the room in his underwear, but Jenny just smiled as she picked up his muddy pants and threw them down the basement stairs.

After lunch, Jeremy went down for a nap and Anna was ready for a break. Jenny and Miriam had been up since 4:30 and were very tired, but the other children were raring to go, so Jenny made a deal with them. If they promised to be quiet and not fight for one hour while she and Miriam took a nap, she'd take them down to the pasture so they could play in the creek. They readily agreed.

At 2:30, Jenny woke Miriam and they packed some cookies and lemonade. They gathered the other children and headed for the creek. When they got there, Jenny pulled some safety pins from her pocket and pinned the girls' skirts up as high as she dared. Then she rolled the boys' pant legs up.

The children had a great time playing in the water. They floated sticks for boats, chased frogs, and watched water bugs skim across the surface. As they were sitting on the bank with their cookies and lemonade, Jenny saw an ATV rumbling across a pasture a short ways away. It was her dad. Since the creek was the same one which ran through the Maas farm, Jenny had an idea. When they got back to the house, she approached Anna with her idea.

"Anna," asked Jenny, "do any of the children know how swim?"

"Heavens, no!" Anna replied. "We haven't got the time or money for things like that."

"Would you like them to learn?"

"I guess so. What do you have in mind?"

"When we were down at the creek this afternoon, I saw my dad one pasture over. Our farm pond isn't far from here. If you give the okay, I'll take the children there and teach them how to swim. Your pond's too small. My mom used to be a lifeguard and I'm sure she'd love to help."

"But we don't have any swimwear," said Anna. "How would they go into the water? The girls couldn't swim in their dresses."

"I've probably got an old suit which would fit Miriam," Jenny responded, "and I'm sure mom could find something for the boys. We could ask the Babsons if they have a small suit for Hannah. I know you want swimsuits to be modest, so I'd wear my most conservative one. It would have to be a two-piece though, since I've never found a one-piece which fits my tall body."

"I'll ask Bob tonight, but I don't see why not," Anna said with a smile.

"Great! I'll have my mom bring over some suits for the children to try on, but let's not tell the kids just yet. Let's surprise them, okay?"

Two days later, Sara brought swimming suits of varying sizes for the children to try on. Jenny took the girls to their room to try some on and Sam quickly found a pair of swimming trunks to his liking, but all of the trunks were too big for Noah.

"Jenny!" he called from the boys' room.

When Jenny arrived, she found Noah holding a pair of trunks up with one hand and wailing unhappily, "They keep falling off!"

Jenny knelt beside him, gave him a hug, and said, "Don't cry. See, there's a string inside which we can tighten, but there's a knot in it. I tell you what. You take them off. Then I'll untie the knot and we'll retie it tighter, okay?"

"Okay," said Noah, wiping his tears.

He let go with his hand and the trunks instantly dropped to the floor. As Jenny picked up the oversized trunks and sat on the bed to start working at the knot, Noah climbed into her lap.

"I love you, Jenny. You're the bestest person I know," he said.

Jenny looked down at the naked little boy, smiled, kissed the top of his head and said, "Thank you, Noah. Now try these on. I think they'll fit better now."

Jenny tightened the string. Though the legs were still a bit big, the trunks would do.

They hurried downstairs, where Jenny asked Anna, "Do you approve?" When Anna nodded, Jenny asked, "Do you want to see what I'll be wearing?"

"I don't want to pry," Anna replied, "but, yes, I would."

Jenny dashed up and put on a modest two-piece. When she went back downstairs, she found everyone in the family room. Jenny was relieved when Anna approved of her bathing suit.

Before they could escape back upstairs to change, Nate arrived. He took one look at Jenny and let out a whistle, making everyone uncomfortable.

The next day was bright and warm, so the children asked their mother hopefully, "Can we go to the pond today?"

"You know it is not can, but may we go to the pond?" she corrected them

"If you have all your chores done and if Jenny's mom can be there, yes," Anna said.

Jenny called her mother and Sara said she'd meet them at the pond.

Everyone rushed up stairs and changed, put dresses and pants over their bathing suits, and started off across the pasture separating the two farms. When they got to the pond, Sara was already there.

Sara began to give beginning instructions on how to swim. Jenny helped Noah, and he clung to her when she took him into water which was over his head. She gently lowered him into the water and showed him how to float on his back. Once he grabbed her top and almost pulled it off, but soon he was swimming with the others.

They stayed for a little over an hour, and before it was time to go home, Sara provided some cookies and punch. Then they said goodbye to Sara and started for home. When they reached the house, Anna listened intently while the kids told her how much fun they'd had; however, looking at them, she knew there would be an early bedtime that night.

After supper, Jenny helped everyone shower and rinsed their bathing suits. She finally took a shower herself, making sure the bathroom door was locked. She didn't want Nate to accidentally barge in as he had done once before.

She was in her nightgown when she hung the suits on the clothesline outside. She knew she was taking a chance, but she didn't want to get dressed just to hang out the swimsuits. To her chagrin, Nate followed and insisted on handing her the suits to hang up.

When he came to hers, he held it up and said, "I'll bet you look mighty pretty in this. I'd like to see you in it. Will you put it on and show me?"

"Never!" Jenny said firmly. "Now get away from me or I'll call Bob!"

"Okay! Don't have a hissy fit," Nate growled as he turned and left.

The next morning when Nate came in for breakfast, he was a different person. He was polite, thanked Jenny for the meal, and never once tried to touch her. Jenny wondered if Bob had talked to him again.

The next weekend, Jenny went home to spend a Sunday with her family. She and Tim were the only ones home, and as they sat on the front porch swing, she told about Nate's advances and touching.

"Sounds like the guy's got a problem," Tim said.

"I know, and I'm a little concerned," said Jenny. "He's a pretty big guy."

"I think you should brush up on your self-defense," Tim suggested. "Let's go out on the lawn."

Tim played the part of the villain, coming up behind Jenny and grabbing her shoulders. She reacted by catching his arm and throwing him over her hip to the ground.

Then Tim approached from the front, grabbed her arms, and held her, saying, "You know what to do, but don't really do it, okay?"

Jenny faked kneeing her brother in the groin, then pulled his arm behind his back and began to push up. Tim faked some pain, but he had to admit the chicken wing hold actually did hurt a little.

"Alright, sis!" he said. "You don't have to break my arm. Just remember to push up until you here a pop. Then run as fast as you can."

As Jenny let go, Tim rubbed his shoulder. "Did I hurt you?" Jenny asked with a smile.

"I think you can handle Nate," Tim said with confidence, "but I hope you never have to do it."

As they went into the house for some lemonade, Jenny said, "Thanks, Tim. I feel safer now."

The rest of the month was uneventful. Nate behaved like a perfect gentleman. On the last Thursday of July, as the kids were practicing their swimming skills at the pond, Sara suggested they put on a swimming show for their parents the next Saturday. The children eagerly agreed.

On Saturday afternoon, everyone drove to the pond instead of walking and the adults, including Nate, sat around the picnic table to watch the show. The children and Jenny went behind the van, and one by one, the children modeled their swimwear. Jenny went last, wearing the modest two-piece, but even her suit showed plenty of skin.

Jenny quickly waded waist deep into the water, knowing Nate was watching her intently. At the same time, Anna was also watching Nate, but she said nothing.

Jenny called Noah to start the show, saying, "Okay, Noah, swim over to me."

Noah dutifully splashed to Jenny's side, where she had him float on his back, tread water, and then swim back to the shore. When Noah emerged from the water, everyone applauded.

Next came the girls, who swam out to where Jenny was waiting, using a freestyle stroke to swim to the dock, a backstroke to return to Jenny, and a breaststroke to head back to the beach. They took deep bows as everyone applauded.

Sam finished the show, swimming out to Jenny with smooth and measured strokes. He demonstrated all the strokes, then swam to the dock, climbed the ladder, ran to the edge, and dived back into the pond. He swam under water all the way to Jenny. They both disappeared under the water, finally surfacing close to the beach. As Sam and Jenny emerged from the water, the other children joined them. They all bowed as their audience gave them a standing ovation.

As soon as she got to shore, Jenny wrapped herself in a big towel and handed towels to the others, saying, "You all did great! Now, how about some food?"

The next evening Jenny and Nate sat together on the pond swing. Nate was a perfect gentleman. As they talked, she learned he'd had a difficult childhood. His mother had died when he was quite young. His stepmom had two daughters and didn't appreciate boys. Nate said he got along well with his stepsisters, but his stepmom made him feel like an outcast. Jenny felt better knowing Nate was trying to do the best he could, given his background.

As the summer wound down, Anna was scheduled to return to Rochester for one more checkup. She and Bob would be gone for three days. Jeremy was sent to his aunt's and the rest of the kids stayed home. Jenny saw no reason to worry.

The first two days went by quickly. Nate even helped with the dishes one night. On the third day, the girls wanted to make the house spic-and-span before their mother came home. So everyone worked hard all day.

To reward their efforts, Jenny gave each child a jar for catching lightning bugs. It was great fun, but at 9:00 Jenny announced it was time to count the bugs. Since Sam had collected the most, he got to sit next to Jenny while she told a bedtime story. Her stories were entertaining because she updated old favorites to reflect modern times. Even Nate turned off his mp3 player and listened.

It was well after 10:00 by the time everyone was finally in bed. Nate retired to his room. She went downstairs, took a shower, and put on her nightgown. The night was warm and she knew she'd be glad to get back home so she could wear her shorty pajamas. There was nothing wrong with the way the Beamers lived, but she looked forward to returning to a less restrictive lifestyle.

She decided to walk barefoot down to the pond swing. A cool breeze would feel good as it touched her skin. Lightning bugs sparkled in the air as Jenny sat on the swing and rocked gently. She pulled the hem of the nightgown above her knees and unbuttoned the top two buttons.

The moon was full and was reflected on the pond's surface. She closed her eyes, enjoying the stillness, not realizing Nate had heard the screen door close as she left the house. From his window, he had watched Jenny make her way down the path to the swing. He had left his bedroom and followed at a safe distance. He also watched her pull up her nightgown and undo the top buttons.

A moment later, Jenny thought she heard a noise. At first she thought it was a deer or a rabbit, but when she turned to look, she saw Nate approaching the swing. She quickly pulled her nightgown down and redid the top button.

"Hi, Jenny," Nate said as he drew closer.

"Nate, how did you know I was here?" Jenny asked nervously.

"I followed you when you left the porch."

"You mean you've been watching me all this time?"

Nate nodded and said, "You're beautiful, Jenny. I love to watch you. I watch you with the children. I watch you cook. I watch everything you do."

"Well, thank you. Nate," Jenny said, trying to collect herself. "I do my best."

"May I sit with you?" Nate asked.

"I suppose so," Jenny replied, sliding over to make room.

Nate sat and they talked for a few moments. Nate put his hand on her leg. She lifted it, but he then put his arm around her shoulders.

"You know, Nate. I think I'd better get back to the house. We've got a long day tomorrow."

She tried to get up, but Nate grabbed her arm and said, "Please stay."

"No!" Jenny said, trying to free herself from his grip, but he stood and twisted her arm behind her.

"Let me go, Nate!" Jenny said firmly. "You're hurting my arm!"

"Not until—"

"Not until what?"

"Not until we talk some more."

Nate quickly grabbed Jenny's other arm and also pulled it behind her back. With one of his strong hands, he held both of her arms in place as he started to stroke her hair. The more she struggled, the tighter he held her arms together.

As Jenny started to scream for help, Nate shoved a hankie in her mouth. She tried to spit it out, but she couldn't.

"Now, Jenny," Nate said menacingly, "I think I'd like to see you with this nightgown off." She shook her head furiously, but Nate ignored her. "All summer I've been watching you and I've seen the shadow of your legs through this nightgown. Now I'm going to see you without it."

He reached out, unbuttoned the nightgown, and slid it off her shoulders. The gown fell to her elbows and waist. He had to let her hands go to strip it completely off, so he grabbed her hair and yanked violently.

"I'm going to let one arm go and you're going to let the nightgown fall, do you hear me?" he snarled.

He released one arm and Jenny pulled it free of the gown. Then he grabbed her arm again and released the other one, but Jenny caught the nightgown before it fell completely off.

"Let it go, Jenny. Let it drop all the way off," Nate said, squeezing and twisting her other wrist.

A moment later, the gown fell to the ground. He grabbed her free arm, spun her around, and jerked her arms away from her body. He had her just where he wanted her—naked and under his complete control. He scanned her body up and down lecherously.

"I'll take that rag out of your mouth if you promise not to scream," he said. "The kids are asleep, and there's nothing they could do to help you, anyway."

As Jenny nodded, Nate bent over and pulled the hankie from her mouth with his teeth.

"Nate," Jenny said with surprising calmness, "you really don't want to do this, do you?"

He tried to kiss her, but she turned her head. He backed her up and pinned her body against one of the oak trees. The sharp bark cut her back as she struggled. He brought her arms down to her sides and tried to kiss her again, but she again turned her head.

"Okay, we'll try something else," Nate sneered.

He raised her arms above her head, held them with one hand, and slapped her face with the other. Jenny immediately stopped struggling and looked him directly in the eye. The look of fear was gone, replaced now by anger. Nate looked down and was consumed with the idea of kissing her naked breasts.

"You know, Jenny, you're better than any of those women in *Playboy*, and you're right here in front of me," Nate said hungrily. "I want to feel your body against mine."

As he leaned forward, he changed his grip to hold her wrists with one hand so he could fondle her with the other. As he moved his feet apart to gain better footing, Jenny brought her knee up sharply into Nate's groin. His leer instantly changed to surprise and pain as he let go of her hands and doubled over in pain.

Jenny then sprang forward, whipped Nate's right arm behind him, and pulled it up until she heard a pop. As Nate screamed in pain, Jenny let go, put her foot on his rear end, and gave him a swift push toward the pond, sending him sprawling into the water.

She quickly retrieved her gown and slipped it over her head and waited until Nate's head popped to the surface. She didn't want to be responsible for a drowning.

Nate's face was a mask of pain as Jenny laughed and turned back toward the house, calling over her shoulder, "Next time pick on someone you can handle! Goodnight!"

She ran to the house and made her way to the boys' room. She scooped up Noah, carried him across the hall, and gently laid him in her bed. Then she returned, woke up Sam, and half carried, half dragged him to the girls' room.

"What's going on, Jenny?" Sam asked sleepily.

"Nate and I had a little fight. Now I want you to lay down on the floor by my bed and go back to sleep. I'm going to lock the door."

Sam curled up on the floor with the pillow and blanket Jenny gave him as she locked the door and wedged a chair under the doorknob. Then she crawled in beside Noah and waited.

After awhile, she heard Nate stomping up the stairs. He tried the door, and when he realized he wouldn't be able to open it, she could hear him curse. Then she heard him storm back to his room, followed by a lot of rummaging noises. Finally, he stomped down the hall and out the front door. After what seemed like forever, she dozed off, hugging little Noah in her arms.

In the morning, the girls were surprised to find Sam and Noah sleeping in their room. It was also 7:30 and Jenny was still in bed.

Miriam tiptoed over and tapped Jenny on the shoulder. "Jenny, wake up. It's 7:30."

Jenny opened her eyes and saw both girls standing in front of her.

"What's going on, Jenny?" asked Hannah.

"It's a long story," Jenny said, sitting and laying Noah gently back onto the bed.

"Why are Sam and Noah in here?"

Jenny jumped up, saying, "You didn't unlock the door, did you?"

"No," Miriam replied. "Why is it locked?"

"I was afraid Nate might harm the boys, so I brought them in here to keep them safe."

"Why would Nate do that, Jenny?" asked Hannah.

"I'll tell you later. Now I have to find out where Nate is. I want you to lock the door behind me. Do you understand?"

Miriam and Hannah agreed as Jenny picked up a baseball bat from the corner and crept out into the hall. She cautiously headed for Nate's room. She had to make sure he was gone before she tried calling her mom from the downstairs phone. She peeked into his room, and quickly realized all the noise she had heard was Nate packing. His dresser drawers were open, the door to his wardrobe was ajar, and his suitcase was gone.

Still on edge, Jenny slowly descended the stairs, slipped on her tennis shoes, and started toward the barn. The cows were there, patiently waiting to be milked. She peered over the barn door. She was about to call Nate's name when Hannah came running into the barn.

"I thought I told you to stay in your room!" Jenny yelled.

Hannah was undeterred. "Jenny!" she said. "Look what we found on the kitchen table. It's a note from Nate. He's gone."

Jenny looked at the note. It read:

Dear Aunt Anna and Uncle Bob,

My dad wants me to come home immediately. Thanks for keeping me this summer.

Nate.

Jenny took Hannah by the hand and made it back to the porch before she collapsed on the steps and began to sob uncontrollably. Miriam put her hand on Jenny's shoulder while Hannah caressed her hair. None of them noticed the blood spots on the back of her nightgown or the bruises on her wrists and face.

Noah crawled into her lap and said, "Don't cry, Jenny. I'm right here. I'll protect you."

Jenny looked down at Noah and hugged him tightly. As she looked at the children surrounding her, she said, "I love all of you so much."

"What happened, Jenny?" Miriam asked.

"Nate and I got into a big fight and he tried to hurt me—but I hurt him, too. Let me tell you the whole story. The truth is always the best."

Jenny told them the whole story, and ended with how she had kicked him and pushed him into the pond.

"Did you kick him in the nuts?" Sam asked. His eyes wide with excitement.

Jenny looked at him in surprise, then smiled proudly and said, "You bet I did!"

"Good," Sam said as everyone laughed.

As the clock in the hall chimed 8:00, Jenny exclaimed, "We've got to get going. We've got a lot of chores to do. Everyone upstairs to change."

Jenny followed the kids upstairs, but her back hurt from being scraped against the oak tree the previous night. When she entered the girls' room, Miriam and Hannah were already in their underwear and putting on their dresses. As Miriam's head poked out of the top of her dress, she noticed Jenny standing by her dresser wearing only her underpants.

Miriam saw Jenny's back was full of cuts and scratches. "Jenny!" she shrieked. "Your back is a mess. What happened?"

"Nate shoved me against a tree," Jenny replied. "It hurts, but I'll be alright."

"Hannah, run downstairs and get some hydrogen peroxide out of the medicine cabinet," Miriam ordered. "I'll get some water and a towel. Jenny, you lay face down on your bed and we'll fix you up." Then she noticed Jenny's face and said, "One of your eyes is black and blue. Did he hit you?"

As Jenny nodded silently, Miriam turned and left the room quickly, leaving the door wide open. When Sam came out of his room across the hall, she saw Jenny lying on her bed, but just as he was about to enter the room, Miriam caught him.

"Samuel Amos, don't you dare go in there," she said firmly. "Can't you see Jenny doesn't have any clothes on? You take Noah and go do your chores. As soon as I take care of Jenny, Hannah and I will milk the cows. Now git!"

"But I was just worried about Jenny," Sam said, almost in tears.

Jenny turned her head toward him and said, "It's alright, Sam, I'll be alright in a bit."

As Sam turned to leave, Noah appeared at the door, then ran right past Miriam and was soon standing by the bed. As he looked at Jenny's back, he touched her hair with his little hand.

"Jenny got an owie. Does it hurt?" Noah asked, his voice trembling.

"Yes, a little," Jenny replied. "Why don't you help Sam do chores while Miriam and Hannah fix my owie, okay?"

Miriam herded the boys out, and gently washed Jenny's back. Hannah brought the hydrogen peroxide and Miriam poured small streams of it on Jenny's back. It burned, causing Jenny to wince, but only for a few seconds.

Then Jenny turned toward Miriam and said, "You'll make a great wife and mother someday."

As Jenny sat up, swung her feet around, and started to push off the bed, Miriam noticed her bruised arms and wrists and asked, "Is that where he grabbed you?"

"Yes, and they really hurt right now. I guess I was too pumped up to notice before."

"Well, you just lay back down," Miriam said. "I'll set the alarm for thirty minutes while Hannah and I do chores. You just rest. We'll come and get you."

As Jenny sank back onto the bed, Hannah pulled the covers over her legs and hips. Jenny's back was too tender to be covered. The girls quietly slipped out the door, leaving Jenny to doze off. When they returned, Jenny was dressed and starting some laundry.

Miriam scolded, "I thought I told you to rest. We'll take care of everything."

"Listen, little lady," Jenny countered, "I'm still the boss around here until your mom gets back. I'm just a little sore. Thanks for taking care of my back."

Just then, they heard the sound of crunching gravel from outside. Bob and Anna were home. Miriam forgot about Jenny and ran out the door to greet her parents. Anna was holding Jeremy. They had picked him up on the way home.

As the children surrounded her, Anna announced she was completely cured and everything was going to be like old times again. When she saw Jenny come out onto the porch, she looked shocked.

Anna hurried to the porch and, seeing Jenny's bruises and black eye, she exclaimed, "Jenny, what happened to you?"

Before Jenny could answer, Hannah said, "Jenny got in a fight with Nate and he hurt her, but she beat him up and he ran away. See? Here's the note he left."

"Is this right, Jenny?" asked Anna.

"Yes," Jenny said weakly. "I'm so sorry. Please forgive me."

"Sorry? What for?"

"For causing Nate to leave."

"Don't you worry about Nate!" Anna said sharply. "I never trusted that boy. He had all those girlie magazines in his dresser. I knew he was no good. Let's go inside so I can see where he hurt you."

Once inside, they went into Anna's bedroom, where Jenny took off her dress and turned around. When Anna lifted Jenny's camisole, she gasped, "My lord, girl. When did this happen?"

"Last night."

"Lay down on my bed and I'll cover you with a towel. Do you mind if Bob sees your wounds? I'll just take off enough towel to show him."

Jenny shook her head.

After Anna had covered Jenny's back with a towel, she called Bob into the room. He was shocked when he saw the extent of her injuries.

"Oh, lord! He didn't—" Bob started to ask.

Before he could finish his question, Jenny interrupted. "No, he didn't, but I'm sure he would have tried if I hadn't fought back."

"Jenny, will you tell us everything before I call his father?" Bob asked. "I mean everything. I'll go into the kitchen while Anna helps you dress, then I'll come back, okay?"

"Yes, sir," Jenny replied.

When Bob returned, Jenny told the entire story and apologized for going outside in her nightgown, ending by saying, "I'm sorry. I should have known better."

Bob shook his head in disbelief. "He had no right to harm you, regardless of what you were wearing. I'm going to call his father right now. Have you called your folks about this?"

"I called home, but they're at my Aunt Sue's. The only one home was Tim, and he said they'll be home tonight."

After Bob left the bedroom, Anna gave Jenny a gentle hug, being careful of her wounds. Jenny put her head on Anna's shoulder and cried. Her ordeal was finally over and she was safe.

"Oh, Anna," Jenny sobbed, "it was such a beautiful night and the pond was like glass with lightning bugs reflecting in it. I just wanted to enjoy it. I'm so sorry."

"Nonsense, girl!" Anna said. "When Bob and I were first married, we sat in that same swing. The moon was full, so I suggested we take a dip in the pond, and that's just what we did! I don't blame you a bit." She paused and added with a smile, "You know, our religion may require dressing modestly, but we're still human beings. My goodness! How do you think Bob and I had five kids? Now, what do you say we go eat some lunch?"

Jenny wasn't very hungry at lunchtime, but by supper, things had calmed down and everyone gathered around the table and held hands while Bob gave the blessing.

"Heavenly Father, thank you for all the blessings you've bestowed on us. Thank you for healing Anna. She's a complete woman again and we're all grateful. Thank you for our children—they're our pride and joy. Lastly, thank you for sending Jenny to us. Without her we couldn't have made it. Thank you for her parents, who were kind enough to let us have her. She's been like a part of our family for the last three months. Now we ask that You heal her wounds and that You'll help her not be bitter. Finally, bless this food and have it nourish our bodies. In Jesus' name, Amen."

When he had finished, everyone chimed in, "Amen!"

The next morning, Anna called Sara and she rushed right over. Jenny took Sara to the girls' room and Sara was shocked, but grateful it hadn't been worse than it was. When Sara asked Jenny if her back was all that was scratched, Jenny pulled down her underpants and showed her the cuts on her bottom. Miriam hadn't checked below Jenny's waist.

As Anna went for some more hydrogen peroxide, Sara had Jenny strip completely and lie on the bed. When Anna returned, she and Sara dabbed at Jenny's wounds.

When they had finished, Sara said, "You'd better stay here until it all dries." Then she added, "And the next time you want to go swinging in your nightgown, maybe you should do it in our yard. You were a brave girl and I'm proud of you."

"Okay, I'll stay here till it dries," replied Jenny, "but will you close the door when you leave? I think Sam and Noah saw enough of me yesterday."

Sara and Anna went back downstairs, and though they closed the door, they didn't lock it. About fifteen minutes later, Jenny heard the doorknob turn and the door open slowly. She knew Noah had come into the room from the sound of his bare little feet on the floor.

When he reached the bed, he touched her long brown hair and said, "Jenny, it's me, Noah. I brought you something."

It didn't seem to bother Noah that Jenny was naked. She reached out and pulled him close, asking, "What did you bring me, hon?"

"I bring you some flowers. I hope they make you get better," he said with a smile.

The paradox made Jenny smile. She'd been attacked by an oaf who had stripped her naked, and now she was getting flowers from a four-year-old who didn't even seem to notice that she had nothing on.

As she rolled over and swung her feet to the floor, Noah proudly held out his flowers. Then he crawled into her lap and put his head on her breasts. She hugged him and kissed his little head as she rocked back and forth, feeling his warmth against her chest.

He looked up and said, "I love you, Jenny. I'm sorry you got hurt."

"Thank you, Noah," Jenny said, hugging him again, "but now you have to go. I need to get dressed. I'll see you in a little bit, okay?"

Noah left, but he was hesitant. Then Jenny got dressed and went downstairs.

When Jenny walked into the kitchen, Sara said, "Anna's wondering if you could stay another week. She has windows to wash and wants to paint the children's rooms. You can take it as easy as you want, until you're feeling better. Your dad and I are taking Ed up to Iowa State on Tuesday. On Wednesday, your dad wants to visit an old roommate who has cancer. I'm sure you'll find it more exciting here with the Beamers."

"Sounds fine with me," Jenny agreed. "No sense going home and sitting around being bored."

"Good," Anna said. "I'll tell the children. I'm sure they'll all be happy."

* * *

The last week went fast as Jenny, Anna, and the girls worked hard, painting in the morning and washing windows in the afternoon while the paint dried. Bob and the boys picked tomatoes, peppers, and cantaloupes for the farmers market, but they only went to Iowa City and Davenport.

On Saturday morning, Jenny rose early. Her folks were coming at 3:00 that afternoon to pick her up. The Beamers had invited them to a picnic before they took Jenny home.

Although she didn't say anything about it, it seemed to Jenny they were making an awful lot of food for just the two families. As Jenny helped Anna make the preparations, she asked, "May I ask you a question?" when Anna said yes, Jenny asked, "Have you heard anything about Nate?"

Anna paused and said, "His dad called last night and told us Nate made it home on Tuesday. On Wednesday, he and his stepsister, who's eighteen, were home alone. She went upstairs to take a shower, but she didn't lock the door. Nate barged in and attacked her. He beat her up pretty badly and raped her. He's in jail now and will probably go to the Eldora juvenile home. You were a very lucky young woman to have escaped the way you did."

"That's so sad," said Jenny. "He could have been such a nice guy."

They ate a light lunch and set tables up outside. It was past 3:00 and Jenny's parents weren't there yet, which made Jenny nervous. Her folks weren't usually late. At 3:30, the Maas car finally pulled up the drive, followed by Jenny's brothers and Carol in the pickup—but there was also a long line of other cars behind them. As dozens of members of Beamer's church got out of their cars, Jenny realized why they'd been making so much food all day.

Before the picnic started, Anna stood and asked for their attention.

"My friends," she began, "we're gathered here to say goodbye to the sweetest girl I know, Jenny Maas. She started out as a neighbor's daughter, but now she's a part of our family. God sent her to us when we needed her most, and she pitched right in. One day she picked beans in the rain so Bob could make it to the farmers' market. She even taught our children how to swim. We'll never forget her, and we all hope you'll visit us often." Then she said, "Now the children each have something they want to give you."

First, Miriam gave Jenny her gift. When Jenny unwrapped the paper, she found a monogrammed handkerchief. Hannah presented her with a clay-fired bowl which had the words "I love Jenny" around the outside. Sam gave her a hand-carved walking stick so she could walk through the pasture to visit them. Finally, Noah gave her his most favorite toy tractor so they could play together whenever she visited.

As Jenny gave each child a hug, tears rolled down her cheeks. Then Bob and Anna asked Tim and Ed to go to the workshop and bring a box from the workbench. When they returned, they were carrying a large wooden chest.

As they set it on the porch, Bob said, "This is for you, Jenny. It's a hope chest. All young women in our congregation receive one when they turn sixteen. I know we're a little early, but Anna and I never would have made it through this summer without your help. Fill this hope chest with things precious to you, and when you find the right man to marry, we know he will be the luckiest man on earth."

Bob held Jenny's hand and his voice cracked as he added, "We're all going to miss your smiling face. Please come back soon."

After the applause had died down, Jenny stood silently for a few moments collecting her thoughts, then said, "When I came here in June I didn't know what to expect. I came in my jeans and a t-shirt, and when the church women came to help wearing dresses or skirts, boy, did I feel out of place—but you always made me feel at home. Then along came Beulah and her sewing machine to make me some dresses and skirts and blouses. She even made me some underwear."

As the crowd chuckled, Jenny continued, "I've learned so much from all of you this summer, and I had so much fun with the children. Miriam and Hannah will always be my little sisters, and Sam—Boy, the girl who catches him will be in for a treat. He's so handsome. Finally, there's my little Noah. I'll miss him more than I can ever say."

Noah smiled happily as Jenny turned to the Beamers and said, "Anna, I hope your health will be good forever, and Bob, I'll help pick beans anytime, but I'll probably keep a raincoat with me, just in case. Thank you all."

There was another round of applause as Bob raised his hands and said, "Okay, I'm going ask our Father Almighty to bless this food before we eat. Everyone, let's bow our heads."

After the main meal, everyone had some homemade ice cream

and cake. Ed and Tim loaded Jenny's hope chest into the back of the pickup and headed for home with Carol. The last to leave were Jenny and her parents.

Jenny climbed into the backseat of the Buick and looked out the rear window as they drove away while the Beamer the family stood on the front porch and waved. When she finally turned toward the front, Jenny wondered if she'd ever experience such a wonderful time again.

Chapter Twenty-One
Jenny's Next Summers

The episode with Nate made Jenny leery of young men for awhile—leery enough that both Jenny and Sara enrolled in a self-defense class at the Muscatine YMCA. Every Monday they put on their white suits and practiced the art of defending themselves, though they hoped they'd never have to use the skill.

The summer she spent with the Beamers reinforced Jenny's desire to work with children. The next summer, Jenny worked for the Muscatine Parks and Recreation Department in the lead position for a three-day-a-week morning youth program at Musser Park.

She was nervous as she waited for kids to show up the first day. The program was to start at 9:00, and she waited until 9:10, but no one had come. She was about to leave, when four little girls wandered over and asked Jenny what the park playtime was all about. Jenny told them there would be games, crafts, and story reading, followed by snacks.

One of the girls looked at Jenny and said, "But we're hungry now. Our moms have gone to work and our breakfast was a can of pop and a piece of pizza."

Jenny looked at the little girl and asked, "What is your name?"

The girl replied, "My name is Lucinda, and this is my friend, Izzy.

The third added shyly, "I'm Sophia Taylor. I don't have a mom. She left a long time ago. I live with my dad and grandma."

Finally, the last girl said, "I'm Julie. I live with my dad. My mom had cancer and died last year."

Jenny looked down at the girls, then introduced herself. "I'm Jenny. I live on a farm outside of town, and it looks like we have four hungry girls here. What do you say we skip the games for now and go right to the snacks? We can always play games later."

Jenny broke out the juice and cookies and the girls ate happily.

They sat and talked about their lives and what they wanted to be. Before they knew it, it was 11:00 and time to end the session.

Jenny stood and said, "I'll tell you what, girls. Next time I'll bring a real breakfast. We'll eat first, then we'll do other things."

The girls smiled and vowed to return the next morning.

When Jenny got home in the afternoon, she explained the situation to her mom. Then she asked, "Do you think we could make something nutritious for the girls tomorrow, Mom?"

"I think we could do something with eggs and bacon, or maybe some milk and cereal," said Sara.

On Wednesday morning, Jenny loaded up her supplies; however, when she arrived at the park, she was surprised to see not just four girls, but ten.

"We hope you don't mind, Jenny, but we brought some of our friends," Sophia said.

"No," said Jenny with a smile. "I think I have plenty, and there might even be enough for seconds."

The morning went fast. When the session was over, Jenny asked the group if she could expect any more children on Friday.

"Can I bring my little brother?" asked one little girl.

"Can I bring my cousin?" asked another.

"If they're seven or older, they can come," Jenny assured them.

Jenny returned home and discussed Friday's prospects with Sara.

Sara suggested, "Maybe you should talk to your boss and see if this can be a regular part of the program. If they approve, we may have to involve Grandma Madge and Emma."

Jenny went to the phone and contacted her supervisor, who said it would be acceptable, as long as the food remained hot or cold as required. Jenny would also have to clean the tables and benches afterward.

On Friday, Sara went with Jenny to the park. They had estimated they'd see fifteen children—but there were twenty. While Jenny was helping the kids do crafts, the minister from the Musserville Church came to visit. She knew many of the children and told Jenny she'd help the next week, and if it rained they could use the church's fellowship hall.

Jenny contacted her friends Yolanda and Maria to see if they could volunteer to help. The next week, the number of children reached thirty. Jenny contacted several churches to see if they could donate food or volunteer to help. The response was overwhelming.

A short time later, Jenny's supervisor asked if she'd like to start a similar program at Madison school on the north side of town. Jenny accepted the challenge. She recruited more volunteers and more food was donated by local grocery stores.

By the end of July, Jenny's crew of twenty volunteers from ten churches was feeding seventy-five children at Musser Park and forty more at Madison three mornings a week.

On the last week of the program, a reporter from Channel 6 arrived to do a story on Jenny's program. The report was aired on a Wednesday evening and the very next day NBC's *Today Show* also aired the story. Someone from the show called and asked Jenny to come to New York City to be interviewed. Jenny declined, saying she had her children to take care of. The producer did convince Jenny to do an interview in the park with all her children. The show also pledged $10,000 for the program.

Jenny had become a star. The park board was so impressed by her work, they named the program *Jenny's Kids*. T-shirts were provided to all volunteers and children with the Jenny's Kids logo on the front. The city council gave her an award for good citizenry and she was selected as one of four recipients of the annual Governor's Award for Community Achievement. She and the other three honorees were guests at a banquet with the governor and his wife at Terrace Hill.

The next summer, Jenny returned to her children in the park program she had started the year before. Jenny's Kids spread from Musser Park to Madison School to a new group in West Liberty at the fairgrounds. There was talk of having a group in Columbus Junction. For an eighteen year old she was very, very busy.

One warm day at Musser Park, Jenny was about to start serving breakfast when a car with chrome rims and a fancy paint job pulled up. Four young men got out and sauntered over to the shelter house. Jenny recognized one of them from high school. His name was Alfredo Masserazi. She had sat next to him in one of her classes, and he had always made her nervous.

The four young men stood watching for a few minutes, until Jenny finally asked, "May I help you?"

Alfredo said, "Yeah, we came for breakfast. We heard it's good.

We'll just take this breakfast pizza and leave."

"No!" Jenny snapped. "Those pizzas are for the children. You can have some if there's any left over."

"No," Alfredo said with a sly smile. "I think we'll just take ours now, if that's all right with you."

As Alfredo reached out to grab a box of pizza, Jenny lunged forward and grabbed his arm. "I said you'll have to wait until the kids are fed."

Alfredo shoved Jenny aside and again reached for a pizza box while one of the volunteers dialed 911 for help.

Jenny again grabbed his arm, this time shouting, "I said no! Now please leave."

Alfredo raised his arm as if he was going to hit Jenny, but she stood her ground. As he started his swing, Jenny's self-defense training kicked in. She caught his hand and twisted his thumb violently, sending him to his knees. Cursing, he jumped up and lunged at her, but Jenny grabbed his arm and flipped him over her hip. The move dislocated Alfredo's shoulder, causing him to scream in pain as he landed with a thud against a shelter post.

"Get her!" Alfredo yelled to his buddies.

"No!" one of them said. "I'm leaving, and listen—I hear sirens. The cops are coming! Let's get out of here."

While Alfredo struggled to get to his feet, the others hurried to the car and sped away, leaving him behind.

As one of the older volunteer's helped Alfredo to his feet, she said firmly, "Now you just sit on this bench and wait for the police. Shame on you, Alfie. You just wait until I talk to your mother. She'll know what to do with a bully like you!"

The woman was Alfredo's Aunt Lila, and he knew she meant business. A few minutes later, the police arrived and put Alfredo in the back of a squad car. They smiled as they heard the story of how Jenny had handled Alfredo with ease. They also assured Jenny they'd be checking in more often on her morning programs.

The next week, however, the same car pulled up one morning at Musser Park—but there was a difference. This time only three young men got out and walked toward Jenny.

Instinctively, Jenny got out her cell phone, but before she could begin dialing, one of the young men said, "Wait, Jenny. We're here to help. Me and the boys want to help with the games and food. We can play catch and help with the ballgames, if you wouldn't mind."

Jenny studied the group apprehensively, then asked, "Where's Alfredo?"

"We don't hang out with Alfredo no more," said one of the young men. "Me and the boys don't like men who pick on girls." There was a long, uncomfortable pause, after which he looked directly at Jenny and asked, "Will you give us a chance to prove we mean what we say? I promise, we ain't as bad as we seem."

Jenny sighed, looked at the other volunteers, then said, "Well, maybe it would be good for the program. Some of these kids have older siblings who aren't exactly good role models—but if any of you mess up, I'll call the cops. Agreed?"

The young men all agreed, and it proved to be a good decision for everyone. The young men eagerly pitched in to help with the games and crafts and Jenny was surprised by their gentleness and ability to relate to the children. Those three young men would return from time to time to help for the next three summers.

Jenny continued to head the summer program. The only difference was she was paid for her efforts. The Parks Department applied for a grant to receive assistance and the program was well funded. Still Jenny relied on many volunteers and the churches to help. She felt it was how she had gotten started and it was how it would remain.

Chapter Twenty-Two
The Wasp Nest

Carol, who was now Ed's steady girlfriend, arrived at the farm early one Saturday morning and entered the kitchen, saying cheerfully, "Hi, Mrs. Maas!"

"Good morning, Carol. My, you're up and around early this morning."

"Yeah, I know, but I had nothing to do, so I decided to bum around with Ed today. Do you think he'll mind?"

"Heavens, no, he'll be glad to have someone here. Tim's up fishing with Brad in Minnesota. Jenny stayed at Amy's last night. They're going to Six Flags with Amy's folks for a couple of days, and Paul and I are heading for his sister's in Waterloo in about two hours. That means Ed will be all alone this weekend, so I'm sure he'd appreciate some company."

"Is it all right if I stay overnight then?"

"Sure. You can sleep in Jenny's room, as always."

"Where is Ed, anyhow?"

"He and Paul are sorting some steers before we go."

Just then the backdoor opened and Paul walked in. He said hello to Carol, then turned to Sara and asked, "Honey, can you come out and help us for a minute? We need a gate holder."

"I'll be there in a minute," Sara said. "Just let me get some boots on."

"Can I help?" Carol asked.

"The more the merrier," Paul said with a laugh as he walked back out.

When Paul had left, Sara looked at Carol and asked, "Are you sure you want to come?" "You might get dirty."

"That's fine," replied Carol. "These are old jeans, and I didn't wear a good blouse today."

"Okay then, I'll find you some boots," said Sara.

The two women entered the feedlot and slogged across the wet manure-filled floor. With so many cattle, it was impossible to keep the lot clean for long. It had also rained overnight, so the surface was slicker than usual.

"What are you trying to do?" Sara asked the men.

"We need to get these smaller steers into the next lot before we leave. They're getting pushed out and they're losing weight," Ed said, smiling to acknowledge Carol's presence.

"Is there anything I can help with?" Carol asked.

"There sure is. You can help Mom with the gate. Dad and I will sort out the smaller steers and when one gets close, you open the gate and let it through, then close it again. The gate's kinda heavy, though."

Sara and Carol took their position at the end of the gate. Ed and Paul proceeded to cut out five steers. The first ones went easily, as if to say, "I'm glad to get away from these bullies." However, the last steer wanted to stay where he was. The men finally got him cornered.

"Open the gate a little wider, hon," Paul called over his shoulder as he watched the steer.

Sara and Carol opened the gate slightly and as they did, the steer charged through, throwing mud and manure into the air. Paul grabbed the gate and helped pull it shut, not realizing Carol was still hanging on to it. Her feet slid out from underneath her and she went down, falling stomach first into the gooey, stinky slime.

Ed hurried over and helped her up, asking, "Are you okay?"

"Yes, I think so," Carol said as she wiped at the brown stuff covering her front, "but I'm a mess."

To her credit, Carol didn't cry or cuss.

"Well, we'd better get this poor girl cleaned up," Sara said. "Ed, help her out of the lot. I'll meet her in the garage."

"In the garage?" Carol asked, looking at Sara.

"Yes. I'll go to the house and get one of my robes. When you get into the garage, tell Ed to get out, then take off your clothes and put them in a bucket. Put the bucket outside the garage door. After that, I'll show you the shower in the basement while Ed throws your clothes over the clothesline and sprays them with a hose before I wash them for you."

Ed helped Carol out of the lot, but they stopped on the way to the garage so Carol could wash her arms at the water hydrant. Ed also took his handkerchief, wet it, and wiped her splattered face.

"I look horrible, don't I?" Carol said with a smile.

Ed nodded and replied, "Yes, you do."

Brown ooze was starting to run down inside her jeans and Carol was afraid of what she might find when she took them off. Ed led her to a clean spot in the garage, and turned to go.

"I'm sorry this happened to you, but you'll be okay," he said as he was going out the door. "Mom will take care of you. Actually, you're lucky. Mom used to make us undress by the back door. Then we'd have to wait naked outside until Mom arrived."

Carol smiled. She couldn't imagine having to take your clothes off outside. In town someone would certainly see you. This would be a new experience. Just as Carol started to pull her t-shirt off, the garage door opened again. With a playful grin, Ed asked, "Do you need any help getting your boots off?"

"Get out of here!" said Carol, looking at him over her up-stretched shirt.

Seeing she was only partly dressed, Ed turned and left, but she pulled her shirt back on, walked over, and opened the door, where she found Ed waiting outside.

"Yes, I do believe I could use some help with my boots," she said coyly.

Ed found a bucket for her to sit on and helped her out of the slimy boots, but by the time they'd gotten them off, his own jeans were also covered with manure.

Shaking his head and smiling, he said, "Well, looks like I'll need to clean up, too."

Carol thanked him and went back into the garage, where she removed all her clothes except her underpants. She decided against taking them off because she didn't want to be completely naked. Carol put her clothes in a bucket and set it outside the garage door, as Sara had instructed. Then she huddled behind the family car while she waited for Sara to show up with a robe.

When Sara finally appeared, she looked at Carol and said, "You poor girl. You must be freezing. You could have waited until I got here."

Sara wrapped the robe around Carol and gave her a hug, but she was surprised when Carol began to cry. "What's the matter, hon?" Sara asked.

"I'm sorry for causing so much trouble," Carol said through her sobs.

"What trouble?"

"Everyone had to stop what they were doing to help me."

"Nonsense," Sara said. "We're just glad you didn't get hurt."

"But you made me go to the garage and take off my clothes. You're not mad at me?"

"Of course not, you're probably lucky I didn't tell you to get undressed by the back door. That's what I would have done when the kids were younger."

"I know," said Carol with a smile. "That's what Ed told me."

"Look, Carol," Sara said, "I love you like one of my own kids and Paul does, too. Any girl ,who would come out here and help work cattle in a sloppy feed yard has to be special. If I came on too strong, I'm sorry. I hope you'll forgive me."

"Gee, Mrs. Maas, I didn't know you cared that much," said Carol. "I do love this place, and I love Ed. I hardly ever see my dad, and when he's home he just sits in front of the TV. My mom's more concerned about her friends and her social life than me, so your family is very special to me."

"Well, let's see if we can get you cleaned up now," Sara said with a smile, "and next time, you don't have to take all your clothes off in the garage, okay?"

Sara put her arm around Carol and they started toward the house. Ed stepped in and could tell Carol had been crying.

"What's the matter?" he asked, obviously concerned.

Sara just smiled and replied, "Her feelings got hurt, and I'm afraid I was responsible for that, but I think we've got it patched now. Right, Carol?"

"Right," Carol answered with a smile of her own.

Sara ushered Carol downstairs to a large room Carol had never been in. Whenever she had stayed before, she always showered upstairs. On one side of the room were the washer and dryer, accompanied by a double sink. On the other side were a folding table, three chairs, and an ironing board. The toilet was hidden in a closet-like space in the corner and the shower was across from it. The showerhead resembled a sprinkling can head. Instead of a curtain, it had what looked like an old barn door hanging across the opening. The door was about four feet tall and ended about eighteen inches from the floor. There was a wooden grate on the floor to protect feet from the cold concrete.

"I think I have to use the restroom," Carol told Sara.

"It's right over there in the corner. Give me your underwear before you go in. I'll turn the shower on so it'll be ready when you come out. I'm going to presoak your clothes before I wash them. I'll be right here at the sink."

When Carol was finished in the restroom, she slipped into the shower. The warm water felt heavenly as it poured over her head. For about a minute she just stood with her eyes closed and let the water warm her whole body. She found some shampoo and washed her hair. As she peeked over the door, she saw Sara was sorting clothes—wearing only her underwear.

When Sara saw Carol looking in her direction, she said, "I got my clothes dirty, too, so leave the water running. I'll come in right after you. You can dry off with one of those big towels, and wrap up in it. The little towels are for your hair. If you want, you can wait for me and we'll go up together. I'll run interference in case any of the men are present in the house."

Suddenly there was a knock on the door. "Who's there?" called Sara.

"It's me, Mom," Ed replied. "I've got Carol's jeans and blouse rinsed out. Do you want me to bring them in or leave them out here?"

"Leave them outside the door," Sara said. "We're both naked in here, so you better git!"

Turning back to Carol, Sara said with a smile, "See what I mean? You never know when one of the men will show up. I've been caught several times, and they always think it's amusing."

Carol finished, stepped out, and grabbed a big towel. Then Sara stepped into the shower. A short time later, Sara and Carol headed up the basement stairs.

At the landing, Sara said, "We didn't get done a moment too soon. Here comes Paul. You go on upstairs and dry your hair. You'll find Jenny's dryer on a shelf in the bathroom. I need to talk to Paul for a second."

Carol quickly went upstairs to the bathroom; and before she turned on the hair dryer, she heard Sara telling Paul she'd be sending some clothes down the chute. As she started drying her hair, Sara poked her head in the door.

"Find everything?" Sara asked. "I had to tell Paul to put some clothes on before he came up, since we have a guest. Sometimes the men come up with nothing on, especially when they're in a hurry."

When Carol went into Jenny's room, the only clothes she had left to wear were a red-and-white sundress.

Sara poked her head out of the bathroom as Carol walked down the hall and said, "That dress looks good on you."

"Thank you," Carol said. "I hope Ed likes it, too."

Paul was standing in the kitchen when Carol walked in. He said with a smile, "If any of your clothes are beyond cleaning, you just go buy some new ones and we'll take care of it, okay? I'll put it on Ed's bill. He has a couple other things to finish up outside, so make yourself at home. It'll be a half hour or so."

"Okay, Mr. Maas," Carol replied.

"Carol, if it's all right with you, I wish you'd call me Paul," Paul said as he turned to go upstairs.

Carol sat on the kitchen stool as she waited for Sara to come down and start packing the food for their trip to Waterloo. As Sara came in and went to work, Carol asked, "Anything I can do to help?"

"Why don't you get four apples out of the fridge and chop them? I'll find the rest of the ingredients for an apple salad. If we make enough, you and Ed can have some, too. Are you sure you're okay? You know farmers. Most of the time all they think about is crops and livestock, but if a wife or girlfriend gets hurt, they melt like butter in the sun."

"Oh, I'm fine," replied Carol, "but I sure was a mess a few minutes ago."

By the time Paul came back downstairs, the food was ready. He and Sara said goodbye and left Carol alone in the house.

Ed finally came in after about an hour. "Why don't you put that casserole in the oven?" he told Carol. "I'll get cleaned up and put on some better clothes."

When he finally came back into the kitchen, the casserole was nearly ready. Carol had set the table.

After they had eaten and put the dishes in the dishwasher, Ed yawned and said, "How about a nap on the couch?" Then he added, "Oh, and you look great in that dress. I've never seen it before."

They went into the den and turned on the fan. Ed then spread out on the couch, his long legs extending over the armrest. As Carol snuggled against him, the fan blew the dress up past her knees.

"Why don't I get behind you? I don't like the fan blowing directly on me," she suggested.

"Okay, sounds good," Ed agreed.

They switched positions and cuddled on the couch. Carol loved the manly smell emulating from her partner. She wrapped one arm around his waist and pulled him closer. They were soon sound asleep. They woke up about four o'clock.

"How about taking a ride out to the pasture and check the cows?" Ed asked. "I think you can ride in the go-getter in your dress."

"I guess I'll have to," Carol said. "I just remembered I didn't put my other clothes in the dryer."

"Okay then, let's go."

As they headed toward the pasture, Ed circled around until he found the cows under a grove of trees. He took a head count and headed to the pond. He stopped by the gate and checked the water tank at the bottom. Carol walked to the pond. She'd been here before, but only briefly.

She walked out onto the dock, took off her sandals and sat on a little bench between the posts. A few minutes later, Ed joined her. He put his arm around her shoulder and they were just about to kiss when Carol let out a scream and began swatting at her legs. Soon Ed yelped, too. The air was full of wasps, and they were mad.

Ed grabbed Carol's hand and hollered, "Jump!!"

They both jumped feet-first off the dock. When they surfaced, they could see the angry wasps still swarming around the dock.

"We can't go back there," Ed said. "We're gonna have to swim to the beach."

As they walked out onto the sand, Ed said, "Boy, I've never tried to swim with my work boots on before."

Carol said, "That's nothing! You should try swimming in a dress!"

Carol's dress clung to her body like wet tissue paper. She was barefooted. While Carol wrung the water out of her dress, Ed unlaced his boots, took them off, and dumped the water out.

Forgetting who was with him, Ed quickly removed his shorts and t-shirt and said, "Man, those wasps got me a couple times." The boxers he was wearing clung to his skin.

"You've got a couple bad ones on the back of your leg," Carol pointed out. "I wonder what mine look like?"

She lifted her skirt just enough to see several stings on her leg. There were also two on her shoulder.

As she turned to show Ed, she jumped up on the picnic table and screamed, "Snake!"

Ed followed Carol's eyes and saw a large bull snake slithering through the grass. "He won't hurt you. It's just a bull snake."

"I don't care," said Carol. "I don't like snakes."

Ed kicked at the snake and it scooted away in the tall grass. Then he turned and held out his hand to help Carol down. As she stepped down, she slipped and fell into Ed's arms. She was trembling.

"It's alright now," he said reassuringly. "The snake is gone."

He put his arm on her shoulder and slipped her shoulder strap to ease the stings. With his other hand, he felt along her back and found that the zipper of her dress had lowered during her swim. Instead of zipping it up; however, he took it lower—all the way to her waist. Carol never said a word, but she was shivering.

Ed put his hand inside the back of the dress and continued around her waist. The shoulder strap had already been dropped on the side where the stings were, and soon the other strap also slipped down. Carol looked into Ed eyes, then stepped back, allowing the dress to fall to the ground. Then she picked it up and spread it on the table.

Carol then turned to Ed in just her bikini underpants and a strapless bra. They studied each other for a moment. Ed reached out and pulled her close. He had seen her many times in a bikini which revealed much more; however, seeing Carol in just her underwear was different somehow. As he held her, he toyed with the idea of unhooking her bra, but changed his mind. This wasn't the right time.

Finally, he said, "Well, I think we'd better go back and get you into some dry clothes."

Carol nodded and turned to pick up her dress.

"Wait a minute, honey," Ed said. "Come over here, please, and turn around."

She did as he asked, and with her back to him, she felt his finger run along the top of her bra strap. He stopped at the clasp, and she felt a rush go through her body. Was he going to unhook it?

As she put her hand to her chest, she heard him say, "There you go. I didn't think you'd want to take this pond moss with you."

As she turned, he held up a glob of moss in his hand. With a sigh of relief, Carol said, "Of course, not. That looks gross."

Back at house, they headed for the shower again. Carol put her dress in the washer and turned on the drier to dry her other clothes. Ed waited outside the laundry room while she showered.

When she finally appeared, wrapped in a big towel, she said, "I'm sort of out of clothes. I guess I'll put on my pajamas."

"Go ahead," Ed said. "I've got to run by the feedlots."

When Ed returned from chores, Carol was coming down the stairs in her pajamas, which consisted of a short nightgown and some undershorts.

"Do you suppose Jenny has some sort of a cover-up I could put on?" Carol asked. "This is kind of revealing."

"Get one my shirts out of the closet," Ed replied. "Jenny's always raiding my room for them, and if she can do it, so can you."

Carol dashed upstairs and rummaged through Ed's closet for a shirt. She found one with long sleeves which covered her nightgown perfectly. By the time she went downstairs, Ed had showered and was dressed in shorts and a shirt with the sleeves cut off.

"Why don't we get a pizza out of the fridge? We can eat on the front porch," Ed suggested.

As the sun got lower in the sky, they ate the pizza. They laughed and joked about the day's events. Carol said, "You know I left my sandals back on the dock. Do you think it would be safe to go back and get them?"

"We'll have to wait until it's almost dark," Ed responded.

"May we go to the dune you're always talking about?"

"Sure. I'll bring up the go-getter. We'll have to put some insect repellent on and I'll take the fogger. The mosquitoes are bad out there this time of day. When we used to go there for picnics, we always had to fog for bugs first. It keeps them away for an hour or so."

They drove out to the dune, where Ed went ahead to set up the fogger and to spread a blanket on the bench. Carol followed shortly. They sat together as the sun disappeared below the horizon. Carol leaned on his shoulder and slipped off the shirt so she could feel the breeze through her pajamas.

As Ed put his arm around her shoulders and gave her a squeeze, Carol asked, "Do you think I could be a good farm wife?"

"Sure, you'll be great," said Ed. "You don't get too excited, except for snakes, maybe. You're willing to tackle just about anything and you like animals."

"Where do you think we'll live?" Carol asked. "Will we have to live with your folks?"

"No, there's not enough room for that," Ed replied. "I talked to Dad and we might be able to live at Mrs. Becker's. She is getting older and she's thinking about moving to an assisted care place in Muscatine. It's an old house, but it's nice inside."

"How long will we have to wait?"

"Well, you've got two more years at Drake and I've got one more at Iowa State."

"I suppose you're right. It does seem like a long time, though," Carol sighed. "You are going to marry me, aren't you?'

"You're darned right I am!" Ed exclaimed. "I've got too much invested in you to quit now."

Carol looked up at him and said in mock disgust, "So I'm just an investment, huh? Don't forget, I'm the business major. So I should be the one checking you out instead."

She stood up and pulled Ed to his feet. Then she felt his ribs, checked his teeth, and ran her hand down his back and the back of his leg. She stood beside him, measuring herself against his height.

"Well, I guess you'll do," she finally announced, giving him an elbow in the ribs.

Ed feigned a painful injury and doubled over, falling back down onto the blanket. Carol dropped to her knees, and when she was close enough, he grabbed her, pulled her down beside him, and kissed her.

When he began to tickle her ribs, she said, "Okay, I give up. Stop! I can't take any more."

Ed rolled over and hovered above her, Carol unsnapped his shirt and slipped it off. She liked the view of his muscular chest.

"You know, Ed, you're quite a gentleman," Carol said. "When you got me out of my wet dress this afternoon, I was almost naked. You could have done anything you wanted with me, but you just acted as if you were my big brother and were more concerned about my not getting chilled. Now we're on a blanket on a sand dune in our pajamas. I mean, in town I couldn't go out my back door dressed this way. The one thing I love about this place is you can be so free. Did you ever run around with nothing on? Did you ever skinny-dip? Your mother told me that your dad and you guys sometimes run upstairs naked. Have you ever seen Jenny without clothes on? I've never seen a man naked. In fact, I'd hate to see my dad naked. He is so fat."

"Boy, you're full of questions. Yes, when I was a kid, sometimes I'd only put on underwear after I showered. One time Mom had us all playing in the rain in our pajamas. Though I was only ten, I'll never forget seeing my mom in her wet pajamas. She even played football in the rain and her top came unbuttoned, but it didn't seem to bother her at all. She just rebuttoned it and kept playing. Yes, I skinny-dipped several times, but only with other guys, and yes, we men do sometimes run upstairs naked when we think no one is home. Yes, I've seen Jenny naked. She fell into the cow water when she was eleven and we had to strip her clothes off to take care of a bad cut in her leg. Now, why do you ask?"

"Have you seen her recently?" Carol asked. "I mean, after all, she's all grown up now."

"Only briefly. She likes to dash from the bathroom upstairs to her room. Sort of a free spirit, like Mom."

"Do you think I'm a free spirit?"

"Actually, I hope you're a little more conservative."

"Conservative!" Carol said with a look of surprise. "Okay, was there anyone else? I don't want you to keep anything from me."

Ed rolled on his side and said, "Well, there was Renee Miller. I dated her in high school, right before she left for a summer job in Wisconsin—and when she came home in August, she dumped me. I guess I wasn't wild enough for her."

"You dated Renee Miller, of the infamous Miller sisters?" Carol said, even more surprised than before. "I don't believe it! My cautious, cool Ed dating one of the Miller girls! Even my little school in Wilton knew about those girls. How did you get to know her? I want to hear it all."

"There's nothing much to tell," Ed said. "I met her at basketball practice. She always had to wait until her dad went home, so she'd either be in his office studying or sitting in the bleachers watching practice. She seemed like a nice girl. Heck, she was the coach's daughter."

"Okay, get to the good part," Carol urged.

"We started dating as sophomores and dated until the end of our junior year. The day before she went to Wisconsin for the summer, she tried to seduce me in her room; but I rejected her advances, and it made her mad. She continued to try and undress me, but I wouldn't let her— that was the last we ever spent any real time together."

"Did you see her in school the next year?" Carol asked.

"Yeah, we actually went to a movie the next August when she got back; but she was as cold as an iceberg. Later, she asked to see me in the coach's office and thanked me for being so honorable with her. Apparently, some guy in Wisconsin had almost raped her that summer. Believe it or not, she's now dating a boy from her church's youth group."

"Boy," said Carol, shaking her head, "I'm proud of you for keeping your wits about you. I've heard some wild tales about the Millers."

Carol smiled and gave Ed a look he'd never seen before. Then she said, "Get ready! Here comes Carol Renee."

She giggled and began to tickle him in the ribs. Ed tried to grab her arms, but she was too quick. Carol rolled him over on his back and pinned his arms to the ground, then hovered over him on her hands and knees.

She looked at Ed's eyes and saw he was looking down. Following his gaze, she saw her nightgown had worked up her back and was dipping deeply, giving him a good view. She let go of his arms and smiled impishly. He raised his hands, ready to pull the top down her back, but Carol quickly ducked down and back, leaving Ed holding her top in his hands.

She dropped down on his naked chest and kissed him. Then they lay still for a few moments, not knowing what the next step would be.

Ed closed his eyes, savoring the feeling of her bare skin against his. Carol rolled off and stood up. Then she pulled Ed to his feet and they embraced. It was a wonderful feeling. There was no one to bother them. They were completely alone.

Because Ed was about six inches taller, Carol stepped onto the kid's bench and put her arms around his neck. She looked deeply into his eyes as Ed moved his hands over her shoulders and down her back. She rubbed her breasts across his chest as his fingers found their way to the waistband of her pajama bottoms. He ran his fingers along her smooth hips; then ever so slowly, he worked the pants down by running his fingers back and forth along the elastic, watching her eyes to see if she would tell him to go no further.

She didn't.

The bottoms slipped off her hips, then dropped to her ankles. She lifted her feet out of the pajamas, smiling all the time. Carol then untied his shorts and pushed them down to his knees, where they dropped the rest of the way on their own. Carol's eyes were focused on the first naked man she had ever seen, and she could see he was ready.

She whispered as she pressed against him, "Honey, we shouldn't. Not now. I know it feels right, but it isn't, is it?"

Ed held her as tightly as he could. The rush was over.

She looked into his eyes and whispered again, "You're not angry with me, are you?"

"No," he said simply. "We should wait until we're married. It will be tough after this, but we can do it."

Ed backed away and grabbed his undershorts. Then he reached behind the bench and pulled out several tissues from a little wooden box, which he used to wipe Carol's tummy.

"Who put the box of Kleenex behind the bench?" Carol asked with a giggle.

"Well, Mom said it was because every time we kids came out here we had to blow our noses, but Dad said it was Mom's idea. Apparently, when she was pregnant with Tim and I was small, the three of us came out here one night. Mom had to go to the bathroom and had to go in the cornfield. She complained that she had no toilet paper, so Dad gave her his old hankie. The next time we came out here, the box had been installed, and it's been there ever since."

Carol began to laugh. "That's the wildest story I've ever heard; however, coming from this family, I believe it."

They looked into each other's eyes for a long time, neither of them wanting to break the spell. Finally, Ed moved back and held Carol at arm's length, his eyes moving up and down her body. Everything about her was beautiful.

At the same time, Carol scanned his muscular frame, until she saw the blackened toenail on his right big toe.

"What happen to your toe?" she asked.

"I dropped a wagon tongue on it two days ago, but it's alright now," Ed said. Then he added, "I guess it's time to go get your sandals."

"I didn't notice your toe until you had all your clothes off," Carol teased. "Maybe we should do this more often."

Carol enjoyed the freedom of her bare skin and the coolness of the breeze. She skipped down the deer path which led to the cornfield, calling for Ed to follow as the knee-high grass tickled her legs.

"You don't want to go into a cornfield with nothing on," Ed warned. "The leaves will cut you and the pollen will make you itchy."

Carol stopped, turned, and said, "Maybe you're right. It does look kinda dangerous."

Ed watched with pleasure as she returned. In the moonlight, he could see her hair flowing across her shoulders. Her breasts swayed slightly as she walked. He wanted to hold her for hours, but he dutifully held out her pajamas as she drew nearer.

Carol smiled, knowing he was mesmerized by her body. Instead of getting dressed, she began to walk back to the go-getter with her clothes in her hands. As she slowly walked in front of him, Ed realized that he'd never appreciated the beauty of a woman's back.

When they reached the go-getter, Carol turned and said, "One more kiss, Eddie. I wish this night would never end."

Ed dropped the blanket in the back and embraced Carol. He would never forget this night. They dressed and headed back toward the pond. Ed crept out onto the dock and grabbed Carol's sandals. He put the go-getter in gear and they tore back to the house.

As they walked hand-in-hand toward the house, Carol squeezed Ed's hand. "This has been quite a day, hasn't it?"

"Yes, it has," Ed replied with a smile.

* * *

When she woke up the next morning Carol heard Ed rustling around in his room across the hall. She called, "What are you doing?"

"I'm going to get those wasps. They'll be cold in the morning."

"May I come along?"

"Sure, but we've got to get moving right away."

Carol quickly got up and put on her chore clothes. They weren't ironed, but at least they were clean. She found Ed downstairs, dressed in his swimming trunks.

"Are we going swimming?" she asked.

"No, but I figure if I don't get all the wasps the first time, I can at least jump in the pond wearing the proper clothes," he chuckled.

She smiled as she thought about the previous day's adventures. She followed Ed outside, where he filled a gallon container with gasoline. Then he found a coffee can.

"What's that for?" Carol asked.

"It's a farmer's wasp killer. You catch the wasps sleeping and douse them with gas. Now let's get going before they wake up."

At the pond, Ed filled the coffee can with gas, and slowly walked out onto the dock. He leaned out over the bench and saw the wasp nest covered with wasps. He quickly threw the gas onto the nest and wasps began to drop off. Only then did he motion for Carol to join him.

After she had cautiously made her way to his side, he showed her that the few remaining wasps were trying to fly; but as soon as they took off, they fell into the water. They could see fish gobbling them up as soon as they hit the surface. Ed pulled a putty knife out of his pocket and scraped the nest from the bench.

"Well, that's that," he finally announced. "Ready for some breakfast?"

"How about church? Maybe we should go—after yesterday, I mean," Carol suggested.

"Okay, yours or mine?"

"Yours. My church is having some kind of a potluck and I'm not fond of potlucks. They're for old people."

"Okay, mine it is," said Ed. "Will you wear that red dress you had on yesterday?"

"I guess so," she said. "It's either that or my pajamas. That's all I brought."

"Super! Let's go eat breakfast at Ernie's."

* * *

Carol wowed all the young men at church with her dress. Several girls also complimented her. She and Ed went to lunch with some friends. When they returned home, Jenny was there.

While Ed changed into some more comfortable clothes, Jenny looked at Carol and asked, "Don't you have anything else to wear? You look a little dressy in that, but I'll bet Ed likes it."

"I don't have anything else here except the clothes I did chores in this morning."

"And they're probably all dirty, right?" Jenny asked with a smile.

"Well, not as bad as yesterday," Carol replied with a laugh. "You should have seen me. Your mom made me strip down in the garage."

"Really?" Jenny asked in surprise. "I've had to strip down out there a few times myself. It's sort of fun running into the house in your underwear, though."

"That was the problem. I thought she meant for me to take *everything* off, so I did. I was standing there with nothing on, hoping Ed wouldn't open the door. Your mom finally brought me a robe, and now that I look back, it was kinda funny. Your mom took great care of me, though. She washed my clothes, started a shower, and told me to wait until she showered so she could check upstairs before I went up wrapped in a towel."

Jenny laughed and said, "Yup, that's my mom. She didn't wash your back, did she?" She's been known to do that too. What happened the rest of the day?"

"Oh, you'll never believe what your brother and I did."

"Try me."

"When we went out to check the cows, I had to wear this dress because all my other clothes were in the laundry."

"Oh, brother, this could be good. Tell me everything."

"I sat on that little bench at the pond while he checked the water tank. Just as he came over and sat beside me, we were attacked by wasps. They got under my dress and stung me on my legs and some got into Ed's pant legs. Ed grabbed me and we jumped into the pond. Ed had to swim to the beach in his work boots!"

"Oh, my! What happened next?" Jenny asked.

"Ed took off his boots and socks—then he dropped his shorts so I could see his stings! I was wringing out my dress when a snake jumped out of the grass, so I jumped up on the picnic table."

"Wow! This just keeps getting better!" Jenny said her eyes getting wide open.

"Ed kicked the snake into the grass. When he helped me down, I sort of fell into his arms. For some reason, he undid my dress. We stood there holding each other in just our underwear. I mean, I just had a bra and pants on, so he really got an eyeful—but your brother just hugged me and said he thought I should put some clothes on."

"That's it?" Jenny said, somewhat disappointed. "Nothing else?"

"Nope, he's such a gentleman."

Hopefully, Jenny asked, "Did anything else happen yesterday?"

"Well, yes," Carol said hesitantly, "we went out to the dune at sunset, but I'll tell you about that some other time."

"Okay, but I can hardly believe what you already told me. We should find you some more comfortable clothes, though. They'll be a little big for you, but you can cinch them up." Jenny looked at Carol and asked, "Say, if your jeans and blouse were in the dryer and your dress was in the washer. What did you wear to the dune?"

"My pajamas."

"What did Ed have on?"

"His pajamas. Why?"

"Just wondering." Jen said with a knowing smirk. "Did you keep them on?"

"I'm not going to answer that," Carol replied with a smile of her own.

Once Jenny had found Carol some clothes , she sat on her bed while Carol changed and was very quiet. Just before they headed back downstairs, she asked, " You didn't. Did you?"

Carol didn't reply. She just smiled, but she could feel her face getting warm.

Paul and Sara returned from Waterloo, bringing two pizzas with them.

As Sara poured some lemonade, she asked Carol, "Did you and Ed have a good time?"

"Yes, we did. I love this farm. You can be so free here."

As Jenny tried to stifle a laugh, Sara looked at the two girls and smiled. "I love this place too, and I love you, too, Carol. I hope you and Ed will do well here. I'm sorry about the episode in the garage, but you're alright now, aren't you?"

"Oh, yes," Carol said, smiling broadly. "Needless to say, I'll never forget my first full weekend on the farm."

Seizing the opportunity, Jenny said, "Let's eat on the porch and then you can tell Mom and me all about your night on the dune. Okay, Carol?"

"The dune?" Sara asked, looking at Carol playfully. "Did you go to the dune?"

"Yes," Carol said shyly, feeling her cheeks getting warm.

"Well, that does it then," Sara announced. "We've got you hooked. Once you've been to the dune, you can never leave. I love it. Paul and I had some great times out there. He proposed to me there and we spent our first night together on that pile of sand. We played Adam and Eve the whole night, if you know what I mean," she added with a knowing wink.

"Yes, Sara, I know exactly what you mean," thought Carol.

Carol and Ed were married as soon as Ed graduated from Iowa State. Carol finished her degree at St. Ambrose University in Davenport the following year. Their wedding was the social event of the year in Wilton—Carol's mother made sure of that.

The best part came after the rehearsal supper. Ed convinced George and Thelma Nopoulos, who owned the Candy Kitchen in Wilton, to open the restaurant just for them. They were to serve the guests whatever kind of ice cream treat they wanted.

For three years after their honeymoon, Ed and Carol lived in the house Mrs. Beamer had vacated. They built a new home just a half a mile from the old home place, where they raised their own children—Aaron, Isabelle, and Isaac.

Chapter Twenty-Three
Reunion

Tim's injuries were mostly healed by Fall. His ankle would always be tender and it often bothered him playing intramural basketball at Iowa State. His roomie, Duane Kester, was from a little town in northwest Iowa called Odebolt. He was enrolled in the agronomy department.

Tim started in mechanical engineering, but midway through the semester, Duane invited him to a meeting of the Agronomy Club, where Dr. Harold Theissen of Pioneer Hybrid International was scheduled to speak. Tim had met Dr. Theissen briefly at the plant in Durant.

Dr. Theissen's presentation intrigued Tim. Afterward Tim chatted with him and several faculty members from the agronomy program. During Christmas break, he decided to change his major to agronomy with a minor in genetics.

As he threw himself into his studies, Tim became a hermit. Duane tried to encourage him to attend mixers with women on campus, but Tim still hadn't gotten over losing Kate. Ed sometimes visited his brother to cheer him up, but it didn't help.

One day, Carol, who was going to Drake University in Des Moines, invited the Maas brothers to a sorority party. She fixed Tim up with Ellie, one of the prettiest girls in the house. Tim was cordial and polite, but didn't warm up to Ellie. After they'd been talking for awhile, Ellie asked Tim if there was something wrong with her.

"No," he replied. "It has nothing to do with you. It's something you wouldn't understand."

"Try me," urged Ellie.

Tim sighed and said, "Have you got an hour?"

Ellie looked at him and said, "Well, it sounds like something you should talk about with somebody. I'm game."

Ellie and Tim found a quiet corner and he poured out the entire story. By the time he had finished, Ellie was in tears.

"Oh, Tim," she said softly, dabbing at her eyes, "I can see how much you loved her; but you're still young, and there are hundreds of women who would like to be with you—me included. I've only known you a little while, but I like you. I don't mean to sound pushy, but you have a whole wonderful life ahead of you, and you have to live it."

"Thank you, Ellie," Tim said, nodding in agreement. "I know what you're saying is true, and I will try to change. I just need some time."

Ellie couldn't stop herself. She leaned over, kissed Tim on the cheek, and gave him a quick hug. She felt sorry for this complicated young man.

Time heals all wounds, the saying goes, and Tim took his time getting over Kate. In fact, it took two years for him to finally come to terms with his loss. In the meantime, he enjoyed agronomy, where he could mingle with people, and especially women, without feeling any pressure. Several women were interested, but Tim never allowed any of them to get too close.

During the summer between his junior and senior years, Tim interned at the Pioneer Seed Corn production plant in Hedrick, Iowa. He found a small apartment in Ottumwa and kept himself busy.

The week before the start of detasseling season, he was in charge of getting the machines ready. He worked with two others, fueling, greasing, and changing oil in the tractors. While he was standing between two machines, another of the workers swung a boom around, which caught Tim in the back of the head and knocked him unconscious.

When he came to, he was on a gurney in the ER of the Ottumwa hospital. Looking up, he saw a tall blond woman standing above him, listening to his vital signs through a stethoscope.

"Where am I?" Tim asked, squinting against the bright lights.

"You are in the hospital, Mr. Maas," the woman replied. "I'm Angie Haftner, your nurse. You received a severe blow to the back of your head and we'd like to take you to x-ray. Is that alright? We've already called your parents."

"Okay, you're the nurse," Tim said groggily, then went back to sleep.

Angie shook him gently to wake him, saying, "Tim, we have to get you into a hospital gown. Gloria and I will help. Can you sit up?"

Tim didn't reply, so the nurses raised him up as best they could and removed his shirt. Then Gloria slid his arms into a gown and tied it behind while Angie removed his shoes and unbuckled his belt and jeans. It took both of them to slide the jeans off.

As they were just getting him ready to wheel to the x-ray room, Tim opened his eyes again, looked into Angie's face, and asked, "Do I know you from somewhere?"

"Yes, but it was a long time ago," Angie said. "We can talk about it when you get back."

Two technicians then whisked Tim off to take the x-rays.

At that moment, Sara was in the garden on the farm with Carol. Carol loved gardening, but had little knowledge of the subject, and Sara was enjoying being able to be her teacher. She saw a lot of herself in Carol—a town girl who had married a farmer without any thought of how it was going to affect the rest of her life.

Sara heard the phone ring, but ignored it at first. After it rang many times, she thought it might be Paul needing some help, so she went back to the house and answered it. Picking up the receiver, she said, "Hello, Maas residence."

"Is this Tim Maas's mother?"

"Yes."

"This is Joe Harper from Pioneer in Hedrick. Your son's been in an accident. He received quite a blow to the back of the head and he's in the Ottumwa hospital. My assistant is with him right now, but the doctors would like for you or your husband to come as soon as possible. I don't think he's in any danger, but they need someone to authorize any procedures that may be necessary. May I tell them you'll be here as soon as possible?"

"Yes, by all means!" Sara gasped. "Someone will be there as soon as possible, but it's about an hour and a half away. Thanks for calling, Joe."

"I'll be waiting at the reception desk, wearing a green shirt," said Joe. "See you soon."

Sara ran back out to the garden, saying, "Carol, Tim's in the hospital. Paul's in Cedar Rapids for a meeting and Ed has to do chores. Can you go with me? We may have to stay overnight."

"Sure, Sara, I'll go home and get some clothes, and you pick me up. I know where Ed is. I'll tell him about Tim and he can get hold of

Paul."

She picked up Carol and they headed toward the hospital. Sara had been to Ottumwa several times when she was working on Susie's wedding, therefore the road was familiar. Conversation was sparse on the way.

After Tim returned from x-ray, it took four aides to move him from the gurney to a bed. A few minutes later, Angie returned, asking Tim, "How are you feeling, Mr. Maas?"

"I've got a headache and my vision seems fuzzy."

"Well, I suppose that's to be expected. You took quite a hit to the head, from what I hear," Angie said. Then she smiled and added, "You asked me earlier if you knew me. Well, you once wrote a song called, "The Girl with the Golden Hair" Do you remember the girl who played it?"

"Yes. She was Angie Vander Ploog. She studied music at Luther. How did you know her?"

"Boy, you really must have been hit hard!" Angie said with a smile. "I'm Angie Vander Ploog Hafner. I'm the girl you wrote the song for. I still have it and I still play it from time to time. It's the prettiest song I've ever heard."

Tim was still confused. "What happened? You were going to study music."

"I know," Angie replied, "and I did go to Luther for one year. I loved Decorah, but I had two problems. First, I had a boy friend in Oskaloosa, or so I thought. Second, the other students in the music department were far better than me. I guess I just wanted to play. I didn't really want to study music. So I quit and discovered a love for nursing. I love helping people."

"You said something about a boyfriend," asked Tim. "I take it you got married."

"Yes, and I thought he would be my one true love, but I soon found out differently. He was abusive and he used to hit me. I thought my Christian values would rub off on him, but I was wrong. One night I followed him in my car. He picked up an old friend of mine and they went to a restaurant. I stayed outside for a long time, trying to build up the courage to confront him. I finally went in and asked for him. They said there was no one there by that name. I pushed past the maître d' and looked for myself—and he was there, except he was using another name.

"Boy, was he surprised to see me! We had an argument and he hit me hard enough to put me in the hospital. The cops came and arrested him, but I didn't press charges. I just wanted a divorce. It was a good thing we didn't have any kids. He left town with my friend and I haven't seen him since."

"So, you're not married now?" Tim asked. "It's too bad it didn't work out."

"Well, we live and learn, right?" Angie said with a smile and changed the subject. "Okay, Tim Maas, I've told you my life story. What's been going on in your life since we last saw each other?"

"Oh, nothing much, one more year at State and I'll be out in the real world."

"Oh, there's gotta be more than that," Angie said, but before Tim could answer, she interrupted, "Oh, here comes Dr. Hansen. I'll talk to you later, okay?"

Dr. Hansen smiled as he looked at Tim and said, "Well, Mr. Maas, we'd like to keep you overnight to monitor you. We want to make sure there's no brain damage. You took quite a blow, but your safety helmet probably saved you from getting seriously hurt. I'll check in on you before I go home."

When Sara and Carol arrived at the hospital, Joe Harper was waiting for them. "They have Tim in room 330," he said. "I'll take you to him."

Sara followed Joe down hall, not knowing what to expect. The last time Tim was in an accident was the night Kate was killed.

"Hi, Mom," Tim said as he saw her come into the room.

He was somewhat sedated, but coherent. His head was shaved and wrapped in gauze

"Hi, son!" Sara said, moving quickly to his bedside. "What happened? Does it hurt?"

As Sara kissed her son and sat on the edge of the bed, Carol found a chair. Then Tim explained what he knew about the situation. He didn't remember the ride to the hospital.

As they talked, there was a gentle knock on the door. It was Angie.

As she walked into the room, Angie smiled warmly and said, "Mrs. Maas! Do you remember me? I'm Angie Vander Ploog, from church and music camps."

"Sure I do!" replied Sara. "Angie, this is Carol Maas."

"Tim, you didn't tell me you were married," Angie said in surprise.

Carol laughed, "No, I'm Tim's sister-in-law. I married his brother, Ed."

"Oh, okay," Angie said, looking somewhat relieved. Then she turned to Sara and said, "Mrs. Maas, we're going to keep Tim here a day or so. He might have had a concussion or other brain damage. It's just precautionary, though."

"That's fine," said Sara. "Carol and I are planning on staying. Is there a motel close by?"

"Yes, there's a good one about a mile away. It's called Sleepytime and it's actually run by my aunt and uncle. I'm sure they'll take good care of you," Angie said. As she turned to leave, she looked at Tim and added, "I'll see you in the morning, Tall Tim, the giraffe man."

Sara and Carol stayed until 8:00 and left for the motel. Their room had only one bed, but they made do. In fact, they laughed at the thought of sleeping together while their husbands were sleeping alone.

Sara turned out the light, and as they lay in the darkness, Carol said, "Sara, I want to tell you I think more of you than I do my own mother. Your family took me in like I had been there all the time. So I'd like you to be the first to know. I'm pregnant! You're going to be a grandma."

"You're pregnant?" Sara said happily. "Does Ed know?"

"Yes, but he's the only one—until now."

Sara flipped on the light on the nightstand, threw off the covers, got out of bed, and danced a jig, singing, "I'm going to be a grandma! Whoopee!"

After her exuberant display, she quietly sat on the edge of the bed, and asked, "When are you due?"

Before Carol could reply, Sara said, "Wow! Wait until Paul hears this. I'm so happy for you and Ed."

Carol didn't want to embarrass her mother-in law, but she had to laugh at her excitement. Sara got back into bed and turned out the light, but it took another hour before they finally fell asleep.

The next morning they found Tim in good spirits. His pain had lessened and the swelling at the back of his head had gone down.

Dr. Hansen stopped by, checked Tim over, then said, "I think we can release you this afternoon, but don't go back to work for at least two days, and don't drive till next week. I want to see you next Wednesday. If everything's okay then, you can drive and go back to work as normal."

"Great!" said Tim, "If I feel good enough Monday, can I go to work? My boss says he could give me some light duty and one of the other employees could drive me around to check fields."

"Yes, but be careful."

When Dr. Hansen left, Sara asked, "Just how do you think you'll take care of yourself and get to work?"

"Angie was in early this morning and she has the next three days off," Tim replied. "She says she'll check in on me and drive me around. I'm sure someone at Pioneer will pick me up for work next week. I don't think I need to go home." When he had finished, he paused and asked, "So what do you think, Mom?"

Sara looked at Tim, then at Carol. Just as she was about to answer, Angie walked into the room.

"Hi, Mrs. Maas, Carol. Do you think Tim and I can handle the next three days?"

Sara glanced over at Carol again and saw that she was smiling. "I think you two can handle it," she said. "If you need any help, I'm only one hour and a half away." Looking at Tim, Sara added, "Carol and I will go shopping for some quick meals and then come back to take you to your apartment. Oh, by the way, I think Carol may have something to share with you."

Carol was beaming as she announced, "My illustrious brother-in-law, you are going to be an uncle next March."

Tim smiled broadly as he exclaimed, "Really? That's great. Uncle Tim. Sounds good to me. Congratulations."

By 4:00 that afternoon, they had Tim settled back into his apartment. Angie arrived from work just as Sara and Carol were saying their goodbyes.

As they drove away, Sara told Carol, "I think Tim will be fine. Did you see his face light up when Angie walked in? She may just the person to pull Tim out of his depression. The Lord works in mysterious ways, doesn't He?"

Carol answered, "Amen to that, sister—I mean, grandma."

They both laughed. Despite the scary start, it had turned out to be a pleasant outing.

Angie planned on staying at Tim's apartment until he was ready for bed. When he said he wanted to shower, she said, "Sorry, but you can't get your head wet for several days. Do you want me to stay and make sure you can get it covered properly?"

Together, they used an old bowl cover to put over Tim's head. As Angie got the shower ready, Tim stood in the doorway in shorts and an old shirt.

When he wobbled a bit and grabbed the sink, Angie asked, "Are you okay?"

"Just a little dizzy," Tim replied weakly.

"Maybe I ought to stay here tonight," Angie suggested. "I could sleep on the sofa." Before Tim could respond, she added, "Remember, I'm off tomorrow. I brought pajamas and a change of clothes. It looks like you'll need some help getting your pajamas on after your shower. Where are they?"

"I just have a t-shirt and sleeping shorts," Tim replied. "They're in the closet, hanging on the door."

Angie disappeared into the bedroom and came out with Tim's sleeping clothes, then led him to the bathroom. She pulled his shorts down before he sat on the toilet stool and helped him with his t-shirt, leaving him sitting in just his undershorts.

"Okay, stand up!" Angie said matter-of-factly.

He looked at her for a moment, then stood so she could strip off his boxers.

"Listen, I've seen dozens of naked men in the last two years, but I must say, you're the tallest one." Angie said with a laugh. "Now get in the shower."

When Tim was finished, Angie handed him a towel and went back out to the living room. When Tim emerged, she held up his shorts and motioned for him to drop the towel.

When he resisted, she shook her head and said, "Okay, you hold the towel while I pull your shorts up for you."

When the pajama shorts were in place, she grabbed the towel and threw it across the room. Then she said she was going out to her car for her clothes. As Tim made his way to the sofa, he smiled, realizing Angie was always a step ahead of him. She never seemed to stand still. She was always in motion and always trying to do things the most efficient way.

When Angie came back in, her sleeveless blouse was already

unbuttoned and she was holding it together with her left hand. By the time she reached the bathroom door, her top was already half off. It was a perfect example of what Tim had just been thinking.

A few minutes later, she emerged from the bathroom wearing a nightgown which barely covered her knees. She could tell by the look on Tim's face he was surprised. She went to him and bent over just enough to show him some cleavage. She turned around, flipped up her gown, and mooned him.

"You see, Tim?" she said with a smile when she turned back around. "Christian women aren't totally stuffy. We like to have a little fun, too. In fact, my mom told me it's bad for your health to go to bed in your underwear. I'm sure she never did, and I won't either. I really should wear pajamas because I can't find nightgowns long enough to cover me completely. You don't' mind though; do you? "

Tim shook his head no. He enjoyed viewing this long-legged blonde in a short gown. What man wouldn't?

The sofa could be turned into a bed, and after they found some sheets and a blanket for Angie, they each fell asleep in their own beds.

Early the next morning Tim heard Angie in the kitchen. He found her there, still in her nightgown, setting the table for breakfast. The morning sun shone through the window—and through Angie's nightgown—and Tim liked what saw.

"Going to be a warm one today," Angie said, smiling warmly. "I decided not to get dressed until later. I hope you don't mind."

"Not at all, you look fine to me," Tim said with a grin.

Angie teased Tim a bit by pulling her nightgown close around her bottom before she sat down. "Do you think you can dress yourself?" she asked.

"Yeah, I think so," Tim replied. "Thanks for staying over. It was nice to have you here."

Angie stayed the entire day, cleaning the kitchen, the bathroom, and the refrigerator. That night she returned to her little house in the town of Agency, just east of Ottumwa.

On Sunday, she asked Tim if he'd go to church with her. He'd have to sit with some of her friends because she was the church organist. Tim gladly accepted her invitation.

When Monday morning arrived, Tim's boss picked him up for work. He got a ride home with a co-worker and he was pleasantly surprised to find Angie there, making supper.

On Wednesday, Dr. Hansen said it was okay for Tim to drive again. He added that Tim was a lucky man, because the accident could have been much worse.

Angie and Tim saw each other often during the next month. One day they went to Oskaloosa so Tim could meet her parents. They remembered Tim from church camp and kidded him about how much shorter he was then.

August 15th was to be Tim's last day at Pioneer for the summer. He wanted a week free at home before he returned to school. On his last night, Angie had him over to her house for supper. As he helped her do the dishes, she looked out the window above the sink and sighed deeply.

"What's the matter, Angie?" Tim asked.

She was silent for a moment, and when she finally spoke, her voice cracked. "Tim, I don't know how to say this, but I'm really going to miss you. I've had such a wonderful time this summer. I know a little about how you felt when you lost your girl friend. I felt empty when I got divorced. It just seems like we've known each other forever." She paused, then said, "I guess what I'm trying to say is that I'd like our relationship to continue. I'm hoping you feel the same."

There was a long silence. Angie hadn't looked at Tim during her speech and she was afraid to turn around, for fear he wouldn't be there if she did. Then she felt his hand on her waist. As she turned, Tim lifted her into the air and kissed her. He hugged her tightly and sat her down on the counter.

They held the embrace for a long time, and then Tim said, "I want it to continue, too. I was afraid maybe you weren't ready yet, and I didn't want to push you."

"Oh, my sweet Tim," Angie said. "You can't imagine how happy I am to hear you say that." Then she smiled and added, "You know, either you squeezed the pee out of me or I'm sitting on the dishrag."

With a laugh, Tim let go and Angie slid off the counter. The back of her shorts was soaking wet. The dishrag was stuck to them.

"I guess I'd better change these before you go," she said, turning toward her bedroom.

In typical Angie fashion, she had her shorts almost to her knees even before she reached the bedroom. When she returned, she shook her head and said, "I guess I should be a little more careful. I forgot I wasn't alone."

Tim smiled and said, "You know, my dad once told me he could still picture the color of my mom's underwear the first time he saw them. Yours were pink, and they said *Tuesday* on them. There was a small hole on the right side. I'll never forget them."

As Angie's cheeks turned red, Tim added, "But to change the subject, my parents and Ed and Carol are going to my Uncle Tom and Aunt Kristie's in Pella on Labor Day. How about you go to your folks' place in Oskaloosa and I pick up you up there for the weekend?"

Angie leapt into his arms, saying, "Most definitely! I'll take some vacation days!"

* * *

The next time Tim and Angie met was in Pella, where Angie met the rest of the family. They also spent Thanksgiving, Christmas, and New Year's Eve together. On Valentine's Day, Tim asked her to marry him, and she accepted. The reunion was complete.

Tim was scheduled to graduate in May and already had a job with Pioneer Hybrid International. He'd be working in Johnston, Iowa, at Pioneer headquarters. Since he'd be very busy early on, he and Angie decided to wait until August to be married.

During the July 4th holiday, Tim went home and Angie visited him on the farm. It was late morning and Sara and Paul had gone to Waterloo to see Aunt Sue. Ed and Carol were picnicking with friends and Jenny was also gone.

Tim asked Angie to wait on the front porch while he finished unloading the side dressing fertilizer applicator. She was sitting on the swing when she heard him call, "Angie, I need help!"

"Where are you?" she shouted, jumping out of the swing.

"Over by the shop, I'm pinned under the applicator!"

When she reached him, she saw his leg caught under the tongue of the fertilizer rig and he was sitting in a pool of fertilizer, trying to reach the shut-off valve.

"Angie, turn that valve off—quick!" he said urgently as he pointed to the valve lever. After she had shut the valve, he said, "Now go in the shop, and behind the door you'll find a tall jack. It has holes punched along its shaft. Get it and come back—and hurry. This fertilizer is burning my skin."

Angie rushed into shop, found the jack, and hurried back to Tim.

In the process, she got grease and dirt on her clean shorts and top. Tim instructed her on how to set up the jack and pump the handle. Slowly the tongue lifted and he was finally able to pull his leg free.

Angie tried to help him to his feet, but the slick liquid caused her to slip and fall. Now she was also covered with fertilizer. The second time they were successful in standing. Leaning heavily on Angie, Tim hobbled across the farmyard and into the house. Angie stood in front of him so he could lean on her as he went down the stairs to the basement shower.

As Tim sat on a chair, he said, "I've got to get these clothes off fast. The last time something like this happened, I got a bad burn and a rash."

Angie pulled off his shoes and socks, then unbuckled his jeans and stripped them off, followed by his t-shirt. She went into the shower stall and turned on the faucets.

When she turned back, she found him standing naked, but only for a moment. As he rushed past her and got under the shower, he said, "Sorry if I surprised you, but this stuff burns like fire." Before Angie could reply, he added, "You'd better take a shower, too. This stuff is really caustic."

Angie stepped out of the laundry room to wait, but a moment later, she heard him call again. "Angie, I can't reach the soap. It's outside the stall."

"Do you need me to wash your back?" Angie asked.

"Yes, please," Tim said. "I can't reach it, and I need to remove all the fertilizer. The last time this happened, Mom helped me; however, I was only ten. "

Without hesitation, Angie stripped to her underwear and stepped into the stall. She could feel her own arms and legs beginning to sting from the fertilizer, so she knew it was important to get Tim's back washed thoroughly. Tim turned his back and she immediately went to work.

Finally, she said, "I think you're good to go. If you step out, I'll finish washing myself."

Tim complied, and when Angie had finished her shower, he handed her a towel over the shower door. She wrapped herself up and they headed upstairs, but Tim needed help because his leg was still very tender. As they walked, Angie had to readjust her towel several times.

She knew Tim was actually hoping it might fall off. It was a good thing Sara believed in large towels. Just as she was walking into Jenny's room, she let the towel fall—but all Tim saw was her bare behind.

As she shut the door, Angie said, "Sorry, but you'll have to wait until we're married to get the whole picture."

Tim smiled. He could hardly wait.

The wedding was held in early August, after detasseling. It was a small affair, with just Angie's family and the Maases. The Beamers also brought Mrs. Becker. Angie's sister, Beth, was maid of honor and her friend Shelia from work was her bridesmaid. Ed was the best man and Kent Paustian was the groomsman.

Since it was Angie's second marriage, she didn't think it proper to wear a white gown, so she wore a light blue cocktail dress. Tim wore his best suit. The reception was held in the church fellowship hall. Ed and Beth made toasts and after the traditional garter and bouquet tosses were done, Tim and Angie visited every table to thank everyone for coming.

At 7:00, Tim was ready to leave, so he scooped Angie up and carried her out to the car. As everyone laughed and applauded, Angie waved goodbye.

Just outside Oskaloosa, Tim stopped, took off his jacket, and replaced his shoes with a pair of loafers. As they continued down the road, Angie removed his tie and unbuttoned the top several buttons of his shirt.

"Where are we going, my new husband?" she asked.

"A special place. You'll find out soon enough," he said evasively.

Between Sigourney and Washington is a long straight, stretch of highway, Angie asked, "Do you mind if I take off my pantyhose? They're awful hot."

"No," Tim replied, "Do you think you can get them off?"

Angie unhooked her seatbelt, pulled her skirt up as high as she could, then began tugging and squirming until she finally got the pantyhose down to her ankles. She kicked off her high heels and threw everything into the backseat, then pulled her skirt down to just above her knees.

"Boy, this feels better," she said, "but you'd better keep your eyes on the road, partner."

He smiled and shot back, "How can I when you're stripping in the seat next to me?"

"This is just a preview, my friend," she teased. Then she added, "I think I'll take a little nap. It's been a long day. Is that okay?"

"That's fine," Tim replied, "but pull your dress down a bit. You're creating a distraction."

Angie smiled, did as Tim requested, and was asleep before they made it to Ainsworth. She even snored a little. Outside of Muscatine, he turned onto County Road X54, and just as they were turning off the blacktop, Angie woke up.

"Where are we? Hey! We're almost to your farm!'" she said, answering her own question. "You're taking me to the dune, aren't you? We're going to spend our wedding night in a bean field, just like your folks, right? I love it! This is going to be fun."

Tim stopped by the shop and picked up some blankets and a camping lantern he had stashed in a cupboard. Then he and Angie loaded the go-getter and headed for the dune. When they arrived, Angie jumped out and raced barefoot to the top of the dune, holding her dress up high as she waded through the tall grass.

When she stopped, she turned to Tim and said happily, "Isn't this beautiful? I'm so glad you brought me here!" She twirled around, her arms outstretched, saying, "Look at me, world. I'm Mrs. Tim Maas! I married the most wonderful guy in the world."

As Tim approached with the blankets and lantern, Angie turned toward him. When he had set everything down, she threw her arms around his neck and kissed him.

"This is the greatest day of my life," she whispered. "Did you see all those children the Beamers have? I want that many. I want five kids—two boys and three girls."

Tim said nothing as he basked in the glow of her excitement. He tried to slip the sleeves of her dress off her shoulders, but they were too tight, so he turned Angie around and tried to unzip her dress. The zipper was balky in his nervous fingers, but he slowly managed to pull the zipper to her waist. He decided while he was back there, he'd also unhook her bra.

She giggled, then turned back to face him. Ever so slowly, he slid the sleeves down, and the dress followed. She gazed into his eyes as he pushed the skirt down beyond her waist. Once it was all the way down, she stepped out of it and stood before her new husband completely naked.

Tim took a step back to get a better look at her body, and Angie struck a pose for him, cocking one leg to the side and placing her hand behind her head. "Well, do you like what you see?" she asked.

"Oh, very much so," Tim said, then he added in surprise, "Didn't you wear any underwear today?"

"Yeah, but I ditched them when I took off my pantyhose," she confessed playfully.

Tim laughed. That was so typical of Angie.

He started to take his shirt off, but Angie stopped him, saying, "Wait a minute! I get to do that, but first I've got to pee. Where do you do that out here?"

Without a word, Tim reached behind the bench, grabbed some tissues, and pointed to the bean field. Giggling, Angie tip-toed through the switchgrass, which was short at the top of the dune; then the switch grass became waist high as she neared the bean field.

Tim watched her disappear into the beans, and watched again as she made her way back up the dune. As she came closer, the moonlight highlighted her breasts, her tummy, her pubic hair, and the rest of her lovely body. He let her undress him and they embraced for a long moment until she pulled him down on the blanket and they made love for the first time.

Tim pulled a large quilt over them and they fell asleep. Sometime in the early morning, Angie woke up, and tickled Tim awake. They made love again, even more passionately than the first time. Although it was early, the air was warm. Angie said, "I'm roasting. Let's go swimming, honey." Before Tim could remind her they hadn't brought bathing suits, she added, "And who needs a bathing suit? We're all alone, so let's go skinny-dipping. I've always wanted to do that."

They rolled up the blanket and climbed into the go-getter with nothing on. The seats were damp, but the breeze felt good as they drove. When they arrived, they ran hand-in-hand into the water, gasping as the cold water washed over their naked bodies. They only swam for a few minutes, then headed back toward the house, still dripping wet.

As they passed through the pasture gate and headed down the lane, Tim stopped the go-getter and turned off the lights. They had forgotten to latch the gate and the heifers from the lot were meandering down the lane ahead of them. Tim put his finger to his lips as if to tell

Angie not to say anything. With the go-getter lights off, they made their way past the grazing cattle. Because it was still dark, the heifers didn't realize the tall corn stalks weren't a fence.

Once they were on the other side of the herd, Tim parked the go-getter across the lane and said quietly, "If we don't scare them, maybe they'll go back to the pasture. We'll just walk up and shoo them back."

"But I don't have any shoes on," Angie said.

"You don't need them," Tim replied. "The lane is plain dirt, no rocks. Just watch for fresh cow pies."

They quietly moved toward the cows, and to their relief, the cattle began moving back toward the open gate. Everything went well until two of the heifers went behind the gate and found themselves trapped.

Tim said, "Angie, you stay right there. I'll go into the cornfield and get ahead of the cows. Then I'll then try to chase them out from behind the gate. As soon as I say okay, you turn on the lantern and put it in the middle of the lane. Then stand behind the light, wave your arms, and start hollering."

Angie nodded as Tim disappeared into the corn. She heard him walking through the stalks, and heard him say, "Okay!"

As the heifers started to move out from behind the gate, Angie set the lantern down and turned it on. Immediately, the cows started toward the light.

Tim shouted, "Wave your arms and yell! Make yourself as big as possible!"

Taking off Tim's shirt, which she had been wearing, Angie flapped it in the air and shouted, "Hey! Hey, cows!"

The heifers looked at the naked lady waving a white shirt and stopped in their tracks. Then they turned and high-tailed it back to the pasture. As Tim ran over and slammed the gate shut, he was laughing so hard he could barely latch the chain.

"What made you do that?" he asked, shaking his head and wiping his eyes.

"Well, I thought maybe a naked lady would be scarier than just a white shirt."

They laughed all the way back to the go-getter, but their laughter subsided quickly when they rounded the corner to the farmyard and saw Tim's parents' car sitting by the gate.

"Oh, my gosh!" Tim said. "I forgot about Mom and Dad being here."

"Well, I can't go in wearing nothing but your shirt," Angie said.

"We'll have to grab your bag and sneak into the basement," Tim said. "We can take a shower and then sneak up to my room. Mom probably already knows we're not in there because I left the door open."

They made it to the basement and took a shower together. Angie took out a conservative long nightie. Tim dug out some shorts and a shirt. They were trying to be quiet, but it was difficult because Angie couldn't stop giggling. It had all turned out to be quite an adventure.

As they crept up the stairs, they heard footsteps upstairs in the kitchen. Then Sara called softly from the landing, "Is that you, Tim?"

"Yes, Mom, we'll be right up."

As they sat at the kitchen table, Sara smiled and said, "Big night last night, huh?"

"Oh, Mrs. Maas, we had a wonderful night!" Angie said happily.

Sara smiled broadly and said, "Please call me either Sara or Mom—I don't care which. After all, you're a Maas now and part of our family."

"Okay, uh, Sara," Angie said. "Tim surprised me by taking me to the dune, and we slept under the stars. Did you ever do that?"

Sara smiled again, remembering her first night with Paul. "Yes, I've done that. In fact, your father-in-law and I did the same thing, and it was wonderful. Tell me more."

Tim looked slightly embarrassed as Angie began to fill in the details. "It was so warm, we didn't need clothes. I had to go to the bathroom, so Tim found some Kleenex and pointed toward the bean field. I'd never gone potty in a field before. Early in the morning, we made love again, and I got so warm we went swimming—and we didn't wear any clothes!"

Sara nodded her understanding as she delighted in how happy her new daughter-in-law was. She knew Angie was going to be a fun addition to the family.

"Now here is the funniest part," Angie said, continuing her story. "When we came back from the pond, the cows were out, and we got them all back in except for two. Tim went into the cornfield and turned them around, and then I stopped them and chased them into the pasture."

Smiling slyly, Tim said, "Angie, honey, tell Mom just how you did it. I think she'll get a kick out of it."

"Do you think I should?"

"I'm sure Mom will understand."

'Well, Sara, as the heifers came toward me, I got a little scared, so I took off Tim's shirt and started waving it at them—and waving that shirt did the trick."

As Sara laughed, Tim added, "But you're still not telling it all, babe. Mom, she wasn't wearing anything under my shirt. She was stark naked. It was quite a sight!"

Sara laughed even louder and hugged Angie, saying, "Welcome to the crazy Maas family. You're not the first woman to chase cattle in your nightgown or your bare skin. I've done it a couple of times myself. Country life can create some crazy situations. If you get this family started telling stories, you're going to find some of them can be a bit embarrassing."

As Tim and Angie had breakfast, Paul came in and sat at the table with a smirk on his face. He had been listening in on the conversation from the den, and it reminded him of his first night with Sara.

"I think Angie and I will stay here today before we head out on our honeymoon," Tim said. "We can get a good start for the Black Hills tomorrow. Right now, I could use a nap."

Angie added, "And for the first time, I'll get to sleep with you and not in Jen's room. She snores, you know."

Everybody laughed. Sara and Paul had gotten used to being around quiet, reserved Carol, but they both realized Angie was going to add more spice to their lives.

Chapter Twenty-Four
Jen Meets Josh

Jenny followed her brothers to Iowa State. She enrolled in Agriculture Education and lived in Linden Hall. She was still wary of young men and didn't want to get serious with anyone.

One Saturday afternoon in February, the Cyclones were playing basketball against a major rival, Kansas State, at Hilton Coliseum in Ames. The place was packed and Jenny and her roomie, Tanya, were sitting in the top section. Behind them sat three young men they gauged to be veterinary students by their conversation.

The game was close for the first few minutes, then Iowa State fell behind. The coach must have chewed some butt at halftime, because the Cyclones rallied in the second half; and with three minutes left, they took the lead. After a great play, the guys behind Jenny and Tanya jumped up. Hollering and cheering, one of them forgot he had a bag of popcorn in his lap and it showered down on the girls. He apologized and began to brush the popcorn out of Jenny's hair and off her back. When Jenny turned to say something to him, she stopped. He was tall, like her brothers, and had a cute smile.

Instead of scolding him, she said, "Don't worry about the popcorn. I know it was an accident. Oh, and by the way, I'm Jenny."

"I'm Josh—Josh Wulf. I'm a vet student," he said self-consciously.

"I'm in Ag Ed." Jenny added as the crowd roared again. State was now ahead by two points with only ten seconds left. K-State drove for the basket and put up a three-point shot. Everyone held their breath as the shot clanged off the rim and sailed up over the backboard. The Cyclones had come back to win! As everyone celebrated, Josh hugged Jenny and kissed her cheek. She kissed him back.

"How's about you girls coming with us to Pizza Hut for supper?" Josh asked. "We'd go somewhere else, but they'll all be crowded."

Tanya looked at Jenny, who nodded, then said, "Sure, why not? Let's celebrate."

Jenny and Josh hit it off immediately, and by the end of the evening, Jenny knew all about Joshua Wulf. He asked her for a date to the next women's basketball game, then to a movie, then on an ice skating date.

When spring came, it was open house time at Iowa State, called VEISHEA, a busy time on the campus with parades and displays. Josh took Jenny to Stars Over VEISHEA, the huge student presentation on stage at the auditorium. The flowers and budding trees on the campus were conductive to romance. An Iowa State tradition held that kissing a girl under the Campanile sealed a couple's devotion to each other, and many couples get engaged there. Sometimes it got so crowded you had to hang on to your girl tightly or you just might end up kissing the wrong one!

Josh was from Osceola, where his dad, Fred, was a prominent businessman. His mother, Cora, worked at the bank. He had three sisters, Lisa, Linda, and Louise. Two of them were married and the third was in the Navy. He had two nephews and two nieces. He liked animals, which was why he was becoming a veterinarian. They had a summer house in Missouri, on the Lake of the Ozarks.

Their relationship grew stronger as the years progressed, but the summers were long. Jenny had her job with the Parks and Recreation board and Josh worked with silo building crews, so they seldom saw each other. They were both grateful for e-mails and cell phones. Jenny would graduate before Josh because vet school took at least six years.

Jenny visited Josh's home several times and found his dad to be a caring person who loved to help people. He had also been mayor of Osceola for two terms. On the other hand, Josh's mother was a neat freak. Everyone had to take off their shoes before entering the house and the grandkids weren't allowed in the formal living room except on Christmas Day.

Jenny never saw Cora in blue jeans or a sweatshirt. She was a sweet person and seemed to be in good shape, although Jenny figured she never mowed the lawn or did any yard work. Josh also visited the Maas farm. He loved talking to Paul about cattle and he loved the relaxed atmosphere of the Maas family.

As fate would have it, Jenny's vo-ag teacher was getting ready to retire the year Jenny graduated, and the Wilton school was happy to replace him with someone who knew the area. The transition went smoothly.

Josh interned at the Eldridge Clinic when he graduated and was hired by the Walcott Clinic. It meant he'd be close to Jenny. One afternoon in early July, Sara and Paul were having lemonade on the front porch. Jenny was off checking her students' progress toward their fair exhibits.

When Josh's pickup pulled into the driveway, Sara called out, "Hi, Josh! We're out on the front porch. Glad to see you. How's about a piece of apple pie? I just baked it. Jenny isn't here right now."

"Sure, Mrs. Maas, thanks," Josh said, climbing the front porch steps.

As Sara disappeared into the house, Josh sat in a rocking chair beside the swing. He and Paul visited about the weather and corn prices until Sara returned with three pieces of apple pie topped with vanilla ice cream.

As Josh ate, he said, "Mr. Maas, I came here today knowing Jenny would be away. I wanted to ask you something."

"Go ahead, Josh, but please call me Paul," Paul said.

"Well, as you know, Jen and I have been going together for some time and I love her very much. I've got a good job at the Walcott Clinic now. I was wondering if it would be alright with you if I asked her to marry me. I promise I'll take good care of her. What do you say?"

Paul looked at Sara, who smiled back at him. Then he said, "Well, Josh, this is a big step. Getting married means living with one woman forever. It's God's plan."

"Yes, sir. I understand that," Josh replied.

Paul held out his hand and they shook hands as Paul said, "We'd like nothing better than to have you for a son-in-law. I'm sure you and Jenny will make a wonderful couple, so if you're asking for our blessing, we're happy to give it. Welcome to the family. When do you plan to pop the question?"

"Thank you," Josh said, sounding relieved. "Next to my parents, I think you two are the greatest. Next week the West Liberty Fair will be over and Jen will have a break before the state fair. I'm hoping she'll find time to go with me to my parents' house at the Lake of the Ozarks. There's a spot on the lake where the sunsets are gorgeous. That's where I plan to ask her."

"I like it," said Sara with a smile. "It sounds like a special place, just like our dune."

"Well, I'd better get going," Josh said. "I'm supposed to be at the Beamer's next. Please don't tell Jenny I was here."

"We won't," said Paul, winking at Sara.

Not more than ten minutes after Josh left, Jenny returned home. As she went into the kitchen, she called, "Hey, Mom, how come there are three pieces missing from the pie instead of two?"

Sara replied, "Your dad liked it so much that he had two pieces." Then, changing the subject, she asked, "How was your day?"

As Jenny came out onto the porch with her own piece of pie, she said, "Busy. One more day at the fair and then I'll have entries to process for the state fair on Monday. By Tuesday, I'll need a break."

"I'm sure you will," Sara said.

"Josh called from work and said he's coming over tonight," Jenny said as she sat in the rocker. "He's taking me to The Eagle's Nest, so I better go get cleaned up. He'll be here at six."

As Jenny finished her pie and stood to go back inside, Sara said, "Dad and I are going to play cards at Petersen's tonight, so we'll be home late."

Jenny was ready at six, but Josh still hadn't arrived. At 6:15, he called to let her know he was at the Beamer's helping with a sick cow and still had another call to make. At 7:30, Josh still hadn't shown up.

Finally, at nearly 8:00, she saw Josh's pickup pull into the driveway. Jenny ran to the gate and found he was still in his veterinary coveralls—and he looked exhausted.

"I'm sorry, Jen," Josh said, "but I've got to take a rain check on our date. Bob Beamer's cow is having trouble calving, and I'm just getting back from the clinic after getting some supplies."

"It's okay, Josh. I understand," Jenny said sympathetically.

Josh left and Jenny returned to the house, where she met her parents, just getting ready to leave. Seeing that Jenny was fighting back tears, Sara asked, "Can I be of any help, honey?"

"I don't know, Mom," Jenny said softly. "This is the third time we've had to change our plans because of a cow. I get all dressed up and then he can't make it. I love him, but maybe I'm not cut out to be a vet's wife. I don't know what to do."

"Jenny, I had my times with your dad. We'd plan something, then a piece of machinery would break down and he'd either be late or not show up at all. I remember one month at harvest time, he couldn't see me for three weeks. At first, I was frustrated, but then I decided if I was really in love with him, I'd go to the farm and help him. It was the best decision I ever made. I got all dirty and we were both exhausted when we were done, but at least we were together. After that, dates just didn't seem so important anymore."

"Do you think I should help Josh?"

"I think you should try it. It might help you make a decision later on."

Jenny smiled through her tears and said, "He said he was at Beamer's. If I'm quick enough, maybe I can change clothes and get over there in time to help somehow."

"Maybe," said Sara, "but be sure to wear boots."

Jenny quickly changed into jeans and an old t-shirt and headed for the Beamer's. She knew the farm so well she went straight to the barn where she knew Josh would be.

When she walked in, she said, "Hi, Josh, can I help? I figured if you couldn't come to me, I'd come to you."

Josh was surprised, but happy. Mr. Beamer greeted Jenny, but he didn't dare let go of the rope harness on the cow's head.

"Okay, Jen, you can go to my truck and bring my big syringe and some tri-sulfa-penicillium. I'll also need another plastic sleeve."

Jenny went to the truck and found what Josh had asked for. When she returned, Josh told her to pull the cow's tail up over its back, this would pinch a nerve and make the cow unable to move her legs. Jenny pulled up with all her might as Josh stuck his arm inside the cow.

"I need some twine!" Josh said a few moments later.

"I'll get it!" yelled Sam, who had come to the barn when he saw Jenny's car pull into the driveway.

Sam ran to the end of the alley and found some clean baler twine, and as he came back, Josh said, "Sam, I need you to take over for Jenny. Jenny, go out to the truck and get my calf puller. It's behind the seat."

By the time Jenny returned, Josh had the calf's feet secured with the twine. He adjusted the puller and cable, then gently guided the calf out while Jenny cranked the calf puller. The cow let out a bellow, then a moan as the calf passed through the birth canal and flopped out onto the ground.

Josh cleared the mucous from the calf's nose. Jenny handed Josh a syringe filled with antibiotics. Josh gave the calf an injection and helped it to its feet. Before Bob released the cow, Josh inserted some antibiotic capsules into her uterus. Bob loosened the rope and the cow immediately turned and began licking her new baby.

As everyone stood admiring their work, Josh said, "I think she'll be fine, Bob. I'll check back tomorrow."

Jenny and Josh returned to the truck, and by the time they had gotten cleaned up, the whole Beamer family had joined them. Although Jenny's jeans and t-shirt were a mess, everyone hugged her and asked how she was doing.

She winked at Josh and said, "I'm doing fine, now that I've become a vet's helper."

Josh added, "We've got to get her into some official coveralls, though."

Just then, Josh's radio crackled and his associate, Grant, said, "Josh, I finished at Henry's early and I'm on my way to the Plett's. You'd better take care of that good-looking gal of yours."

Everyone laughed as Josh picked up the microphone and said, "Thanks, Grant, but Jenny's right here. She just helped me pull a calf at Beamers. We'll have to get her some coveralls. I kinda like having a pretty assistant working with me."

"10-4," said Grant with a laugh. "I'll see you in the morning."

Josh followed Jenny home, where she said, "Why don't you stay here tonight? I'll see what's in the frig for supper—after I take a shower. You can wear some of Tim's clothes."

Jenny hurried to the basement to clean up, then wrapped herself in a towel and headed upstairs, where she met Josh at the top of the stairs. He enjoyed seeing his girl dressed only in a towel.

"You'll find a towel on the dryer. I'll send some shorts down the clothes chute," Jenny said as she whisked by him.

Jenny was fixing some eggs when Josh entered the kitchen. She was wearing her nightgown and slippers.

"No sense dressing at this hour," she said matter-of-factly.

He sat on the stool and watched as his soon-to-be-fiancée cooked. When she opened the refrigerator door, the light shone through her gown, leaving little to the imagination.

As they ate, Jenny knew her mom had been right. She was much happier working with Josh than waiting for him. Jenny rinsed the dishes and put them in the dishwasher. She dropped a fork. As Josh bent down to pick it up, Jenny couldn't resist the opportunity to give him a squirt from the sink. He jumped at the cold water, then grabbed the faucet hose and gave her a shot. Soon they were both soaked. Jenny giggled, but not Josh. Jenny's gown was wet and clung to her body like nearly transparent wet tissue paper. Jenny stopped giggling when she realized what Josh was looking at.

Then she pulled the fabric away from her body, held it out, and said, "Well, now. I guess I'd better go change."

As she turned to leave, Josh caught her and pulled her close, saying, "First we've got a floor to mop up. Where's the mop?"

"In the hall closet. I'll be right back," she answered.

"Hey, are there more shorts for me? I'm wet, too, you know."

"I'll bring something of Tim's down for you."

Jenny didn't realize Josh was watching as she left, but he clearly saw her slip her nightie over her head before she hit the stairs. Smiling broadly, he found the mop and was almost finished with the floor by the time she returned.

"I see you've got it all done," Jenny said. "Sorry, but I couldn't find my summer PJs, so I had to wear this old nightie. I hope it isn't too risqué. Here's some of Tim's PJs for you."

Josh only smiled again because the nightie was thin and lacy and the slits on the side showed she wasn't wearing underpants, but Jenny didn't seem to mind. She accidentally mooned him several times as they worked, but Josh said nothing.

He did tell Jenny they should wash his clothes before morning, since he wasn't going home. They went down to the laundry room and put his dirty clothes in the washer. It would be about a half hour before they could be put into the dryer.

It was too chilly outside to sit on the porch, so they went into the den where Jenny snuggled close to Josh's body. After Jenny had come to help him at the Beamer's, Josh wondered if he could wait as long as he had planned to get married. They were almost asleep on the sofa when the washer alarm went off.

Half asleep, Jenny stumbled over a footstool, sending her nightie up over her back, exposing her behind. As she quickly pulled it down, Josh laughed, then followed her to the laundry room and watched as she put his clothes into the dryer, seemingly oblivious to his presence. He got several nice views of her fanny as she worked.

As they started to head upstairs, Jenny said, "You go first. You've seen enough of my behind for one day."

Before going up to bed, she turned on the back porch light and the microwave light over the stove for her parents when they returned. Then she shut off the kitchen light and hall light.

At the top of the stairs, Jenny asked, "May I ride with you tomorrow? I have a day off."

Josh smiled and replied, "Sure, but we have to be in Walcott by eight."

They held each other in the dark hallway and ran their hands over each other's bodies. Jenny easily slipped Tim's big shorts down Josh's hips and pulled him close.

Josh whispered, "What would happen if I untied these little bows on your shoulders?"

"Maybe you should untie them and find out," she whispered back.

When he untied one side, nothing happened, but when he untied the other, the nightgown fell to the floor. They stood skin-to-skin caressing each other until Jenny began to pull Josh toward her room. They were just sitting on the edge of her bed when they saw headlights flashing through the window.

"Damn! My folks are home," Jenny said. "I guess we'll have to put this off till later. Sorry, honey. We'd better get our clothes from the hall. I'll see you in the morning."

"Okay," he said, "but first, one more kiss."

By the time Sara and Paul reached the top of the stairs, the lovers were in bed, pretending to be asleep. Sara found a note on her pillow that read:

"I took your advice and had a wonderful time. Josh stayed overnight. Needs breakfast at 6:30. Going to ride with him tomorrow. Love you, Jenny."

Sara smiled. She knew Jenny was going to be fine.

Jenny rode with Josh the next day. He dropped her off at home at about seven. There wasn't room in the crowded truck to get a goodnight kiss, so Jenny walked around to Josh's side and kissed him through the open window.

"Say, would you like to go to the lake next Wednesday?" he asked.

"Sure, I need a break before the state fair."

"We'd go down Wednesday and stay till Sunday."

"Fine, I'll be ready."

The next three days seemed to drag, but on Wednesday morning, Josh picked up Jenny at eight. When they arrived at the lake house at 2:00 that afternoon, Cora came out to greet them in her usual way— immaculately dressed and not one strand of hair out of place.

"Welcome, Jenny," Cora said sweetly. "Josh, put her bags in the girls' room. She can sleep with Megan and Sophie."

"But, Mom, why can't she sleep in the guest bedroom?" Josh asked.

"Lisa and Lyle are coming for a few days and they'll need the guest room," Cora explained. Then she turned to Jenny and asked, "You don't mind sleeping with the younger girls, do you. Jenny?"

"Not at all, Mrs. Wulf," Jenny replied. "I spent an entire summer babysitting and sleeping with a couple of small girls, so it won't bother me at all. How old are they?"

"Ten and thirteen."

"We'll get along just fine. Don't worry."

Josh wasn't happy about the sleeping arrangements, but he let it go. When Lisa and Lyle arrived with their two girls, the girls were excited about the prospect of sleeping with Josh's girlfriend. Jenny's experience with young girls paid off, and they became instant friends.

The first day, the whole family went boating on the lake. The second day, Jenny offered to take Megan and Sophie to a water park in the afternoon. Josh began to get nervous. Would he run out of time before he could ask Jenny to marry him?

Friday morning, after a short swim in the lake, while Jenny, Cora, and the girls played Parcheesi, Josh and Lisa sat on the deck. Taking a deep breath, Josh asked, "I don't want to sound unkind, but when are you and Lyle leaving?"

"Probably sometime today. Lyle has to get back for Saturday

church services and also for Sunday. You know the life of a minister—no weekends. Why?" Lisa replied.

Speaking softly, Josh said, "Don't tell anyone, but I want to ask Jenny to marry me out at the cove, so I need some time to get her alone."

"Why, Josh, my little brother!" Lisa exclaimed, and lowered her voice to barely above a whisper. "So you're going to pop the question. Praise the Lord! We were wondering when this would happen. She's a real catch in my book. Congratulations! Is it okay if I tell Mom? She can keep a secret."

Josh agreed, but the rest of the day seemed to drag. Finally, Lisa and her family said their goodbyes and headed for home.

After they had gone, Josh said, as casually as he could, "Well, I think Jenny and I will take the boat out to the cove."

"Great! We'll go with you," said his dad.

As Josh looked shocked, Cora came to his rescue, saying, "No, Fred. We have dishes and some picking up to do. I think you and I should stay here."

When Josh and Jenny reached the cove, Josh turned the boat toward the west, then rummaged around in a side compartment and found a blanket. "Let's sit on the front deck and watch the sun go down," he suggested.

As they settled down onto the blanket and Jenny leaned back on the windshield, Jenny looked over and saw Josh wearing a strange expression. He knelt beside her and said, "Jennifer Julia Maas, I love you with all my heart and soul. Will you marry me?"

Josh opened a small box, which revealed a diamond ring. She held out her hand and as Josh slipped it on her finger, she said, "Oh, yes! I'll be glad to marry you."

Then she pulled him to her and kissed him. Josh joined her on the blanket and they held each other tenderly as they watched the sun set. As they continued to embrace, they failed to realize how close they were to the edge of the bow. A big pontoon boat went by, and the wake began to rock the boat violently. Jenny lost her balance and although Josh reached for her, she fell into the water with a shriek. Josh jumped in after her.

When they surfaced, they looked at each other and began to laugh. They swam around to the back of the boat, where Josh hoisted himself up and threw a rope ladder out for Jenny. They laughed until their sides hurt. After the sun was down, it began to get chilly.

"We'd better head for home," said Josh.

Shivering, Jenny asked, "Are there some more blankets?"

"I'm sure I can find something," Josh answered.

He dug through the side compartments and found a sweatshirt, a t-shirt, and some swim trunks.

"Here, you put on this sweatshirt and I'll get the blanket from the front. I can wear these old trunks."

When he returned, Jenny had removed all her wet clothes except her underpants. She was about to pull on the sweatshirt when she saw Josh staring at her. She instinctively covered her chest with her arms, but a moment later, she dropped her arms and stood before him naked to the waist as if to say, "Here I am. I'm yours, body and soul."

Josh continued to stare, drinking in her beauty. It was everything he had ever imagined. He held out his arms and she fell into his embrace.

They kissed briefly. She backed away, saying, "You're cold, too. Get some dry clothes on, quick."

She put on the sweatshirt and wrapped the blanket around her legs while Josh stripped off his shirt, then his shorts. He was down to his jockey shorts and Jenny wondered what he would do next. When he turned and told her to cover her eyes, she did—almost—as he stripped off his underwear and started to slip into the swim trunks.

As he slid his second foot into the trunks, his toe got caught in the lining and he stumbled forward, hitting his head on the side of the boat.

Jenny screamed, "Josh, are you all right?"

Stunned by the fall, he didn't answer for a moment. Jenny rushed to his side. She could see he had cut the side of his head, and it was bleeding profusely. She grabbed the t-shirt and pressed it against his head as he lay on the deck moaning.

He whispered, "Jenny, we've got to get back. Call my dad on the cell phone."

"Okay. I think I can drive the boat," Jenny said. "We'll call him when we get closer, okay. Right now we need to get you back as soon as possible. Let's get your trunks on first."

Once the swim trunks were in place, Jenny covered Josh with the blanket, then slipped into the captain's chair and switched on the dash lights. Following the instructions on the dash, she started the motor, turned on the running lights, and pushed the throttle forward. The motor roared to life and they headed for the dock.

As they got closer to shore, she called Fred's cell phone. "Mr. Wulf, this is Jenny. Josh fell and hurt his head. We're about a half mile from the dock, but I don't know if I can bring the boat in alone. Can you meet us at the dock?"

"Yes," Fred said. "Do we need an ambulance?"

"It wouldn't hurt. He's cut pretty bad right above his eye. Okay, I can see the dock now."

"I'll be there. Cora will call 911. Stay calm. You can do this."

As Jenny throttled back, the boat slowed almost to a stop. She was relieved to see Fred on the dock, waving his arms. He called her cell phone and talked her in. While he and a neighbor grabbed the ties and secured the craft, an ambulance pulled up to the dock. The EMTs loaded Josh into the ambulance and headed for Osage Beach, followed by Fred.

As the sound of the siren died away, Cora hugged Jenny and said, "My land, girl, you're almost naked. Let's get you into the house before you catch your death of cold."

With Cora's arm around Jenny, they walked around the house and finally came to an enclosed deck. The deck was just outside the master bedroom. Two sides were enclosed by junipers and the third by a lattice fence. The house itself was the fourth wall. "Jenny," Cora said, "Wait here for a second. I'll go in and get a washcloth. I don't want you marking up my carpet with your dirty feet." Cora disappeared and soon returned. "Take those filthy clothes off out here and put them in this garbage bag."

Jenny protested, "Undress out here? On the deck? Outside?"

"No one can see you," Cora said. "I make Fred undress out here all the time. Now hurry and get out of those clothes. I'll get you some towels and turn the shower on."

Jenny didn't have much choice, so she waited shivering in the cool night air until Cora returned, saying, "Come, come, girl. We mustn't waste water."

Jenny followed Cora into the master bathroom, where Cora waited for her to finish, watching intently. Jenny had her back toward Cora most of the time, and Cora noticed the small scars on Jenny's back.

"May I ask where you got those scars, my dear?" Cora asked.

"It a long story, but I was attacked by a young man one time and he scraped my back against an oak tree. The scars have always been a reminder to be careful with men, and I always have—until I met Josh. He's so kind and considerate, and he treats me like a queen," Jenny explained. Then she added, "Oh, that reminds me. Before all this happened, Josh asked me to marry him at the cove!"

Cora didn't look surprised as she examined the ring Jenny proudly displayed above the shower wall.

"Yes, I know," Cora said without much enthusiasm. "Lisa told me yesterday. Welcome to the family, Jenny. We all love you."

Jenny thought, "Well, at least I have her approval."

As Jenny stepped out of the shower, Cora handed her a soft robe to wrap in as she went back to her room. Jenny put on her own nightgown and robe before returning to the family room, where Cora was waiting.

"Tell me, Jenny," Cora asked. "How come you were wearing only a sweatshirt and panties? Maybe I shouldn't pry, but I'm curious."

Jenny explained how she had fallen into the lake and Josh had jumped in to save her, although she left out a few details about what had happened just before Josh had gotten hurt.

"You were a brave girl, Jenny. I certainly would have panicked," Cora said, and the subject was dropped.

In about an hour, Fred and Josh returned. Josh had thirteen stitches above his eye, which was swelling shut, and twelve more stitches in his ear. He also had a cracked collar bone and a separated shoulder. His left arm was in a sling. He looked as if he'd just returned from a war zone, but he was in surprisingly good spirits. It was 11:00 when everyone decided to go to bed.

Josh said, "Mom, Jenny can sleep in the guest bed now that Lisa's gone."

"No," Cora said sharply. "She stays where she's at. I just changed the bedding in the guest room."

"Then she can have my bed."

"You'll take your own bed. You're going to have a hard enough time sleeping as it is."

"But, Mom—"

"It's okay, Josh," Jenny said. "Your mother's right. You'll sleep better in your own bed."

"Well, before I go to bed, I need a shower. All I've had on for the last three hours is a pair of Dad's trunks. I felt pretty stupid going into the ER wearing nothing but a blanket and swimming trunks," Josh said firmly.

"I'll help you get set up, dear. How are you going to keep your head dry?" Cora asked.

"I'll put a plastic sack over my head," Josh replied. "You just go on to bed."

"Come on, Cora," added Fred. "He's a big boy now and he can take care of himself."

"No, I'm going to help," Cora snapped.

Fred just sighed and left as Josh headed down the hallway, followed by his mother and Jenny. Jenny ducked into the girls' room while Cora went into the bathroom with Josh. He let her help him with his sling, but he stood still as Cora started the water.

Cora turned and said, "Come on, son. Let's get you into the shower."

Josh looked his mother squarely in the eye and said firmly, "You can leave now, Mom. I'm twenty-five years old and I can take care of myself. Now go!"

"Well, I never! I was just trying to help," Cora sputtered. "I guess I know when I'm not wanted."

Cora stormed down the hallway. Jenny lay quietly in her room. When she heard the shower turn off, she tiptoed to the bathroom door. She cracked the door open and said softly, "May I help you, honey?"

"Yes," Josh said, "I can't find my pajamas. I know Mom brought them in, but with only one eye I can't see them."

"Are you decent?"

"Yes."

"Okay, I'm coming in to help you look."

They looked around the bathroom, but the PJs weren't there. Jenny went across the hall to Josh's room and found them. Apparently, Cora had tossed them into his room on her way down the hall.

When Jenny returned to the bathroom, she asked, "Do you need help putting these on?"

"Yes, especially the top and this sling."

"Do you think you can get the bottoms on?" Jenny asked. "I'll help you get your feet in and pull them up under your towel—and I promise I won't peek."

" But you saw me just hours ago."

" That was an emergency."

"Well, this is sort of the same," Josh teased. "You can close your eyes if you like, but then you'd have to feel your way around."

Josh dropped the towel and Jenny pulled the pants up as fast as she could. She was smiling all the time. After all, she was almost his wife.

When he was finally dressed, Josh thanked Jenny and added, "Oh, and I really like your nightie. Why does it have all those buttons on the front?"

Jenny smiled and replied, "I wore nightgowns when I worked for the Beamers. When I went to college, my roommate wore a short nightgown, so I found this one. It's comfy and it has wide shoulder straps to hold it up. It doesn't dip too much, either. When I went home one weekend, I showed it to my mom, and she just laughed. She said it was a nursing gown for mothers who breast feed. When the baby wants milk, you just flip it open and let it nurse. I was a little embarrassed, but it's easy to put on, so I kept it. Either way, I'm glad you like it."

Jenny then helped Josh to bed and went back to hers. At 1:30, she heard Josh cry, "Jenny, come on! Keep going."

Jenny jumped up and hurried to his bedside. He was reaching out with one hand.

She grabbed it as he said, "Don't look at me!"

Confused, Jenny said softly, "I'm here, honey. What don't you want me to see?"

It was then she realized Josh was talking in his sleep. She held his hand close to her chest until he awoke, looked at her, and asked, "Jenny, what are you doing here?"

"You called me," Jenny said. "I think you were having a bad dream."

Josh said, "I was. We were on the boat and it caught fire. We had to swim to shore and when we got there, I had no clothes on, but you were fully dressed. I was so embarrassed."

Jenny smiled and said, "You almost got it right. Go back to sleep. I'll have my cell phone by my bed if you need me."

Shortly after Jenny drifted off to sleep, her cell phone rang. It was Josh. She hurried to his room, where she found Josh lying in bed with no covers on and his top unbuttoned.

"I'm so hot, Jenny," he said, "and my shoulder aches. Is it time for another pill? Help me take this top off."

Jenny helped him remove his top, then gave him another pain pill and waited for him to calm down. As she was standing by his bed, he reached out and put his hand on her gown, saying groggily, "I like your nightie. It's so soft."

She waited until he was asleep, then bent over and kissed his cheek before leaving to return to her own bed. It was five in the morning and the sky was just beginning to lighten. She decided to go to the bathroom, and just as she was coming back out, she heard Josh moving around in his bedroom. When she peeked in, she saw him sitting on the edge of his bed.

"Going somewhere?" she asked.

"To the bathroom."

"Need some help?"

"This I can do myself."

She watched him struggle to his feet, but he stumbled. Jenny rushed to his side to steady him. Josh put his arm around her waist and hobbled to the bathroom. As Jenny lifted the lid, he told her again how much he liked her nightgown.

"I think this is where I leave. Hang onto the sink if you have to. I'll be back when I hear the toilet flush," Jenny said as she stepped out of the room.

As she helped him back toward his bedroom, Josh's arm was higher on her body and he playfully fingered the side of her breast all the way back.

"Aren't you getting a little frisky?" she asked.

When Josh was back in bed, Jenny ran her fingers through his hair as he put his hand on her leg. Jenny giggled quietly.

"What's so funny?" he asked.

"Just this. We've been engaged for less than twenty-four hours and we should be all lovey-dovey. Instead, I'm sitting here helping my fiancé take pain pills and go to the bathroom. What a start, huh?"

"I guess you're right. It isn't the most romantic situation."

Jenny continued to play with his hair. She coyly unbuttoned two buttons at the top of her gown. Two at the bottom were already undone. He moved his hand to her midsection and played with a button, but it was difficult working it through the hole with only one hand. He kept at it, and soon he had three buttons undone and his fingers were stroking her smooth tummy.

Jenny never said a word. She'd let him play if it made him feel better. There were only five buttons left of the original twelve to be unbuttoned. Finally, he had them all, and Jenny smiled. He separated the sides and Jenny let the gown fall off her shoulder. Her breasts rose and fell as she breathed. When he touched her nipples, she closed her eyes and sighed. He caressed the skin between her breasts and moved his hand down to her tummy, making circles around her belly button with his finger. He, too, closed his eyes and let his fingers do the talking. Then he reached as far as he could down her leg and ran his hand back and forth on the outside of her leg, as if petting a cat. She stiffened for a moment, then relaxed again and sighed. He slowly moved his fingers back and forth inside her thigh, each time coming closer to her crotch.

She moved her leg sideways, but just as he was about to massage her crotch, she turned, opened her eyes, and said, "I think I'd better get back to bed now."

She stood, but when she turned, Josh got a full frontal view.

"You're definitely the female of the species," he said with a wide smile.

"Well, you're definitely the male," Jenny replied as she bent over and gently patted the huge bulge in his pajama bottoms. "Maybe we should get together sometime."

"Maybe."

Jenny then picked up her gown and disappeared out the door.

When Jenny awoke, she smelled coffee from the kitchen. She put on her robe and slippers and padded out, expecting to see Cora, but she found Fred.

"Sleep well, Jenny?" he asked cheerfully.

"Sort of, but Josh got me up a couple of times. He was in some pain," Jenny replied.

"Jenny, I want to ask you a question, and I'd like you to give me an honest answer."

"Okay, I'll try."

"Did Cora make you wash your feet before you entered our bathroom last night?"

"Yes."

"Did she make you undress on the deck and put your clothes in a garbage bag?"

"Yes," Jenny said hesitantly, "but I didn't mind. Why do you ask?"

"I found your shirt and underwear in a bag on the deck this morning. She makes me do that all the time. I want to apologize for Cora's behavior. Please don't hold it against Josh."

"I'm fine, Fred. Don't worry about it."

"Why don't you go check on Josh?" said Fred. "If he's still sleeping, let him sleep. He needs the rest."

As Jenny turned to go to Josh's room, Cora entered the kitchen dressed in slacks, matching shoes, and a color-coordinated blouse. Her makeup was perfect.

'Good morning, sweetie," she said to Fred.

"Cora, we have to talk," Fred said softly/

"Talk about what?"

Fred looked at her sternly and said, "Cora, I've loved you for nearly forty years, and I still love you dearly, but this neat thing has gone too far. You won't even let your grandchildren walk into the living room. I've heard them call you Gramma Neatnik and Granny Cleanup behind your back. They don't even like coming here. If it wasn't for Jenny, their vacation would have been awful. Either you change your ways or you can stay home from now on, do you understand? I won't leave you, but I want my old Cora back—the one who used to laugh and play and go fishing with me. I want the Cora who wore her pajamas to breakfast— the Cora who used to wear old blue jeans and tennis shoes. Leave that stuffy old bank. We don't need the money. We can even go to counseling if it will help. I just can't take this any more."

"Sweetie, I just try to keep the house clean," Cora said, obviously shocked.

"I know, but you've got to let us live a little," Fred said, shaking his head.

Tears began to roll down Cora's cheeks. "Okay, sweetie, I'll try," she said softly.

Fred stood his ground. "Oh, no! Don't give me that sad look. Things have got to change!"

"May I ask how?"

"First, I want you to apologize to Jenny for the way you acted. Second, I want you to go back into our bedroom and come back in your pajamas and slippers. Third, I want you to stop treating Josh like a five-year-old. You've got to start letting your hair down. Put on an old t-shirt after breakfast, without a bra. I want my old Cora back!" Fred said, wiping away his own tears.

Jenny discreetly left at that point and checked on Josh. When she returned, she sat with Fred in silence until Cora entered the kitchen—wearing a pair of silk pajamas and nothing else. She was even barefoot.

She apologized to Jenny, then walked over to Fred, kissed him, sat in his lap, and said, "I'll try to do better, sweetie. Really, I will."

The three of them drank some coffee and were eating some breakfast rolls when Josh walked in wearing just his pajama bottoms.

"Where's your top?" asked Cora.

"I got too hot last night, so I had Jenny help me take it off. Then I took some more pain medicine and it solved the problem. Jenny was a big help," Josh replied.

"I'm sure she was," Cora said, looking at Jenny and smiling, "and I'll bet she didn't mind it a bit." Before anyone could say anything in reply, she continued, "You know, before Fred and I were married, he worked on a road construction crew. He fell from a bridge one day and broke his arm and several ribs. At the time, he was working closer to my home than his, so he stayed at my place for several days and I got to nurse him back to health. I remember some awkward moments, but in the name of nursing care, we made it through. I must admit, though, it was nice to wash his back for the first time." Then she looked at Fred, winked, and said, "I haven't done that in a long time."

Turning a little red, Fred said, "Now, Cora, let's not say too much more. The kids might get the wrong impression."

Everyone laughed and the mood was light as Cora asked coyly, "Tell me, Joshua, how did you manage to stumble on an open deck last night?"

Josh now felt his own face redden. "Well, Mom, we were both wet and cold since we fell into the lake. I found Jenny the sweatshirt and when she went below to change. I stayed topside. I got one leg in the trunks fine; but I caught my toe on the lining and I fell forward hitting my head on the engine compartment."

"So," Cora said, smiling broadly, "Jenny caught you with your pants down, I assume."

"Yes, Mom, I guess she did."

Cora stood, walked over to Jenny, and hugged her. Then she kissed her on the cheek and said, "Jenny, you've been a blessing in disguise. If I had been you, I would have run away, but you stayed, and I want to thank you from the bottom of my heart. I realize now how much I have to lose, and if I don't change, it will all be gone. When I get back to work on Tuesday, I'm giving my notice. Things are going be different from now on. I'm going to be the old Cora again."

By the time Cora had finished, everyone was crying. Now it was time to start cleaning up the house and grounds before they went home. When Fred and Josh went outside to get everything ready, Cora walked Jenny back to her room.

When they neared the bedroom door, Cora whispered, "Do you mind showing me your nightgown? I'm assuming you didn't wear a robe all night. I'll tell you a little secret. I showered with Fred when he was injured. We had to dream up stories to tell my folks, so they wouldn't catch on."

As Cora giggled like a schoolgirl sharing some embarrassing secret, Jenny looked at her future mother-in-law—and saw her with new eyes. As Jenny loosened the belt and slipped off the robe, Cora took a step back to get a better look.

"My, that's a nice nightgown," Cora said approvingly. "I bet it's comfy." Then she leaned in close and added, "But next time, re-button the buttons straight—and get all of them."

Jenny looked down to see what Cora was talking about—and saw the buttons were at least two holes off, and four of them weren't buttoned at all.

"Okay, I will," Jenny said with a broad smile.

They changed clothes and went out to help the men clean the boat. Cora even found some old jeans and tennis shoes. Although she didn't wear a t-shirt braless, she found an old halter top which Fred found more than acceptable.

After lunch, Josh announced he needed a nap.

"I think you both could use a nap," Cora suggested, looking straight at Jenny. "Why don't you use the guest bedroom? Just throw back the quilt. Fred and I will finish cleaning the boat while you sleep. Who knows? Maybe I can talk him into taking me out to the cove for the sunset." Then she looked at Fred, winked seductively, and added, "And, sweetie, when we get there, I think I'll need you to fix the clasp on my halter top, okay?"

Jenny and Josh slept for three hours. When they went out to the dock, they realized Cora and Fred had taken the boat. Cora and Fred returned after dark. Cora's hair was a mess, she had an old beach towel thrown over her shoulder. They both had gotten sunburned, but didn't care. They were both smiling from ear to ear.

As they stepped on the dock, Cora announced, "We went for a dip in the lake."

"But, Mom, you didn't take any swimwear," Josh teased.

"I know, and that made it even more fun," Cora said, throwing her arms around Fred.

Sunday it was time to head home, and when Jenny and Josh pulled into the farmyard (with Jenny at the wheel), Jenny parked the car and ran toward the house, shouting, "Mom! Dad! Guess what? I'm engaged!"

As they sat on the front porch, Sara and Paul tried to act surprised when Jenny thrust her new diamond ring out for them to see.

"My, my!" Sara said nonchalantly. "And when is this wonderful event taking place?"

"Oh, Mom. I don't know yet. Sometime next year, I suppose," Jenny said. "We haven't planned that far ahead."

At that moment, Josh finally came limping up to the porch in his sling and bandages.

Sara looked shocked as she asked, "What did she do, beat you up and *make* you propose?"

Josh laughed. "No, Mrs. Maas, I had a little accident on the boat after I asked Jenny to marry me."

"Sit down beside me, honey, while I tell them the whole story," Jenny said happily, "because it'll take a while."

Chapter Twenty-Five
Carol Speaks Out

The Maas family was content; however, things changed at the July farm meeting held at Ed and Carol's house. Ed and Paul were discussing the purchase of a new planter and tractor when Carol joined the conversation after putting the children to bed. Sara had made some coffee.

"How come Sara and I don't get to be involved in this conversation?" asked Carol.

Paul was flabbergasted and Ed looked shocked. "I don't know, honey. I suppose we just thought you didn't care."

"I know I'm not here all the time, but because of my job, I save this operation some $7,000 a year in health insurance. I don't mind doing it and I like my job. Because I live on a farm, I work on all the farm accounts. Bob apparently thinks I have more of an idea of what it takes to work on farm accounts. He thinks I know all the terminology. I try to keep up with the government programs and markets. I know Ed sometimes get frustrated with me for asking him, but I ask many questions to be in the know.

I have one account where the family comes in at the end of the year for tax advice, the son's wife doesn't have a clue what's going on. She's a teacher and doesn't get involved in her husband's business—but someday she'll wish she had. I feel sorry for her, and I don't want to be like her. I want to be a real part of this farm operation."

"Honey, maybe we could discuss this later," Ed suggested.

"No, Ed," Paul said. "Carol's right. She should know what's going on and have a say in what happens. I remember after your mom had spent hours driving tractor and cooking and housekeeping, my Dad and I started buying equipment and spending money. It was your grandmother who exploded, and she jumped all over Dad and me, saying we were more concerned about a new tractor than about a new kitchen for your mom. We agreed she was right—and your mom got her kitchen. You and I need the input from our partners."

Then Paul turned to Carol and asked, "What do you think about getting a new planter and tractor?"

"Well, I did some research," Carol said, surprising everyone, "and I found out a new twelve-row planter costs about $9,000 per row. That's $108,000, and a bigger tractor to pull it is somewhere in the $75,000 range. Together they would be close to $185,000, right?"

As both men shook their heads in agreement, Carol continued, "I know we wouldn't have to borrow all the money; however, it's a cost to the farm because the money can't be used for something else. The cost would be a minimum of 5 percent, or $9,250 per year. Assuming depreciation and payoff, the total interest bill would be close to $40,000 over a five-year period, and if interest rates go up, so does the investment cost."

Paul and Ed listened attentively as Carol went on. "I searched some online farm machinery sites and found several used twelve-row no-till Kinze planters. I know they're not the green-and-yellow ones they sell in Durant, but they're comparable. In fact, Kinze was a pioneer in no-till planters. I found a Kinze planter for $50,000 near Ames. It also has a blue tractor to go with it, but I'm guessing green is the only color for this farm. I found a 2005 200-horsepower John Deere in Kalona for $40,000. Both pieces together would cost $90,000, which is half of what they'd cost new. I found others, but those were the best."

Sara smiled broadly. Her normally quiet daughter-in-law had set the men on their heels.

Paul looked at Carol and said, "Good work. I'll be the first to admit I didn't think you were that interested, but I apologize for being wrong. She's terrific, isn't she, Ed?"

Ed didn't know what to say. He'd never realized Carol had been feeling left out.

Paul asked, "Is there anything else you have on your mind, Carol?"

"Yes, there is," Carol replied. "Ed and I have worked here five years. I know it takes time to work into a farm operation; but I've seen many sons live under their father's thumb. I'm not saying Ed's that way. You and he have a great relationship and do most things together. We know we'll have to wait a few years until we can take over, and we don't have enough money to expand without your and Sara's help. I guess I'm more concerned about what happens to us if something awful happens to you, Paul."

Carol paused briefly, took a deep breath, and plunged forward. "The partnership arrangement is dangerous. If you should die, Ed and I would have to buy out Tim and Jenny or at least buy the machinery from Sara. I doubt we could do that, so the farm might have to be dissolved. I think we should look into a C or S type of corporation, or maybe a limited liability corporation. Bob knows some good corporation lawyers. Do you think it might be a possibility?"

Paul studied Carol's face and realized she had given it a lot of thought, but no one had ever questioned his decisions before. Sara was always informed and generally agreed with him, but she seldom challenged his business dealings.

Paul nodded and said, "Why don't we think this through? Carol, I'm sure you know a lot about corporations, but machinery might not be your field of expertise."

Sara immediately jumped into the conversation. "Now look here, Mr. Land Baron. Carol has obviously done her homework better than either you or Ed. You get caught up in new equipment fever with Jake at John Deere. Maybe you should look into Carol's ideas."

"Okay," Paul conceded. "I'll tell you what. Ed and Carol, you check on the various choices for planters and tractors, while Sara and I investigate incorporating the farm. It's a big decision. Dad and I got along for years with a partnership, but maybe it's time to do something different. If that's acceptable, we'll review all this at next month's meeting."

Ed looked at his dad and asked, "If Carol and I find a planter that's not green, are you okay with it?"

"Sure," Paul said. "The color of the paint shouldn't be a factor, but a good dealer is important."

"Do you mind if we find a planter online?" Carol asked.

"Not at all," Paul replied, "and Carol, could you get us some information on corporations? I'd like to study it more. Now let's close this meeting and have some ice cream."

As Sara and Paul walked out to their car, Sara gave Carol a thumbs-up when Paul's back was turned. Ed was beaming. He was finally going to get a chance to make an important decision for the farm.

The next Thursday morning, Paul was sharpening lawnmower blades. He didn't see Dan Petersen and Everett Niles walk into the shop. He jumped when Dan tapped him on the shoulder.

"What can I help you guys with?" Paul asked.

Dan said, "Paul, we know you've never been involved in county politics, but we're hoping we can convince you to come to the Republican picnic next Thursday. Senator Grassley will be there, along with several other legislature members. We know you have an issue with people who want to curtail livestock expansion, and this would be a place to express your views. We'd like you and Sara to come. It's $20 per person for a steak dinner. What do you think?"

Paul was a little taken back, but then he said, "I'll give it some thought. I'll need to discuss this with Sara first. Can I get back with you?"

"Fine," said Everett. "Hope to see you there."

The men talked about the weather and prices for awhile, then left. They met Sara as they pulled out of the driveway, and though they waved at each other, neither of them stopped.

As Paul helped Sara carry groceries into the house, she asked, "That was Dan Petersen, wasn't it?"

"Yeah, he and Everett invited us to the Republican picnic next Thursday at the fairgrounds. Senator Grassley will be there. I'd like to go. Would you like to go with me?"

"I guess so," replied Sara. "Maybe it's time we took more interest in what's going on politically."

At the picnic, Sara saw many women she knew. While she was catching up on their lives, she noticed Paul and several other men having a heated conversation.

On the way home, she asked, "What was the discussion about? It looked pretty animated."

"It was about the right of farmers to do what they want without rules and regulations. The idea of shutting down livestock operations, because they smell, has to be addressed. I say future expansion should be regulated, but existing buildings and lots should be left alone. Homeowners, who build in the country next to a livestock farm and expect no odor, shouldn't be able to sue the livestock producer."

"I agree," said Sara. "I'm glad we went. I even got to speak with the Senator. He's nice, and very knowledgeable."

In July, it was Muscatine County Fair time. The Maases always went on Friday and Saturday for the 4-H and open beef shows. On Friday, they ate lunch at one of the church stands. After the 4-H show, they headed for the craft and 4-H project building.

As they walked by the political tents, Nate Howell, George Maas' replacement after Georges' death, asked if he could speak with Paul. Paul agreed, and Sara decided to go watch the baked goods and garden contests. Paul joined her about a half hour later.

"What did Nate want?" asked Sara.

"He just wanted to thank us for attending the picnic and to tell me how much he thought of my dad," Paul explained.

The next day, after the show was over, Sam Samuelson asked if they wanted to stop for a bite at a Mexican restaurant. While they had dinner, the issue of farmers' rights was discussed. They got home later than usual, but their chores were few and easy.

On the way home from church the next morning, Sara noticed Paul was being very quiet. She asked, "Is there something on your mind, hon?"

"Sort of," said Paul. "This corporation thing is bothering me. I know it's the right thing to do, but implementing it bothers me. I'm just not used to relying on someone else to make decisions—and Carol's so smart and talented that I'm afraid I'll look old and stupid."

"Don't worry, hon," Sara reassured him. "It'll all work out, but I must admit Carol surprised me, too. She's really sharp when it comes to taxes and financing."

The following weekend, Ed asked Paul if he could do chores for a couple of days. He, Carol, and the kids could visit Tim in Des Moines. He didn't say anything about a planter deal he was working on with a farmer near Montrose.

Paul said, "Sure, why not?"

Ed and his family left Thursday afternoon. They planned to stay at a hotel with a water park. Tim and Angie would be joining them just to get away from the house.

When they met at the pool, Ed asked Tim, "Do you want to look at a planter with me tomorrow morning over by Montrose? Carol found it on the Internet."

"Sure, but since when do you get to buy things?" Tim asked in surprise. "Is it green?"

"No, it is a Kinze, but Dad's alright with that," Ed replied. "I told the manager we could be there by 10:00."

"I'll be ready," said Tim.

Carol was sitting at the edge of the pool, playing with little Isaac, when Angie walked in. Angie wasn't wearing a swimsuit and it was obvious she'd put on some weight.

Carol looked at her and said, "Angie, you're pregnant."

Angie smiled broadly and announced, "Yes, and it's twins—boys!"

"Wow! When are you due?"

"November 25th—Paul's birthday. Won't that be great?" Angie said excitedly. "How are things going on the farm?"

"Well, okay, I think."

"What do you mean, you think?"

Carol told Angie the whole story, then said she didn't think Paul had taken her idea well. "You know, Angie, if something happened to Paul, we'd all suffer. It probably wouldn't be a problem until Sara died, but the inheritance taxes would be terrible. It would affect not only Ed and me, but you and Tim and Jenny, too. We'd probably have to sell part or all of the farm just to pay them."

"I hear what you're saying," Angie said sympathetically, "I didn't realize the government could tax us that much."

"Paul said he'd think about it," Carol went on, "and I really hope he will. If you think about it, Ed's really just a glorified hired hand. I know we'll have to wait a while, but I've seen too many sons wait until the dad decides to let go—and then they find themselves in their fifties and the dad still rules the roost. I hope the idea doesn't cause too much friction, but I really think it's important."

Angie said, "Tim and I would never want to harm you and Ed. Do you think if I talk to Tim, he might be able to help?"

The next morning, Tim and Ed headed for the Epworth Land Company near Montrose, where Jeff Epworth showed them the planter. He claimed it had been rebuilt just before Kinze asked his operation to try a new twenty-four-row machine, and they liked the new machine so well they bought it.

As Jeff showed Tim all the monitors and gauges, Ed checked the frames and boxes, and everything looked fine. Jeff then offered them a package deal. The tractor used to pull the planter was also for sale and already set up with all the monitors and pumps to run it. Ed and Tim were impressed, but the tractor was blue, not green. This meant Ed would have to clear the purchase with Paul. Ed told Jeff he'd call him Tuesday morning to confirm the deal.

On the way back to the hotel, Tim asked, "Are you and Dad having problems? Angie told me Carol's concerned about the future. Do you think I should talk to Dad?"

"Well, Carol and I talked about different ways to approach Dad, but she surprised me by being so direct. I think Dad will understand in time, but he's been the boss for so long it'll be hard for him to change. We'll just have to be patient. I'll let you know what happens after the next farm meeting."

On Saturday morning, Paul was restless and got up at 5:00. Sara heard him in the kitchen, but by the time she came downstairs, she found him on the porch with a cup of coffee.

"Couldn't sleep?" she asked.

"No, too much on my mind."

"Can I help?"

"I don't know. Say, it's supposed to be hot today. How's about checking the cows early? Let's talk while we ride. A ride in the pasture always helps me think. It is so quiet out there."

"Okay. I'll get some clothes on."

"No," Paul said with a smile. "Let's go in our pajamas. No one will see us."

"Really?"

"Yes, really. Are you getting conservative in your old age?" Paul teased.

"No," Sara said firmly. "Let's go. I'm game if you are, Big Boy."

They drove the go-getter all around the pasture and checked the cow water. They stopped by the pond. As they sat on the dock, Paul started to talk. "Nate Howell is retiring and he asked me if I'd consider running. It would mean quite a bit of time away from the farm, so I'm thinking maybe it's time to let Ed and Carol take over the reins."

"If you're asking for my opinion, I approve," said Sara. "I think it's great you replace your dad. Having Ed and Carol take over the farming is the right thing to do. They need a challenge and we need to slow down."

Paul looked at Sara, kissed her, and said, "I love you. You're the greatest."

He smiled mischievously and pushed her into the water. She came up sputtering. She glared at him, and grabbed his leg and pulled him in. They stripped off their pajamas and skinny-dipped for a half hour. It was something they hadn't done for a long while—and it helped relieve their stress.

When Ed and Carol arrived at the farm meeting on Monday night, they found Paul grilling burgers. As they sat at the table, everyone started talking at once.

Sara held her hand up and said, "Let's put numbers in a bowl and then draw. Number one will go first."

Sara drew the number one, so she announced, "I suppose Ed and Carol already know this, but Angie called this morning and told me she's pregnant with twin boys. She's due on your birthday, Paul. Wouldn't that be something?"

They chatted about Angie for a few minutes. Ed took his turn. "Well, Carol and I found a planter and a tractor near Montrose. Tim went with me to see it, and though it's really nice, it's blue. The price is $90,000 for the package. Carol also went online and found out our six-row no-till is worth about $10,000. So, Dad, what do you think? I told the guy we'd let him know Tuesday morning."

"Blue, huh?" Paul said, frowning as if he was making a tough decision. Then he smiled and said, "The neighbors will talk, but let them talk. I say buy it."

As Ed and Carol beamed, Paul delivered his news. "Well, I have two things. The first one is: I wonder if it would upset you and Carol if I ran for county supervisor. It would mean more time away from the farm, and I won't do it if you think it'll jeopardize the farm.

"The second one is: if I win the election, I'll be gone a lot, so I talked it over with your mom and we think it's time to turn the management of the farm over to you and Carol. I spoke to Joe Farley at the bank and he says in today's world incorporating is a good idea."

Paul looked at Carol and said, "Oh, and I guess there's a third thing. Carol, I need to apologize if I hurt your feelings at the last meeting."

Carol smiled and said, "You don't need to apologize, Paul. I know I was a little brusque, and what you just said has helped me make a decision, too. This morning we had a meeting at work. Mr. Billingsley wants to sell the business because he has cancer. He asked the financial advisors, Perry and Nathan, if they wanted to buy the company. He also asked Reuben and me. Reuben said yes, but I told them probably not. I also told them I wanted to be at home more, and they asked if I'd consider working with their farm clients from home and come in to work one day a week. I think I'd like to give it a try, and I could do our farm books, too."

There was a brief silence before Sara said, "I think that's a great plan. You can help Ed and still be a part of the accounting business."

Carol looked at Paul and said, "I think you'll make a great supervisor, and if you'd like, I'd be willing to run your campaign. This county needs good leadership, and you'd be great."

"Thank you, Carol. I accept your offer," Paul replied happily.

The next morning, Ed called and purchased the planter and tractor while Paul went to the courthouse and filled out the necessary papers. Carol told her new bosses she'd accept their offer. Sara was happy because the family was all working together—and because she was going to be a grandma again.

During the fall, Carol phased out of her job and trained a new CPA. In November she cut back to two days a week. She also ran Paul's campaign which he easily won. By December, Carol would be working only one day a week at the office. The rest of the week, she worked from home. She had clients visit her at home during school hours instead of at the office.

On November 25th, Angie had twin boys as scheduled. They named them Harlan and David—and there were lots of children and toys for Christmas that year.

The farm incorporation was completed by January, with Ed as president and manager. Paul was sworn in on the first Tuesday in January.

At the first supervisor's meeting, John Worthington, the man Paul had defeated for the supervisor position, was being harassed by neighbors and an animal rights group. The neighbors didn't like the smell of his hog units, so they contacted PETA to help shut him down. Somehow PETA had taken some photos of a dead hog and what they thought were crowded pens. The issue was finally resolved, but only after weeks of difficult negotiation. Since John had been there first and received glowing health reports from the local veterinarian, the suit was dismissed. The supervisor's passed ordinances to clarify the right for livestock producers to raise animals in Muscatine County. Paul was the voice for the embattled farmers. He influenced the urban supervisors to follow his lead. Muscatine County became a bellwether for the state

As Carol began doing taxes that spring, her new bosses asked if she could handle thirty clients instead of her agreed-upon twenty. They didn't want to lose good farm clients. She increased her office hours from one day to two a week. She promised to continue that schedule until April 15th.

Chapter Twenty-Six
The Dune is Re-Visited

March started with calving and although the number of hours Carol spent helping Ed increased, she loved it. She even became adept at driving a skid loader—a far cry from her first day helping sort cattle when she took an embarrassing spill. Carol changed her day at the office from Monday to Wednesday because Paul's meetings were always on Mondays.

Fall harvest began with cutting silage, and Carol pulled loads to the silo for Paul to unload. The soybean harvest came early. On a warm Monday in mid-October, Ed was combining the last bean field. Sara was helping her mother in Muscatine, so Carol's mother was babysitting Isabelle and Isaac.

At 3:30, Carol decided to take some refreshments out to Ed, but when she arrived at the field, the combine was going away from her, so she waited. She tried to call Ed on his cell phone, but he didn't answer.

When he returned again, Carol stepped out of the tractor to flag him down, but as he got closer, he wasn't looking up. It was then that Carol remembered something her mother-in-law liked to say: desperate times call for desperate measures. She grabbed her pink sweatshirt from the cab and laid it on the top of some uncut beans.

The combine reel grabbed the shirt, whirled it around once, then sucked it into the throat of the header. Ed quickly shut off the head, but it was too late. The shirt was already inside. Five seconds later, the straw chopper was spitting pieces of pink fabric out onto the ground.

At that point, Ed finally saw Carol standing by the rear tire of the tractor, wearing a bright pink tank top and jeans and holding a glass of lemonade.

He shut off the combine and jumped out, saying, "I saw you behind me, but I wanted to fill the hopper before I stopped. Why did you throw your sweatshirt out? Now it's all shredded."

"I was just trying to get your attention," Carol teased. "I'm glad I didn't have to take any more of my clothes off."

Ed gazed at his wife and smiled. You'd never know she'd had three children. Her body was still as tempting as a strawberry ice cream cone in July.

"We could have lunch at the dune," Carol suggested. "It's on the edge of the field."

Ed replied, "Yeah, I could use a break, and the combine needs to cool off anyway. The dust in the radiator coils is making the engine run a little warm. As soon as the sun goes down the air will cool."

At the dune, Carol pulled out the lunch basket and an old blanket. Ed finished the round and stopped the machine at the edge of the bean field. She was spreading the blanket over the old bench when he walked up behind her and grabbed her waist. As she spun around, he pulled her close and kissed her.

"Why did you cover the bench?" he asked.

"I figured it would be covered with bird poop and I didn't want to sit on it."

Ed sat down and took off his shoes and socks. "My feet are burning up. The cab is cool but the floor is hot. It must be all those hydraulic lines."

As he wiggled his toes in the cool sand, Carol handed him a bologna sandwich. Ed wolfed down the sandwich and started on a piece of German chocolate cake. Then he lay back on the bench and closed his eyes. After Carol had put the food away, she sat down beside him and they both napped for a few minutes. Carol woke up first and saw Ed was smiling in his sleep.

She nudged him and asked, "What are you smiling about, honey?"

"You and me," Ed replied. "Remember the day you came to the farm? First you fell in the manure, then you got stung by the wasps, and all you had left to wear were your PJs. We came back to get your sandals in our PJs and ended up here at the dune."

"Do I!" Carol said with a laugh. "Somehow we both ended up naked. It was the first time I'd ever seen a naked man—but you were a fine specimen, with those skinny, hairy legs and those pecs. Wow! It was the greatest night of my life up to that point."

"Yeah," Ed agreed. "It *was* something else."

Carol looked at her husband again and said playfully, "You know, we could finish what we started that night."

"Really?" Ed said, looking at Carol in surprise.

"Yes," Carol said. "Come on, Ed, let's do it."

Carol untied her shoes and took them off, followed by her socks, and she already had her jeans to her knees before Ed finally realized she wasn't kidding. Then she turned and began unbuckling his belt and pulling at his zipper. As she bent down to tug at his pant legs, Ed playfully pulled her top over her head. Then he stood, stepped out of his jeans, and pulled off his t-shirt.

As Ed embraced her underwear-clad body, Carol could tell he was in the mood. She escaped his hold and turned around, letting him do the honor of unhooking her bra. She slipped off her underpants and helped Ed out of his briefs.

They embraced again for a long moment, then Carol grabbed the blanket and spread it on the ground. In the warmth of the October afternoon, they made passionate love. When it was over, they lay close together, looking into each other's eyes and smiled. It was wonderful to do something spontaneous and different.

Then Carol looked at her watch, which was sitting on the picnic basket and said, "Oh, dear. It's 4:30. I've got to go. My mom has to leave at five."

"Yeah, I suppose we should break this party up," Ed conceded, "but I could lay here with you all afternoon."

They kissed again, then stood and started getting dressed, giggling like teenagers who had just done something naughty without getting caught. Carol put the picnic basket back into the tractor cab, but before she climbed in, she turned and gave Ed another kiss.

"You know, Mr. Maas," she said with a wink, "we should do this more often."

"Anytime you're ready. Mrs. Maas."

Ed started the combine and headed back to the field. Carol pulled the full wagon to the buildings.

As she was unloading the picnic basket from the tractor, Sara arrived and said, "You guys had a picnic, I see."

"Yes, Ed said he'd be done around 7:00," Carol replied. "Tell Paul the wagons can sit until tomorrow."

Sara said conspiratorially, "Do you always wear your tank tops with the tag on the outside?" Carol blushed a little as Sara winked and added, "I think maybe there was a little more to it than just a picnic."

Carol admitted Sara was right, she pulled off her top and put it back on—this time with the tag on the inside. She knew she couldn't go home dressed that way. Sara might understand, but her mother wouldn't.

As she watched Carol readjust her top, Sara smiled and said, "Paul and I have had some wonderful times on that dune. Sex in the outdoors is kinda fun, isn't it?"

Carol nodded and replied, "Yes, it really is."

Chapter Twenty-Seven
Overworked

Carol helped Ed with chores often because Paul was at meetings or hearings. The Iowa legislature was trying to eliminate funding for some county programs, which also meant Sara and Paul spent many days in Des Moines.

February was busy. Carol's clients had received all their tax forms and she regularly had appointments from 10:00 in the morning until 3:00 in the afternoon. Carol's mom came to the house at 7:00 to help get Aaron off to school and babysit the other two while Carol and Ed did chores.

Carol was glad she only had three farming corporations using the fiscal year system. What she hadn't planned on was for one of those corporations to become a nightmare. One of the sons was getting a divorce and his ex-wife's lawyer was out to get her share of the corporation's assets.

The family finally agreed to buy the ex-spouse out, but Carol had to let the court know the current value of the corporation's stock. She spent many hours going over assets, land values, machinery, livestock, and crop inventories. The value eventually gave the ex-spouse a tidy payoff—plus alimony.

The days were long and some of the meetings had to be held at night. Carol had to be present at all of them because she was in control of the figures. By mid-March, the matter was settled, but the judge asked Carol to present a few more facts the following day, which meant a trip to the client's lawyer's office in Davenport.

She called at 10:00 that night and told Ed she was on her way home; however, when the evening news was over, Carol still hadn't arrived. Ed tried her cell phone, but got no answer. He wasn't concerned because Carol hated to talk and drive, but at 11:00, he began to worry.

At midnight, he called Paul and woke him up. "Could you and

Mom come over and watch the kids? Carol still isn't home and I'm getting worried. I'm going to go look for her."

When Paul and Sara arrived at Ed's, Paul said, "I'll go with you. Mom can stay and listen for the phone. Did you call the sheriff?"

"Yes, and they said they'd check the road. I called the Thompsons and he said she left two hours ago. They're willing to start at the city limits of Davenport and check from their end."

Carol had left at 10:00, driving down old Highway 6 to Wilton, she turned onto Highway 38. She was fighting sleep. Her hectic schedule was finally getting to her. She turned on the radio and cranked it up, then opened the driver's side window.

As she began to feel a bit more alert, she closed the window again, thinking, "I should be able to stay awake until I get home."

She dozed off for just a second, and when she woke up, the van was tumbling down a steep bank. The van rolled twice and finally came to rest on its side in a small pool of water.

Carol found herself hanging by her seatbelt. The side door had been sprung open by the impact and dust filled the air. The top of the van had collapsed and the windshield had been reduced to a few pieces of jagged glass around the opening.

She unhooked her seatbelt and as she fell, she felt a sharp pain in her right leg. It was still caught under the dash. Water had seeped into the van and it was cold against her shoulders as she tried to decide what to do next. She decided to jerk her leg free with one hand, but even though it did come free, the motion was accompanied by an even sharper pain. She screamed in pain. The leg was also bent at an odd angle. She figured it was broken.

When her leg popped free, she had tumbled into the water, ripping her slacks and cutting her leg on something sharp on the way down. She looked at the open side door—her only means of escape—and spent many minutes struggling to pull herself out of the van.

When she finally fell onto the ground beside the van, she lay for a long time, weighing her options for what to do next. She finally tried to stand, but her right leg collapsed beneath her. She reached out to steady herself as she tried again, but her hand touched the hot catalytic converter, burning her palm. She screamed in pain and again fell to the frozen ground.

As she lay helpless, the cold began to seep into her body. She could only hope someone would find her before she froze to death. She considered taking off her wet jacket, but decided she would be in even more danger of freezing if she did.

Grabbing handfuls of brome grass, she began to pull herself up the long slope, her broken leg dragging behind her. Although she had many other injuries, they all paled in comparison to the pain in her leg. Her fingers began to bleed from hanging on to the sharp blades of grass. She could only pull herself a few feet before she had to stop and rest. She removed the shoe from her right foot because her ankle was swelling badly.

After many arduous minutes, she finally reached the roadside and dragged herself to the shoulder of the highway. She'd then have to wait for the next car to see her.

Meanwhile, Ed and Paul had already passed the scene of Carol's accident, not knowing she was lying at the bottom of the ravine. There were no skid marks to alert them, just tufts of brome grass waving in the breeze. They met the Thompsons, who had seen nothing on their end. They decided to turn back and retrace their paths.

Finally, Carol saw headlights coming down the highway. With great effort, she raised her body up to try to flag the vehicle down. To her relief, the car slowed, and screeched to a stop. A man got out and ran to Carol's side while his wife waited in the car. It was Bob Beamer.

Bob knelt down to help the injured woman. He didn't recognize her until Carol said, "Please call my husband, Ed Maas."

Bob sprinted back to the car and got out his cell phone while Anna hurried to Carol's side, where she cradled Carol's head on her lap. At that moment, Carol passed out.

Bob called 911 and ordered an ambulance. Then he brought a sleeping bag from the trunk and covered Carol's shivering body. An Iowa highway patrolman arrived first and directed traffic as they waited for the ambulance.

By the time Paul and Ed arrived, EMTs were putting Carol into the ambulance. Ed told the officer the injured woman might be his wife, so the patrolman let them through. Just as Ed approached the ambulance, Carol opened her eyes briefly and saw him. She immediately began to cry. Against all odds, she had been saved!

Paul told Ed, "You go with the ambulance. I'll stay and help here."

After Ed and the ambulance left, Paul and the officer searched the scene for any of Carol's belongings. They found her purse, her laptop, and briefcase, along with a few other things from inside the van. The van itself was a total loss.

When the ambulance arrived at the hospital at 1:30, two nurses and a man dressed in scrubs hurried out to help. They rolled Carol into the emergency room while Ed went to the admitting desk. When he reached the cubicle where Carol was lying on a gurney, the nurses were covering her with blankets. They had cut off her wet clothes and dressed her in a hospital gown. Her body temperature was ninety-six degrees.

"Where's the doctor?" asked Ed.

One of the nurses said, "The doctor went home, so there's no one here at the moment. The PTA has a sick child, so she's not here, either."

Ed couldn't believe his ears. No doctor in the ER? How could that be?

When he hurried back to the admitting desk, the receptionist asked, "Who's your family doctor?"

"Dr. Barnes."

"I'll call her immediately," the woman said, "and then I'll call my supervisor."

Dr. Barnes arrived in about thirty minutes and immediately began to bark orders for x-rays, blood tests, and burn salve. Not only was she appalled by Carol's condition, but also by the lack of emergency care. When Carol was finally stable and her body temperature had returned to normal, she was moved to a room, heavily sedated. Only then did Dr. Barnes have time to give Ed a full report.

"Carol has a broken tibia, several cracked ribs, a sprained ankle, and seventy-five stitches in her head, legs, and hands. Her right hand has first degree burns. She'll be here for several days," said Dr. Barnes. "She's lucky to be alive. It was only because she managed to climb up to the highway that someone was able to find her. She definitely had a guardian angel watching over her tonight."

Dr. Barnes later filed a formal complaint against the doctor who had gone home early that night and against the hospital. She also threatened a lawsuit. It was a scandal that would rock the town of Muscatine for months afterward.

Chapter Twenty-Eight
The Last Chapter

It took several months of therapy for Carol to recover, which meant she wasn't available for spring work. A wet April allowed very little field work to be done, so when the weather finally dried out, all the work had to be compressed into a few days. Because Paul was only there four days a week, it was Sara and Ed who carried the majority of the work load.

One day, Great-Grandma Madge came out to babysit so Carol could see if she felt well enough to help. Carol was happy to discover she could run the skid loader, which allowed her to help Sara clean lots.

One Friday evening, Paul helped Ed with the planting. It was 11:00 before he finally came through the kitchen door. When he was ready for bed, he complained of his arm being sore and how it had gone numb while he was driving the tractor. Sara rubbed his arm with some liniment and gave him two Tylenol, and in the morning, Paul's arm felt better.

As spring progressed, Paul complained several times of headaches and numbness in his arm, but he attributed it to overwork. On Sunday during Memorial Day weekend, Sue and Jeff came to the farm for a picnic. Ed put Jeff to work hauling round bales with Paul, but they quit early enough to have a wiener roast before Sue and their crew had to go home.

Because of the holiday, there was no board meeting on Memorial Day, which was fine with Paul. Things had been more intense than he had anticipated. The following weekend, Sara and Paul went to Pella and got home late Sunday night. The next morning, Sara was fixing breakfast while waiting for Paul to come down. He was supposed to be in Muscatine by eight.

She hollered up the stairs, "Your eggs are ready, Hon, you had better hurry."

"I'll be right down," Paul called.

A few moments later, Sara heard a loud crash and a thump. She ran to the stairs and found Paul lying at the bottom.

"Honey, what's the matter?" she said, kneeling by his side. "Are you hurt?"

Paul looked up and tried to speak, but his eyes were blank and his speech was slurred. He tried to right himself, but couldn't. Sara ran to the kitchen and called Ed on his cell phone. He was checking cows in the pasture.

"Ed, come quick!" Sara exclaimed. "I think your father has had a stroke or something."

Ed said, "I'm on my way, Mom. Have you called 911?"

"Not yet."

"Call them!" Ed said urgently. "I'll call Carol. I'll be right there!"

Within minutes, Sara heard the go-getter slide to a halt outside and Ed was by her side seconds later. As he was cradling his dad's head and shoulders, Carol arrived. She had left Aaron in charge. The kids would be alright without her for a few minutes. On the way over, she had phoned the Beamers, and Anna rushed to the Maas farm to babysit.

Carol turned off the burners on the stove. The eggs were burnt and the smoke alarm had gone off. After she had climbed onto a stool and shut it off, she could hear sirens in the distance.

As EMTs loaded Paul into the back of the ambulance, Ed encouraged Sara to ride with them. He and Carol would call Jenny and Tim. They'd join her at the hospital as soon as chores were done.

Paul had another seizure on the way to the hospital. He was rushed into the emergency room, where Dr. Barnes administered some drugs. By the time Ed and Carol arrived, Paul was in the ICU, Sara at his side.

Ed had seen his dad in such condition before. He remembered being worried when his dad was bleeding, but this time he was even more concerned. How would he be able to farm without his dad's advice?

The next morning, Sara, Ed, Carol, and Jen met with Dr. Barnes. Hannah Beamer was babysitting Ed and Carol's children until this crisis was over. Dr. Barnes suggested they get advice from a specialist in Iowa City. Since Paul's condition was fragile, a specialist would have to come to Muscatine.

When Dr. Wong diagnosed Paul, his conclusions were not promising. Paul would be severely paralyzed, but the full severity wouldn't be known for a few weeks. It would be followed by a long period of recovery—if recovery was possible.

Tim arrived that evening as the family gathered outside the ICU to discuss the future. They'd take turns staying with Paul. Sara would take the night shift, Jenny the morning, and Carol the afternoon. Grandma Madge would fill in when needed.

Carol hired Hannah Beamer as a nanny so she could stay at the house full-time until the crisis had passed. Although Ed tried to get the farming done, his mind was never quite clear. One day, he mixed up the wrong herbicide and almost put it on the wrong crop. He forgot about the cow tank one morning and let it run over, which made a huge mess in the lot.

Jenny continued working on her wedding plans, but her heart was no longer in it. It was possible that her dad wouldn't be walking her down the aisle.

"Why don't we postpone the wedding until Dad gets better?" Jenny asked Sara one day.

"No, your dad wouldn't want that. Let's just pray he'll recover enough to be there," Sara replied. "The wedding needs to go on as planned."

June 16th was a warm and humid day. Sara had converted the dining room into Paul's recovery room. A contractor came to discuss adding a ramp onto the front porch. It wasn't the way Sara had always dreamed it would be as they got older, but she was determined to take care of Paul as long as possible. Her vow had been "in sickness and in health."

As she walked into the hospital the next afternoon, she noticed thunderheads building in the west. She checked in on her husband, but he was simply lying quietly. The only noise in the ICU was the humming and beeping of the various machines.

Jenny was also there, and she suggested they go to the cafeteria for supper. The sky outside was dark and ominous. While they were eating, the lights flickered and went out—but the hospital's generators immediately kicked in and restored the power.

For some reason, Sara knew she needed to return to the ICU. When she and Jenny arrived, they saw staff members shouting orders and readings at each other. Looking at the monitors, Sara saw only flat lines—and she knew what had happened.

Jenny hugged her for a moment. Sara broke free and hurried to Paul's bed, pushing one of the nurses aside, saying, "Let him go. God has called him home. He'll be waiting for me when it's my time. He promised me that, and he's never let me down."

Silently, the staff members began to gather up their equipment as Sara held Paul's hand and gently kissed his forehead. "Goodbye, my love. I'll see you in heaven."

Jenny approached the bed slowly and put her arms around her mom's shoulders. Through her tears, Sara said, "We have to call Ed and Carol, and then Tim and Angie and Sue and Jeff."

Ed and Carol were the first to arrive. Ed broke down and though Carol tried to console him, she was grief-stricken as well. Paul had been more of a father to her than her own dad.

A short time later, Tim and Angie arrived. It was almost as if God had notified them, because they were already on their way to the hospital when Sara called. Angie led Carol into a family waiting room, where they talked and cried together.

Ed helped his mom fill out the necessary papers and everyone headed home. There would no longer be a need to remodel the downstairs or the front porch. Now they would be discussing funeral plans.

They planned a large visitation at the church. This way, visitors could sit and wait instead of standing in long lines. Visitation started at 3:00, but the last mourner didn't leave until nine.

Jenny was up early the next morning. The sky was blue and clear. She hurried downstairs, but Sara wasn't in the kitchen. The knife drawer was open and there was a note on the counter that read: "Went to the dune. Thought Dad might be there."

Jenny panicked. Was her mom going to do something drastic? She slipped on her tennis shoes and ran toward the dune. Several times her feet caught in her gown, causing her to stumble and almost fall. She gathered her gown up around her waist.

"I'm glad nobody's around," she thought as she continued to run. "Running with my nightgown above my waist must be quite a sight."

She found Sara sitting on the bench, a bouquet of flowers in her hand.

"Mom, are you all right?' Jenny asked breathlessly.

"Sure. Why, is there a problem?" Sara asked.

"Well, the knife drawer was open in the kitchen and I was afraid you were going to do something terrible," Jenny explained.

"Oh dear," Sara said apologetically. "Did I leave it open? I'm sorry. I got out the kitchen shears to cut these flowers. They were your dad's favorite. I brought them here to show him."

As Jenny joined her by the bench, Sara said, "Come and sit with me. I think Dad will be here soon. I had a dream last night. Your dad told me he wanted to say goodbye properly, since he didn't get to do that at the hospital."

As Jenny held her mom's hand, a gentle breeze began to swirl across the field, rustling the leaves of the cornstalks. "Ah, here he comes now," Sara said, smiling happily. She looked at her daughter and said, "Now, Jenny, I'm going to do something and it's going to seem peculiar, but don't try to stop me."

"Okay, Mom," Jen said, though she was thinking, "What could be more peculiar than what she's already doing?"

As Jenny watched in silence, Sara stood, unbuttoned her pajama top and took it off. Then she removed the pajama bottoms and stood naked in the morning sun.

Without looking back at Jenny, Sara said, "Your dad and I stayed out here all night on our wedding night, and when the sun came up, we stood here together, naked before God and all of creation, vowing we'd serve Him and take care of this land. I want to say goodbye to Paul the same way. That breeze is Paul, saying goodbye. I can feel him."

Wiping her eyes, Jenny said, "I'm sure Dad's here. I'd like to say goodbye, too—but if it's okay with you, I think I'll leave my nightgown on."

"You can do whatever you want," Sara replied. "Your dad won't mind—although he *has* seen you naked, you know."

"But that was when I was little," Jenny said. "I'm not a little girl anymore."

As Sara and Jenny stood shoulder-to-shoulder, the breeze advanced up the slope of the dune and playfully blew Jenny's nightgown up past her knees. Then it seemed to swirl away, finally slipping off into the cornfield.

"Goodbye, Big Boy," Sara said softly. "I'll see you later."

"Goodbye, Dad," Jenny added. "We'll all miss you."

Mother and daughter stood silently until they heard Ed's pickup pull into the farmyard. He'd be looking for them. Sara put her PJs back on and they turned back toward the house. They met Ed by the barn.

"Where have you two been?" Ed asked. "I've been calling and calling."

"We've been to the dune to say goodbye to Dad," Jenny explained. "It was beautiful."

Ed nodded his understanding and said, "Well, we have to hurry. The service is at 10:30 and the pastor wants us there by 9:30."

By 10:30, there was standing room only at the church. Sandi Anderson, a family friend, sang an old hymn and a new one called, "Anywhere with Jesus, I Can Safely Go."

As Pastor Tom began the ceremony, he looked directly at the family and said, "Farming is a lifetime occupation. You don't change jobs every ten years. Once a family starts a farm, it's handed down from generation to generation. Paul and Sara are the third generation. Paul's grandfather came here from Germany and established the Maas farm. It was passed to his son, George, and George handed it to his son, Paul. Paul, by the grace of God, now has given it to Ed, and so the tradition lives on. Ed and Carol are the fourth generation, and if the tradition holds true, their children will represent the fifth generation.

"I envy farmers. Even in my occupation, God has called me to serve several different congregations. Many of you have changed jobs over the years, but not farmers. Farmers and their families are the foundation of our community. Most of them believe in Jesus and God, and I know that Paul took his job seriously. He understood it wasn't his land—it was God's. He was just a steward of the land.

"Sara told me the morning after their wedding, the two of them made a vow to the Almighty that they'd cherish His land. They'd raise a family and be fruitful, and that, brothers and sisters, they have done— and in a fine way.

"Of course, it's a mystery why God called Paul home. We all feel it was much too early, because Paul still had much left to do here on earth. We can never know what God has planned for us. John 1:5 says, "God is light and in him is no darkness." Even in this dark time for the Maas family, they must continue to take comfort in that light. I challenge everyone here to support the Maas family in their time of grief. We all know time heals all, and we'll have times of grieving. We'll all have happy times, and we'll all have times of stress. No matter what, we must trust in Jesus to carry us through. Sara, Jesus is your Rock and He will be there for you. You and Paul have done well in beginning the fourth generation. God bless you and your family."

Tim then delivered his father's eulogy. He spoke slowly and deliberately. When he had finished, he walked over to the casket, bent down, and said softly, "Goodbye, Dad. I love you."

Paul Maas was buried in the family plot at the Wilton Cemetery.

Two days after the funeral, Sara was fixing some coffee when she saw Ed's pickup pull into the yard. Carol got out and hurried toward the barn.

Sara poked her head out the back door and called, "Where's Ed?"

Carol turned and said, "He's in bed. I told Hannah to stay until he got up. He's just worn out."

"And how about you?" Sara asked.

"I'm okay," Carol replied. "Just a little tired."

"Hang on! I'll come out and help. I can still push buttons, you know!" Sara called as she stepped out onto the porch.

After they'd finished the chores, Carol decided to check the cows, and Sara asked if she could ride along. They found the cows and calves by the pond.

Carol stopped the go-getter on the top of the hill and said, "Isn't this a beautiful spot?"

"Yes, it's always been one of my favorites," Sara said, looking around with a smile. "I'm glad you like it, too. You know, you and I have a lot in common. We were both city girls and we both had careers outside of farming. We both married farmers, and we both love this spot."

As Carol nodded in agreement, Sara continued, "Farm wives are really the backbone of agriculture. They take care of their husbands, they bear the children, and like Pastor Tom said, they begin the next generation. You and Ed are going to do fine. My heart is heavy, but I have to move on with my life. This farm is yours now. Paul and I trust you to take care of it—just like we did."

When Sara and Carol returned from the pasture, Ed and the children were waiting by the barn. Aaron and Izzy were hanging on the gate and Isaac was perched on his dad's shoulders.

The fifth generation of Masses was well underway.

About the Author

Bob Bancks is a retired farmer. He grew up on the family farm and continued to work the land after his father's death as a result of a farm accident. As a child, he played in the large pastures and the small farm creeks. Haymows and hog wallows were also sources of adventure. The stories of the Maas children are based on experiences of Bob's own childhood.

He and his wife, Jane, worked together all their married lives. Seldom were they ever apart. Living with his best pal 24–7 seemed to fit them, for they have been together for more than fifty years. Their children, though all boys, also lent their adventures to some of the episodes in the book.

CPSIA information can be obtained at www.ICGtesting.com
Printed in the USA
BVOW03s1858061113

335516BV00001B/3/P